More praise for *Contrition*

"In *Contrition,* Maura Weiler creates a tapestry woven of spirituality, artistic ability, and family bonds. This poignant and riveting debut novel delivers a rich voice and compelling characters. A must-read."
—MIKE BEFELER, author of *Mystery of the Dinner Playhouse*

"A haunting, spiritual journey through darkness and light, Maura Weiler's *Contrition* tells the story of twin sisters separated at birth, their shared commitment to God and art, and the sorrow and vulnerability each learns about herself as they come to know one another. Moving and bold."
–JIM RINGEL, author of *Wolf*

"*Contrition* is a lively tale of twins separated soon after birth and then reunited in a cloistered monastery in Big Sur. *Contrition* explores the perils and pulls of art, faith, and fame. Smoking, drinking tabloid writer Dorie McKenna specializes in crafting wacky tell-alls about fake two-headed goats for *The Comet*, but when she begins to immerse herself in her long-lost sister's world of silence, self-abnegation, and prayer, she finds genuine stories she doesn't want to embellish, a call to pursue something higher, and nuns who lead her down a countercultural path to happiness."
—JENNY SHANK, author of *The Ringer*

CONTRITION

MAURA WEILER

CONTRITION

MAURA WEILER

INFINITE WORDS
NEW YORK LONDON TORONTO SYDNEY

INFINITE WORDS
P.O. Box 6505
Largo, MD 20792
http://www.streborbooks.com

ISBN 978-1-59309-648-9
ISBN 978-1-4767-9345-0 (ebook)
LCCN 2014943300

First Infinite Words trade paperback edition April 2015

Cover design: Kristine-Mills Noble
Cover photography: Nun © istock.com; picture frame © Shutterstock.com
Book design: Red Herring Design, Inc.

10 9 8 7 6 5 4 3 2 1

Manufactured in the United States of America

To Christine Taber

Your friendship and talent are missed; your inspiration lives on

ACKNOWLEDGMENTS

Heartfelt thanks:

To my first readers, Ann Buchanan, Michelle Topham, and Louise Weiler, who saw me through multiple "nunumentary" drafts as I separated the detail from the drama; to the writers in my first critique group, Will Baumgartner, Lisa Golloher, Julie Paschen, and Rick Schwartz, who taught me the novel craft; and my second, Sara Alan, Carrie Esposito, Susan Knudten, and Gemma Webster, who taught me the art of emotion.

To Nick Arvin, Mike Befeler, Eleanor Brown, Erika Krouse, Laura McBride, Jim Ringel, Jenny Shank, and Rachel Weaver for their guidance and generosity. To Lighthouse Writers Workshop founders, Andrea Dupree and Michael Henry and their staff, for both the outstanding writing community they foster and the tranquil writing space they provide.

To the teachers who believed in me: Paula Zasimovich Ogurick, Rita Green, and William Krier; and to the one I am still learning from, William Haywood Henderson. To my agents, Sara and Stephen Camilli, and editors, Zane, Charmaine Parker, and everyone at Infinite Words/ Simon & Schuster, for their faith in this novel.

To Chad, Gianna, and Aliyah, for the deep joy, frequent laughter and unconditional love that make me whole, and to my parents, Claire and Nick, for their support and tireless enthusiasm. To my extended family and friends for their countless pep talks, feedback on the book, and willingness to listen.

I owe the details of the cloistered tradition to the hospitality of many religious orders who shared their sacred space and often their stories as I researched this novel in California at the Abbey of New Clairvaux, the Carmel of Saint Teresa, the Monastery of the Angels, the Monastery of Poor Clares, the New Camaldoli Hermitage, the Old Mission Santa Barbara, and Saint Andrew's Abbey, and in Colorado at the Abbey of St. Walburga.

Special thanks to Sister Kathleen Bryant, RSC, both for her discernment seminars and her insightful book, *Vocations Anonymous*. Additional publications I found helpful included *The New Faithful* by Colleen Carroll Campbell, *St. Benedict's Rule for Monasteries* as translated by Leonard J. Doyle, *Nuns as Artists* by Jeffrey F. Hamburger, *Music of Silence* by David Steindl-Rast with Sharon Lebell, and numerous pamphlets provided by the religious communities I visited.

My utmost gratitude goes to my friend, the late painter Christine Taber, who shared her artistic process with me before her untimely death and whose abstract paintings inspired the art descriptions in the novel. This book is for her. And thanks to Bill Turner at the William Turner Gallery for allowing me the space to grieve and write about Christine's paintings both as they hung in his gallery and for months beyond.

PROLOGUE

I rarely speak now. And I never write. Not after what happened.

A year ago, I wrote too much: sentences that ran across the page with the kind of passion only a hungry, young journalist can muster. Declarations I thought would make a difference.

They made a difference all right. My words of sincere praise led to crushing loss. So I stopped using them. Most slipped away in the silence, but there are a few stubborn ones still demanding a voice.

Today, I feel compelled to pick up my pen and use them up. I have enough words left for that.

CHAPTER ONE

Nuns terrified me with their year-round Halloween costumes and severe shoes. Even after eight years of Catholic school, I still found their built-in piety intimidating. Never mind that I was a twenty-six-year-old woman approaching the convent where my twin sister lived. I may as well have been a ponytail-pulling, seven-year-old being marched to Principal Sister Helen's office back at Sacred Heart Elementary in Calabasas.

I wondered if Candace, now called Sister Catherine, would be home. Then I remembered that a cloistered nun never left her convent. I wasn't ready to meet the twin whose existence I'd only recently learned about, but I wanted to see where she lived a life so different from my own. I would drive by, take a look, and leave without ever getting out of the car.

At least that was the plan until I found the top of the driveway impassable. A waterlogged pothole larger than my Jetta stood between the convent and me. The recent rains had been very thorough.

I rolled down my window and peered into the night. The mist kissed my face while the compound's eight-foot adobe walls blocked my view. I'd have to get out of the car and walk to the wrought-iron gate if I wanted to see anything. I assessed my wanna-be Armani suit and determined that it needed dry cleaning anyway.

As I opened the door and stepped out into the rain, I considered the day's assignment. As expected, the piece on the unlucky goat that had brought me to Big Sur wasn't going to be the breakthrough story I'd been looking for to expedite my escape from tabloid hell, but it *had* brought me to the place I'd been avoiding for the last four months–a convent where my past and future would collide.

That morning, Phil Stein, editor-in-chief of the West Coast's premier gossip sheet, *The Comet*, had picked his way through the paper-strewn, fire hazard of a newsroom and stopped at my friend Graciela's cubicle.

"Find out more about this two-headed goat, Sanchez," he ordered, waving the blurry snapshot and accompanying letter in his hand.

Graciela and I shared a look over the low cube wall between our desks. "Find out" was Philspeak for "fabricate."

"Maybe it talks," Phil added, skimming the letter.

"Or predicts the stock market?" Graciela said in all seriousness while inhaling a brownie. Reed thin, Graciela functioned, albeit rather spastically, on a pure sugar diet.

"Uh, uh." Phil shot her down with his trigger finger. "Guinea fowl did that last year."

"Too bad." She set aside her snack with effort and picked up the phone.

"Drive up to Big Sur." Phil hung up Graciela's phone before she could dial. "Goats give poor phone interviews."

"Did you say *Big Sur*?" Graciela looked at me. Even though months had passed since I'd located my twin, she realized I hadn't met Sister Catherine. "*Muy interesante.*"

It was interesting, all right. And terrifying. Shortly after my adoptive father passed away earlier in the year, an estate lawyer had contacted me to disclose that my late biological father was the renowned abstract artist Rene Wagner. Before I could react, he added that my biological mother, an aspiring poet named Lucy Gage, had died giving birth to not one but *two* babies.

I was a twin. My adoptive parents had told me how my mother died but never mentioned that I had a sister—something they probably didn't know themselves given that names and most details were withheld in my closed adoption. Absorbing this after being raised as an only child rocked my sense of self much more than learning that my biological father was famous.

In some ways, it was a relief. If the connection many twins describe is real, it explained why I sometimes felt pain without an injury, laughed for no reason, and knew odd facts I hadn't learned, like where to find the best surfing waves in Malibu. Maybe the urge to find my biological parent—something I felt strongly but had never mustered the courage to pursue—was really the urge to reconnect with my twin.

The Wagner biographies I'd read didn't mention me or my relinquishment but did say that the hard-drinking Rene raised my sister, Candace, until he died of cirrhosis of the liver when she was seventeen.

I knew there were good reasons why my birth father chose adoption for me and kept my twin. I also knew I was probably better off as a result. But the fact that I didn't exist to him, at least not on paper, was a permanent punch in the gut.

Candace disappeared from public records shortly after Wagner's death. It took some sleuthing and called-in favors to learn that she entered the cloistered Monastery of the Blessed Mother in Big Sur after her high-school graduation, later taking the name Sister Catherine and making her solemn vows.

In the last few months, I'd compiled enough information to write my own book about my birth father if I'd wanted to. But writing Wagner's biography would involve tackling his alcoholism, revealing myself as the child he'd put up for adoption, and meeting the twin he'd kept, none of which I felt ready to do. I'd had a great childhood as Connor and Hope McKenna's adopted daughter, and I didn't see the point in dredging up my or Rene Wagner's past, much less my sister's. Yes, I was curious about Candace and wanted a relationship with her—maybe too much. What if I overwhelmed her with some irrational belief that she should be the mother, father, and sister I'd never known all rolled into one? I doubted I would be that needy, but until I felt ready to meet her with no expectations at all, it wasn't worth the risk that I'd freak her out or have her dismiss me as my birth father had.

On the other hand, my coworker couldn't believe I hadn't met my twin yet and had no qualms about handing off the goat assignment to help make it happen.

I shook my head at Graciela and mouthed, "Don't you dare!"

"I'd love to go to Big Sur, Phil, but here's the thing." Graciela tapped her watch and ignored me. "It's almost noon and that's a twelve-hour round-trip. I can't leave Sophie in daycare until midnight. Daycare means day*time, comprende*?"

"Pesky children." Phil huffed with a grandfatherly smile.

"Why don't you send Dorie?" my coworker asked, all enthusiasm. "She likes field trips."

I shot daggers at Graciela with my eyes. She batted her lashes and made me laugh.

"Fine." Our editor wheeled around and handed me the farmer's blurry snapshot and accompanying letter. "Bring a camera, McKenna. Need better pictures."

"Well, you know you won't get those from me," I said. My picture-taking skills ranked among the worst in the newsroom.

"They'll be good enough." Phil didn't bother hiring real photographers since most pictures were digitally altered later.

"How about I interview him on the phone and have him text better photos?" I offered.

"Not gonna work," Phil said. "He describes himself as technologically challenged."

"Isn't Highway One closed from the mudslide damage?" I asked, attempting to switch tactics.

"It reopened last Thursday," Graciela said, her eyes shining.

I wished I could match her excitement over the possibility of me meeting my sister, but I could barely process it. My birth parents were both dead, yet there was this living person with a direct connection to them whom I could actually talk to if I wanted to. Did the ghosts of our parents follow her around? Did they follow me?

"So there's nothing keeping me from going to Big Sur." I scowled and eyed the pack of cigarettes that California state law forbade me from smoking inside the newspaper's bullpen. "Oh, joy."

"Surprised." Phil tilted his head and considered. "Thought you'd jump at the chance to get out of here."

"Are you kidding?" Normally he'd be right, but today staying put sounded better than driving to a place I'd been avoiding. "I relish every moment I have at the feet of a newspaper god such as yourself."

"Nice try." Phil dropped the letter and photo on my desk. "Put in for mileage and take tomorrow morning off to recover."

The morning off wasn't a generous gesture on Phil's part. He didn't want to pay the overtime.

Still, as assignments went, it wasn't a bad one. I wasn't proud of my job, but it paid the bills, though barely. I spent my off hours writing serious articles in hopes of selling them to legitimate newspapers, but so far I hadn't had a freelance story get noticed by a paper of record. In the meantime, I stuck to mostly animal and alien stories at the tabloid. As long as my subjects couldn't read or didn't exist, they couldn't sue for libel.

Six hours of driving produced a decidedly one-headed goat with a softball-sized lump above her left ear, but Phil would want to run the story anyway. We'd already covered all the true animal freaks of nature within a 500-mile radius and were scrounging for items until the next breeding season produced a new crop of genetic anomalies.

"That looks painful," I said, wincing as I scribbled notes in my palm's-width reporter's notebook.

"Doesn't hurt her a bit," the goat's gap-toothed owner explained. "Vet says it's a benign tumor."

I had to admit that two-year-old Carmie seemed comfortable enough to be bored by the prospect of her imminent fame. I pulled a digital camera from my bag, and did my amateur best to keep my disabled fingers out of the way while I snapped pictures.

I was born with a crippled right hand. The thumb curled under my first two fingers and over the second two, forming an awkward fist. I had mobility in my index and middle digits thanks to multiple infant surgeries, but the others were useless. I'd devised ways to do most everything people with normal hands could do, but photography was a particular challenge.

"Do you think she'll make the cover?" the farmer asked.

"Depends on how realistic we can make it look in Photoshop. But my editor loves this kind of stuff."

The farmer threw his head back and crowed in delight.

"Whoo hoo! Wait 'til the guys at the diner see that I got you into *The Comet!"* he said to the goat as he patted her second "head." "It's way better than when Stan Mitchell's cow was in that stupid feed store ad, huh, girl?"

Carmie nuzzled into his hand, apparently a willing exploitee in her owner's game of one-upmanship. Or maybe she was simply looking for food.

"Hang on," the farmer said, pulling a black Sharpie from his pocket and drawing two eyes and a smile on the goat's lump. He stepped back to admire his handiwork. "Much better."

"I don't think it gets much better than this," I said, gesturing toward the landscape.

I snapped a few more pictures of Carmie and then took a shot of the expansive ocean view from the lush pasture. A light rain tangled crystalline drops in my eyelashes as I admired the sunset. People had told me how beautiful Big Sur was, but words couldn't capture its graceful splendor. Huge redwoods nestled against mountain cliffs on the east side of Highway One; the ocean crashed against a rocky beach on the west. Even the soggy evidence of the recent mudslides couldn't detract from its majesty.

"This is some prime real estate for a goat," I said.

"Don't I know it?" The farmer pulled his black cap lower on his forehead as the mist dusted it gray. "I'd build condos but for the zoning laws."

"I'd buy one." I could afford an imaginary condo.

Afterward, I started my car, lit a cigarette, and drove into the growing darkness. A couple of miles down Highway One, I saw a large, wrought iron cross and a sign that read "Monastery of the Blessed Mother." I hadn't noticed it on the drive up, obscured as it was by a hedge on the south side.

I squeezed the steering wheel and silently cursed Graciela. I hadn't planned to look up Sister Catherine, a.k.a. Candace Wagner, but now that I was mere yards away, the desire to see where my twin lived overwhelmed me. What did her home look like? What did the home she grew up in look like, for that matter? How would our lives be different if we'd grown up in that place together?

Without thinking, I stubbed out my cigarette, turned my car off the road, and chugged up the steep, switch-backed driveway.

CHAPTER TWO

Walking toward the monastery, I stepped carefully to avoid the muddy patches of ground. Damp salt air rose from waves that spilled onto rocks far below, mingling with the cool rain and heightening the pungency of the anise and fennel that grew along the edge of the pockmarked driveway. I skirted the pothole, arrived at the gate, and peered through the bars. The drizzle and the distance made it impossible to see more than vague outlines of a building. I half considered ringing the nearby doorbell, but gaining entrance would mean interacting with a nun. Before I could decide, a diminutive sister who looked about sixty emerged from the murk carrying a pink umbrella.

A chill crept up my neck. I wanted to bolt, but my legs shook too much to carry me away.

"Can I help you, Miss..."

"Uh, McKenna. Dorie McKenna."

"Well, hello, Dorie McKenna. I'm Sister Teresa."

When I searched the woman's eyes and found no flash of recognition there, I concluded Sister Catherine and I probably weren't identical. I wondered if my sister told people that she was a twin or if she even knew it herself. Considering the circumstances, I wouldn't blame her if she kept it a secret. I hadn't told many people.

Sister Teresa offered her hand to shake. I reached over and grasped her right hand sideways with my left, pumping it up and down as warmly as physics allowed. I'd learned that attempting to shake with my weak hand led to a frowning revelation for anyone unaware of my handicap, not to mention jangling joint pain for me. The sister took my left in her right as comfortably as if that was how all handshakes were conducted. Nun or no, this woman was all right by me.

Sister Teresa's white wimple and black veil covered her head, neck, and ears. Rain-fogged, cat-eyed glasses framed her face, while a set of rosary beads and a massive ring of keys like the ones janitors wear hung from the knotted linen cord that belted her coarse gray habit. The only flesh exposed was her slender face and hands. She wore what looked like a gold wedding band on her left index finger. To whom was she married? God?

"I heard your car coming up the driveway and thought I'd better have a look-see," she said, pulling her cloudy glasses down her nose and squinting over them at me. "What brings you out on such a night as this?"

"I uh, well, um, wanted to stop by because...er..."

I bit my lip. Suddenly I was afraid to say that Sister Catherine was my twin. What if she didn't want to meet me? I wasn't sure I could handle that.

Sister Teresa waited for me to continue with kind eyes. Unnerved, I said the next logical thing that sprang to mind.

"Because I'm interested in becoming a nun," I blurted.

I took a step back. Where the hell had that come from? The ruse rolled off of my tongue with an ease that suggested I'd said, or at least thought it, before. I cringed. *The Comet* had made me a little too adept at lying. Now I had offered a whopper.

"A vocation is a beautiful thing," Sister Teresa said. "Fortunately, this is the right place. Unfortunately, it's not the right time. We're closed. Can you come back in the morning?"

"I'm headed back to Los Angeles in a few minutes." I started to leave. "So I'll come back another day."

"Nonsense." The sister took her giant key ring and unlocked the gate. "I can bend the rules for a new recruit. Come on in out of the rain and we'll have a chat."

I glanced at my car. Too late to turn back now.

The gate swung open with a haunted-mansion creak. Sister Teresa beckoned me with a smile and indicated that I should join her under the umbrella. Despite her attempt to put me at ease, I tasted the acrid tang of old fears as I followed her, and unconsciously slowed my steps to a principal's-office pace.

"'Course, it'll just be me. All of the other nuns are sequestered," Teresa said as the gate clanged shut behind us with unsettling finality. "As Extern Sister, I deal with outside business and visitors."

So I couldn't see Catherine even if I'd wanted to. I let out an involuntary sigh of both relief and disappointment.

"You'll have to come back on Visiting Sunday and meet some of the other gals," she said. "Get a wider perspective on our life."

With that, the possibility of meeting my twin reemerged, as thrilling and intimidating as ever.

A large courtyard surrounded by the arched walkway of a Spanish mission building subtly revealed itself in the darkness. I followed the rattle of the sister's key ring past shadowed trees and statuary and jumped when a red bottlebrush bloom grazed my cheek. I was grateful when we arrived at a narrow, blue door under an arch.

As we wiped off the mud from our feet on the doormat, I realized another bit of Sister Teresa's flesh was exposed. She was barefoot.

Lack of the ugly-but-sensible footwear I associated with nuns didn't appear to bother her. In fact, this woman seemed more comfortable in her own skin than most people. Her rain-washed cheeks suggested the dewy aura of an expectant mother. Despite her age, there was an undeniable, youthful exuberance about her.

Sister Teresa opened the door to reveal a modest sitting room divided by a floor-to-ceiling metal grille. Despite its elaborate decorative touches, the cold steel of penitentiary bars came to mind. Separate exits and straight-backed chairs on either side suggested a prisoner's visiting room. The nun's key ring now reminded me more of a jailer's than a janitor's.

"The sisters visit their families here in the parlor once a month." Sister Teresa pointed to the visitors' chairs and motioned for me to sit. "Vatican II said we could take the bars down, but we didn't want to bother with the trouble and expense."

"Don't you find them oppressive?" I took a seat on the public side of the bars where we'd entered and shook off the shivers, relieved that she hadn't led me to the church. The last time I'd set foot in a church was one of the worst days of my life, and the sitting room was unsettling enough.

"You'll be surprised how quickly you forget they're there." The nun sat in the chair beside me. "I'd offer you a cup of tea, but we only have a few minutes to talk before Grand Silence begins, so let's get right to it."

"Grand Silence?" I asked.

"With the exception of the prayers of the Divine Office, we don't speak between nine p.m. and six a.m. to allow time for contemplation."

"Divine Office?" I repeated, a human parrot.

"We gather in the chapel seven times a day for prayer, beginning with Vigils at twelve twenty a.m. and ending with Compline at seven thirty p.m." She picked up a copy of the daily schedule from a side table and handed it to me. "But enough about us. Tell me about your vocation."

"I um, well..." My eyes darted around the room in search of something that might help me figure out what to say. They came to rest on a large painting of the *Madonna and Child* hanging on the cloistered side of the room. Bingo. "Ever since I became a Catholic, I've felt a strong connection with the Blessed Mother."

I left out the fact that I wasn't Catholic anymore. The extern smiled and nodded encouragement.

"I think maybe it's because I never knew my birth..." I looked through the bars at the *Madonna and Child* again. The stylized figures and ethereal background gave the Biblical theme a distinctly modern patina, while the painting's midnight-blue fabrics and daybreak-gold haloes warmed the cold room. The Virgin Mary's expression suggested a serenity I wasn't sure existed in reality. I felt myself relax. "My birth mother."

"That makes sense." Teresa nodded. "Mary is Mother to us all."

"She is, isn't she?" I said without shifting my gaze from the painting. Between researching my birth father's work and being college roommates with an art major, I understood enough about paintings to know that this one was exceptional.

With her huge, almond-shaped eyes, long nose, and rosebud mouth, the Madonna appeared so tranquil that I wanted to trade places with her. I hadn't been able to track down a photo of my biological mom, but I'd always pictured her wearing this same composed expression. My eyes flicked to the baby Jesus, whose face hinted at a sadness not shared by His mother. Seeing the Madonna holding the child on her lap, I thought of my mothers, the one I'd known and loved and the one I would never meet, and realized that no matter how tightly my adoptive mom held me, I'd never found peace. The baby in the painting seemed to understand. I saw the tension in His hands. His left hand grasped His mother's for extra support, while His right hand...*curled into a partial fist, with the thumb tucked under the extended index and middle fingers.*

I gasped and reared back.

"What's the matter, dear?" Sister Teresa peered over the top of her glasses at me.

"I have to go." I stood up and fled the room.

The drizzle swelled to heavy rain. It transformed the ground into a slogging, primordial muck that threatened to suck the shoes off my feet as I ran through the courtyard. I scrunched up my toes for leverage and managed an awkward, flip-flop gait to keep my loafers on. It wasn't until I arrived at the exit that I found Sister Teresa had relocked the gate after admitting me.

The nun arrived a few steps later, her bare feet better suited to muddy conditions. In her haste, she'd left her umbrella behind and was as drenched as me.

"Are you sure you're in a state to drive?" Teresa paused before she unlocked the gate. "You seem upset and the rain is blinding. I'd be happy to make up the bunk in the visiting priest's quarters for you."

"I'm fine, really," I said, glad the rain obscured my tears as she turned her key in the lock and strong-armed the heavy gate open. "I'm sorry to make you come out in this mess." I slipped through the threshold. "Thank you for your hospitality."

"Be sure to come back again when you're feeling better. God bless you, Dorie," she said as she closed the gate behind me.

Already soaked, I marched straight through the giant pothole to get to my car.

Sister Teresa was right. I wasn't okay to drive. Even if I was, I didn't trust my elderly Jetta on the winding road of a muddy cliff in the dark and rain. I couldn't go home, but I couldn't bring myself to return to the convent either, especially since it would mean dragging the nun out into the weather again.

I searched through my bag, found a cigarette and then discovered no amount of shaking could produce enough fluid to spark my plastic lighter. My Jetta's lighter had broken years before. Resigned, I curled up in the back seat of my car and closed my eyes in what amounted to an act of faith. The sleep that often eluded me at home wouldn't come in a cramped car with a metal roof that amplified the storm. Then again, I wouldn't have slept well anywhere that night.

The painting haunted me. What were the odds that someone displaying work at the convent would depict a hand that looked exactly like mine? Had Sister Catherine painted the *Madonna and Child*? It was nothing like Rene Wagner's abstracts, but wasn't it at least possible that my twin was a painter like our father? I was a writer like our mother.

CHAPTER THREE

The arthritic falsetto of rusty wrought iron startled me awake. I looked at my watch—five a.m. The rain had stopped. It was still dark, but stars shone through the trees and residual moisture sparkled on silvered stems and blooms. I saw the silhouette of Sister Teresa opening the gate.

I pulled on my shoes, patted my tangled hair, and met her in yesterday's sodden clothes. She jumped when she saw me but soon smiled. I blinked to moisten my dry contact lenses and started to speak.

"I'm feeling bet—"

The nun raised a finger to her lips and then pointed to her wrist where a watch would be if she wore one.

I kicked myself when I realized that Grand Silence didn't end until six. My questions about the painting's origin would remain unanswered for at least another hour.

The chapel bell rang five times. The extern's hands pressed together, and a tip of her head toward the sound told me that the bell was a summons to prayer and that I was welcome to join them. I nodded reluctantly. Anxious as I was to ask Sister Teresa about the painting's creator, I was hesitant to go where she was headed.

Ever since I'd walked away from religion, I'd found myself unable to enter a Catholic church for any reason. Now curiosity about my twin became reason enough.

I discovered the public entrance to the chapel a few doors down from the parlor, took a deep breath to counteract the pounding of my heart, and walked inside on trembling legs. Stepping inside a Catholic house of worship after years of weaving tabloid tales smacked of a fallen woman seeking redemption. Even worse was the fact that reparation wasn't my purpose. I was simply there to spy.

I lost my nerve when I found the place empty. I was about to make my getaway when, keys jingling, Sister Teresa entered through a side door and grinned at me. I smiled weakly and sat down in the nearest row, assuring myself things would be fine. I didn't have to participate. I simply had to survive. At least the pew was uncomfortable enough to keep me awake.

The softly feminine chapel was shaped like a cross. White trim accented pale, yellow walls and huge, stained-glass windows still blackened by darkness. Calla lilies festooned the altar in spare, elegant arrangements and a sunburst-shaped gold vessel about a foot high rested on a white, lace altar cloth. In the center of the sunburst, a tiny glass window displayed the Eucharist.

Behind me, a spindly spiral staircase rose to meet a wall of organ pipes. Before me, a floor-to-ceiling metal grille, like the one in the parlor, divided an area to the left of the altar from the rest of the church. Wooden shutters ran the length of the grille and obscured whatever was behind it.

Sister Teresa finished preparing the altar and left me alone again. I sneezed, producing a thunderous echo in the empty space. Five minutes passed. Maybe there wasn't a service after all?

An unseen door squeaked. The candles cowered as a rush of cool air blew in from behind the shuttered grille. Then the shutters opened at the hands of a nun on the other side to reveal several pews and a small organ. One sister was already seated there; another dipped her fingertips into the holy water at the door and crossed herself as she entered the separate, holy space.

I slid to the end of my own pew and craned my neck to see around the corner as the nuns filed into the enclosed area. There were sixteen in all, most of whom wore eyeglasses. An 80 percent myopic population seemed disproportionate until I realized a vow of poverty didn't allow for contact lenses or laser surgery. How did these nuns manage to get their eyes checked if they never left the cloister? Or their teeth cleaned? I saw the glint of gold wedding bands as they flipped the pages of their prayer books.

I wondered which one of them was my twin. The only picture I'd found of Candace in the Wagner biographies was a black and white snapshot of our father helping her fly a kite on the beach when she was twelve or so. Between the wind whipping her long hair and the distance from which the picture was taken, I couldn't see enough of her face to determine if we were identical. Now I figured we probably weren't given that Sister Teresa hadn't seemed to recognize me, but maybe Catherine and I had some similar features that would help me pick her out.

Most of the nuns were too old or too young to be her. One elderly sister occupied a wheelchair, her hunched back forcing her to stare at her own knees. Another still suffered from adolescent acne. Several bent their heads in prayer, making it impossible for me to see their faces behind the drape of their veils. Sister Teresa was easy to pick out thanks to the clatter of her key ring. She winked at me through the grille.

A young Filipina woman in a distinctive blue jumper and crooked veil cued the gray-clad nuns with an organ chord. They began to sing.

Praise God in His sanctuary:

Praise Him in the firmament of His power.

Praise Him for His mighty acts:

Praise Him according to His excellent greatness.

The sisters' timeless, celestial song sent the good kind of shiver down my spine, and soon the grille seemed less about keeping the nuns in than keeping the world out. I felt a deep stillness in that secluded space that I'd never felt anywhere else. Something about their song and being up before the sun made me see life in a new way—a world full of quiet possibility—if only for a few measures of music. The soothing chant commanded my exhausted body to nap despite the unforgiving pew. Every time I dozed off, my stomach growled and woke me up.

Dawn arrived and set the stained-glass windows afire with images of female saints. Several locals joined me on the public side of the chapel. I flinched as a bell rang and an aged priest shambled out to the altar for Mass, his gold-embroidered garments a stark contrast to the poor habits of the sisters. This service was different.

Regina coeli laetare, alleluia:

Quia quem meruisti portare alleluia

The fact that the priest spoke in Latin gave me a break from the guilty feelings I typically felt sitting through Mass, mainly because I couldn't understand most of what he said. His one-line sermon, "Try to love today," was the only English spoken in the service, and it wasn't long enough to trigger any Catholic guilt. If I ever attended church on a regular basis again, this was the priest for me.

Too tired to pray, I went to communion more to get a better view of the nuns than to fulfill any sense of duty or desire for grace. The tiny wafer eased the acid in my empty stomach somewhat, but the trip to the altar to receive it didn't deliver the glimpse of Sister Catherine I'd hoped for. No amount of stretching and squinting helped me see the veiled sisters' faces behind the grille. I felt frustrated knowing I was in the same room with my twin, yet couldn't identify her.

A fresh wave of exhaustion hit me when yet another prayer service followed Mass. Terce, as the schedule called the third of the seven hours of the Divine Office, turned out to be blessedly brief.

After the service, a nun closed the shutters again, preventing further spying. Sister Teresa disappeared behind them before I could get her attention. Impatient for answers, I knocked on the sacristy door to ask the priest about the painting in spite of my aversion to the clergy.

Introducing himself as Father Charles, the reverend was happy to chat as he put away his vestments in a room with more drawers and cupboards than an Old-World apothecary shop.

"I suppose I know the sisters as well as anybody." The priest's words rolled off his tongue with a gentle Georgia twang in charming contrast to his High Mass Latin.

"I say Mass here every morning and hear their confessions twice a week. Not that they've got much to report." He scratched his bald spot. "Asking a nun to avoid sinning is like telling a landlubber to avoid swimming. Sure, the sisters manage a venial now and again, but nothing for the tabloids."

I squirmed and tried to reassure myself that he couldn't possibly know where I worked. "Are any of them artists? I saw a beautiful painting in the visitor's parlor."

"Oh my, yes." He folded his embroidered stole and placed it in a drawer. "Gift shop is fulla pictures for sale."

That was all I needed to hear. Anxious to see more paintings, I said goodbye to the priest without remembering to ask him if he knew who had painted the *Madonna and Child,* probably because part of me already knew. Once outside, I went in search of Sister Teresa or the gift shop—whichever came first.

The courtyard that had been so forbidding in the darkness was resplendent in daylight. Lemon, lime, and apricot trees punctuated the spectacular ocean views. Camellia, bougainvillea, oleander, and dozens of other West Coast varietals I couldn't name bloomed everywhere, their delicate fragrances competing with the earthy, wormy smell that followed a night of rain. A black-and-white cat sat as still as the surrounding religious statuary and stared into a burbling fountain teeming with koi fish.

I found Sister Teresa and the gift shop at the same time as she prepared to unlock the door and open for business.

"Welcome back." Teresa grinned. "Feeling better?"

"Yes, thanks," I said to be polite. As friendly as Sister Teresa was, I still felt my unease around nuns kick into high gear. "Sorry about my hasty departure last night."

"No need to be sorry." Teresa reached for her key ring. "Considering a vocation is a scary business."

"Yes, it is." I guessed it was almost as scary as looking up your long-lost twin. "And seeing my handicap depicted on the baby Jesus in that *Madonna and Child* painting was pretty unsettling." I held up my right hand to show her.

My impaired hand didn't fit neatly into any diagnosis. The most likely cause was a brachial plexus nerve injury incurred during birth. Three surgeries and ongoing physical therapy produced some improvement, but not the full recovery that had been expected. Over the years, new ingredients like arthritis, atrophy, and symptoms of ulnar neuropathy stirred the soup, leaving doctors unable to find a recipe for a cure.

"Oh, but it shouldn't be, dear," the nun said, holding my hand with both of hers. "The peace sign is a common gesture of blessing that appears in a lot of Christian artwork."

I felt like an idiot. Of course it was. I'd made a big deal out of nothing. Just because my father was an artist didn't mean my sister was, too. The baby Jesus' gesture was a fluke.

"Sister Catherine has at least one figure giving that blessing in each of her paintings," Sister Teresa said.

Or not.

"'Course, she would never call them 'her' paintings," the nun continued as she flipped through dozens of keys. "She says it's God painting through her."

God, or the father, anyway, I thought. *Our father.*

"So the *Madonna and Child* painting is hers." I found myself unnerved, delighted, and envious all at once. "Sister Catherine's, I mean."

"Yes."

My mind reeled. Did the baby Jesus' grip in Catherine's painting mean she knew about my hand, or did she suffer from the same disability? My adoptive parents had told me that my birth father tried to keep me but got overwhelmed and ended up choosing adoption when I was six weeks old. He was struggling to manage my recurring infections from a prior hand surgery and didn't have the money for the additional operations that the government would cover if I were made a ward of the state. As a closed adoption, he wasn't told the names of my potential adoptive parents, nor did they know his. But he was told that my adoptive mom was a nurse, and the agency said that my mom's ability to care for me convinced him that I would be better off with them.

That was all my parents knew. When Wagner's estate lawyer later told me I was a twin, he explained that back when Catherine and I were born, my father was an unknown painter living in his tiny art studio because he couldn't afford two rents. I guessed that when he realized he couldn't afford two children either, he chose to keep Catherine because she was healthy and had fewer medical bills. Assuming she wasn't similarly handicapped, then my twin must know about my hand, and in turn, me. Or did she?

Teresa stopped searching her key ring and tilted her chin toward me. "Do you know her?"

"Oh, no. No, I don't." I shook my head a little too vehemently. "And yet the painting feels familiar somehow."

"Catherine has a gift for touching people on a personal level." She put a hand to her heart. "Her work moves me."

"Father Charles said there are paintings in the gift shop."

"Plenty. Lots of the sisters paint during recreation hour." The extern resumed flipping keys until she came up with the one that turned in the lock. "Once in a harvest moon we sell one."

My eyes devoured the walls for more artwork as soon as the nun opened the door. Unfortunately, they remained hungry.

There were paintings all right, but they were staid, pedestrian affairs and not very good. Flowers, wishing wells, and dogs were the dominant subject matter. The colors were standard, predictable, primary. A well-stocked book section, handmade crafts, assorted religious items, and some random rummage sale pieces rounded out the vaguely musty merchandise.

"I don't see anything similar to the *Madonna and Child* in here," I said, trying and failing to hide my disappointment.

"Oh, you wouldn't." Teresa shook her head and straightened a bookshelf. "Sister Catherine doesn't display her paintings in the public areas and she *never* sells them."

"Really? Why not?"

"Says they're never finished. She often traipses around in the middle of the night to fiddle with them some more."

"But the one in the parlor is perfect," I protested, almost fearing for the piece.

"Which is why I take it from the wall and stash it in the public bathroom every night hoping she'll forget about it."

"I see." I smiled, suddenly very fond of Sister Teresa. "And they're not for sale?"

"Nope. Whenever I sneak one of her paintings into a public area like the parlor, a visitor offers to buy it, but Catherine always refuses." The extern spit-polished the figures in a ceramic nativity scene priced at $19.95. "A shame, really. She would probably be excused from her kitchen job and get to paint full time if she'd let us sell them."

"May I speak with her?" I asked and then panicked. But I calmed down when I realized that I had found a safe way to see my sister without having to reveal our true relationship right away. I could meet her and get a sense of her first. Then if she seemed open to it, I would tell her who I was. "I mean, uh, maybe she'll make an exception about selling that *Madonna and Child*."

"You can meet her on the next Visiting Day, but I doubt she'll sell the painting and I know she won't speak to you." Teresa set the baby Jesus figurine back in the small, wooden manger. "Sister Catherine has taken a vow of silence. It's not required in our order, but she seems to prefer it. She's a bit of an odd duck who goes her own way, God bless her, but a true child of our Lord."

Odd duck. If that was Sister's Teresa's polite way of saying Catherine was stubborn, my twin and I had a lot in common.

"She doesn't make it easy for fans of her work, does she?" I pursed my lips in frustration.

"I'm pretty sure her idea is not to have any fans."

Too late.

"Would you mind if I took one last look at that painting before I leave?" I asked.

"Help yourself. The parlor's open."

"Thanks." I stepped outside.

The courtyard walk from the gift shop to the parlor afforded a stunning view of the ocean. I couldn't imagine what it was like for the nuns to live that close to the Pacific, and yet be unable to dip their toes into it. I crossed the sand outside my Venice Beach apartment every morning just to touch the water.

Back in the parlor, I tried to memorize every detail of the painting but got caught up in the emotion it evoked instead. Love, pride, envy, and understanding superseded line, color, texture, and content at every turn. I pulled out the camera, planning to photograph the *Madonna and Child*, but the battery light dimmed and died as I turned it on. Disappointed, I clicked it off. Next I tried to take pictures with my phone—also dead after almost twenty-four hours of roaming in search of Wi-Fi.

I wasn't disappointed for long. As I zipped the camera back into my bag, there was a rustling of fabric. The door on the cloistered side of the grille opened to reveal a young nun carrying a mop and bucket. Her hair was brown to my blonde, her eyes blue to my green, but a quick glance at her jawline, freckles, and height was all it took for me to know she was my sister.

Sister Catherine crimped her brow and stared at me for a moment before waving her apologies and turning to leave.

"No, please wait," I said, my skin feeling prickly one moment and numb the next as adrenaline swamped my veins. I shoved my weak hand into my pocket before she saw it. "Can I ask you a quick question?"

My twin paused, set down her bucket, and turned to me with a smile. She looked about as tall as my five-foot-ten and was as thin as Sister Teresa. Her pale skin, accented by a lock of brown hair that slipped out from under her veil, softened her posture of humility. Her expression had a quiet radiance that surpassed even that of the Madonna's in the painting. I found her beautiful in a way that transcended physical traits and rested in what looked to me like... well...joy.

"Is that your work?" I pointed to the *Madonna and Child* with my strong hand.

Catherine startled at the question. Her eyes flicked to the art, then back to me. She nodded a bit sheepishly and broke into a beatific grin. So this was definitely my sister. I couldn't help noticing her well-formed, perfect hands.

"It's amazing," I said. "Would you be willing to sell it?"

My twin shook her head. I was neither surprised nor disappointed, considering that I couldn't afford such a painting anyway. For me, this one-sided conversation was an excuse to stare. Was it the same for Catherine? Maybe my twin sensed that our incidental meeting was somehow important but didn't quite know why. I, on the other hand, knew exactly why I gaped. I was looking at the first person I'd ever met who was biologically related to me.

I tried to open my mouth again and tell her that we were related, but the words camped in the back of my throat and refused to exit. What if she wasn't ready to hear it? Did she know I existed? If so, how did she feel about being the one our father kept when he gave me away?

The staring continued. It didn't matter that Catherine and I weren't identical. It was enough that we were sisters. Seeing this woman, whose freckled nose, straight posture, and crooked smile matched my own, I felt grounded for the first time in my life. The emotion of the moment made my throat tighten into a cough. When I unconsciously pulled my weak hand out of my pocket to cover my mouth, Catherine's gaze went straight to my disfigurement.

Panic clouded her eyes and chased the smile off of her face. Her whole body constricted. She picked up her bucket and rushed out of the room, sloshing water in her wake.

"Sister Catherine, wait!" I called out, feeling pretty shaky myself. "It's okay. I'm your..."

But she was gone.

CHAPTER FOUR

Stung, I wandered out to my car, where a red-tailed hawk and a turkey vulture shared the sky overhead.

No matter how many times I was reminded of the circumstances of my adoption, or acknowledged to myself that it really was in my best interest, the irrational part of me never understood how my father could let me go. Catherine's swift exit made me feel rejected all over again. And that pissed me off. Graciela had insisted that meeting the twin my father kept would help me sort out my feelings about being adopted, but instead I felt even more confused.

How could she, my flesh and blood, run away like that? I couldn't tell for sure if Catherine knew we were sisters—she was out of the room before I'd had the chance to tell her—but I had to assume she did given the way she panicked when she saw my hand.

It wasn't unusual for people to react inappropriately to my disfigurement. People giggled or blushed, said the wrong thing in an effort to say the right thing, stared at it or pointedly avoided staring. Normally, I wrote it off to nerves or discomfort in the face of disability. But Catherine's extreme reaction, combined with the fact that she painted a hand shaped just like mine in all her art, led me to believe that she knew I was her twin.

I hesitated before starting my car and driving away. Angry as I was at Catherine's reaction, I ached when I left her. I'd found and lost my twin in a matter of seconds. It was unsettling. I felt like I'd left some part of myself behind in that parlor, a rare flicker of true, raw emotion, a profound connection, before I'd had the chance to fully experience it.

Still struggling with my feelings, I arrived at my affordably dingy apartment a few hours later. I walked past my front door and out onto the sand toward my favorite place to think—a cluster of jagged boulders near the shoreline. Several large rocks were balanced, one on top of another, to form a totem that stood six feet tall. Similar totems towered nearby. Together they made up a circle big enough to walk around inside. Smaller stones had been piled into sturdy cairns that marked the perimeter.

The effect was elegant, dramatic, and always changing. Whenever the wind upset the tenuous balance of a totem or shifting sands scattered a cairn, someone walking by built it up again into a different configuration. It reminded me of Stonehenge, except that these feats of engineering withstood the test of time not through the staying power of the rock, but that of the human spirit.

I sat down among the stones, mourning the hoped-for relationship my sister didn't seem to want. Admittedly, the urge to connect hadn't been strong until I found myself driving to Big Sur. And in her defense, Catherine didn't get any warning or time to prepare herself for our meeting. Maybe she would warm up after recovering from the initial shock of seeing me. But what if she didn't? How much of a relationship could I have with a cloistered nun anyway?

Still, even if she didn't know who I was, what the hell was her behavior about? How did she get to act all holy and pull this *my-paintings-are-for-God* routine and still be that rude? Aren't nuns supposed to be extra nice to people? I'm the one our father gave up, and now she's literally running away from me? It wasn't fair.

Furious all over again, I stood up and pushed over the nearest totem. The rocks fell with a muffled thud that was just satisfying enough to goad me on. I knocked over every totem there, ignoring the battering of my legs and feet when stones bumped my body as they fell. Finally, a sharp-edged rock tumbled too close, slicing skin and pounding the top of my foot so hard that I cried out.

I dropped to the sand and cradled my injury, tears of pain streaming down my face. I cried for a long time, longer than I needed to. A fist-sized purple bruise formed around a garish, bloody cut, but it was a shallow wound that wouldn't slow me down much. Yet I cried on, not so much for my foot but for me and the family I would never know—the mother who died the day I was born, the father who took himself out of my life long before he died, and the living sister who panicked and ran when she saw me. Sitting there bleeding, I threw a pity party with myself as the guest of honor and the fallen rocks as the only other attendees.

After about twenty minutes of feeling incredibly sorry for myself, I remembered the painting. If Catherine didn't want to get to know me, I could at least get to know her artwork. Seeing the *Madonna and Child* was as close to a religious experience as I'd ever had. I wanted to see more of her paintings, all of them, inspiring and humbling as I knew it would be. I'd spent years nurturing whatever seedling of writing ability I'd been born with, only to be instantly cowed by Catherine's enormous artistic talent. It made me wonder why I bothered to write at all.

And yet, the only way I could think of to process my overwhelming feelings about my sister was to write about her and her art. For me, writing wasn't so much a choice as a need. It was the way I made sense of life, and the only way I knew how to sort out this new reality. Most of my personal writing remained hidden in my notebooks, but in this case I felt compelled to introduce my sibling's genius to the world. Twin or no, if I was moved by her painting, others would be also.

My skin tingled with the exhilaration of considering writing Rene Wagner's story only to discover a better one in Catherine's. The only new angle I could add to Rene's multiple existing biographies was my relationship to him, something I couldn't be articulate about yet, if ever. But no one had written about Catherine's amazing artwork—paintings that demanded attention no matter who her father was. I wouldn't even need to reveal that we were sisters if she didn't want me to. Phil would reject the serious, scandal-free article, leaving me free to pitch it to more legitimate publications. That elusive landmark story was staring me in the face.

That is, if I could convince Catherine to let me tell it. Frustrated as I was by her intentional obscurity, and as much as I felt that her paintings should be seen, I also had to accept that she'd probably say no. But in many ways the story would be incidental. Researching it would provide the excuse I needed to spend more time with my sister. Even a one-sided relationship would be better than nothing.

As I began to rebuild the first totem I'd knocked over, I realized I hadn't smoked a single cigarette since the night before. Nor did I want one.

Miracles never ceased.

I was so excited when I returned to the newsroom late that afternoon that my words chased each other out of my mouth. "I can't tell Phil she's Wagner's daughter because I don't want him to find out *I'm* Wagner's daughter, and I want to make sure he'll reject the story, so—"

"No worries there. Good journalism doesn't sell tabloids, so Phil will reject it just like he rejects every idea you're enthusiastic about," Graciela said. "We both know that the only way to get *el Jefe* to agree to a piece is to act like you don't want to write it. Then he'll immediately know it's worthless trash and assign it to you."

"Sad but true," I agreed. Our editor only endorsed whatever we appeared to be against.

"Speak of the devil..." Graciela said without turning around to look. The scent of stale cigar smoke preceded Phil by about ten yards. "Remember, keep up the enthusiasm and you're home free."

"That won't be hard," I said. It was impossible for me to act nonchalant about a story that mattered to me.

"Got my goat?" Phil asked when he arrived at my cubicle.

"I wish." I handed him the two-headed goat story fresh from the copy department. He snatched it and began scanning.

"The pictures should be back from photo any minute," I said.

"Wanted this for today's edition." The editor's eyes advanced down the page.

"Didn't you get my message about the weather cond—"

"Mmm-hmm. Just stating the facts out of an inflated sense of self-importance." He flipped to the second page and continued reading. "Next trick: feigning interest in your well-being. Tired?"

"Exhausted, but I stayed overnight at a convent and I think there's a story there. One of the nuns is an incredible painter and—"

"Can't use it," he said.

Graciela struggled to suppress a grin.

"Why not?" I asked, half-smiling myself. "She's really tal—"

"Don't care." Phil flipped to the next page. "My mother paints. Unless this nun paints porn..."

"She does religious subjects."

"There's a shocker. Do said subjects cry actual tears? Do they have real, or at least convincingly faked, stigmata?"

"No." I watched Phil's anemic interest bleed out of him.

"Then forget it." The editor tossed the goat story on my desk. "Looks fine. Proof it and get it to layout."

"But her stuff is amazing," I said, laying it on for extra insurance. "I think it may be—"

"Got a title? How about 'Two-Headed Goat Butts Heads with Herself?'" He patted himself on the back. "Use it."

Graciela's grin busted out across her face as Phil walked away.

"Nice work, *chica*," she said. "Now you're ready for the big leagues."

"Yep." I gulped, suddenly needing that cigarette after all.

"I don't see what you're so hyped about," Matt, my former boyfriend and current next-door neighbor, said through a mouthful of *huevos rancheros* on the sunny patio of the Rose Café. Those waiting for tables at our favorite Sunday morning breakfast spot stood ogling other people's pancakes and snorting with contempt at anyone who lingered too long over emptied plates. "*The Comet* would never run a serious piece, and even I know the odds on somebody picking it up freelance are way shitty."

"Thanks for the vote of confidence," I said over the din of clattering dishes and Sunday chat.

"I just want you to be realistic about your chances."

"I am. I'm doing it as much to get to know my sister as I am to get published."

"Well, that makes more sense to me," he said, shuffling through the stack of newspapers that crowded our table. Matt was the only other person I knew who still liked to read hard copies of the weekend papers. "I just wish you would get to know her on her terms."

"She's not really offering any terms," I said. "So I'm making them up as I go."

He shrugged, snapped open the *Los Angeles Times*, and dove in, his bed head hair sticking up over the paper. Sunday was the only day Matt had to catch up on errands and the news of the world. His job as a film production assistant kept him in a sort of suspended animation. The work hours were so insane that the rest of his life got dropped.

"We landed another probe on Titan?"

"A week-and-a-half ago," I said.

"Really." He whistled and resumed reading.

We reached that point in our meal where those waiting for a table could justifiably scowl at our indifference to their plunging blood sugar levels. I used my fork to cut off two more bites of my French toast and called for the check. I always ordered soft foods at restaurants so I didn't have to struggle to use a knife in public.

"Time to go, Mr. Current Events," I said.

"Yes, Ma'am."

Matt and I headed for our apartment building. We walked arm-in-arm not because we were in love, though we may have been once and might still be on a good day, but because I had to lead him like a blind man as he continued to read the paper.

Our Venice neighborhood was half-gentrified, half-terrified. The ocean views, art galleries, and multimillion-dollar renovations collided with regular drug deals, tattered homeless wandering the streets, beach hippie culture, and crumbling, rent-controlled apartments like the ones Matt and I occupied.

"Curb," I warned when we reached a corner.

"Tornado hit South Dakota." Matt felt for the curb with his foot and stepped up as he folded the newspaper to a new section. "Political crisis in Indonesia."

Matt had been between films back when I'd moved in across the hall from him two years before. That left us plenty of time to get to know each other and start dating. I tried not to fall too hard for him, sensing that neither his personality nor his profession left room for any real intimacy. When he got his next movie gig three months later, I found myself playing the part of a production widow trying to have a relationship with someone who was either absent or asleep. I hung on for another three months, but it wasn't working. We broke up, remaining friends and neighbors, sharing newspaper subscriptions and Sunday mornings. I wallpapered over my real feelings as best I could with a confident, bold pattern befitting an independent woman who accepted that the man she loved would never want the same things she did—at least not at the same time.

Having already lost four parents, the idea of building a family both fascinated and freaked me out. I craved the connection, while fearing the possibility that I could lose that new family, too. I wasn't in a huge hurry to get married and have kids, but I knew, based on prior comments, that Matt was in no rush at all, not to mention that he wasn't my boyfriend anymore. I would probably need to look elsewhere when I was ready to risk it. In the meantime, I hoped to get to know the one family member I'd just learned I had, if only during short visits in the cloister parlor.

"Wildfires are burning up Florida." Matt shuffled along and kept reading. "Flooding continues in China."

When we arrived outside our building, I slipped my arm out from his and left him standing beside the mailboxes just to see what would happen. Thirty seconds passed before he realized where he was and followed me inside.

I managed to fool myself, but nobody else, about my affection for Matt. In the year and a half since we'd broken up, I dated only rarely and always compared other guys to him. Meanwhile, "trust-me" brown eyes and an affable manner made it easy for Matt to meet women in the scant free time he had.

"Earthquake in Afghanistan," I heard him mutter in the hallway as he opened his apartment door.

Once in a while, he got involved with someone. The potential girlfriend usually bailed after two weeks of Matt's schedule and I got my best friend back. So in the name of friendship, I led him around by the nose while he eyeballed the paper, but I didn't feel too bad about leaving him out on the curb.

"Where's Evan?" Matt asked an hour later when I let myself into his apartment. He sat straight up from the couch where he'd been lying on what I hoped was a pile of clean laundry. His staring eyes were open, but he wasn't awake. "I've got to get him to the set!"

"Shhh, you're okay. It's Sunday." I helped him lie down again. "You and Evan have the day off."

Evan Cole was the twenty-seven-year-old star of the action movie Matt was working on. Matt had been assigned to be the actor's personal production assistant. Evan was low maintenance, but Matt took his job seriously in hopes of impressing the producers and promoting his own fledgling directing career.

I folded a sweatshirt and positioned it behind Matt's head. We had planned to play tennis, but the man clearly needed his rest. I scanned his bachelor-chic apartment, which, despite a weight bench occupying the space where a kitchen table should be and a home theater set-up worth more than the rest of the contents combined, was still cozier than my own apartment across the hall.

The scuttled tennis game meant my whole Sunday now stretched before me in open invitation. I decided to drive up to Big Sur. It wasn't Visiting Sunday at the convent, but then I didn't feel ready to see Catherine again anyway. Instead, I would photograph the *Madonna and Child* so I could ask my art-dealer friend Trish's opinion of it and have a copy for myself. The warm feeling I got whenever I looked at the Virgin Mary's expression was something I wanted to have available at all times. Was that how Catherine imagined our mother?

CHAPTER FIVE

Arriving at the convent, I headed straight for the visiting room as the songs of five o'clock Vespers floated out of the chapel. I tried not to worry when the canvas wasn't on the parlor wall. When it wasn't in Sister Teresa's nearby bathroom hiding place either, panic set in just beneath my rib cage. I paced the courtyard for eight chain cigarettes waiting for Vespers to end and was in the chapel the moment they did.

"I don't think she took it down to work on it this time." Sister Teresa collected and slid the hymnals down one of the public pews toward me.

"Well, that's a relief. At least it hasn't been altered," I said, stacking the hymnals in a pile at the end of the row. "But where is it? She didn't change her mind and sell it to someone else, did she?"

"Not exactly, no." The extern paused, as if unsure of how to break the news to me. "My guess is that she gave it away."

"She *what?*" Panic turned to fury, dropping down from my rib cage to burn a hole in my belly. "But why would she give it to someone else when I would have been happy to pay at least what I could afford for it?"

I forgot about the incoming hymnals and unconsciously tapped a cigarette out of the pack, further agitated when I realized I couldn't smoke it inside.

"Oh, she didn't give it to a person." Teresa approached and gathered the neglected books. "She gave it back to God."

I dropped the cigarette and looked at her, uncomprehending.

"Art supplies are pricey." The nun picked up my cigarette and whisked the unlit tobacco under her nose with what looked like lust if I hadn't known better. "We can't keep up with the demand at the rate Sister Catherine goes through them, so she recycles canvases."

"As in paints over them?"

Sister Teresa nodded and handed the cigarette back to me. "I kept that one around longer than usual, but she always finds my hiding places eventually."

I sat down in the front pew, speechless but not silent, as I burst into tears. Intellectually, I knew an article about an artist who blithely destroyed her own work was that much more compelling. Emotionally, I'd formed a personal bond with the painting. My family that never was had just lost an heirloom.

"I feel your pain." Sister Teresa sat beside me and put a hand on my shoulder. "We strive for detachment from material things here. Sister Catherine gives us a chance to practice that skill more than some of us have a mind to. Can't say I've gotten very good at it."

"I'm sorry." I wiped my eyes with the back of my strong hand. "It's just been a long time since I've gotten that excited about anyone, I mean, anything. I can't believe it's gone."

"Do you remember what it looked like?"

"More or less."

"Then it's still here." The nun tapped her temple. "And here." She touched her heart.

"But what if I forget?" I was in no mood for sentimentality now.

"Then God will put something better in its place."

I was still unconvinced. We sat there for several minutes before Sister Teresa spoke again.

"Come with me." The extern stood and led me out of the chapel, her keys jangling out the cadence of her stride.

"I don't get it." I rose and followed the nun into the courtyard. "How could an artist bear to lose her own work, much less destroy it herself?"

"From what I can figure, Sister Catherine values the *act* of painting, not the outcome. The creation process is her method of prayer, a direct appeal to God, who replies in colors and shapes. Once their conversation is over, Catherine considers the finished piece incidental."

"But that's tragic."

"Maybe," Teresa said as we passed several of the closed courtyard doors. "Sister Catherine doesn't show or sell her paintings because she doesn't want to be given the credit for them. In order to keep the channel clear for God to work through her, she paints as often as possible, even, and sometimes especially, if that means recycling canvases."

I found it all very noble and maddening at the same time. "It's selfish to squander such an inspired vision of God." I stomped along in my heavy-soled loafers. "How anyone with such a gift could just throw it away is beyond me."

"Who's to say she's throwing it away?" Teresa stepped lightly in her bare feet. "Maybe God is audience enough."

"What kind of God would ask an artist to destroy a part of herself?"

"I don't think God made that request so much as Sister Catherine took it upon herself to reuse canvases." Sister Teresa led the way to the parlor door. "At any rate, faith and love often result in some sort of personal sacrifice."

"Personal sacrifice, sure, but what about everyone else? People would be inspired by Sister Catherine's work. If it's not hers to take credit for, then why does she get to decide what happens to it?"

"Who do you think should decide?"

I couldn't answer that.

We entered the parlor.

"Make yourself at home." The nun gestured to a chair. "I'll be back in a jiffy."

Teresa disappeared through the cloister door. I sat and waited. The Shaker chair was even more uncomfortable than the church pew. Scanning the walls for more paintings, I found only picture windows and a framed religious print of the Sacred Heart of Jesus. It seemed heartless of Him to reclaim the painting just as it was restoring my faith in, well, something.

Ten minutes later, Sister Teresa reentered, this time on the cloistered side of the room. From behind the bars, she revealed a canvas she'd hidden under the folds of her habit.

"Sorry it took me so long. I had to find one small enough to smuggle."

I jumped up and put my face to the grille so the bars didn't obscure my view as Sister Teresa pulled out the unframed oil painting depicting the *Annunciation*. At twelve-by-eighteen inches or so, it was much smaller than the *Madonna and Child*. Mary knelt before the Angel Gabriel, whose silken wings fluttered against a dreamscape where soft, gray brushstrokes suggested fading fireworks on a misty night, melting away into the gauzy beauty of a blackened sky over a depthless ocean. It didn't take me long to find what I was looking for: the angel held his hand over Mary in the gesture of blessing that resembled my handicap.

The painting triggered both my secular and spiritual sensibilities. The sanctity of the scene transcended religious fervor and rested in tranquility. I saw the fearsome news that she would bear the Son of God reflected in the Virgin's eyes, yet her open-armed posture was one of acceptance. My recent distress disappeared and a feeling of peace washed over me.

My eyes moved from the painting to Sister Teresa, who nodded in recognition of our mutual awe.

"Would you mind if I took some pictures?" I pulled out my digital camera.

"I suppose that would be all right, provided they're only for your personal use. Mind you don't get me in the photo—my hair's a mess." Teresa winked and held up the painting for my clicking camera.

"I wasted a lot of valuable class time in grammar school wondering what the nuns' hair looked like under their veils," I admitted.

"Those were sisters. Only cloistered religious are called nuns. My hair is wash-'n-go short, if you must know. Whom should I fix it for?"

"Sometimes I wish I wore a veil." I pushed a long blonde strand out of my eyes.

"Join us and make bad hair days a thing of the past. When do you feel the call most strongly?"

"The call to what? Cut my hair short?"

"To a religious vocation."

"Oh, God, never," I spat out and then cringed, wanting to chew up my words and swallow them again. "I mean, never before now. I hope that's not a bad thing. I just didn't see myself that way until uh, the other night in the rain."

I took pictures faster.

"I see." Sister Teresa glossed over my abuse of God's name and focused on my answer. "That's nothing to be concerned about. We all hear the call in God's good timing."

"Last picture." I snapped it. "Thanks."

"My pleasure." A visibly relieved Teresa lowered the painting.

"How did you hear the call?" I asked.

"I felt drawn to the church from my childhood on." The nun set the painting down and shook out her weary arms. "My mother was quite religious herself and thrilled that I tried to be good and holy. Until I said I wanted to become a cloistered nun, that is. Then she wrote to the Pope and told him to talk me out of it."

"Really? Why?"

"Despite Mary's Immaculate Conception, my mother was reasonably sure my becoming a Bride of Christ wasn't going to produce any grandchildren for her. Plus, she wouldn't see me much if I entered the cloister, and I wouldn't be around to take care of her in her old age. So anxiety played a big part."

"What did you do?"

"I listened to her. I went to college, then got a job, and set about looking for a husband, but I knew I was doing it for her and not me."

Teresa pointed to the exits. We walked through the doors on our respective sides of the grille and reunited in the courtyard.

"Finally, in my mid-twenties, I couldn't ignore it any longer and joined the novitiate." The extern smiled, blushed, and shook her head in apparent disbelief over her good fortune. "You can't imagine the joy and gratitude I felt when I was accepted into the community."

"Your expression pretty much sums it up." I slowed my step, touched by Sister Teresa's quiet humility. "What did your mother do when you joined?"

"Didn't speak to me for a year." The corners of Teresa's mouth tightened. "Nearly broke my heart. We made our peace after that, and I did get special dispensation to go care for her when she was dying since I was an only child."

"I'm sorry." Realizing I wasn't ready to leave yet, I sat down on a stone bench among the hibiscus bushes.

"Every woman has her own struggles when she enters." The extern took the seat beside me and worried a salmon-colored bloom between her fingers. "Sister Carmella wanted to join us at age fifteen, but Mother insisted that she finish high school first. Sister Scholastica visited the convent as a prospective right out of college, then took thirteen years to think about it before she returned."

"Do you ever regret your decision to become a nun?" I couldn't help asking. The black-and-white cat glared at me from across the koi fish fountain.

"Regret it? Never. Doubt it? Often." The extern shooed away the contemptuous cat with a flick of her wrist. "Three of the women who took their initial vows with me have since left the order. I wonder at times if I shouldn't have left with them, but I believe in the power of prayer. My daily recital of the Divine Office isn't going to change the world, but maybe it will ease someone's suffering, and that's good enough for me." She tossed the flower into the water, where it floated in languorous circles. "What is your present career?"

"Well..."

I struggled with how to answer. After my first visit to the convent, I had decided not to tell anyone at the cloister about my job, my potential article, or even my relationship to Sister Catherine for fear it might further limit my access to the art and the artist. Confessing that my vocation story was a ruse to see my twin wouldn't help my credibility, and I trusted the silent Sister Catherine wasn't telling anyone whatever she might know. Yet I readily revealed my career to the extern.

"I'm a journalist and—"

"Is that right? A journalist came here in the fifties to interview a few of us and put together a book," Teresa said.

"Did you give an interview?" I asked.

"I did." Teresa frowned. "But I wish I hadn't. He didn't exactly misquote me, but I think he missed the point."

"Oh, he knew what you were trying to say." I definitely wouldn't tell the extern about my possible article now. "He just twisted it to fit the point he wanted to make. That's what we journalists do. Sometimes I wonder why we bother to conduct interviews when we've typically written the piece in our heads long before meeting the interviewee."

"And here I thought he was just a little slow. Now I understand why several sisters refused to speak with him." She plucked another hibiscus. "I wouldn't do it again, but back then I was flush with enthusiasm for my new life and I thought the book might help attract more women to serve our Lord."

"Did it?" I asked.

"We got a lot of nibbles, but none of them panned out. Those who enter and stay feel the call long before they read or hear about us. The call comes from within, the rest is just reinforcement. I'm sure you're a much nicer journalist than he was."

"Actually, I'm worse." I avoided her eyes. "I'm a tabloid journalist."

"Well, if being a tabloid journalist is what you feel called to do, then you're serving God," Teresa said, gently setting the second hibiscus bloom afloat in the fountain.

"Maybe." Part of me liked writing for a tabloid. It provided a wide canvas for the overactive imagination I'd developed as a child fantasizing about what my birth parents were like. The rest of me was disgusted and ashamed that I traded on half-truths and hyperbole for a living. I stood up and headed for my car. "I'd better go before it gets late."

Scant radio and phone reception on the long drive home gave me plenty of time to ponder the merits of my occupation. Did God call *anyone* to write for tabloids? I certainly didn't feel fulfilled by tabloid journalism, or even straight journalism.

I had originally wanted to write books. Going the starving author route after being a starving student would have put me over the edge, not to mention sent my student loans into default. I decided journalism was steadier. Steady or not, though, I was often in danger of defaulting anyway. Careful as I was, loans and life in a large city made solvency a constant challenge. In addition to addressing my need to have a relationship with a sibling who didn't appear to want one, I wondered if publishing the article would improve my financial situation. Maybe I'd conquer my discomfort around nuns along the way.

CHAPTER SIX

I opened the door to *The Comet*'s darkroom around midnight and found Rod, the gangly photography intern, scrambling to cover some print work before the light damaged it.

"Sorry, Rod. I forgot to knock."

"No worries." Rod grinned and turned down the ska music blaring from his iPod speakers. "I forgot to lock the door."

Rod, a college junior, took *The Comet*'s unpaid internship in photojournalism hoping to beef up his portfolio. Instead, he found himself relegated to both old-fashioned film processing and high-end Photoshop manipulation in an airless room where the chemicals couldn't help but go to his head.

"I have a favor to ask." I tossed him the memory card full of pictures of the painting. "Could you choose the best one of those and make me an eight-by-ten?"

"Take me about half an hour to get to it." He turned his music back up and got to work.

"Thanks. Coffee?" I gestured drinking.

He nodded. "Lots of cream."

I left him to his computer and his chemicals and returned twenty-five minutes later with the biggest cup of coffee 7-Eleven had to offer. This time I knocked but got no answer. The music was off and I wondered if he'd left. Freeing up my left hand to open the door, I found

Rod sitting there staring at several eight-by-tens of the *Annunciation* pinned up on the clothesline for display. The fluorescents were on at full wattage, yet the prints held up as well as the painting had. Rod didn't notice me until I stood beside him.

"Holy shit," was all he could say.

"Exactly. The artist is a nun."

"For real?" He pulled the prints from their clothespins. "She's wicked good. How do you know her?"

"I don't," I lied. "I came across her work by accident."

"Right on."

I half-thought I saw Rod's gaze shift from the Angel Gabriel's curled hand to my own, but maybe I was paranoid.

"I printed a couple for myself," he said. "Hope that's cool."

I hesitated, remembering Catherine's distaste for exposure, but then rationalized that it was okay since Rod had already seen the image anyway.

"Sure, as long as you don't show anyone else." I gathered up the pictures. "She's very private about her stuff."

"I won't."

"Thanks for the quick turnaround, Rod. I owe you one."

"No, you don't." He waved it off. Young, green, and new to the tabloid universe, Rod was the only person at the paper whose favors were freely given. Everyone else demanded reciprocity at the worst possible moment.

As I stuffed the photos into an envelope, Rod flipped through his own copies.

"Damn," he muttered, shaking his head.

Encouraged by the photographer's enthusiastic response, I drove straight from *The Comet* to my friend Trish's house in Laurel Canyon.

Trish was a highly successful art dealer who trotted the globe scouting pieces for film actors and directors who had the money to spend, but no time to follow the auction circuit. The clients got valuable paintings and sculptures they liked, and Trish got to save her commissions for the gallery she hoped to buy someday. She also acquired enough frequent flyer miles to send the entire population of Sweden around the world twice.

It was after one a.m., but Trish was always up late thanks to chronic jet lag. I jumped when she cracked the door wearing a Maori war mask, her curly, red hair framing it like a mane.

"Is this a bad time?" I asked.

"No, I'm not having kinky sex with the gardener, if that's what you mean. Not that I would mind. He's quite the hottie." Trish undid the chain, opened the door, and pulled off her mask in one fluid motion. "I'm trying to scare you, the hypothetical intruder."

"Do hypothetical intruders ring the doorbell?"

"Polite ones do."

"Where's Fritz?" I asked.

"Broken."

Fritz was Trish's Rottweiler, or rather, the electronic barking machine that went off when her doorbell rang. Living alone in the City of Angels hadn't imbued her with a sense of safety, particularly since what appeared to be a high-end drug dealer had recently bought the house next door.

"Did you check his batteries?"

"Yeah, they're fine. It's probably his wiring. The tech said I might have to put him to sleep." She wiped away a fake tear.

"Can't you get another one?"

"I suppose." She heaved a theatrical sigh. "There's a new Great Dane at Radio Shack, but puppies are so much work."

"Well, I've got something that'll cheer you up," I said, holding up the photos.

"Wow," Trish said a few minutes later. She sat curled up on her living room sofa, and peered at the prints through the rectangular black frames of her glasses. "Her sense of perspective is incredible—really groundbreaking. Talent certainly runs in your family, Dorie."

"So it would seem." Trish was the only one besides Matt and Graciela who I'd told about my birth family. I was glad she validated my opinion of the picture but couldn't help wishing I'd inherited a bit of Wagner's talent myself. "And you agree that the angel's hand is a common gesture and not a reference to me?"

"Absolutely. It's all over religious art. The fact that Sister Catherine uses it in her paintings doesn't mean she knows who you are."

"Given the way she reacted to seeing my hand, I'm not so sure."

"But you are sure she doesn't have a gallery rep?" Trish asked, not one to dwell on personal issues when there was money to be made.

"That I am sure of."

"She does now." Trish rubbed her palms together. "Wait until the art world finds out that Rene Wagner's daughter paints as well as he did. They'll go crazy."

"Not yet," I reminded her. "You can't tell anybody about this until after my story breaks... *if* it breaks."

"Sure. Fine." My friend pushed her lower lip into a pout. "But, after that, I plan to take at least half the credit for discovering her."

"Fair enough." I smiled.

"What are her other paintings like?"

"I've only seen one other, but it was just as amazing." I relaxed into the luxury of a distressed leather chair that easily cost more than I spent on a month's rent. "The photos don't capture the emotion. You should see the original."

"I intend to. Along with everything else she's ever done."

"That could be a problem. I can't officially meet her until the convent's next Visiting Sunday and then only if she agrees to see me, at which point she still won't actually *speak* to me, given her vow of silence."

"She's taking the whole reclusive artist thing a little far, wouldn't you say?" Trish flipped to the next print.

"I'm as frustrated as you are."

"Well, if I can't see the stuff, I'll settle for pictures of everything for now."

"That'll take some time, but I'll get them," I promised, having no idea how I would accomplish it.

"How many does she have?"

"I'm not sure. She has this nasty habit of painting over completed canvases to save money."

"Shut up!" Trish's jaw dropped in horror. "Painting over old canvases is terrible for the longevity of the work."

"Is it? I knew it was bad for the original painting to be lost. I didn't realize it's bad for the new painting as well."

"It's disastrous." She jumped up and grabbed an art book from the shelf. "Unless the artist soaks the canvas and scrapes off the original ground and paint completely, ghosts of the old painting will eventually show through the new one."

"Look." Trish paged through the book and showed me two photographs of the same oil portrait taken years apart. "You buy a clean portrait and ten years later, a tree pops up on the guy's forehead. Not exactly what the collector paid for."

The subject of the painting had the outlines of a maple bursting from his frontal lobe in the second photo.

"That looks painful," I said.

Based on the little I knew about Sister Catherine—and God, for that matter—I guessed they would like such unexpected effects. Trish clearly didn't endorse the posthumous reinvention of paintings, however, so I kept my thoughts to myself.

"For Christ's sake, somebody get the woman some fresh supplies." Trish returned the book to the shelf.

"I've thought of that, but I can't afford it," I said.

"I can. You fly, I'll buy." The art dealer went to her desk and signed a blank check. "Make sure you get the best pre-primed linen or cotton duck. Winsor and Newton Artists' Oil Colour. And sable brushes."

Trish ripped out the check and handed it to me.

"I'll pay you back," I said, not sure how I would manage that either.

"No need. Just bring me the receipt so I can write it off on my taxes. Does she have a good easel?"

"An easel won't fit in my car," I said.

"Forget the easel. But buy everything else. Jesus. Wasting such talent on subpar materials is a shame."

"I know. And Trish?"

"Mmmm?" she said as she leaned over another print.

"It's probably not a good idea to take the Lord's name in vain if you ever meet the nuns. Just a little tip I learned the hard way."

"Good point, good point. I'll keep it clean. If I like the rest of her stuff and she has enough pieces ready, we'll do a show. Religious art can sometimes be a tough sell, but your sister's sensibility is hip enough to give her paintings a wide appeal."

"Hold on there." My spine stiffened. "I'd love to feature you as the expert opinion in the article, but don't get your hopes up about a show."

"You can't dangle this in front of me and then say I can't do anything with it. My clients will eat this up. How many frequent flyer miles do you want for this? Or would you prefer a finder's fee?"

"Not gonna happen." I said, feeling protective. "I guarantee she'll refuse to sell."

"Oh, I'll make her sell. Money talks, honey."

"Not to silent nuns with vows of poverty it doesn't."

"There'll be more for us, then."

I shook my head. "You're shameless."

"What? You get to exploit your sister and I don't?"

"I'm not exploiting her." At least I hoped not. "I won't print the article without getting her permission first. In the meantime, I'm getting to know her in the only way I know how under the circumstances."

"Did you ever consider us artsy types might want to get to know her and her work, too?" Trish took off her glasses. "Don't be so selfish. At least *I* can make her a little money."

"Money is useless to her."

"I don't care if she uses it or not. She can burn it for all I care." Trish tossed the print onto her coffee table. "As long as I get my percentage first."

"How much money do you need?" I looked around at the Spanish revival house replete with California Craftsman furniture and an original Diego Rivera over the fireplace.

"I dunno. More than I have?"

"Now who's the one being greedy?"

"*Moi?* Always. Time for a drink to celebrate." Trish cracked open a bottle of Glenlivet and poured us each a belt.

"What happened to us?" I asked. "You wanted to paint and I wanted to write books. When did that change?"

"When we ran out of Ramen noodles."

I chuckled in uneasy acknowledgment as we clinked glasses and downed our scotch.

"So," Trish said, swirling the ice in her glass. "I assume you'll want to visit with another Wagner since you're here?"

"Yes, please," I said.

Trish rose, and I followed her to the dining room, where she rolled a china cabinet out of the way and keyed in the security code to her climate-controlled storage vault. My breath quickened as the door swung open to reveal the painting that had changed everything.

I may not have inherited my birth father's talent, but I did inherit one of his paintings. Respecting the privacy rules of the closed adoption to the end, Wagner had instructed his estate lawyer not to contact me until after both my adoptive parents had died. When that time came nine years after Wagner's own death, the main point of the lawyer's call wasn't to tell me who my biological family was, but to inform me that I was the inheritor of one of Wagner's masterpieces, an abstract entitled *Shift*. Shocked, thrilled, and way too nervous to keep something that valuable at home, I put the painting in Trish's art vault and paid it frequent visits.

I peered into the vault and saw *Shift* nestled between a blood-orange Rothko and a kaleidoscope-colored Kandinsky. Black, white, and gray circles of paint floated up from a murky swath of ebony that covered the bottom quarter of the canvas. Thin, horizontal lines blurred the image slightly, as if warped gas station squeegees or snails had passed over the wet canvas and left tracks. As I stared, the image seemed to move–a babbling brook full of tadpoles playing bumper cars, cells bouncing against one another under a microscope. Birth and life in all its exuberance.

I usually didn't care for abstract art, and yet I'd been fascinated by Wagner's work long before I learned he was my father. Most abstract paintings frustrated me because they seemed too easy for the artist to render and too difficult for the viewer to decipher. But here, understanding felt effortless, the experience collaborative, even strangely familiar.

"It's in excellent condition," Trish said, reflexively going into sales pitch mode even though she'd already shared everything she knew about the painting with me. I let her continue because she loved talking about it and I loved hearing it. She picked up the canvas for better viewing. "So beautifully done. His use of light is inspired. I'd have to get an appraisal, but based on its size and quality, I'd say it's worth at least a million dollars."

"So you've told me," I said. That kind of money would take care of my Stanford loans, plus a lot more. But selling my only tangible link to my birth family was the last thing I wanted. "I'd like to keep it if I can."

My eyes swam into the canvas and lost themselves there. Beyond shapes and paint, the piece was pure emotion—mine or my father's, I wasn't sure which. I couldn't shake the feeling that I'd seen the image somewhere long before I'd encountered it on canvas. In the painting, I saw my fantasy life as an artist's daughter presented in muted oils. I felt the exhilaration of a two-year-old blowing bubbles at my first swim lesson, the ecstasy of a six-year-old running through the lawn sprinkler, skidding on flattened grass slick with moisture and mud. I sensed the strength in fragile things and the weakness in strong ones. Just as I had with Catherine's *Madonna and Child*, I stared at Rene's *Shift* and tried to imprint every brushstroke on my mind, hoping it would provide me with some insight into my birth family.

"I think you should keep it." Trish examined the back of the canvas. "But will you be able to cover the inheritance taxes on something this valuable?"

"Good point." I frowned. "Probably not."

"Well, you don't have to part with it just yet." Trish placed the painting back against the wall. "Nothing's due until tax day. I'll put some feelers out in case you decide to sell. Meantime, you enjoy it."

It wouldn't be difficult. I looked back at the painting. The writer in me stood agape at such skillful communication with no words at all. My father hadn't bothered with color or recognizable images, yet managed to say more than everything I'd ever written put together.

CHAPTER SEVEN

"No way," Matt marveled when he found me up and fully dressed in the gloomy apartment hallway at four thirty in the morning. Five a.m. call times during the week made it impossible for him to sleep in when he wanted to. "Has hell frozen over?"

"Close. I'm going to Mass again," I said. "It's Visiting Sunday and Sister Teresa's Diamond Jubilee celebration at the convent."

"Diamond? That makes her—"

"Over eighty," I said. We almost bumped heads bending down to grab our newspapers. "The woman hardly looks sixty years old. Turns out she's been a nun for longer than that."

"The Lord takes good care of His women. Or so I've heard." Matt handed me *The New York Times Magazine* and *Book Review* pull-outs. "I was going to make you breakfast."

"You were?" I'd never known Matt to make anything besides Pop-Tarts and chocolate milk. Of course, that may have been what he had in mind. I passed him *The Los Angeles Times* Sports and Business sections. "To what do I owe such an honor?"

"I thought eating here might reduce my chances of being left out on the curb after the meal."

"Sorry about that." I laughed. "Can I take a rain check?"

"It never rains in Los Angeles."

"I'll take a sun check then." I turned a circle in my black turtleneck and demure skirt. "Do I look okay for church?"

"Looks good to me. 'Course I'm just a pagan." Matt frowned. "Who am I going to play with on my day off if you're bailing again?"

"You could come with me. I could use some moral support."

"Already plenty of morals to go around at the convent." He raised his hand in benediction. "Go with God."

I arrived for ten o'clock Mass with three minutes to spare. Enough garden flowers festooned the chapel to make the potted begonia I'd brought as a gift look paltry. The special recognition of Sister Teresa's anniversary made the service more personal and enjoyable. Father Charles' sermon, "God Bless Sister Teresa," once again set the standard for brevity.

Despite the brief sermon, the service still gave me plenty of time to get nervous about my first chance to formally meet Catherine. Was my interest in her paintings enough, or would I have to admit we were twins in order to see her? I still felt I could write a better article if I didn't acknowledge our relationship just yet, given that Catherine didn't seem to want to hear about it at our initial meeting. But part of me really wanted to get it out in the open.

After Mass, I found Sister Teresa on the public side of the parlor encouraging the guests to eat from a continental breakfast set out for her celebration. Based on my brief chats with the extern, I knew the *petit fours* and cucumber and mint sandwiches were much more extravagant fare than the perpetually fasting, vegetarian nuns allowed themselves.

"Congratulations," I said to the guest of honor. "Sixty years is quite an accomplishment."

"Oh, not really. Spending my life serving God is hardly work. On the other hand, sharing close quarters with fifteen other women can be rather..." Teresa's keys jangled as she chuckled. "Well, maybe it *is* an accomplishment."

"For you." I held out the begonias.

"Thank you, but I can't accept them. Our vow of poverty forbids individual ownership."

"But..." My shoulders slumped as I thought about the money I had put down at Art Mart for painting supplies a few days before. "How can you take donations if no one can—"

"We may accept donations and gifts to the convent as a whole, but not personal gifts," Teresa clarified.

"Okay, then these are a donation to the whole convent."

"Now you're talking. In that case, *'we'* thank you." She took the flowers and inhaled their fragrance. "We'll all enjoy them in the garden."

I pulled the art supplies from where I had stowed them in the corner and presented them next.

"I know you said Sister Catherine, I mean all the sisters, were short on supplies. Since I didn't know her preferences, I bought several different types of paints, thinners, and brushes. At the very least she, er, everyone, can use the canvases and the stretchers."

"We thank you." Teresa accepted the supplies, leaned over, and whispered, "I promise Catherine will get first crack at them."

"Is she here?" I scanned the knot of sisters gathered on the cloistered side of the grille to share in the celebration.

"Oh, no. She won't come out with all these people around. She's already congratulated me privately. But why don't you hold on to the art supplies and give them to her, I mean *us*, personally?" The extern gave the supplies back to me with a wink. "I bet I can convince her to meet you a bit later when things quiet down."

That was all the encouragement I needed. I sat and waited as a parade of relatives and friends came and went. At lunchtime, the entire extended family of a young local nun, Sister Carmella, arrived, bringing food and speaking Spanish as they filled the visiting side of the room to capacity. A toddler got passed from lap to lap to be cooed over, his feet never touching the ground. An older child climbed through a window to play ball just inside the garden as her grandmother clucked out a warning to be careful.

"Ever since we were kids she wanted to enter." The young nun's sister handed me a plate of *carnitas* as she spoke.

"She knew even then?" I asked.

"Mmmm-hmmm. You can see the convent from the house where we grew up."

The woman nodded toward the teenage Sister Carmella hugging relatives through the grate. Everyone laughed when she got to the end of the line of people and then went back to the beginning to start all over again.

"You're still here?" Sister Teresa asked when she came in to tidy up the parlor a few minutes before five and found me alone. "I told Sister Catherine you were waiting hours ago. Did she ever show?"

"No, but it's all right. Sister Carmella's family fed me very well." I patted my stomach and got up to leave.

"Hold on there. Let me see what I can do. But don't expect too much from her. She's very shy." Teresa started to exit and then turned back to me. "Oh, and try not to give her credit for the paintings. Focus on telling her about your vocation instead."

"Got it." As I watched the nun leave, I realized that in order to make Catherine more comfortable, I was going to have to go deeper into my vocation lie. I wasn't sure how I would talk my way out of that fiction when the time came.

Moments later, I heard Sister Teresa talking to someone in the hall outside the parlor.

"Just see her and make an old nun happy. Consider it my Jubilee present."

The door opened and Teresa and my sister entered the room. As soon as Catherine spied me, she dropped her gaze to the floor and shifted from foot to foot. Her cheeks went rosy with what might have been anger, embarrassment, or both. When she looked up again, I thought I saw confusion in her eyes, but she mustered a nervous grin with that crooked smile I recognized as my own.

All the jealousy and rejection I felt after our first meeting disappeared. I was just so happy to see her again. I wanted to speak but was afraid to say the wrong thing and snap the thread of connection her smile had established. Did she know we were twins? I still couldn't tell for sure and didn't want to ask in front of Teresa, who didn't seem to notice the high emotion in the room.

"Sister Catherine, may I present Dorie McKenna," Sister Teresa said.

Catherine nodded in acknowledgment and looked away. She didn't need to worry about seeing my deformed hand again. I was careful to keep it in my pocket this time. My twin's own hands were hidden behind the paint-smudged blue smock that protected her habit.

"Dorie is considering a vocation with us," Teresa continued.

I stiffened as my lie was repeated back to me, and tried to think of something to talk about besides my phony vocation.

"I'm so glad to meet you, Sister Catherine," I said, extending my left hand through the grate. My twin didn't take it but displayed her own to indicate that it was sticky with pigment.

"You'll have to excuse Catherine. She paints up until the very last minute before prayers," Teresa said. "I'm afraid I interrupted her."

I had decided to discuss the rituals at the cloister that resonated with me, but the minute Sister Teresa referred to Catherine's painting habits, I lost my cool and went exactly where the extern had asked me not to go.

"I think you're extremely talented," I blurted, giddy as a teenager meeting her pop star idol. "Your paintings are stunning."

Catherine's whole body tensed as the eggshells I had been walking on broke under the weight of my compliment. Catherine frowned, folded her arms without thinking about the paint now smearing her smock and didn't respond. When Sister Teresa elbowed her, Catherine unbent her frown but didn't smile as she dropped her hands to her sides and nodded to the extern.

"Sister doesn't like to take credit or praise for her work. She believes God works through her," Teresa reminded me.

"Yes, well, it's certainly beautiful," I said, kicking myself and yet unable to stop complimenting her. "I've brought you and uh, the other sisters some fresh supplies." I turned my back to Catherine and picked up the sacks of canvases, oil paints, and brushes from where they leaned against the wall. "I hope they're the right kind."

I slipped the cumbersome items through the space between the bars with my good hand, but my twin kept her arms firmly at her sides. After several agonizing seconds, Sister Teresa took the supplies.

"We thank you very much, Dorie." Teresa juggled the shopping bags. "I'm sure Catherine and the other painters here will enjoy these. Won't you, Sister?"

Sister Catherine bowed and nodded her head.

"I'm glad. I look forward to seeing more of your work in the future," I said, having given up on avoiding the topic.

I hoped seeing more of the art would include seeing more of the artist. The walls Catherine had built between us seemed higher than those surrounding the cloister. Not that I blamed her—my enthusiasm was pretty obnoxious.

The first bell chimed for Vespers. Sister Catherine looked to Sister Teresa with pleading eyes as if to say, "May I go now?"

"Well, we'd better give Sister time to clean up for prayers," Teresa said.

"Nice to meet you," I called out as Catherine disappeared.

"As I said..." Sister Teresa shrugged, "She's very shy and doesn't respond well to praise of her work."

"I understand." I was fairly sure shy had nothing to do with it. "Thank you so much for the introduction."

I headed to Vespers myself to get another glimpse of my twin. Her height made her easy to pick out among the nuns lighting candles in the darkening chapel. Catherine kept her eyes on her prayer book, but I kept mine focused on her throughout the service, as if staring would provide the answers our brief meeting hadn't. Why was it so difficult for her to accept praise of her work? Why did she react to me as she had? Given that she'd had some time to process our first chance meeting by now, I'd thought she might somehow silently acknowledge our relationship during this visit. When she didn't, I wondered if maybe she didn't know who I was after all.

My sister was the first to exit the sanctuary at the conclusion of Vespers. I smiled, hoping that she was in a hurry to break in the new supplies.

When I walked out to my car, I heard a racket coming from the side of the parking lot behind the cloister wall. I peered through the gate and saw Sister Catherine, her face glistening with tears and sweat. She was dealing with the supplies all right—by tossing the new brushes, paints, and canvases into the dumpster.

I felt a smile creep onto my face uninvited. I'd always been strangely detached from most material things, and I liked that my sister displayed the same trait, even if it was at my, or more correctly, Trish's expense. I suppose I could have taken her rejection of the supplies personally, but I was determined to stop assuming I knew what Catherine thought about me.

CHAPTER EIGHT

"Check out Father What-A-Waste." I showed Graciela the pictured author of an article entitled "Celibacy: Is It Right for You?," a square-jawed, blue-eyed priest handsome enough to make a grandmother blush. "That's just cruel."

"Madre mia." Graciela leaned on my desk, took one look, and waggled a lacquered fingernail at the newsroom's polyfoam ceiling to indicate the sky beyond. "God's got some nerve keeping *that* all to Himself."

"God's keeping the hotties pure, and my sister is keeping her art unseen." I chewed the end of my pen. "Not fair."

"How did she like the supplies? Was she thrilled?"

"Don't tell Trish, but she threw them out," I said, smiling again.

"In the *trash*?" My coworker dragged her eyes away from the priest's photo and puzzled at my odd grin. "Why aren't you upset?"

"At least she didn't paint the canvases first—that would have been way more painful," I said. My detachment from material things didn't extend to sentimental items like my family's artwork. "And I like a challenge."

While I respected Catherine's efforts to keep her work for God alone, I really believed that in the grand scheme her paintings would be even better prayers if she shared them with the world. My task was to persuade her of that.

"She's challenging, all right." Graciela rubbed her stomach. "You want to go grab some ice cream?"

"No thanks." I set down the pen and turned to my computer. "I'm leaving for another artist interview in twenty minutes."

Since my access to Catherine was limited, I'd met with a former priest who sculpted and a sister who made stained-glass windows, hoping to gain some understanding of how each one's religious vocation affected the creative process.

"Oh, yeah? Who's headlining 'Dorie's Holy Roller' tour today?" Graciela asked.

"Sister Barbara Nolan. She sells her pottery on the Internet."

"Fear factor on a scale of one-to-ten?" Graciela knew how much nuns flustered me until I got to know them.

"Five. She sounded pretty nice on the phone."

"Not bad." Graciela checked her watch. "You still have time for ice cream."

"I wish. I have to write up this piece on psychic tree frogs before I can leave."

"Well, you, or maybe the tree frogs, know best." Graciela grabbed her bag. *"Adios, amiga."*

As Graciela left, I pounded out the frog story in fifteen minutes. Since I'd discovered my sister's paintings, my regular *Comet* assignments had taken an interesting turn. I found it more difficult to write unscrupulously after witnessing the hyper-ethics of cloistered nuns, but I had no problem being sloppy in my haste to get back to researching Catherine. The combination resulted in articles that were the equivalent of a cherubic, wholesome child with chocolate pudding all over her face.

My editor had been less than pleased with the change.

"If I wanted Pollyanna amateur hour, I'd read the Girl Scout newsletter," Phil had said in response to some of my recent stories. "Juice it up, McKenna."

Chain-smoking, I chose my streets carefully in South Central. Sister Barbara may have been a fear factor of five, but her convent's location in an infamous neighborhood bumped my gauge up to ten. Graffiti-covered highway underpasses, boarded-up buildings, and a wailing police siren did little to ease my anxiety.

I pictured the convent as a boxy brick structure with a large cross on the front; similar to church buildings I'd seen in suburban parishes. Instead, the address I'd been given matched a freshly painted, two-story house sandwiched between a liquor store and an empty lot where corroded shopping carts went to die. A barbed wire fence surrounded the house's quarter-acre of property. I parked on the street, climbed out of my car, and rang the bell.

"You must be Dorie," said a smiling woman with a salt-and-pepper ponytail after she opened the door. A small, gold cross dangled from a chain over her faded Lakers T-shirt and clay clung to her jeans where she'd wiped her hands. "I'm Sister Barbara."

"Hello." I extended my left hand, surprised by the sister's casual appearance after the habits of the cloistered nuns. The secular clothes made her seem more approachable. "Thank you for seeing me."

"My pleasure." Unlike Sister Catherine, Barbara took my hand with her own left and shook it with no excuses or apologies for the clay under her fingernails. "So you want to know what it's like to be both a Sister and an artist, huh?"

"And how you balance the two." I nodded.

"Come on back and I'll show you where I do my dirty work."

The ceramics studio consisted of a sagging one-car garage that leaned to the left as if whispering a secret to the backyard tomato plants. Inside, clay pots in various stages of completion lined a set of unvarnished shelves. A wheel, a stool, and a kiln shared the floor with a salvaged kitchen cabinet and buckets of water and glaze. A Spanish talk station crackled over a portable radio.

"This is some good stuff." I wandered from pot to colorful pot. The work was simple and solid.

"Thank you." Sister Barbara set a lump of clay on the wheel and sat down on the stool. "Basic pieces sell the best—mugs, bowls, and the occasional chalice. The proceeds finance our soup kitchen down the street."

"Do you make pottery full time?"

"I throw and fire pots in the morning, help my housemates Sister Cindy and Sister Joan serve and clean up lunch for our soup kitchen guests at midday, then come back here to the studio for a couple hours of glazing in the late afternoon."

"Do you enjoy the work?" I asked, though the care with which Sister Barbara handled her materials had answered my question.

"I love it, sometimes too much. It can be a struggle to keep my pottery within the context of my higher calling to serve God." Sister Barbara lifted the gold cross that hung around her neck and kissed it. "At one point I gave up pottery for five months because I sensed that it had become too important to me."

"Wow." I couldn't imagine Sister Catherine being able to stop painting for five minutes, much less five months. "How did that go?"

"It wasn't easy," Barbara said. "The time away helped me realize that the meditative aspects of pottery-making were integral to my prayer life. But not every artist feels as strongly connected to her work as I do."

That was true. The stained-glass artist I'd interviewed saw her work as nothing more than a service she was obligated to perform, if not necessarily enjoy, to help support her religious community. The sculptor I'd met was more like Sister Barbara, drawing sustenance from the often tedious, sometimes painful, and occasionally exhilarating artistic process. It fed his soul, and, he admitted, his ego. He had left the priesthood to pursue his sculpting full time.

"I'm no great artist, but people buy it because it's for a good cause," Sister Barbara said.

"Are you ever reluctant to sell your art?"

"I keep a couple of things for myself here and there, but generally I try to sell as much as I can." The sister dipped her hands in a bucket of water and moistened the clay on the wheel. "It's tough. Sales vary, so I don't know what our income will be from one month to the next. But between my pottery and donations, Sister Cindy manages to keep the soup kitchen going. Why?"

"The cloistered nun I'm writing the article about refuses to sell her paintings even though I get the feeling her religious community could use the money."

"Everyone's situation is different," the potter said. "Is she fulfilling her regular duties in the convent otherwise?"

"According to the extern sister, she's doing more than her share."

"Who pays for her supplies?"

"They're donated." I picked up a small, blue pot I particularly liked. "All the nuns are welcome to use them. Or reuse them, in Sister Catherine's case. She paints over her work to recycle the materials. Do you do that?"

"There's no reusing clay once it's fired, but I can't imagine intentionally ruining something salable." Sister Barbara spun her wheel via a foot pedal and hunkered down over the lump of soft clay before her. A bowl soon took shape. "What your Sister Catherine does with her paintings is between her and God. Selling the art you produce in your spare time certainly isn't a requirement in any religious community that I know of."

"But your pottery—"

"Serves a different purpose. Apostolic orders like mine focus on community outreach. My pottery helps make the soup kitchen possible. A cloistered order focuses on prayer. From what you've told me, Catherine's paintings are a pure form of prayer. Why change what's working?"

"Is it working?" I frowned, not surprised by Sister Barbara's answer, but not ready to accept it either. I set the blue pot back on its shelf. The potter saw my expression.

"Sorry to disappoint you, but that's what I think." Sister Barbara's hand slipped and the emerging bowl warped. "Oops."

The roar of a revving engine followed by squealing tires pierced the dusk.

"You'd better get going." Sister Barbara wedged the misshapen clay together again and started over. "I don't want you getting lost around here after dark. Feel free to call or come back anytime if you have more questions."

I thanked her and drove home.

The sculptor, the stained-glass window maker, and Sister Barbara had all agreed that Catherine wasn't obligated to show or sell her paintings. Yet each one was more than willing to sell his or her own art. None of them went so far as to destroy good work just to reuse the materials. On that point my twin stood alone.

CHAPTER NINE

On his next day off, Matt powered through his errands so we could visit an illuminated manuscript exhibit at the Getty Museum in the afternoon and catch a Kurosawa film that night.

"It was unnerving," I said on the tram ride up to the Getty from the parking lot. "The religious artists who aren't cloistered were really open and friendly. We tabloid journalists aren't exactly used to being trusted. Not that we should be."

"I'm sure it helps when they know you aren't writing an article about them specifically," Matt said as we arrived at the hilltop museum and exited the tram.

"Yeah, but it makes me want to be worthy of their trust."

"That's not a bad thing, is it?"

"Not usually." I bent down and dipped my hand in the fountain that tripped alongside the museum's main staircase. "But at *The Comet*, hyperbole is in my job description."

"Are the other artists as good as your sister?"

"Nobody is as inspired as Catherine, but some are quite talented. Not one of them was willing to take credit for his or her artwork. Even the sculptor who'd left the priesthood still insisted it was God's work and he was merely His instrument."

"Maybe that's why they're gifted—God is showing off because He knows He'll get the acclaim," Matt said. We reached the Getty's soaring atrium entrance. "Nothing like assembling a solid PR team. Singing the boss's praises can only help their chances of getting into that big studio in the sky," he added as he opened the door for me.

Inside the illuminated manuscripts exhibit, I marveled over tiny masterpieces wrought on sheepskin by medieval monks. Rich, textured shades of burgundy, azure, salmon, and purple combined in intricate, painstaking patterns to adorn the parchment. Often the borders were even more stunning than the pictures they framed. The violets, poppies, peacock feathers, and dragonflies appeared real enough to be plucked from the page.

"Somebody put a hell of a lot of time into those books," Matt observed when we wandered the manicured grounds afterward.

"And for what?" I asked. "To be closed up on some shelf for hundreds of years where no one can see them?"

"The manuscript owner saw them, and you're seeing them now."

"One page at a time," I complained.

"Nothing like scarcity to keep you wanting more." He paused on a garden terrace to take in the expansive view of city and sea as yet another fountain murmured behind us. The late afternoon sun hung over the Pacific like ripe fruit. "Take the Getty here. Limited parking guarantees that it'll always be a hot ticket. It's all about marketing."

"And you can't beat the admission price."

I admired the artful combination of stone, water, light, and space at the free museum. Like the cloister, the Getty extended an invitation to slow down, breathe, and appreciate, but I found that hard to do whenever I thought about yet more amazing art going unseen.

"Okay, fine," I said over soup and sashimi at Hurry Curry of Tokyo an hour later. Waiters with steaming bowls of noodles slipped smoothly through the narrow aisles without bumping tables or elbows. "I'll agree that those manuscripts are getting their due in museums now, even if they have been hidden between bindings for centuries. But the thing is, when Catherine paints over an image, that's it."

"It's still there." Matt sipped his Asahi. "It's just hidden under a layer of paint instead of a book cover. Painters reuse canvases all the time."

"Only when they've made a mistake or didn't like the first painting. Nobody paints over a masterwork unless they're trying to hide it from marauders or something."

"Which is sort of what Catherine is doing if you think about it," he said.

"I can't think about it or I'll never have the nerve to write the piece."

"It's your conscience." Matt drained his beer and set the bottle back on the table with a thud that reminded me of a judge's gavel.

It *was* my conscience, and it was a constant worry. But I wasn't ready to let go of the opportunity to get to know my sister, much less write a piece that could lead to a real job.

"Anyway, you're wrong." I stabbed another piece of sashimi with a chopstick, happy with a one-handed meal that didn't entail cutting my food. "Catherine paints over them with stuff at least as good. So once she's covered the original, it's gone. Nobody's going to ruin the one on top to get to it."

"If they really want to see the one underneath, they'll use an X-ray," he said.

"It's not right. She's doing significant work that should be preserved for posterity. What if great religious artists like Fra Angelico or the monks who illuminated those manuscripts had ruined their own art? There wouldn't have been anything to exhibit today."

"And we'd be none the wiser," Matt said. "Let's say that your sister *is* doing significant work. She's under no more obligation to unleash it on the world than I am to make people read my bad poetry."

"You write poetry?" I asked.

"I used to when I wasn't working so much." Matt gulped a mouthful of noodles.

"I want to read it!" My voice rose an octave.

"You will not be reading it." He blushed. "Anyway, I threw it out."

"No, you didn't."

"Can we get back to the subject here? Even if Catherine did want to preserve her art, she might not succeed. For all we know, there was a sculptor greater than Michelangelo whose body of work happened to be the victim of a nasty earthquake. Or maybe your sister's stuff does survive, only to have the fickle art world decide it isn't all that great in a few years." Matt pointed his chopsticks at me. "Nobody knows what's good, what's bad, or what will last. All we have is right now. And Sister Catherine is living in the now if anybody is. The rest of us should be taking notes."

"If you believe what you're saying, why aren't you shooting your own movie? You have more than enough money saved to make your short."

Matt put down his chopsticks and wiped his mouth with his napkin. "Touché."

"I'm sorry, Matt. I didn't mean to—"

"No, you're right. You're absolutely right." He leaned back in his chair. "I am completely full of shit."

"At least you've got talent. All I've got is the desire to capitalize on someone else's."

"Uh, uh. You're not getting away with that. You're a great writer, and you're doing what you love for a living, which is more than ninety-nine percent of the population can say. I'm not sure a piece about your sister is the best choice, but I guess you have to follow your gut. Don't ever lose your passion, Dorie. It's the best thing about you." Matt pulled out his wallet as the check arrived. "I've got this."

"Thanks." I melted, then froze, suspicious. "Okay, what's going on? You're buying me dinner and giving me amazing compliments."

"Is that so unusual?"

"Unusual? It's unprecedented."

Matt laughed and paid the bill. "You've been so busy researching this story that I hardly see you. I'm just enjoying the time we do have to hang out."

"I guess there is something to be said for scarcity." I melted again. "Thanks for dinner."

As I felt my shoulders relax and ease into the softness of the moment, I watched Matt's shoulders and jaw contract.

"Yeah, well, don't think you're not paying for the movie," he grumbled with a gruffness that couldn't negate all the nice things he'd said before.

Matt stood up and strode outside without waiting for me.

I gathered up my coat and reprimanded myself. It wasn't paying for the movie that bothered me—I had planned to do that anyway. It was falling for the vintage Matt mind game. It had new grass and pretty flowers on it, but it was the same old trap. He'd dangle intimacy in front of me with sweet words and kind gestures, then snatch it away the moment I concluded it was safe to reach for the bait.

For some reason this most recent game didn't hurt as much as usual. I took my time leaving the restaurant. After all, I had the car keys.

CHAPTER TEN

"The sisters are having a grand, old time with the art supplies you gave us," Sister Teresa reported when I found her watering the parlor plants on the next Visiting Sunday. "We have lots of new paintings up in the gift shop, thanks to you."

"But I saw Sister Catherine throw them out," I said, confused enough to confess I'd been spying.

"She did." Teresa smiled at my admission. "Since they weren't hers to dispose of, Mother Benedicta made her retrieve them."

I hadn't met Mother Benedicta, but I liked her already. Sister Teresa handed me the narrow watering can through the bars of the parlor grille and pointed to the peace lily behind me.

"Why didn't Catherine want them?" I doused the plant.

"Oh, she wanted them all right. She wanted them too much."

I passed the watering can back to Sister Teresa and wrinkled my forehead, mystified.

"Those supplies created a desire in Catherine. A desire she wished to be free of."

"But is that the right way to avoid temptation—by not exposing yourself to it?"

"Whatever works, I say." Teresa tipped the watering can over a ficus. "Is it any more 'right' to dangle a chocolate cake in front of someone on a diet?"

Mmmmm, cake. My stomach growled. The night before, I'd spent my grocery money on a room at the nearby inn so I could be at the convent bright and early for services. I reasoned that if Catherine saw me in the chapel, perhaps she'd be more inclined to see me in the parlor. But my twin never once looked up throughout morning prayers. I'd trudged to the visiting room afterward more out of a sense of general optimism than any real belief that she'd appear there.

"Given that I'm the one who led her into temptation, I'm guessing Sister Catherine won't want to see me today," I said.

"I'll tell her that you're waiting, but don't expect miracles."

"I'll hang around just in case. If there's anyone else who could use a visitor, I'd love the company." The journalist in me figured I might as well ask the other nuns about my sister as long as I was there.

"I'll see who I can rustle up." Teresa left the room.

I wanted a cigarette but was hesitant to go outside to smoke. What if Catherine came in and didn't find me? I tried to rid myself of the desire and unwrapped a stick of gum instead. Admittedly, I didn't try as hard to avoid temptation as Catherine had—I stopped short of throwing away the pack.

The visiting room seemed larger without Sister Carmella's extended family. Their absence left the sun free to slide around the grille and paint a grid of light and shadow on the now-visible hardwood floor. A small, brown bird trilled on a branch right outside the open window. Even if I didn't see Catherine, this silent, sunny space wasn't a bad place to spend the day. I pulled out a new notebook and wrote down the observations I'd compiled on the cloister and my sibling.

Shortly after noon, I ate the granola bar I'd discovered at the bottom of my purse and opened a novel. Before I found my place, Sister Teresa returned with a young Filipina woman. I recognized her as the organist in chapel, where she stood out among the gray-habited nuns in her navy blue jumper and slightly askew blue veil. She looked about twenty-five, but I'd learned not to trust my eyes when it came to guessing a nun's age.

"Dorie McKenna, I'd like you to meet Melanie Bunye," the extern said. "Melanie came here as a postulant over five months ago. Her family is saving up to visit for her clothing ceremony next week. Meantime, I thought she might get a kick out of you."

"I'll do my best to be entertaining," I said.

The fact that Melanie was a newcomer and had stylish, rectangular glasses supported my emerging Eyeglass Theory. I guessed that the various outdated styles worn by most of the nuns directly corresponded with the decade in which each woman had entered the cloister: pointy, cat-eyed frames on the older nuns who'd entered in the sixties, bulbous, owl-eyed lenses on the middle-aged nuns who entered in the eighties, and lightweight, rectangular frames on young women like Melanie.

"I'll leave you two alone." Teresa winked and turned to leave. "You can't have proper girl talk with an old lady hanging around."

"Congratulations, Melanie." I shook her hand through the grille. "What happens at your clothing ceremony?"

"I choose a new name and receive the novice habit." The woman tried to straighten her postulant veil but only managed to set it further aslant. "Let's hope I can master the veil thing by then. I'm still adjusting to life without mirrors."

"No mirrors anywhere?" I'd thought the absence of mirrors in the bathrooms I'd visited was just an oversight.

"They foster vanity," Melanie explained. "No mirrors only fosters crooked veils."

I laughed. "What's your new name going to be?"

"Sister Dominica. My doctoral advisor was a Dominican priest."

"Do you have a PhD in theology?"

"Physics. I taught for a couple of years, but even then I planned to enter the convent."

"From the lab to the cloister—that's quite a change."

"Not really," she said. "All the marvels of science point to the existence of God, at least for me. The only difficult part was convincing the sisters I could be happy without my career."

"It must have been hard to leave academics to submit to the rules of a male-dominated church," I said aloud without intending to.

"It's not any worse than what I experienced working in science. I'd probably have more of a problem with it if I'd chosen an apostolic order where I was out in the world and found myself hindered by my gender. But I've chosen to make myself as humble and lowly before God as possible. If I were a man, I would've chosen to be a brother, not a priest." The postulant looked at the print of Jesus on the wall and smiled.

"Huh." I leaned back. In an odd way, it almost made sense. I shifted in my seat and craved a cigarette.

"But I absolutely believe women should be restored to the priesthood," Melanie added.

"Restored?" I said a little too loudly.

"Women were ordained as priests up until the fifth century—at least that's what some historians argue. Women baptized, said Mass, you name it. I'd like to believe it's true, anyway."

"I had no idea," I said, wondering what else I didn't know.

"Our own Sister Scholastica is seminary trained and ready to be ordained if it's ever allowed," Melanie said. "We need someone in the monastery to perform religious rites when a priest isn't available. But what about you? How long have you been discerning?"

"Oh, I'm not considering a vocation," I said, and then gulped. I still wasn't familiar enough with my own ruse to answer correctly on the first try. "I mean, I am, but—"

"You ask questions like you are."

"Do I?" That was a frightening thought I wasn't ready to contemplate. I changed the subject. "What do you think of Sister Catherine's paintings?"

"I think they're divinely inspired."

"The very face of God," I said, not previously aware that I felt that way.

The cloister bell rang.

"Already?" I checked my watch. It was 12:30. "I thought the fifth Divine Office wasn't until two o'clock."

"We're having an emergency finance meeting." Melanie made another unsuccessful tug on her veil and rose to leave. "Really nice meeting you, Dorie."

"You, too."

I found Sister Teresa in the courtyard pruning one last bougainvillea vine before the second bell rang for the finance meeting. A light breeze sent tall stalks of pink oleander swaying, while the black and white cat wound in and around the foliage.

"It's so beautiful here that I have a hard time leaving," I said.

"I hear you." Sister Teresa set down her pruning shears. "When I first arrived, I thought this place was *too* beautiful. The fancy estate and the pretty views didn't seem rough enough for a life of prayer and sacrifice. Then the rainy season taught me otherwise."

"Do the storms do a lot of damage to your buildings?"

"To say the least. Our vow of poverty means our finances are precarious by nature. I never guessed the 'by nature' part was meant literally."

"I hope you work it out," I said.

"God will provide." Teresa pulled off her gardening gloves and turned to go indoors. "I'd better be off to the meeting."

"I think I'll sit here a minute." I parked myself on the stone bench beside the fountain, still reluctant to go. "I promise to stay in the public areas."

The extern cocked her head and looked at me. "You know, if you applied for an aspirancy visit, you wouldn't have to."

"Have to what?"

"Leave. Women considering the life may come live and pray with us inside the cloister for a two-week visit to see if it's for them."

"Really." My eyes lit up at the prospect of direct access to my sister and her paintings.

CHAPTER ELEVEN

The moment my self-proclaimed hippie Aunt Martha appeared on the industrial blue carpet at LAX and saw me, she tittered and wiggled her arms aloft in preparation for the long hug to follow. Martha McKenna was a great, theatrical hugger who embraced with feeling, a far cry from the usual air hug most people delivered. Her cut-for-comfort batik skirt pitched and whirled as she squeezed me and swayed side to side. I hadn't seen her since my father's funeral.

"So how's your Wagner?" my aunt asked as soon as we sat down at the nearest airport Starbucks, where she sipped green tea from the travel mug she carried with her everywhere to avoid littering landfills with disposable cups. Her brief layover before her Osaka flight wasn't long enough to allow us to leave the airport for our visit.

"It's good." Unable to wait, I scalded my tongue on my hot chocolate. "I'm afraid to keep it at my house, but I go over and visit it in Trish's vault."

Even though I'd learned my birth father's identity through forces beyond my control, it still felt like a betrayal of my parents to discuss him, the painting, or my twin with my aunt. Martha, however, didn't seem to have any problem with it.

"And how's your sister, the Sister?" Martha chased her tea bag around the mug with a spoon. "Have you looked her up yet?"

"I did, actually."

"Really? What's she like?"

"She's quiet. Silent, in fact."

"No kidding?" Martha asked. "She never speaks?"

"Only in prayer. But her paintings say plenty. She may be even more talented than my birth father. The weird thing is, she doesn't want anyone to know."

I explained Catherine's desire to remain anonymous and my newly hatched plan to pose as an aspiring nun in hopes of convincing her otherwise.

"Sounds pretty sneaky." My aunt looked skyward. "Connor and Hope, you raised a deviant."

"They wish."

Aware of the tendency of adoptive parents to be overprotective, my parents went out of their way to give me freedom. In fact, they were so liberal that the only way for me to rebel as a kid was to conform. I think my goody two-shoes approach to public high school disappointed them.

It was their own fault. College professors both, my parents valued rigorous academics over a school in keeping with their own beliefs or lack thereof, so off to Catholic grammar school I went. At Sacred Heart Elementary, conformity was the order of the day. When I asked if I could receive the sacraments so I wouldn't feel different from the other kids, my parents agreed. I don't think they expected me to actually *like* it, but since they weren't sure about God one way or the other, they concluded it couldn't hurt. I can still remember the looks on their faces when I was baptized in second grade. I may as well have landed on the moon.

"Let me get this straight," Martha said, lowering her chin and peering at me from under her wiry eyebrows. "You're going to pose as something you don't want to be to in order to get your sister to let you publish an article she probably doesn't want you to write?"

"I don't see what the big deal is." I couldn't meet her gaze. "You're about to spend a month visiting sacred temples in Japan and you're not Buddhist."

"The difference being I'm not pretending I want to be a monk to get into them." Martha folded her arms. "If your twin doesn't want people to see her artwork, I'd say it's a pretty safe bet she doesn't want them to read about it either." She pressed her lips together and considered. "Then again, even if going against your sister's wishes is wrong, your religion does have the benefit of confession and forgiveness."

"My *former* religion," I reminded her. "Getting pardoned for my sins would require me to return to the fold."

As a child, I had embraced Catholicism from the beginning, if only to fit in with my classmates. I grew to like the church for offering the structure and discipline I missed at home. There was comfort in predictability. As an outsider tagging along, I never had the visceral, emotional issues that my "cradle Catholic" peers born into the faith sometimes struggled with. I obeyed the laws of the church, but the decision to do so came from me rather than any family obligation. That took away a lot of the pressure. I knew there was a lot about Catholicism I misunderstood or simply didn't know, and I believed there were ways of making sense of the inconsistencies if only I sought them out.

I'd never bothered. I understood that religions are human institutions with failings. I believed the Catholic Church was striving to do a better job of protecting children and fighting for social justice. Yes, I wished that women could be priests and that more of the church's tremendous wealth was spent on educating the poor, but none of my issues with the institution upset me enough to make me leave the faith that had given me the direction my freewheeling family lacked.

Yet the day after my mother, Hope, died, I did leave. No bells or whistles went off. I simply stopped going to Mass and calling myself Catholic. I said it was because I didn't want to dishonor my agnostic mother, but at the time, my real reasons were beyond even me. They still were.

"It's a long shot anyway," I said to Martha. "If by some miracle I get the cloister's permission to make an aspirancy visit, I'm not sure I'll be able to get the time to go. I used up my vacation cleaning out Dad's house."

"Something tells me you'll find a way." Martha checked her watch. "I'd better head back to my gate."

We stood up and gathered our bags.

"How do cloistered nuns support themselves anyway?" Martha asked as she rinsed out her travel mug in the drinking fountain.

"Depends on the order. Usually, they rely on alms and have some sort of cottage industry." I guiltily threw away my empty cup in the trash as my aunt watched. "But their main job is praying the seven hours of the Divine Office."

"Sounds impractical. Shouldn't they be making some sort of tangible contribution instead of just praying all the time?"

"I wonder about that, too." I followed her to the security checkpoint. "Even if the sisters are self-supporting, part of me thinks they should be out there working with the poor or something. If you sign up to be a nun—"

"Then again, just because you can't see the results of prayer directly," Martha interjected, "doesn't mean there aren't any."

I looked at her, surprised.

"I figured Connor and Hope would want me to play the *devil's* advocate since they're not here to do it." She elbowed me in the ribs. "You still believe in God, right, Dorie? You take that on faith?"

"I believe in God. But I don't always understand God."

"Doesn't matter," she said. "What's the difference between believing in God and believing in the power of prayer? You don't have any more proof that God exists than that prayer works."

She had a point. I hated that.

"You take care, Sweetie." Martha delivered another long hug that I relished. "I have a five-hour layover on the return trip, so I'll have time to take you out for a nice meal or something."

"Sounds good. Have fun," I said, waving as she got in the security line.

During the drive home, I lit a cigarette and wondered about the power of prayer. Certainly frequent prayer and meditation are good for a nun as an individual, but did her efforts really make a difference in the world at large?

For my own spiritual practice, I'd fashioned a personal theology out of the void left by my departure from formal religion. I shunned Catholic churches but often stopped by the house of worship of another faith, not for services necessarily, but just to sit in awareness of God's presence. I found a few I liked better than Catholicism and encountered others that I liked less—usually ones where women were not allowed to enter without a male escort, or even at all in some cases—but nothing ever felt quite right.

On such visits I'd relaxed and enjoyed the peaceful atmosphere. But now I wanted to pray, to understand what went on in the minds of Catholic cloistered nuns. I drove past my apartment building and headed for St. Monica's Catholic Church a few blocks away.

I arrived, parked in the church lot, and sat in the car until I'd finished the cigarette. Stubbing it out in the ashtray, I considered scuttling my prayer plans in favor of watching the pick-up basketball game in the park across the street. Eventually, I ambled to the church entrance.

Feeling a little queasy, I opened the heavy, wooden door and entered the vaulted, softly lit structure. I forged on and chose a pew far from the other dozen or so visitors scattered around the sanctuary.

I started with the Our Father and then recited other prayers from childhood. My mind wandered. Next I tried talking to God and asking Him to help people I knew to be in need. That made me feel silly and unworthy. Who was I to ask God for anything? Finally, I sat there smelling the candle smoke and listening to the hoarse whisperings of the bent, old woman several pews ahead of me, the beads of her rosary clinking like a handful of pennies. I watched the brilliant greens, blues, and golds of the frescoes reflect the light. Before long, my breath evened out and my shoulders relaxed. I wondered if maybe I'd been praying all along.

CHAPTER TWELVE

"So you feel you may be called to join us," Mother Benedicta said from the other side of the parlor grille the following Saturday. A large, silver cross hanging from her neck identified her as the head of the monastery. The no-nonsense prioress' face was stern, but the laugh lines around her gray eyes suggested a habit of smiling that I found reassuring. Still, she was not someone to be trifled with. And that was exactly what I was doing.

"Yes, Mother, I—"

"We try to avoid excessive talking whenever a simple nod will do." The prioress held up her hand to quiet me as she checked over my written application for the aspirancy stay. "Silence provides our fellow sisters the quiet space they need for prayer throughout the day."

I nodded.

"You've been in our chapel quite a bit recently. Was that late-night visit in the rain your first introduction to our convent?"

I nodded again.

"Had you discerned your vocation before that?"

"Not really." I was determined not to lie unless it was necessary. "Honestly, I'm not sure if I have one or not, but everyone else keeps asking me if I do."

"I'm not surprised." Mother chuckled. "Having your vocation acknowledged by other people before you recognize it yourself is very common. In the end, it's up to you and God to decide if the life is right for you. Meantime, it's good to have healthy doubts. The ones who don't doubt are the least likely to be happy here."

"I do know that I feel drawn to this place." Also the truth, I reassured myself. "It's so gorgeous."

"We are lucky enough to do God's work in an earthly paradise. But we are not a vacation spot. We're here to pray. Have you explored other religious communities since you began considering a vocation?"

"Yes." I was glad my thorough research had led me to Sister Barbara and the other religious artists. "I've met with a couple of apostolic orders in the Los Angeles area."

"Excellent. I encourage comparison-shopping. How did you find them?"

"Very welcoming. But I prefer the monastic lifestyle," I said, hoping to charm her.

"And why is that?"

I panicked at the unanticipated question and then realized I had an answer.

"Back in high school, I felt some sort of Catholic obligation to save the world, or at least a small part of it." My mind whirled, but I kept talking. "The thought was so overwhelming that I didn't dare begin to try. I imagined that sisters and priests felt even more pressure to pull off peace and justice than the average person."

"We religious carry our share of Catholic guilt," the prioress said.

"The thing is, if prayer really is an effective tool, then the daily recital of the Divine Office is the first manageable approach to the task of world-saving that I've heard of."

"A lot of people draw comfort from knowing we're here," Mother Benedicta agreed.

"I'm one of them," I said. "As much as I appreciate all the good work apostolic sisters and priests are doing out there in the world, I'm personally more attracted to a life of monastic contemplation."

"Speaking of attraction, are you currently involved in an intimate relationship?" the prioress asked.

"No," I answered, after a pause.

"Are you certain?" The prioress wrinkled her brow. "I sense some hesitation."

"I'm sure. But I do have a close male friend."

"Do you hope for more with him? I don't mean to pry, but romantic relationships tend to distract us from a potential commitment to Our Lord."

"No." I shook my head. "We tried that a couple of years ago and it didn't work out."

"I see. The convent is not a haven for broken hearts. Are you aware that we strongly encourage at least a year, preferably more, of celibacy before entering?"

"No, I wasn't." I felt my cheeks grow hot. "But, it's already been um—"

"Spare me the details." This time Mother Benedicta held up both hands to silence me. "Just so you know that for down the road. Do you have any questions?"

"I don't think so." My internal reporter drew a rare blank.

"All right. I'll have to review your aspirancy application and references with the other sisters, but I don't foresee any problems. Most aspirants find the visit helpful in discovering if they're ready to give themselves wholly to God. I hope it will be the same for you."

"Thank you, Mother."

"Let's close our meeting with a prayer, shall we?"

Mother reached through the grille and took my hands in hers with the comfortable acceptance of my disfigurement that I'd come to appreciate from all the sisters. We bowed our heads.

"Heavenly Father, we pray that you look upon Dorie's vocation favorably. Please watch over her as she takes this important step in Your holy service. Amen."

"Amen."

"May the good Lord bless you, Dorie." Mother Benedicta gave my hands a final squeeze and departed.

I walked to the chapel and sat in a pew to gather my thoughts. I thanked God for swaying the prioress and wondered uneasily how I had pulled off my own part so convincingly. I wasn't even sure if I'd been lying. My answers came so effortlessly that I concluded I was either callous—a hardened journalist comfortable bending the truth into whatever shape best suited her purpose, or I was curious—a lapsed Catholic considering not a vacation at the cloister but an actual vocation.

Was I unethical enough for the former? I couldn't fathom the latter. I *was* honestly interested in a vocation; it just didn't happen to be my own. I had asked Sister Teresa and Melanie all the right questions and answered all of Mother Benedicta's more or less correctly because I truly wanted to know what went into my twin's decision to become a nun.

I hoped to learn how the contemplative religious life had come to be such a perfect complement to Catherine's artistic life. Whether my methods for gleaning this information harmed the nuns or not wasn't something I was ready to look at.

Now that Mother Benedicta had agreed to my aspirancy visit, I found myself in the awkward position of needing my boss to approve a research trip for a story idea he'd already rejected.

"How am I going to do this?" I drummed my fingers on my newsroom desk.

"Easy." Graciela tacked her daughter Sophie's latest crayon drawing to her cube wall. "You're going to tell *el Jefe* you've discovered a scandal at the convent and then act like you don't want to cover it."

"I won't have to act," I said. "But what happens when I come back and he expects a juicy tell-all?"

"Then you write a scandal-free, boring article and hope he vetoes it."

"It's not fair to Phil," I said.

"When has he ever played fair with us?" she asked. "If it makes you feel better, you can offer to make up the missed time when you get back."

"That might make it okay." I squirmed, not believing it.

We batted around a few more options. There was the possibility of unpaid leave, but I couldn't afford that. I could pitch a different story he would approve—one about Big Foot sightings in Big Sur, maybe—and then write Catherine's article on the side. That seemed plausible until I realized that the cloister rules would prevent me from leaving to talk to locals or research anything else, even if I did have time between their work and prayer routine. That left us with Graciela's scandal suggestion.

A plume of acrid smoke wafted toward us as our editor's office door opened. Phil felt that California state law did not apply to his cigar habit.

"Here he comes," Graciela said as Phil exited his office behind her. "Just go with me on this."

Out of ideas, I shrugged and nodded.

"Okay," she said. "Tell me when."

I waited for our boss, who was nose deep in a piece of copy, to make it within ten feet of Graciela, and then whispered, "Now."

Graciela stretched and let out a luxurious yawn. "So what's the deal with that cloistered nun running a brothel for priests, Dorie?" she asked in a voice loud enough to break through whatever Phil was reading. "Are you going to write a story about it?"

Our editor slowed his step but continued walking past us.

"Nah," I said. "Sex scandals are a dime a dozen."

Phil stopped, turned and wagged a finger at me. "Blasphemy!"

"What's the pitch?" Phil asked, chomping on his cigar as I sat across from him in his office a few minutes later. The disarmed wires of the smoke detector hung down from the ceiling above his black, lacquered desk. "Lay it out."

I paused, not having really thought through the details of the phony scandal and still uncomfortable using it.

"Well, there's this priest who had an affair with one of the nuns," I began, my stomach churning as if I'd drunk battery acid. "And he realized that the cloister would be a great place to..."

I trailed off and sat staring at my hands.

"Go on," he said, taking another puff and leaning forward in his chair.

I couldn't. I was already bending the truth with the nuns. I didn't want to make it worse by lying to Phil. He may have rejected my pitch about Catherine's art before, but he hadn't heard the whole story.

"Actually, there isn't a scandal," I said. "There's a cloistered nun who's an amazing painter."

Phil leaned back in his chair, closed his eyes and delivered a rattling, fake snore. "Ho hum."

"Hear me out," I said, warming up. "Not only is this nun a great painter, she's also the twin sister I never knew I had."

Phil's eyes popped open. He leaned forward again as I explained who our father was, and how he had raised Catherine and arranged for my adoption after our mother's death.

"Well, why didn't you say so before?" he asked.

"I wasn't sure how I felt about it. I had just met my sister and it hadn't gone so well."

"Exactly," he said, pointing his cigar at me for emphasis. "There's plenty to write about with you reuniting with your long-lost twin, not to mention your mother dying in childbirth and your famous alcoholic father keeping your sister and giving you up."

"So you'll approve it?" I asked.

"On two conditions," he said. "One...you have to deliver a thorough, well-researched article about your sister. Paid for too many 'research trips' where reporters came back with little more than a sunburn. You're going there to work, not party with the nuns. "

"That's fair," I said, praying I could convince Catherine to let me publish. "What's the second condition?"

"It has to be good. Lately, your output has been low and your pieces have reflected an irksome sense of ethics that's downright undesirable in the tabloid business. This article had better knock my socks off or you'll be looking for a new job when you get back."

I gulped and shuffled out, relieved and happy he'd said yes, but unsure that my piece would be up, or, more accurately, down, to *Comet* standards.

CHAPTER THIRTEEN

"Does this mean we can't have sex anymore?" Matt asked, only half-joking as he watched me pack a duffel bag in my spartan bedroom a few days later. Two years after moving in, I still hadn't hung pictures on the walls or softened the lines of the stark window blinds with curtains. An odd sense that I was merely passing through had left me unmotivated to decorate.

"That would imply we were having sex now," I pointed out.

Matt dropped onto my futon, bounced up and down, and beckoned me with a big grin.

"No way." I threw my worn childhood teddy bear at him. "Casual sex with my workaholic ex-boyfriend is a bad idea."

"You never know until you try."

"Oh, I know. I've got too much emotional baggage from you as it is."

"Well, let me lighten your load." He leapt up and took the half-packed duffel from my hands. I tried to take it back, but he held on.

"Seriously." He gripped the bag tighter. "You're not really going to do this, are you?"

"I really am." I wrested the duffel from him with my good hand. "The prioress gave me permission and I'm going."

"Permission to what, deceive her? Do you want to be a nun?"

"No, but I can get better access to my sister and her paintings if I'm inside the cloister. I don't want to publish the article without Catherine's approval." Happy to leave my suits and heels behind, I reached for a clean pair of jeans from the stack of blue milk crates that served as my dresser. "The only way she'll get to know me well enough to give that approval is if I'm inside the cloister. And the only way I can get inside is by pretending I want to become a nun."

"You're obsessed."

"I thought you said I was passionate."

"Now you're just obnoxious. If this is some sort of misguided attempt to get back at the church you left or the father who left *you*—"

"Ouch. You don't pull any punches, do you?" I took a moment to absorb the blow before continuing. It wouldn't have hurt so much if there weren't some truth to his words. "You're giving me way too much credit for vengeance."

"Why do you want to expose your sister? She's perfectly happy not showing her work to anyone."

I couldn't answer him because I didn't *have* an explanation. So I evaded. "Catherine has a responsibility to—"

"To what? Advance your career?" he asked. "Who benefits besides you?"

"The cloister, for one. If I can convince Catherine to sell her paintings, she can help the order financially."

"You've been hanging out with your art dealer friend again," he said.

"Yeah, well, Trish says her clients will pay top dollar for Catherine's paintings. The convent has some serious damage from the last rainy season that they haven't repaired, so I know the nuns need the money. If the show eases their financial troubles, then they'll have more time to pray."

"Top dollar, eh?" Matt gave a grim nod. "A high price will be paid, but not by the buyers. You don't mess with someone else's creative process. Period."

"I know. It's awful, it's lying, it's deceitful– it's all of those things."

"Then why are you doing it?" he asked. "And don't give me your sound bite answer this time. I want the real reason."

"I can't, I don't—"

"Let me take a stab at it then," Matt said. "From where I sit, you're the worst kind of soccer mom. You're projecting your ambition onto a sister who doesn't want or need it. You see her with a talent you wish you had, so you want to live through her or at least prop up your career on her gifts."

"Don't spare my feelings or anything," I said.

"No reason to, because you have your own talent and your own story to tell. Maybe the article you really need to write is the one that explains how you feel about being adopted."

"Oh, please. That'd put people right to sleep." My heart knotted as it did whenever I remembered that I would never have the chance to meet either of my birth parents. "I don't sympathize with my situation. Why would anybody else?"

"You may not think your story is that interesting," Matt said. "But a lot of people can relate to it."

"Maybe other adoptees who don't know who they are, but—"

"I've got news for you, Dorie. Even non-adoptees don't know who they are."

"Well, then a story about Catherine is that much more fascinating," I said. "I may not know who I am, but with a twin I at least get to see who I might have turned out to be under different circumstances. So, in a way, writing about Catherine *is* writing about me, only safer."

"Safer for you, maybe."

I reached for a Marlboro Light and a book of matches. "I'm sorry, but I feel compelled to go."

I struck a match and lit my cigarette.

"How did you get the time off?" Matt took the cigarette from my mouth and stubbed it out in the ashtray. I glared at him and pulled out another. "You're out of vacation."

"Phil thinks he wants to run the article in *The Comet* after all, which I'm grateful for since I couldn't afford this trip otherwise," I said, lighting the second cigarette. "So it's not a vacation, it's research."

"It's dishonest, is what it is." Matt made a grab for my new cigarette, but I moved out of his reach.

"Why are you freaking out on me? I've gone on research trips before."

"This one's different." Matt sat down and hugged the teddy bear. "You're different. I know how excited you are about this article, but pretending you want to be a nun just so you can get close to your sister is taking it too far. It's one thing to exaggerate in a tabloid article, but lying to nuns? That's just bad karma."

"Maybe so, but I'm going," I said, stubbing the cigarette out myself. "I can't explain it. It's like I don't have a choice. If I don't go, I'll always wonder."

"Wonder what? How it feels to be hungry and sleep on a straw mat?" he asked, incredulous. "Wonder how it feels to deceive your sister?"

"Wonder how it feels to *have* a sister, for starters."

"If you're so interested in getting to know Catherine, why don't you tell her who you are?"

"I tried to tell her." I sat down on the bed, deflated. "Based on her reaction, I'd say she either already knows or doesn't want to know. But it's not just about spending time with her anymore. It's about her art, too. I wonder why Catherine's paintings affect me so much. Am I getting out of them what she put into them, or did she intend something else altogether?" I heard my voice rise an octave but couldn't bring it down again. "I wonder why this talent, this gift, this *miracle* was granted to her and not somebody else, how it is she's come to know God in a way most of us haven't. I wonder when I got so damned preachy," I checked myself.

Matt stared at me. "Wow."

"Sorry." I blinked. "I don't know where that came from."

"I do." He dropped the teddy bear and examined his fingernails. "That's exactly what scares me about this trip. You're basically a good person. You don't mess with people. And you wouldn't be pretending you wanted to be a nun, invading these women's privacy, just to see a few paintings and hang out with the twin you haven't even told is your twin. Unless—"

"Unless what?"

"Nothing," Matt muttered and shook his head. "Whatever."

He stood up and walked out of my apartment.

"Matt, wait." I tripped on my bag in my hurry to chase after him, knocking over my milk crate dresser in the process. By the time I picked myself up and got out to the hallway, he was gone.

"Phil threatened to *fire* you?" Trish asked as we walked out of the Rose Café the next morning. She and Graciela had insisted on taking me out for a big breakfast before I spent two weeks limited to the one full meal and two minimal meals a day allowed by the nuns' practice of perpetual fasting. "But I thought you were one of his best reporters?"

"She is," Graciela answered, following us out of the restaurant and over to our cars.

"I was," I corrected. Beach sand blew down the street and worked its way into my contact lenses. "Phil says I've lost my edge, that my stuff isn't racy enough lately."

"He's just trying to scare you," Graciela said.

"It's working." I rubbed my eyes. "I've gone from hoping he'll reject the article to possibly losing my job if he doesn't like it and definitely losing my job if Catherine doesn't agree to let me show it to him."

"Just focus on convincing Catherine and let me worry about *el Jefe*," Graciela said.

"Besides, who cares about Phil when you've got Glen?" Trish pulled a bottle of Glenlivet tied with a red bow from her bag.

"Never mind Glen. I brought you the real essentials." Graciela went to her car and produced a carton of Marlboro Lights and a grocery bag full of Twinkies, Cheetos, and Hershey bars.

"You're too kind." I took the offerings and put them into my trunk alongside my duffel.

"Do you have your camera charger?" Trish asked. "I need decent images to familiarize myself with the paintings before the show."

"If there is a show." I closed the trunk again.

"Oh, there'll be a show." Trish patted me on the shoulder. "Blood is thicker than holy water."

"Not when the blood in question either doesn't know or refuses to acknowledge that we're related." I climbed into the driver's seat of my car. "Matt says what I'm doing is wrong."

"It's completely wrong, but it's the only way, and that makes it okay," Trish said.

"What about you, Graciela?" My coworker's opinion was the one I really wanted. "Would you do it?"

"Well, of course I'd do it, but we're different that way. It depends on what you expect to..." Graciela looked at the sky for a moment before continuing. "*Mira*. You do what you have to do to get what you need from Catherine, but come back the minute you compromise her trust more than you're willing to."

"As long as you get pictures and a signed commitment first," Trish interjected.

Graciela threw Trish a dirty look as I started the car. I heard them bickering as they waved. Silence may not be such a bad thing after all.

The silence became ear-splitting when my radio reception predictably gave out halfway through the drive up to Big Sur. Questions I didn't want to answer popped and bounced through my brain like balls in a bingo tumbler.

I tried to figure out why I was so obsessed with getting the story, even if it meant taking advantage of my sister. Just because I wanted Catherine to get the attention she deserved didn't mean she wanted that attention. What was I really after? Vicarious fame? Acknowledgment from Catherine or my fellow journalists? Love? From whom? Maybe I thought a breakthrough story about a biological family member would somehow justify my existence, or at least serve as a consolation prize for losing that family before I knew I had it. If so, I wasn't sure it was worth the price.

I kept pushing the radio buttons to see if there was any reception to be had. At that point I would have listened to anything to drown out the doubts swirling around my brain. I considered singing, but the only songs I thought of were church hymns I'd learned in school, and they felt a bit *too* appropriate. I left the radio on static just to have some noise.

CHAPTER FOURTEEN

"Some quick ground rules for your visit," Mother Benedicta said as soon as I had settled into a parlor chair that afternoon. "We designed the aspirancy program to help you determine whether you wish to enter our novitiate. You are not here to make friends, nor are you to openly disregard, question, or disrupt our way of life in any way while you're with us. Understood?"

I nodded.

"Excellent. Typically, a sister may communicate with her friends and family once a month. Since you will be here for only two weeks, phone calls, letters, and visitors are prohibited during your stay."

I nodded again, trying not to cringe.

"Those are the caveats for all aspirants." Mother sighed and touched the cross around her neck. "I've recently learned that you are a journalist by profession, so you get an extra one."

I fiddled with a loose thread on my skirt and waited.

"I need you to promise that you won't publish anything about what you see here. We have nothing to hide, but superfluous publicity goes against the spirit of our mission. You are here as a potential member of our community, not as a journalist."

"I understand," I said, hoping I could eventually change her mind. Looking down, I realized I had pulled the hem out of my skirt. The ragged edge hung down like a war-torn flag. "I appreciate your trust."

"Make sure you earn it."

The wailing siren of a passing emergency vehicle rose up from the highway below as I tucked my tattered hemline back in place. The phrase "no-win situation" sprang to mind. Now I had two sisters to convince that Catherine's art should be shared with the public. Short of that, I'd have to keep my promise to Mother Benedicta and somehow persuade Phil that I should be able to keep my job despite refusing to deliver the article. That seemed somewhat possible, if not probable.

I hadn't promised her not to write anything, I told myself, *just not to publish.* I couldn't. Writing was as demanding as any addiction. Even if I made a conscious effort not to do it, I would ultimately find myself compiling the story regardless. Maybe getting Catherine's permission to publish it would enable me to obtain Mother's blessing as well. Maybe not. All I could do was write the best article I was capable of and hope both the sisters and Phil would all agree that it should appear in print. I still would have preferred that Phil reject the idea so I could sell the piece to a more legitimate paper, but now that he had made my job contingent upon delivering the article, I resigned myself to running it in *The Comet.*

"Now that we're clear on that, I can stop being the taskmaster and welcome you to our community." The laugh lines that framed Mother Benedicta's eyes crinkled as she smiled. "It's nice to have you here, Dorie."

"Thank you. I'm looking forward to my stay."

"Our life centers on *ora et labora*—prayer and work. We devote half the day to manual labor as a visible expression of our life of poverty. I think you'll find it very meditative."

"I'm sure I will," I said, believing it.

"I'm assigning you to the kitchen. Tomorrow you may arrive at eight, but after that you're to report for duty at four a.m. to start the baking before Lauds."

My face fell before I could catch it. The early hour was fine, but the word "kitchen" quickly extinguished any hopes of enjoying manual labor.

"I should tell you now that I can't cook at all," I said. "I mean not at all. My hand makes it difficult for me to chop things and—"

"Don't worry," Mother reassured me. "Just do your best. Half the sisters here can't cook either, but we all take turns trying and eat the results gratefully. Eating between meals is frowned upon, but the bakers get an extra cup of coffee to rev them up. Do you drink coffee?"

"I have a feeling I'm about to start."

"No time like the present, provided you leave other vices at the door. I'm sure I don't have to tell you that smoking, drinking, and drugs aren't permitted here."

"I figured," I answered through gritted teeth. I could hear the Marlboro Man, Glenlivet, and Chester Cheetah calling out to me from the car trunk. I ignored them. If I was going to invade the convent, the least I could do was honor their rules, as hard as that would be. I didn't want to get kicked out for bad behavior before getting everything I came for, whatever that was.

"We're not going to go through your bags, but we strongly encourage you to avoid any creature comforts during your stay. Sharing our way of life as completely as possible is the best way to get a real feel for it, and the only habits we can afford are the ones we wear. That's it for now." Mother Benedicta rose to leave. "Sister Teresa will show you around. I'll see you at Vespers."

"Thank you for this opportunity, Mother."

"I hope it gives you some clarity." She padded out of the room on her bare feet.

I hoped I could deal with the hours, the workload, and my guilty conscience.

Out in the parking lot, a turkey vulture turned lazy circles above the monastery. I opened my trunk while Sister Teresa waited to help me carry my things inside. The nun's eyes slid over Graciela's and Trish's care packages.

"My friends don't really understand the nature of perpetual fasting." I pushed the contraband back out of view.

"Most people don't," Teresa said. "My mother insisted I bring a year's supply of her homemade cookie dough. It's probably still in our icebox."

"I did bring donations of my own, if that's all right." I pulled out some additional art supplies but left the cigarettes, alcohol, and junk food in the trunk where they would be less tempting.

"We thank you." Teresa slung the bag of paints and brushes over her shoulder. "But you didn't have to do that."

"I wanted to." What I wanted was to make sure Catherine had plenty of canvases during my stay. I hitched the fresh canvases under my right arm and dragged my duffel bag with my left hand as Sister Teresa watched with amusement. "I didn't know what to bring, so I brought everything."

"You'll be surprised at how little you need."

The nun led the way back to the garden while the vulture surveyed us from the sky.

We stowed my things in Sister Teresa's office. I peered into the adjacent visiting room and saw that the *Madonna and Child* remained conspicuously absent. I wondered what form it took now that Sister Catherine had reclaimed it.

"Ready for the sixty-cent tour?" my hostess asked.

"Just about." I grabbed a stapler from the desk and clamped the jagged hemline of my skirt back in place.

"Well, aren't you resourceful? You'll fit right in."

I felt the weight of the moment as the extern sorted through her keys and unlocked the large door to the cloistered areas. I was about to enter a place few people ever see.

My mind reeled through realistic and fantastic guesses about what the inside of a cloister should look like. Stone hallways lit by dripping candles that tilted in their cobwebbed sconces? High prison windows casting weak beams of sunlight onto rough, cement floors?

The hallway inside the cloister looked a lot like the hallway outside the cloister—plain, whitewashed walls decorated with the occasional wooden cross or devotional image. In contrast to the industrial schoolroom linoleum in the public areas, beautiful hand-painted tiles in elaborate patterns covered the floors. I walked slowly and stared at the ground.

"Divine, aren't they?" Sister Teresa whispered now that we were inside the cloister. "The tile magnate who originally built this as his summer home made sure the place showcased his product. They're chilly on the toes, though. As a barefoot order, we try to touch the earth only on tiptoe as a symbol of our penance and poverty."

I leaned down and touched the floor. It was ice cold. I straightened up with a shudder.

"You can keep your shoes on if you like," she said. "But I suggest you try going barefoot at least once just to see how it feels."

My toes curled inside my footwear at the prospect. "Do you ever wear shoes?"

"We may wear clogs when we're working outside or leaving the cloister, but I'm partial to bare feet."

"When *can* you leave the cloister?" I still wondered about eyeglass prescriptions and dental hygiene.

"As the extern sister, I can leave anytime for errands or what have you."

I amused myself with potential "what have yous" silently. A night at the biker bar? A skinny dip in the ocean? Not likely.

"The cloistered sisters may leave for doctors' appointments, though often the doctors come here to perform check-ups since there are enough of us to keep them busy all day."

"What about voting?"

"Absentee ballot."

"Aha," I said. "And how do you support yourselves?"

"Vow of poverty notwithstanding, it takes money to run this place," the extern said. "I'll show you where we earn it."

Teresa led me through the vegetable gardens to a converted garage on the edge of the cloister campus. Inside, one sister counted clear plastic bags of communion wafers, another packed them into boxes, and a third tracked orders on a computer. I realized what a perfect cover the operation might make. Altar breads made of pressed cocaine came to mind. I shook the thought out of my head and resolved to cut down on action movies.

"We distribute a total of one point two million hosts a month to four different dioceses," Teresa said.

"But we *could* produce up to two million a week and cut our shipping costs in half if we made them here," a sharp-eyed nun wearing little, round glasses said without a pause in her typing. The disparity between her centuries-old white wimple, black veil, gray habit, and the state-of-the-art laptop was almost comical. "Whenever a mudslide washes the road out, the shipments don't arrive from Missouri in time to be sorted. And rates are going up."

"Then why don't you make the hosts here?" I asked.

"The altar bread ovens are too rich for our blood." Sister Teresa rubbed her thumb across the tips of her fingers. "There's one type of oven for white hosts and a different type for wheat. Two ovens mean twice the price."

As we continued the tour, I noticed that nearly every nun I saw had the same smooth skin and otherworldly glow that I'd noticed in Sister Teresa, and, if my Eyeglass Theory was a correct gauge of how long a sister had been in the cloister, looked several years younger than she was. Was it the low stress of their carefully scheduled lifestyle, the Holy Spirit infusing their whole beings, or simply the fact that most cloistered nuns don't spend much time in the sun, that kept them all looking so young? If only they could package and sell *that*, they'd never have to worry about money again.

Teresa took me through the main office, where an apple-cheeked nun sorted dozens of the day's prayer requests as they arrived via post, fax, and email from all over the world, to the laundry and tailor shop, where young Sister Carmella made a show of measuring me for my habit.

"Size eight. Am I right?" Sister Carmella whipped out a tape measure and ran it from my waist to my ankle.

"Well, uh..." I stammered, craving a cigarette.

"She's only joking," Sister Teresa assured me. "You can wear your own clothes during your visit."

I kept hoping we'd run into Sister Catherine along the way and kept an eye out for her. After we'd been through most of the compound and seen or met what seemed like every sister except my twin, it finally dawned on me that she might be avoiding me.

Sister Catherine was absent, but her paintings were displayed everywhere we went. My sibling's work graced the library, infirmary, recreation room, and several offices. Lacking the time to fully appreciate the pictures during the tour, I allowed myself only quick glances as we passed, planning instead to return and savor each canvas later. I did note that every one of Catherine's paintings included a figure with a hand curled in a blessing gesture that resembled my disability.

"This is our entrance to the chapel." Teresa opened a door off the main hallway.

Inside, a middle-aged sister sat in prayer, nodding ever so slightly in acknowledgment as we peered in from the threshold.

"Our special charism, which you can think of as our particular focus—our flair, if you will—is perpetual adoration of the Eucharist,"

Teresa whispered. "We keep a consecrated host on display twenty-four-seven and always have a sister in here keeping it company."

My eyes swept across the familiar chapel, now viewed from the other side of the grille. The late-afternoon sun shone behind the monstrance displaying the Eucharist, giving it a visually divine quality in addition to its symbolic one.

"The chapel used to be the tile magnate's private theater. These backstage wings account for its cross shape. No doubt the Lord knew what its ultimate purpose would be. Still, we said an awful lot of prayers to make up for whatever bawdiness may have taken place on stage here."

"So you converted it in every sense of the word," I said.

"We hope so, anyway." Sister Teresa crossed her fingers.

At the end of the tour, Sister Teresa and I picked up my bag in the office and headed for my room.

"The sisters sleep in one big dormitory, but aspirants get their own cells to make sure they have plenty of solitude for reflection." The extern opened the door to my quarters. "You'll get to know us well enough without being kept awake by the snorers."

I set down my heavy duffel in the small room, happy to have the privacy. The furniture consisted of a dresser, a desk, and a foam pallet on the floor. A picture of the Pope gazed at me from the wall.

"Our order sleeps on straw mats as part of our vow of poverty, but straw is very pricey around here, if you can believe it. So we opted for these fiberfill pallets instead," Teresa explained. "I'm off to prepare the chapel. You have some time to settle in before Vespers."

After she left, I lay down on my pallet and reflected on what I'd experienced so far. For a place that had seemed so mysterious, there were few surprises on the tour. On one level, the cloister was a collection of buildings, not much different from what any Catholic boarding school fortunate enough to occupy a mansion might look like. Take the crosses and religious icons down and it could pass as a secular boarding school.

And yet the cloister was profoundly, inexplicably different. It wasn't the layout or decor that set it apart. It wasn't even the silence. It was the intention behind that silence. I sensed peace, joy, and more than a few internal struggles in it. How many women had walked these halls? How had it changed them? How would it change me?

The bell rang for Vespers. I took off my watch before leaving for chapel but wasn't ready to give up my shoes.

For the first time since I'd arrived, I saw Catherine in the hallway. She was without her paint smock as she walked close to the wall and kept her eyes on the ground. Our strides were evenly matched and we soon fell in step. Rather than acknowledge me, she picked up her pace and beat me to the chapel entrance. Clearly I had a long way to go to win her trust. But how had I lost it? Were my intentions that obvious?

Inside the cloistered area of the chapel, I blessed myself with holy water and bowed before the cross with the reverence the sisters displayed rather than the speed perfected in my childhood trips to church. Catherine headed to what appeared to be her usual place. I scanned the pews and wondered where to go. Sister Teresa was too busy handing out the new missals to notice my confusion, and Mother Benedicta hadn't arrived yet.

A few seconds felt like an hour as I stood there awkwardly. I felt a hand on my elbow and turned to see a radiant Melanie Bunye beside me. She now wore the gray habit and white veil of a novice rather than the blue jumper of a postulant.

"Sister Dominica, I presume?" I whispered.

The new novice grinned and nodded.

I followed gratefully as Dominica led me to a seat in the second pew. Several of the nuns nodded in welcome. Touched by their hospitality, I suddenly found myself trembling with guilt. Touring the cloister hadn't seemed all that invasive. Now I occupied this privileged part of the chapel and prepared to pray with women who had cut themselves off from friends and family but made an exception for me. The women began to chant.

Make a joyful noise unto God, all ye lands:

Sing forth the honour of His name:

Make His praise glorious...

And I began to cry. Not silent tears, but noisy, aching sobs. The sisters continued their prayer, completely unruffled. Not unsympathetic, I could tell, but comfortable with my suffering.

...All the earth shall worship Thee,

And shall sing unto Thee;

They shall sing to Thy name.

My face grew wet and my nose began to run. Sister Dominica produced a tissue from somewhere in the folds of her habit and handed it to me without missing a beat in the chant. Someone behind me put a soothing hand on my shoulder. The gestures made me sob even harder. I was grateful for, if not a little puzzled by, their calm response to my outburst.

The five or six people seated in the public section of the chapel seemed much less comfortable with the situation. Through bleary eyes, I saw the visitors craning their necks trying to spot who was crying. It didn't bother me. I had done the same thing myself even when there wasn't such a spectacle being made. Now it wasn't the sisters, but the gawkers who struck me as a curiosity. I felt safe as I floated in the sea of gray habits. Safe and conflicted.

I made sure to be the last in line in the refectory so as not to accidentally take someone's seat. The three long dining tables formed a U-shape, chairs on the outside only, enabling all the sisters to face one another. A huge picture window occupied the area where a fourth table might have completed the square. A private garden bloomed beyond the glass.

Three open chairs remained after most of the nuns seated themselves. One belonged to Sister Catherine and one to Sister Dominica, who each carried curry-scented bowls of stew to their fellow nuns. The third presumably belonged to me, but which one was it? Mother Benedicta waved and pointed to the empty seat beside her. I slunk down into it and tried to make myself as small as possible.

After my display in chapel, I was embarrassed to be there at all and wished I could go back to my cell. I wasn't hungry for the simple chickpea stew, bread, and cloister-grown orange that constituted my supper. Mother Benedicta asked me to stand so she could formally introduce me to the community.

"I'm sure you've all noticed the new face among us. Let's keep Dorie and her potential vocation in our prayers and do our best to be holy examples of the monastic rule during her visit." Mother gestured that I could sit down again.

I sank into my chair, afraid to return the gazes of the women around me. When I did look up, there were no reprimanding glances, only open smiles. It was as if my chapel outburst had never happened.

The only person who didn't acknowledge me was Catherine. She remained intent on serving the stew. I was glad, as I wasn't sure I could look my twin in the eye without confessing my plans to introduce her and her paintings to a public she didn't want to meet.

I considered getting up, telling all the nuns my motive for coming, and then leaving before I had to deal with the reaction to such a revelation. Instead I picked up my spoon and tried the stew as Sister Carmella read aloud from the writings of Thomas Merton.

Looking beyond the faces, the tables, and the window for the first time since entering the room, I saw one of Catherine's best works hanging on the wall across from me.

At about three-and-a-half by four feet, this depiction of *The Last*

Supper was the largest of all of Catherine's paintings I'd encountered. At the head of the table, Jesus raised His right hand over His disciples in that gesture of blessing so ubiquitous in Catherine's paintings that it had begun to make me self-conscious. I tucked my right hand under the table. It hadn't occurred to me to hide my deformity from anyone until I'd arrived at the cloister. Now I didn't want the fact that my physical handicap matched Catherine's trademark gesture to alert the other nuns to the connection between us.

The Last Supper's colors were beyond gorgeous—Jesus' robe was the silver-white green of a Russian olive tree, the table the rich copper of sandstone, St. Peter's beard the glossy black of a river in moonlight. I stifled a smirk when I noticed that some of the features of the disciples on the canvas were stylized versions of the faces belonging to the nuns seated around the table. Mother Benedicta's gray eyes, Sister Carmella's dusky skin, and Sister Teresa's thin lips characterized St. John, St. Thomas, and St. James, respectively.

More arresting than the colors, the flawless composition, or even the familiar features were the expressions of the disciples themselves. The emotions captured on their faces ranged from terror, pity, and disgust to ardor, resolve, and rapture.

My own emotions ran the gamut as I experienced the power of the painting. I heard Merton's words without absorbing them, ate my stew without tasting it, and now tried to catch my sister's eye without success. Whether or not she looked at me, I hoped she sensed my awe at her achievement.

Finally, Catherine's ice-blue eyes flicked past my own as she turned to reenter the kitchen. Her glance suggested such fear and dread that I wondered if she already knew my plans. If so, I couldn't blame her. If I convinced her to let me publish the article I intended to write, it would be at Catherine's expense.

CHAPTER FIFTEEN

On my way to recreation hour, I came across the black and white cat I'd noticed in the garden on previous visits to the cloister. When I bent down to pet her, she arched her back and hissed.

"Don't mind Penguin," Sister Teresa said when she witnessed the exchange from the common-room doorway. "If she weren't such a good mouser, she'd have lost her status as head house pet long ago." Teresa turned to the cat. "Mind your manners or I'll make you go vegetarian like the rest of us."

Penguin switched her tail back and forth and stalked off down the hall.

In the cavernous common room, the previous owner's legacy extended beyond the tiled floor to include a fireplace large enough to stand in and an elaborately carved, beamed ceiling. The huge room was chilly despite the summer evening, but the cozy chatter of women who only had an hour a day to discuss non-prayer and non-work matters filled the air. The worn, inexpensive furniture included two couches, card tables stacked with every board game invented before 1960, and several reclining chairs that all faced the focal point in the room, a ping-pong table.

"We're rather zealous about our ping-pong tournaments, God forgive us," Sister Teresa said over the hubbub. "Sister Carmella is our reigning champ."

The extern pointed out the teenage nun from the tailor shop. Sister Carmella had traded her tape measure for a paddle as she practiced her game with the apple-cheeked nun I'd seen in the mailroom. Several of the older sisters sat crocheting or knitting while Sister Dominica strummed a guitar and Mother Benedicta stoked a small fire.

I looked around and discovered that Catherine was absent from the gathering. I did notice several easels facing the windows and eagerly strode toward them.

"Is this where Sister Catherine paints?" I asked.

Then I saw the still-lifes and pet portraits in progress there and had my answer.

"No." Teresa caught up with me. "She received special permission to set up a little studio in an old storage closet. Everyone may use it, but the other sisters who paint prefer the light in here."

The nun with the tiny, round glasses who ran the altar bread distribution business set out a *Scrabble* board on one of the card tables and crooked her finger at me.

"You game?" she asked.

"Oh, sure." I proffered my left hand. "I'm also Dorie."

"Sister Scholastica, *Scrabble* devotee *extraordinaire*." The nun shook my hand with a firm grip. "Welcome."

Cheers and sighs over the ping-pong pyrotechnics of Sister Carmella and her latest victim rose up behind us. I smugly assumed that my journalistic prowess would make me reigning *Scrabble* champ inside a week.

Teresa joined us as Sister Scholastica set the tone on her first *Scrabble* entry—*ipsum*. Sister Teresa soon followed up with *veni*.

"For a couple of women who don't talk for most of the day, you two certainly have strong vocabularies," I said over the smacks and pops of the ping-pong match. "I'm a writer and I've never even heard of those words."

"Yes, well, here at the convent we play in Latin," Sister Teresa said with a sly grin. She handed me a dog-eared Latin dictionary.

"Hope you paid attention in Lauds," added Sister Scholastica.

"Sh... I mean, dang," I said. "Can I say dang?"

"You can say it, but you can't use it in *Scrabble*," Sister Teresa said. "No slang allowed."

"No foreign languages either, last time I checked." I arched an eyebrow and flipped through the paperback.

"It's good incentive for our novice to study her Latin," Scholastica explained. "So we bent the rules in the service of God."

"I see." I scowled and settled in for my first *Scrabble* defeat in years.

"It worked, too." Sister Dominica seated herself at the last chair at our table. "I've been furiously conjugating Latin verbs for months and these two still whup me every time."

"We're all here to learn humility." Sister Teresa giggled.

"I got my share of that in chapel today." I put my lettered tiles in alphabetical order. "I don't know what came over me."

"The same thing that came over the rest of us—God's grace." Sister Teresa set down another Latin word—*clamor.* "I cried my eyes out the first day."

"You did?" I asked.

Teresa nodded and chose five new *Scrabble* tiles.

"So did I." Scholastica organized her own tiles into a row.

"Me, too," Sister Dominica agreed. "I don't know if it was terror over what I left behind or joy for my life ahead."

"For me it was both," Scholastica said.

"Heck, I was just thinking about how much I'd miss pork chops." Sister Teresa's eyes got glassy. "I still get choked up thinking about pork chops."

"Don't trouble yourself, Dorie." Sister Scholastica patted my shoulder. "All your tears mean is that you belong here."

Scholastica's assurance was troubling in itself. The idea that I belonged here wasn't one I wanted to entertain. Instead of assuming that God was calling me into the fold, I preferred to write my tears off as guilt over intruding on a sacred ritual for my own selfish ends.

"Look who's decided to join us." Sister Scholastica peered over the top of her tiny glasses and watched Catherine enter the common room.

"Doesn't she usually come?" I asked, following her gaze.

"Mother lets her paint during study periods and recreation hour," Teresa said as a tentative Catherine crossed the room toward the easels and art supplies. "She gets along fine with everyone, but she pretty much keeps to herself even when she's not painting."

"I don't think it's fair that she gets to do her own thing a lot of the time." Scholastica frowned. "What's so wonderful about her painting anyway? We're here to focus on the community, not the individual."

At first I was taken aback to hear harsh words from a nun. Then I remembered mean Sister Agnes back in the fifth grade, who was so skilled at humiliating kids who didn't turn in their homework that I made sure to never be in that category. In this case, Sister Scholastica's humanity was a relief, as I imagined living among saints would be exhausting. If nothing else, it was interesting to find someone who *didn't* like my sister's paintings.

"She more than makes up for her absence here with extra work elsewhere," Sister Teresa said, jerking her head toward my hand and shooting Sister Scholastica a warning glance when she thought I wasn't looking.

I watched a light bulb switch on over Scholastica's head and wondered if Sister Teresa had guessed my relationship to Catherine. If so, when? Was it when she saw how Catherine reacted to me, or earlier? She may have known it the moment she met me. But how could she really know? Catherine and I didn't look all that much alike. Did my behavior give it away? I took a deep breath and told myself I was probably overreacting. Even if Teresa did know, she probably wasn't telling anyone, except maybe Scholastica.

"That's true," Scholastica acknowledged, backpedaling so fast she nearly fell off her metaphorical bike. "She takes double and triple shifts at perpetual adoration..."

"Paints in the middle of the night..." Dominica added.

"When does she sleep?" I asked.

"I don't believe she does." Teresa used a stubby pencil to tally the game points on a pad of paper. "I think that's why she doesn't talk. She's too tired after pouring herself into her work, her prayers, and her paintings."

"Too tired or too cranky." Scholastica wrinkled her nose, apparently unable to dampen her disdain for long. "She's got a temper."

"So do you when you haven't had your coffee," Teresa said.

"That I do." Sister Scholastica sighed. "Now I'll have to stay and say an extra novena after...what is that third Divine Office called again?"

"Terce," I answered without thinking.

"Get a load of her," said Sister Teresa.

"Somebody's showing off." Sister Scholastica laughed.

"I didn't even know I knew that." I felt my cheeks burn. "It's not like I've memorized them or anything, but I guess I did read through the schedule today."

"Maybe you had some divine help," suggested Dominica.

"Reel 'er in, she's a keeper." Teresa scored fifteen points on the word *dominus*.

I shrugged and looked away, almost sorry to learn how much I liked and respected these women. I thought about how disillusioned they'd be once they learned the hidden agenda behind my visit. Sister Scholastica would no doubt have some choice words on *that* topic. I watched Catherine leave the room with a fistful of my donated brushes, glad at least to see her take the gifts she had once rejected.

The bell rang for Compline, the seventh and final prayer of the Divine Office. Carmella and her opponent stopped their ping-pong match mid-point as all the sisters rose and filed out of the room. I started to put the *Scrabble* game back in its box, happy to clear away my miserable performance before suffering official defeat.

"Leave it." Sister Teresa's keys rattled as she stood up. "We drop everything for the bells."

"Besides," Sister Scholastica said. "We'll pick up where we left off tomorrow."

Chagrined, I complied and followed the women to the chapel.

Since the monastery closed to the public at 5:30 every evening, I'd never attended the 7:30 Compline service before. I was alternately curious about the content and focused on avoiding more chapel tears. Taking my seat in the pew, I tried to ignore the article that was writing itself in my head.

Compline turned out to be unnervingly appropriate. Each sister examined her conscience and asked forgiveness for the day's offenses before retiring for the night. As the sisters sang the *Salve Regina*, I realized my crimes were too numerous to count, much less make amends for.

When Mother Benedicta sprinkled everyone with holy water in remembrance of baptism, I had a feeling my own sins wouldn't be washed away unless I came clean with the prioress about my motive for coming to the monastery. The more time I spent at the cloister, the less comfortable I became with my purpose there. I started to wonder what exactly my purpose was.

I walked to my cell surrounded by the silence and scribbled in my notebook until the bells rang for lights out. I counted the chimes—nine o'clock. I hadn't gone to bed before midnight since age twelve but snapped out the light to honor the rhythms of the community.

CHAPTER SIXTEEN

By 9:30, I had paced my cell several dozen times. By 10:30, I was chain-smoking the one pack of cigarettes I'd brought to taper off with. In an effort to avoid the telltale stench, I stood in my bra and panties with my hair tied up under a bandanna and blew the smoke out the small window. I wished I'd thought to buy an e-cigarette rather than fool myself into believing I could quit. Then I noticed the picture of the Pope watching me.

"Go ahead and judge if you must, but you shouldn't be looking at a woman in her underwear, either." I took the photo from the wall and laid him face down on the desk.

My stomach rumbled. I thought about the Hershey bars in the trunk of my car. Only the impossibility of unlocking the massive front gate stopped me from sneaking out to the parking lot to get them. I lit the last cigarette and eyed my duffel bag. After smoking the cigarette down to the filter, I threw away the bandanna, pulled on a clean pajama top, and dug through the rest of my clothes in search of the bottoms.

I heard something sloshing inside the bag as I pulled out the other half of my sleepwear and put it on. Settling my hand around a solid object amid the jeans and sweaters, I found myself clutching a fifth of bourbon that I hadn't packed. The attached note read:

Thought you might need this.

Cheers, Matt

How right he was. It wasn't a chocolate bar or even a booze I liked, but it would do. I pinned the bottle to my chest with my right fist and unscrewed the cap with my left. The scent of black licorice unfurled into the air. Raising the bottle in salute to Matt six hours away, I took a manly swig. It tasted like burnt chestnuts, scorched my throat, and made me cough. My sinuses cleared immediately. One more swallow on an empty stomach and I was downright tipsy.

But I wasn't tired. I was sleepless, hungry, drunk, *and* I missed Matt. I appreciated his gesture knowing how he felt about my trip. I wished I could call him.

Instead, I looked for the only other distraction I could think of. I dug around in my bag again until I located the camera I'd borrowed from Rod. I adjusted it per his coaching and reviewed the lighting tips he'd given me. I planned to photograph all of Catherine's paintings before circumstances or my emerging conscience prevented it. Slipping on my shoes, I opened the door silently but hadn't gone five steps before the noisy clacking of my stacked loafers against the tiled floor forced me to turn back. I kicked off the offending footwear and went out again, barefoot after all.

The smooth, cool tiles felt good under my feet as the scent of night-blooming jasmine wafted in through the open windows. I retraced the steps of Sister Teresa's tour and photographed every one of Sister Catherine's paintings along the way. Only the rustle of my cotton pajamas and the tick and buzz of my camera broke the unearthly silence. Unsure of the dim lighting, my rookie skills and my bourbon-impaired coordination, I took several pictures of each painting using different shutter speeds. At one point I had to duck into an alcove and share the tight space with a statue of St. Someone Or Other as Sister Scholastica passed by on her way to what I guessed was her perpetual adoration shift in the chapel.

Fifty images later, I wracked my brain for other places where there might be a painting. I had risked the creaking doors of every storage closet and still hadn't found Sister Catherine's studio. I was scrolling through the images when I nearly tripped over Penguin. The feline let out a blood-curdling caterwaul.

"Shhh! You'll bust me," I whispered.

Penguin replied with a hiss and reached for the dead mouse I'd unwittingly kicked away from her.

When I saw that the fur my bare foot had touched belonged to something other than the cat, I let out my own screech of horror.

Nonplused, Penguin batted the corpse onto a colorful tile that framed it as its own work of art.

I looked around. No one appeared to be within earshot. Penguin had placed the mouse beside a closed door, reminding me of the way my mom's cat, Socrates, had left dead birds next to the porch door as a gift for her. The familiar smell of the citrus paint thinner Trish used back in college hovered in the air.

"Animal sacrifice went out years ago, you little heathen," I informed the cat. "But thanks for the heads-up."

I checked for light under the door. Seeing none, I turned the handle and stepped carefully over Penguin's offering to enter the confined space. The rough cement floor scratched my bare feet while the citrus thinner assaulted my nose. It was too dark in the windowless room to see more than vague shadows. I threw aside any caution exercised in the previous two hours and flicked on the light switch.

A single, harsh fluorescent rod sent a chemical blue sheen over everything. I blinked and understood why the other sisters preferred to paint by the natural light of the common room windows. I cringed to think what it must've been like to try to paint in such a space and doubted I could get decent photographs given the conditions. After adjusting my eyes to the light, I blinked again for a completely different reason.

The walls were a riot of color, brilliant beyond the handicap of poor lighting. Canvases in different stages of completion hung haphazardly on hooks designed to store mops and brooms. On the back wall, high, slotted shelving designed for buckets and cleaning solvents now held a bunch of paintings tipped up against one another. The paint-splotched edges of the canvases indicated that nearly every one had been used. A dented electric fan provided ventilation, plastic wrap kept the paint moist on a Tupperware lid palette, and an old A-frame ladder served as a makeshift easel. Aside from the lack of natural light, it was a functional little studio.

Never before surrounded by so much of my twin's work, my eyes darted from painting to painting. Dependable as the trademark Ninas in a Hirschfeld, each canvas had at least one figure with a right hand shaped like mine.

As I reflected on the sketch artist who hid his daughter's name in all of his drawings, it dawned on me that the acknowledgment I craved, but hadn't received, in my encounters with my sister existed in every painting she'd ever done. Suddenly, the room full of artwork seemed to close in on me with the affirming warmth of a womb. I sat down in the office chair and hugged my knees to my chest. A lump rose in my throat. Catherine remembered me every time she picked up her brush.

Overwhelmed and uncomfortable with my feelings, I leapt up and began taking pictures of the paintings as fast as the camera allowed. I finished the memory card within seconds but continued to press the button in frustration. Only when I paused long enough to pull out the card did I realize Catherine stood in the doorway staring at me. I jumped and stubbed my toe on the uneven concrete.

"Oh, it's you." I hopped on one foot and forgot that Grand Silence meant just that. "You startled me. How did you know I was here?"

She tugged on her ear.

"I guess I did kinda scream, didn't I? That little thing scared the bejesus...I mean, the daylights out of me." I pointed to the mouse lying in state just outside the door.

The only small object Catherine seemed to care about was the one in my hand. She held out her own hand and waited.

"I'm sorry. I can't give you the card because it belongs to my coworker, but I will delete the pictures." I replaced the card in the camera and deleted the last ten pictures. I knew I should have deleted the rest of the images as well but couldn't make myself do it, rationalizing that it was okay as long as I didn't show them to anyone. "See? Gone."

I leaned over and showed Catherine the word "delete" on the display screen, praying she wouldn't want to inspect it herself and discover the other pictures. She nodded and appeared satisfied. "It was wrong of me to photograph your work without permission, but I couldn't resist."

I tried and failed to curb my used-car salesman enthusiasm. All that practice presenting story ideas to Phil and I still couldn't act nonchalant. I hadn't planned to suggest a gallery show while drunk and guilty of invading Catherine's privacy, but the bourbon forged ahead and I followed.

"Do you have any idea how talented you are?" I asked.

Sister Catherine replied by scooping up Penguin's bounty with an old newspaper and tossing it in the trash.

"You should do a show," I said. "Nobody else paints like this. People need to see how amazing your work is."

Catherine glared at me from under a furrowed brow as she donned her robin's egg-blue paint smock. She lit a candle in the corner of the room, flicked on the electric fan, peeled the plastic wrap from the paint-dabbed Tupperware lid, and chose a brush from several that poked bristles-up out of an old coffee can, all without taking her eyes off of me. Now that I had her attention, I feared it and pinched my arm just to distract myself from the power of her glance.

"Look, I know you don't want to sell your stuff. But think about how much money you'd make for the cloister. I've spoken to an art dealer who's very interested. You wouldn't have to lift a finger on the business end."

My appeal was lost on my sister, whose steady gaze alone made me back out of the room.

Desperate, I considered acknowledging our twinship right then but didn't want to cheapen that moment by throwing it into a sales pitch. Besides, I wasn't sure it would help my cause at that point. Instead I pulled my religious trump card.

"Think about the vocations your art could attract."

Catherine rolled her eyes and shut the door in my face.

"Remind me never to go into sales," I muttered and turned away from the closed door.

Penguin watched me from across the hall.

"What are you looking at?" I asked.

The cat tipped her head and resumed licking her paw, suggesting a response of "Not much."

A moment later, the first bell rang for Vigils. Catherine emerged from the studio and headed to the chapel without further acknowledging me. Sheepish, I followed, both energized by the art and embarrassed by our exchange.

As midnight Vigils began, my energy gave way to guilt over my recent behavior. Between bouts of self-loathing and trying not to breathe bourbon on anyone, I found the mystery of the prayers whispered in darkness enchanting.

I misjudged the distance to my pallet on the floor and literally fell into bed after the prayer service. Too tired to care, I slept well despite a bruised elbow.

When the bells rang at 4:55 a.m., I stared at my phone in disbelief.

I rolled over, swore I'd get up in a second, and promptly dozed off again. When the bells rang a second time, I only had five minutes to get to chapel for Lauds.

"So much for hygiene." I swished a quick glob of toothpaste around in my mouth and swallowed it. As I pulled a pair of jeans over my pajamas, my body bewailed what most would consider an ungodly hour with a wave of nausea. I kicked myself at the thought of my overbaked gallery pitch a few hours before.

With no time to put in my contacts and unable to locate my glasses, I stumbled down the hallway. My impaired vision made my hearing more acute. Outside the windows, dozens of birds sang different songs that somehow blended seamlessly. I decided to buy a bird feeder for my patio at home, preferring birdsong to the all too acoustically accessible whoosh, gargle, and sneeze symphony of my neighbors' morning routines in Venice.

I stifled a yawn and rushed inside the chapel to find all the sisters already washed and dressed for the day. Just as I caught my breath and found my place, they began to sing, not unlike the birds announcing the day outside and every bit as beautiful.

I will sing of the mercies of the Lord forever:

With my mouth will I make known thy faithfulness to all generations.

For I have said, Mercy shall be built up forever:

Thy faithfulness shalt thou establish in the very heavens.

I closed my eyes and truly listened for the first time in my life. Sitting in the midst of the generous voices, the chant had an even lovelier tone than when I'd heard it from the other side of the grille. I hummed along as Sister Teresa helped me find my place in the hymnal.

By six a.m. Mass, I was still tired but ready to grapple with the Latin in my missal. I belted out the songs that were familiar to me with enthusiasm, though often in the wrong key.

Terce followed Mass with a prayer for blessings on the day. The longer I deceived these women, the less I felt worthy of such blessings.

Too nauseated after the morning offices to follow the sisters into the refectory for breakfast, I took a quick shower. My lungs screamed silently for nicotine. I settled for a tall mug of ink-black coffee from the refectory sideboard on my way to report for kitchen duty. It was only eight a.m., but my body insisted the day should be over. I took a swig of the brew and pushed open the kitchen door. Before the bitter liquid could slide down my throat to deliver its much-needed caffeine, I let the door swing shut again and turned back to the refectory wall.

The blank space over the sideboard stared back at me. Catherine's painting of *The Last Supper* was gone. Flooded with guilt over whatever role I may have played in its removal, I prayed she hadn't altered it.

I went into the kitchen and took in the daunting industrial sinks, stovetops, and oven. The moist smell of yeast floated on a current of oven-heated air. At the counter, Sister Dominica peeled potatoes while Catherine kneaded bread dough with quick folds and angry jabs. Judging from the pile of potato skins and the rise in the dough, they'd been at it for a while.

"I thought Mother Benedicta told me to be here at eight," I said. "Am I late?"

Sister Dominica smiled and shook her head, and then handed me a blue smock like the ones she and Catherine wore to protect their habits.

As I put on the apron, Catherine carried a stack of empty mixing bowls still sticky with dough over to the sink where I stood. She placed them in front of me with a clank, but without a word, and returned to her dough. I found the dish liquid and filled the sink with hot, soapy water, grateful for a task I could handle.

"I noticed you took down the painting in the refectory. Are you working on it?" I couldn't help asking despite being unsure I was ready for the answer.

No answer came. Catherine gave the bread dough one last punch and left the kitchen. Soon the sounds of rattling cans and clattering utensils emanated from the pantry down the hall.

"We try not to speak during the day unless it's work-related," Sister Dominica murmured after the artist was gone.

I scowled in frustration and began washing the bowls. After a few seconds, Dominica checked the hallway and shut the door.

"She took them all down," the novice whispered. "Sometimes she removes one or two at a time, but she's never taken them all down at once before. I don't know why she did it."

I knew why, and I was ashamed.

CHAPTER SEVENTEEN

The missing paintings clinched it. I washed the mixing bowls clean, but I couldn't rationalize away my indiscretions any longer. In less than twenty-four hours, my presence had already become detrimental to my sister and her art. I took off my apron, mouthed "bathroom" to Sister Dominica, and left the kitchen in search of Mother Benedicta.

I considered the situation as I walked. Clearly, the more I insisted Catherine share her work with the public, the more she'd make it unavailable. Why was I so driven to expose her against her will?

It wasn't that I felt some higher calling to introduce an important artist to the world, even if she was my twin. I'd simply chosen to react to my sister's immense talent the only way I knew how. I needed to write about the paintings as a way to work through all the feelings they stirred up for me, but did I really need to publish the results? Probably not. I would get by with or without my *Comet* job if it came to that. I always had.

I found Mother Benedicta in her modest office. A perfect calla lily bloom rested in a mason jar on her tank-green metal desk, and the plastic clock on the wall ticked off a military rhythm that matched my racing heartbeat.

"I think I should leave," I said the moment I entered.

"Already?" Mother put aside her paperwork and gestured for me to sit. "You've only—"

"I know. But I came for the wrong reasons."

"We all do, more or less." Mother touched the cross around her neck. "Whether they're delusions of sainthood, suffering, or both, none of us had any idea of what we were really getting into until we got here."

"Delusions of grandeur in my case." I sat down and wound my right foot around the chair leg to anchor myself against squirming. "I came because I wanted to write an article about Sister Catherine's paintings." I didn't see any point in mentioning that Catherine and I were twins. It was bad enough to admit I was there to exploit a nun, much less one who was also my sister.

Not even a hint of surprise flickered across Mother Benedicta's face. "I know you did. You still do."

"On some level, yes." My shoulders relaxed. Apparently I was as bad an actress as I'd always thought. "Which is why you asked me not to publish anything about the cloister."

She nodded.

"And since I've promised you I wouldn't and plan to keep my word, I don't see any reason for me to stay here."

"Don't you?"

I cocked my head and looked at her, confused.

"I'm guessing there is a reason; we just don't know what it is yet. If there wasn't a reason, you would have left the moment you promised me you wouldn't publish."

"I could have lied," I said, again aware that I was still lying about my relationship to Catherine. I decided to admit that too before the conversation ended. "Or maybe I stayed because I wanted to see the rest of the art."

"No." Mother practically looked through me. "You don't lie about the important things, except maybe to yourself. And you knew you'd see all the art eventually, even if you hadn't stayed, given that Sister Teresa shows you at least one painting every Visiting Day."

"It's not Sister Teresa's fault that—"

"That Catherine is an inspired painter? No, I don't believe it is. There's no rule against sharing community property with visitors."

I breathed a sigh of relief and unwound myself from the chair, glad I hadn't gotten the extern in trouble.

"Why else did you stay?" Mother asked. "Why did you apply for a visit at all, for that matter? You could have written an article about your twin from the outside."

"I might have." I thought about my growing pile of journals on the subject and then stopped, surprised, and looked at the prioress. "You know that Catherine is my twin?"

Mother Benedicta nodded. "I saw the resemblance, then confirmed it by checking your birth date on the aspirancy application."

Even though Sister Teresa's warning glance to Sister Scholastica over the *Scrabble* tiles had alerted me to the possibility that the sisters suspected my relationship to Catherine, I still turned bright red when Mother Benedicta said it out loud. She was the first person who had met both Catherine and me to acknowledge that we were siblings. I was both embarrassed that I hadn't told her myself and exhilarated that there was now someone with whom I could openly refer to "my sister" (a phrase that still felt unfamiliar) without having to explain who my twin was.

"Does anyone else know?" I asked, guessing the answer. These nuns lived away from the world, but were by no means unworldly.

"I'm sure several sisters have figured it out. Your hand is in all the paintings; it's hard to miss. Have you talked to Catherine about your relationship?"

"No, but she seems to know."

"She's doing as bad a job of hiding it as you are." Mother nodded. "I've never seen such a case of sibling rivalry."

"We've just met, so we've got some catching up to do."

"Well, I expect you two to hurry up and get things resolved. I didn't grant you an aspirancy visit to watch you conduct a family feud."

"Why did you let me enter at all if you knew Catherine was my sister?" I asked.

"It's not uncommon to have biological sisters in the same religious order. Sisters Soteris and Walburga Saenger lived and prayed among us until they passed on within days of each other three years ago," Benedicta said. "Besides, your sister isn't the reason you're here. You could have acknowledged your relationship with Catherine and gotten to know her on visiting days just as easily as you got to know her paintings."

"That's true, if she was willing to get to know me, which I'm still not sure about. I don't know why I entered. I guess I was curious. Isn't everybody curious about what goes on in here?"

"Yes, but few are take-off-two-weeks-to-fast-and-pray curious."

"Maybe I'm a masochist." *God, I wanted a smoke.*

"Heaven forbid. Masochists enjoy suffering. Contemplatives endure it in order to offer it up to God."

"I wasn't suggesting that—" I wound my foot around the chair again.

"Oh, I suppose we are on some level." Mother leaned back in her seat. "But you haven't answered my question."

"I guess I don't have an answer." I shrugged. "I don't know why I'm still here."

"Well, then I suggest you stay until you have at least one good reason why you *shouldn't* be here."

"I've got two right now. My sister despises me and I don't want to be a nun."

"You and Catherine stand a better chance of making peace if you stay. And you're not a nun, nor will you be at the end of your two weeks."

"I don't ever want to be a nun," I insisted.

"I'm not sure I ever want you to be a nun, either. But you're welcome to finish out the aspirancy visit if you like."

"Why would you let me do that?"

"Because it's not always up to us. One woman here fought the call for years. Gave herself an ulcer not wanting to be a nun."

"What happened?"

"I got tired of drinking Mylanta." Mother patted her stomach and got up. "When God calls, you don't say no."

"But I really don't want to be a nun," I said.

"If that's the case, then you can leave right now with a clear conscience. For whatever reason, God brought you to this place. Whether it was to write an article about your twin or not, I don't pretend to know. I do know that if there's any inkling of 'or not,' I suggest you explore that, because it's not going to go away. If you'll excuse me, I've got a meeting to attend."

Mother Benedicta rose to leave and then paused. "By the way, the inside of any car parked in our public lot is virtually soundproof from the cloister."

The prioress exited, leaving her *non sequitur* behind like Cinderella's glass slipper—interesting but of no immediate practical use. I sat alone in the office, momentarily stunned. I stood up and shot the crucifix above Mother's desk a nasty look before storming out of the room.

Back in my cell, I packed my bag, bundled up the linens for the laundry, put on my noisiest shoes, and click-clacked loudly through the courtyard toward my car. I thought I saw Catherine watching me from a window, but when I paused to look, she'd disappeared. I considered finding her and talking things over, but for what? I wouldn't get any answers from a silent nun.

I was angrier than I had a right to be—at myself, at my ambition, at the world, and anyone in it who crossed me. Who did Mother Benedicta think she was, anyway? Couldn't she have accepted my promise not to publish and left it at that? All I'd wanted to do was come clean and get out of there, and the prioress had to go laying this vocational head trip on me.

Of course I liked being at the cloister. Big Sur was paradise, for God's sake. It was a damned tourist attraction full of campgrounds and national forest, with an eight-hundred-acre nature preserve that happened to belong to cloistered nuns smack dab in the middle of it. I'd discovered my long-lost sister doing some of the most beautiful painting I'd ever seen in one of the most beautiful places I'd ever been. So I was drawn to it. It didn't mean I wanted to be a nun.

Or did it? Maybe I *wasn't* interested in the paintings as a way to forward my career or get to know Catherine. Then why had I gone to such extraordinary lengths to be close to them and her on false pretenses? Whom had I fooled? Maybe the joke was on me.

I heaved my duffel into the trunk, grabbed a pack of cigarettes from the carton, and lit one. I took a long drag, leaned against my car, and waited for a chemical rush that never came. The cigarette tasted like dirt. I threw it down and ground it out with my loafer before opening the car door and sliding into the driver's seat. The moment I shut the door, I understood why Mother Benedicta had made the soundproof comment.

"ARRRRGGGGGHHH!" I bellowed from deep in my gut, smacking the steering wheel with my palm. It felt good. "SHIT, SHIT, SHIT!"

I thought about my options. I'd driven up to the monastery on Saturday so I hadn't missed any work yet. Producing an article for *The Comet* or even for freelance purposes was out of the question now, but maybe if I showed up in the newsroom as usual on Monday, Phil might let me keep my job.

When I went to turn the key in the ignition, I was shocked to find that I couldn't bring myself to start the car. The view of the Pacific beyond my steering wheel hypnotized me and I suddenly realized I didn't want to leave. I shook the thought from my head, reached for the ignition, and tried again. A goldfinch landed on my hood. It blinked at me, its yellow and black feathers dazzling against the backdrop of blue sea. I sat there, captivated.

When the sun grew hot, I climbed out of the stuffy car. Occasional highway traffic hummed below as the wind rustled the laurel trees and cooled the air with a welcome breeze. I wandered into the public garden and sat on a stone bench beside the cloister wall. The decision not to publish relieved my conscience, but staying the full two weeks without producing a story would relieve me of my job. Remaining at the cloister also meant I'd have to reach some sort of truce with Catherine, something I feared as much as I craved.

I took in the orange and yellow marigolds, burgundy roses, emerald ferns, pink impatiens, and purple begonias as cicadas chirruped in a nearby lilac tree and wasps came and went from a small nest under the eaves. A black-headed blue jay tried to peck open a nut with no success and then hopped about, chirping in apparent frustration. I could relate.

I closed my eyes, leaned my head against the wall, and let out a deep sigh. I was tired of the indecision and endless questions taking up all the space in my brain.

"I give up," I whispered.

As my mind quieted, I started to pray without thinking about it—a welcome change from the constant doubt. I kept praying, sinking deeper and deeper.

A bell rang and took me out of my trance. Sitting up, I rubbed my eyes and counted eleven chimes. Over two hours had passed. When the bell summoning the sisters to chapel for the next Divine Office sounded ten minutes later, I calmly got my bag from my trunk and returned to the cloister.

Smuggling the carton of Marlboros back into my room would've been easy enough, but I left it behind. I'd already survived twelve hours of withdrawal, as well as a dearth of food and sleep and a surplus of caffeine. If I was going to be miserable anyway, I may as well quit smoking too. It was just two weeks, I told myself. And it was all about Catherine and her art, even if I couldn't publish. Maybe Phil would accept some other article in lieu of a cloister piece. I doubted it.

"How's the ulcer?" I asked Mother as we walked toward the chapel a few minutes later.

"Haven't had a pain since the day I entered, praise God." The prioress touched the cross around her neck. "How's the lung cancer?"

"I'm working on it. But I don't think I can beat my addiction to Catherine's paintings."

"None of us can. So long as you lose the liquor and cigarettes, we'll get along fine."

"Yes, Ma'am." I checked the back of Mother's head for the extra pair of eyes she apparently had there and then decided to offer up restitution. "I will say the Act of Contrition prayer for violating your ban on smoking and drinking."

"Good idea. And I've got just the thing if you'd like to throw in some penance."

"Whatever you think." I gulped.

Mother patted my shoulder and we entered the chapel together.

Despite my recent crimes, I had to break one more rule of the cloister and talk to my sister as soon as possible. I'd lose my nerve if I waited until recreation hour.

I found Catherine tidying up her studio after lunch. She set down the canvases in her hands when she saw me in the doorway. Her eyes brimmed with tears.

"I'm pretty sure you know that you and I are twin sis—"

Before I could finish, Catherine wrapped her arms around me in a fierce hug I wasn't prepared for. Then she pulled back to look at me as she cradled my deformed hand between both of her own.

"I thought so," I said in a quivering voice. "So our father told you about me and my handicap?"

She nodded and looked at the floor.

"How long have you known? When did he tell you?"

Catherine turned and sorted through several finished canvases stacked against the wall. She paused at one and beckoned me over.

The background of the scene showed only hints of furniture and structures to put the figures in context, but my recent studies of religious art helped me recognize the subject as Mary on her deathbed, surrounded by attendants and angels ready to convey her soul to heaven. Catherine pointed to Mary.

"Okay, yes, Mary is dying, I get that," I said.

Catherine gestured between Mary and herself to suggest a connection.

"Mary talked to you on her deathbed?"

Catherine shook her head and kept gesturing.

"Not Mary. *Our* mother? That's not possible." I smacked my forehead. "Duh. Our father. Our dad told you about me when he was dying."

Catherine nodded vigorously and held up nine fingers.

"I understand. And since he died when we were seventeen, you've known about me for nine years."

Catherine gave me the thumbs up to indicate "yes." I felt a twinge of old pain in my sternum. It hurt to learn she'd been aware of me for so long and hadn't looked for me. Then I remembered that I wouldn't have sought her out, either, if Graciela hadn't arranged it.

"I found out about Rene, Lucy, and you when my adoptive dad died last January," I explained.

She lowered her chin and put her hand to her heart, which I took to mean that she was sorry for my loss. We stood there for a long time. Unsure how to proceed, I decided to tell her everything.

"You probably also know that I'm not here because I want to be a nun," I began.

Catherine nodded. As I explained my real motives, my twin visibly stiffened but didn't look surprised. When I told her I'd decided not to write the article, Catherine mouthed the words "thank you" and hugged me again.

I hugged her back; grieving over the years we'd lost. It was a relief to be close to her, letting our genetic memory take us back to a time before we were born, before the death of our mother and the complication of my handicap took away what might have been and replaced it with insecurity.

CHAPTER EIGHTEEN

Later that day, after the prayers of the 2:30 Divine Office focused on the impermanence of temporal things, I returned to my cell for a lesson in the impermanence of my attention span. Attempting the sisters' afternoon meditation practice of *Lectio Divina*, I opened the Bible, picked a random passage to reflect on, and reminded myself to aim for inner stillness. Emotionally exhausted from the recent events, I grew so still that I fell asleep.

The five o'clock bells woke me with a soothing melody rather than the usual chimes. I followed the sound, a parade of one.

The lights were turned on inside the chapel now and trees cast stained-glass shadows across the pews during Vespers. I joined in the chanted *Magnificat*.

And Mary said, My soul doth magnify the Lord,

And my spirit hath rejoiced in God my Saviour.

For he hath regarded the low estate of his handmaiden:

For, behold, from henceforth all generations shall call me blessed.

When Sister Teresa slid the cloister's gate to a close after the service, I was inside its walls.

That night I went to bed long before the nine o'clock chimes, too tired to write in my notebook. I barely survived midnight Vigils and then returned to my cell and set the alarm for one forty-five a.m. I hoped it wouldn't go off. As penance for the previous evening's smoking and drinking, Mother had "suggested" I take over the two a.m. perpetual adoration shift of a nun suffering from the flu. Contrite as I was, it was still a sobering thought.

"I've never prayed in front of the Eucharist before," I had told Sister Teresa during that evening's *Scrabble* game. "What if I mess it up?"

"Well, if you do, at least there won't be anybody else awake to see you," Teresa said. "Anyway, you can't really go wrong."

"Trust me." I watched the extern set down the word *templum*. "I already fell asleep during my *Lectio Divina*."

"Oh, everybody zzzz's through that from time to time. The meditation lulls you."

"But what do I do for adoration?" I flipped through my loaned Latin dictionary and managed to use my "X" tile with *luxor*. "What do I say?"

"Nothing special, or nothing at all. Most of the time on my shift I just look at God and God looks back."

"There has to be more to it than that."

"Okay, fine," Teresa said. "Sometimes I yell at Him."

"No way."

"Sure I do. Where else can I make noise and bring my problems if not to the Eucharist? It's God after all. He won't break."

"No, I don't suppose He will," I said.

When my alarm went off at one forty-five in the morning, I slogged off to the candlelit chapel in my sweats and T-shirt to relieve Sister Carmella. My predecessor was far too bright-eyed by comparison. I desperately hoped that there wouldn't be more to perpetual adoration than looking at God and letting God look back. That was about all I could manage. My nicotine withdrawal had revealed itself in a headache and a surplus of nervous energy. I wasn't sure I could make it through another minute, much less an hour, without smoking something, anything.

In fact, I was quite convinced I would die if I didn't have a cigarette. Yet I knew how seriously the sisters took this special charism. I decided I would rather keel over right then and there than leave my post and risk offending them again. Not knowing how seriously God Himself took the ritual, I wasn't willing to court His ire either.

Chewing my fingernails, I sat and waited for death, or at least the next wave of nausea. Somehow I made it through the hour. Sister Teresa arrived a few minutes early for her shift.

"How'd it go?" she whispered.

"Ask Him." I pointed to Christ embodied in the consecrated communion wafer displayed on the altar. "I'm guessing He was disappointed."

"Are you kidding? After what you've just gone through to keep Him company? That was a beautiful prayer."

"I dunno, I'm suffering a little nicotine withdrawal."

"I knew you were a smoker and realized what you were in for." Sister Teresa shuddered. "Went through it myself when I entered. Back then nobody knew cigarettes were addictive. Boy, did I find out the hard way."

She sat down beside me and shared the silence for several seconds.

"We don't seek out suffering at the cloister." Teresa put her hands in her pockets. "But when it happens, we try to embrace it and offer it up as a little death to Jesus. It gives us an idea of what He went through."

"I definitely feel like I'm going to die, but I doubt it's as bad as that." I tipped my head to the cross above the altar.

"Remembering the crucifixion helps us keep things in perspective. The other thing to remember is that suffering doesn't last forever, especially when I place the pharmacy orders around here." Teresa placed a hand on my bare arm and guided me to the exit. "Go get some rest."

The extern's pharmacy comment didn't make sense until I was out in the hall and noticed the nicotine patch she'd placed on my bicep.

Back in my room, I discovered a pack of nicotine gum and a rubber band with a note attached:

Wear the rubber band on your wrist and snap it whenever you want a cigarette. It'll give you something to do with your hands. Hang in there, Sister Teresa

Ignoring the rubber band, I ripped open the package of gum, chewed all the pieces at once and promptly threw up.

Vomiting produced some relief, but I was still too uncomfortable to sleep. When a shower didn't help, I slipped the rubber band on my wrist and resigned myself to roaming the halls in hopes of discovering a painting that Catherine had forgotten to take down.

When nearly an hour of wandering produced no stray artwork, I went to the studio. Light and the pungent smell of oil paint emanated from underneath the door and spilled onto the hallway tiles. I pressed my ear to the wood and heard the whir of the electric fan inside but couldn't bring myself to knock. I didn't want to intrude but didn't want to go back to my room either. I eased my spine down the wall and sat on the hallway floor, happy for the company on the other side of the door.

Penguin trotted down the hall bearing her regular offering between her teeth. She dropped the mouse long enough to snarl at me, presumably for occupying her post. When the threat didn't result in my departure, the cat placed the mouse at the door beside me and went off in hunt of further spoils. Too tired to scream this time, I eyed the bedraggled corpse.

"Did you offer your suffering up to Jesus?" I snapped the rubber band on my wrist.

The mouse was beyond reply.

My withdrawal symptoms decreased after a couple of days, but I continued to sit outside my sister's studio door every night after my shift. Previously, I would have knocked until I got an interview. Now I was satisfied to sit outside, writing in my notebook and snapping the rubber band that had become as addictive as the cigarettes it had replaced. I drew strength from my belief that the creative process thrived within.

Filling page after page, I recorded all the experiences I'd normally just chat with Matt about. Phone calls were against house rules.

I wondered if the painting process was anything like journalism. Making entries in a private journal was easy, but I generally put off articles intended for publication as long as possible, even straightforward, puff pieces. I often spent more energy on useless research and stalling than it would take to write the story, until the agony of avoidance became worse than diving in. Once I finally started, it was still a struggle. More than a struggle, it was a daily, monumental effort to overcome my anxiety. Giving meaning to a blank page or a white computer screen was way more than I wanted to face on any given day, yet I felt compelled to do so.

Sometimes, for a few, fleeting seconds, everything flowed. And for that one instant, I felt complete, as though all were right with the world, or at least my place in it. Even a bad day of writing left me with a sense of accomplishment just for showing up. Sometimes the hard days were more satisfying than the easy ones simply because I had survived, endured, and persevered through them. And while they weren't typically the days when the best work was done, they were still necessary. Even if all they produced was thrown out, difficult days made the easy, flowing, miraculous days possible. They laid the groundwork and, to paraphrase Louis Pasteur, prepared me to be lucky.

CHAPTER NINETEEN

Despite our heartfelt acknowledgment of each other in her studio, tension remained high between Catherine and me as we worked together on kitchen duty. While I appreciated her new-found patience with my culinary bumblings, I couldn't help wishing that she would talk to me as she showed me how to slice, dice, simmer, and stir. I knew the basics of her life with our father but not her perspective. I found it exhausting to have so many questions that could neither be asked because cloister rules prevented talking during the day, nor answered because of Catherine's vow of silence.

If anything, physical closeness increased our emotional distance. As much as I wanted to be near my twin to make up for lost time, I was also repulsed and wished for complete independence from her as if I feared letting myself need her. I asked for a switch to the mailroom to give us a break from each other.

Mother Benedicta wouldn't allow the change.

"We all have our cross to bear," the prioress said.

Somehow the closed studio door provided just enough distance between us for me to feel close to my sister and her creative process without intruding upon it.

On the fourth night of my studio vigils, Sister Teresa walked by after her shift in the chapel and found me sitting on the hallway floor writing in my notebook. Her eyebrows darted up and then dropped into frowning disapproval when she realized I was outside the studio. The extern reached for the knob to open the door for me, but I placed a hand on her arm. Teresa shook her head and went to open it again, but I insisted with pleading eyes. Sister Teresa shrugged and left.

Mother Benedicta called Catherine and me to her office the next morning.

"Sister Teresa told me about your nightly stand-offs," the prioress said.

"They aren't exactly stand-offs, Mother," I clarified. "I've never even asked to—"

"You shouldn't have to ask." Mother turned to Sister Catherine. "May I remind you that nothing is our own in the cloister? I allow you that studio with the express understanding that both the room and supplies are available to everyone. Everything is shared, including space. That means no one shall close a door on another member of the community."

Sister Catherine nodded without protest. Mother turned back to me.

"At the same time, I strongly discourage anyone from encroaching on another sister's contemplative process, whatever form that process takes, unless it is absolutely necessary."

I nodded, contrite as a teacher's pet suddenly finding herself in detention.

"I don't want to have this discussion again. I can't believe we had to have it at all." The prioress returned to her papers as Catherine and I filed out of the room.

That night, I found the studio door wide open as I passed after my perpetual adoration stint. I saw the light on inside and smelled fresh paint but still didn't enter. Penguin looked up when I didn't stop. I returned to my room in search of the sleep that continued to escape me.

The next night, a paint-smocked Catherine stood in the studio doorway when I passed by. Her open hands and wide-eyed expression seemed to say, "I've opened the door, why don't you come in?"

I entered with as much trepidation as when I'd stepped inside a Catholic church after eight years away. Penguin watched from the threshold, seemingly hoping for a similar invitation. Inside, I settled into a corner chair and tried to make myself invisible.

There was no need to be inconspicuous. The moment Catherine resumed work on a portrait of the Holy Family, she appeared to forget my presence. I was free to study the emotions playing across her face as she worked—the furrowed brow of intense concentration, the shining eyes of sheer, creative abandon, or a blank expression wherein she seemed to see nothing except the canvas.

The lighting that was so poor when I had photographed the paintings seemed somehow better now. A soft, natural glow bathed the room and highlighted the canvas resting on the easel. Was it moonlight? I scanned the walls for a window. There wasn't one. She hadn't changed the lights—the same merciless bulb burned overhead along with the single candle she kept lit in the corner.

I shifted position and accidentally jostled a low shelf on the wall. Several tubes of paint clattered to the floor, one of which knocked over the burning candle. A startled Penguin jumped in the doorway as I lunged and put out the flame before anything else caught fire, but Catherine didn't flinch. I picked up the scattered vials and realized it was unlikely that my intensely focused sister knew about my hallway vigils until she was reprimanded for them. I probably could have entered the studio and observed her unnoticed from the beginning.

As I sat in the silence, I couldn't decide what was most fascinating—the art, the artist, or the relationship between the two. The contemplative repetition of Catherine's addition and removal of paint was a kind of visual chant—an exchange with an unseen listener who responded in oils.

I concluded that Catherine's process was singular performance art. Unlike actors who conjure sentiment via tidy, preordained actions onstage, my twin waded through the mire of real-world, real-time emotions. The resulting artistic expression seemed to sometimes crash against her technical ability and other times jibe with it perfectly. The work always appeared personal and deeply felt. I realized that any sort of audience, even an appreciative one consisting of only an adoring cat and me, was an invasion.

After an hour or so working on the painting, Catherine removed it from the ladder-turned-easel. She then ascended that same ladder, pulled down a completed canvas from the shelf, climbed to the ground, and set the new piece on the middle rung.

It was the *Madonna and Child* from the visiting-room parlor—intact after all rather than painted over as Sister Teresa had assumed. I couldn't help but let out a little yelp of joy when I saw the glorious painting again.

I reveled in the Madonna's body language—the contentment in her eyes, the warmth with which she cradled her child. Her expression waited for no one but beckoned to all in an effortless invitation to inner peace. Calming reassurances. Restful naps. Time for everything.

Time for nothing. Before I could fully appreciate the image, Catherine dragged a swath of white across the Madonna's face as she started a new painting over the old.

The desecration was swift. I opened my mouth to protest and then remembered that it wasn't my loss to mourn or my place to lecture. The painting belonged to no one, not even the canvas that hosted it, and certainly not to me despite the ache its absence now produced in my sternum. I snapped the rubber band on my wrist, and struggled to deal with a type of loss that the painter herself seemed very comfortable with.

Occasionally, Catherine paused to close her eyes briefly or sit in the broken office chair for a rest while the canvas waited for her. After a few hours, she lay on the floor and took a nap, the concrete not much harder than her own sleeping pallet. Even with her eyes closed, I could see that she was still painting, could hear it in the rise and fall of her breathing, could sense it in her movements, could feel it in her stillness. Then she awoke, drew back the veil of sleep, and looked at the canvas anew. Whether she'd solved whatever creative problem she'd dozed off with I couldn't tell, but she carried on with a new angle, a paler color, a different approach.

Catherine's different approach sometimes involved switching hands. I first thought my twin was left-handed like me, but then I saw her manipulate the brush with her right hand as well. It led me to wonder if the talent for painting wasn't in one's skill or dexterity with a brush at all, but instead in one's ability to see, just as I had begun to realize that writing wasn't about pen, keyboard, or new combinations of words but about listening. Transforming. Translating what you *think* you see or hear into what is actually there. Bridging the gap of perspective.

I imagined the touch of the brush against the canvas, stared at the pure, saturated color, inhaled the heady resin. I savored the breeze in the room, yet held onto the stillness. Sitting in the studio with my sister was the closest I'd ever felt to God. I felt God in the room, smelled God in the paint, saw God on the canvas.

I realized then why Catherine didn't care about the ends. The means were more than enough.

If painting really was in the eye and not in the hand, could anyone become a great artist? Maybe if one learned to see things the right way, the ability to illustrate them naturally followed.

I decided to test the theory myself during recreation hour one evening. While the sisters fixated on the latest ping-pong match, I snapped the rubber band on my wrist and slinked over to the easels by the common room's windows. Not ready to commit paint to canvas, I chose a sketchpad and a box of colored pencils from the available supplies.

I soon discovered that facing a blank sketchbook was just as intimidating as facing a blank computer screen. Unable to bear the void, I reverted to the simple stars, hearts, flowers, and primary colors I'd relied on as a child just to have something covering the unnerving whiteness.

My skill level was right where I'd left it the last time I picked up a crayon or a brush at age twelve. I wasn't surprised but still rattled. Drawing was easier as a kid. Everything was refrigerator-worthy in the eyes of enthusiastic parents.

My own adult eye was far more critical. Now every line, every mark seemed so permanent, so irreversible, so firm a judgment, that I was afraid to make a serious start. At least a writer had the benefit of the delete button. Most artwork can be erased or painted over too, but it will still be there underneath, if only as a groove on the surface, ready to haunt the new image. Did those hidden relics bother Catherine? They unsettled me, almost as much as whatever efforts I decided were good enough to keep. No wonder Catherine wanted to undo any potential permanence by creating new works over old. Maybe recycling her canvases wasn't just about honoring God, but also about avoiding criticism, and acclaim, for that matter. Art was far less daunting when it was temporary.

Finishing my childish drawing of nothing in particular, I ripped off the sheet of paper and crinkled it up in my own version of undoing what I'd done. Yet somehow that seemingly useless first drawing did make the second blank sheet appear less intimidating. Was it because I'd been able to destroy it before anyone else saw it? Or had the amateurish results given me perspective and lowered my expectations? Whatever the reason, I relaxed.

I looked around the room for something to draw. My eyes settled on a coffee mug full of paintbrushes. I resisted the urge to immediately put pencil to paper and toss something off. Instead I forced myself to study the contours of the ceramic, the wispy bristles on the brushes, the dried paint running down the broken handle of the cup until it ended in one perfect drip on the jagged edge, permanently poised to fall but never falling.

I stared. I stared until I saw it differently. Until I could distinguish between what my eyes saw and where my mind filled in the blanks of what I knew was there. The rim of the cup was curved, but to do a correct rendering from my angle, it had to be drawn straight. For a moment, I forgot about everything else except the line. A whole world in that line.

I finished the drawing and found myself surprisingly happy with it. I tucked it in my pocket, unsure whether I would share it with anyone else or not. I definitely wouldn't be attempting anything abstract. Drawing from a model was hard enough. The talent for seeing beyond the visible was beyond me. I left the common room with a whole new respect for my birth father, my sister, and their craft.

CHAPTER TWENTY

A couple of minutes late for recreation one evening, I entered expecting ping-pong but found Sister Scholastica reviewing the monastery budget in front of the entire community. Even Catherine was there, shifting from foot to foot by the fireplace. I turned to leave, assuming it wasn't my business. Mother called out to me.

"Come on in, Dorie," the prioress insisted with a wave of her hand. "If you're thinking about joining us, you ought to know what you're getting into. Please continue, Scholastica."

Sister Scholastica pushed her round glasses further up the bridge of her nose. I lowered myself into a folding chair.

"We've addressed most of the structural damage caused by the last rainy season, but the chapel roof and foundation repairs wiped out our prudent reserve, leaving us with only eight thousand in the building fund," Scholastica said from a podium fashioned from a cardboard box atop a card table.

"As you all know, shipping altar breads was impossible during the two months that Highway One closed due to the mudslide damage," she continued. "The financial repercussions of that closure will continue to plague us for years to come. As for our driveway, we're still short of what we need to make the repairs of the March slides. With rainy season coming again soon, we're in for a lot more of the same. We simply can't afford to sustain that much damage again."

"How can we avoid it?" asked Sister Teresa, her keys jingling with agitation. "The rain's gonna fall."

"We can commission a hydro-geological survey of our water table to see how to reconfigure the road and retrofit the buildings to limit future slide damage. But the study alone will cost sixty thousand—not to mention the cost of the repairs that they'll recommend." Scholastica looked up from her notes and addressed the group. "In short, we can't afford to do the study or the repairs, but we can't afford not to, either."

I watched Catherine stare at the floor across the room. I couldn't tell if she was listening.

"Can't we sell off some of our land?" Sister Carmella asked as she mended a torn habit with tiny hand stitches. "We've got eight hundred acres."

"Eight hundred acres of designated wildlife preserve," Mother Benedicta said. "The reason the Murphy family deeded us the land in the first place was because we promised never to develop it."

"Couldn't the Diocese bail us out?" Sister Teresa asked.

"They're struggling just like we are." Mother rubbed her stomach and grimaced. "Most of our diocese is national park land. There aren't a whole lot of parishes to support us."

"We'll have to cut back on other things, then," Sister Teresa concluded.

"I wish it were that easy." Scholastica shook her head. "Even if we slashed our daily living expenses, it wouldn't be a drop in the bucket."

"The Ladies' Auxiliary's fundraising campaigns and bazaars on our behalf may bring in as much as twenty thousand this year, while our volunteer oblates' activities will give us another ten. But that only meets half the cost of the study," Mother said. "And we don't know exactly how much or how soon those donations will come in."

"Do we have any estimates on the actual repairs?" Sister Dominica tried to straighten her white novice veil without success.

"The study and damage-limiting plans will run us about sixty thousand." Scholastica paused and took a deep breath. "The repairs themselves might cost as much as one point five million."

The normally reserved women all spoke at once.

"So you're telling us we're sunk?" asked Teresa.

"Unless God shows us a way to make a lot of money in a little amount of time, yes," Scholastica said.

"Do we have anything of value we could sell?" Sister Dominica asked.

Scholastica frowned. "Yes and no. We had a collector interested in buying our floor tiles, but it'd be a small fortune to rip them up, and they're so fragile that many of them would be ruined and unsalable anyway."

"What about our antique vestments and altar cloths?" Carmella tied off the thread on the repaired habit.

"Our chapel statuary and reliquaries are worth something, but they've been with our order for over two hundred years and will only fetch a few thousand dollars on the market anyway. So no, not really. We have nothing of value to sell," Sister Scholastica concluded.

I couldn't help but look at Catherine, who quickly turned away when I caught her eye.

"Then what are we going to do?" Sister Carmella asked.

"We've applied for three different loans," Mother said. "If the largest one doesn't come through, we may be forced to move."

A wave of panic passed through the women.

"You're saying we have to leave our home?" Sister Grace, a wheelchair-bound nun in her nineties, asked.

"I'm sorry, but it will be unsafe to spend the winter here if the repairs aren't made," Sister Scholastica explained.

"Where will we go?" asked Dominica. "We're not going to have to split up, are we?"

"The most promising site we've found doesn't have infirmary facilities," Mother Benedicta said. "Our more elderly members may have to stay with other orders."

"But they'll make us sleep in beds and wear shoes," Sister Grace protested.

"If that's what the Lord calls upon us to do. I don't see any other way." Scholastica closed her report. "I'm sorry."

The first bell rang for Compline. Scholastica left the podium. The sisters rose quickly and quietly in response to the call to prayer but shared looks revealed their anxiety. It was the first time I could sense fear among these women who trusted their lives to God. I tried to catch my sister's eye again, but Catherine avoided my look and hurried off.

CHAPTER TWENTY-ONE

Getting used to each other's presence while we worked in her studio built some trust that helped Catherine and I adjust to working together in the kitchen. My sister promoted me from cleanup to food preparation as she taught me to distinguish a potato peeler from a paring knife. Where I'd previously never had the patience for microwave popcorn, I came to enjoy the repetitive, measured tasks involved in basic cooking and baking. There were some things I still couldn't do—like use a manual can opener—but I learned that the proper way to chop involved holding the steadying hand in a position similar to the way my right hand was shaped already.

My twin moved through the kitchen with the same grace that propelled her brush across a canvas. I still wished I could interview her, not for publication anymore, but for myself. Had Catherine ever been in love? How did she discover her talent? Did we all have such abilities but just don't recognize them? Maybe that was what silence afforded her—a finely tuned, creative intimacy beyond what's available to someone deafened by the noise of the world.

I tried to imagine my approach and her answers and then gave up when I realized that the medium was unfair. How could I accurately describe in words someone who rarely used them herself? The visual and culinary arts inform in a way speech and text can't. Until I learned to interpret the world through color, taste, texture, and image the way my twin did, I couldn't fully communicate with her, much less "tell" her story.

Instead, I tried to learn from her ways, appreciating the simplicity of her daily tasks and the level of her labor. I speculated on why Catherine seemed to value baking and cooking as much as she valued painting, concluding that there was a necessary, worthy end to the means of cooking. The food she made fed others' bodies as well as her own. That left painting free to feed her soul.

As someone whose idea of a day's worth was often determined by how many words I'd written, my two weeks inside the cloister taught me the value of a day of no words at all. The silence that initially drove me crazy now brought peace and freedom. I saw how hard such absolute quiet would be to accomplish in the secular world. No wonder the nuns chose seclusion.

When the days were long and daylight lingered after the gates were locked to visitors, several of the sisters walked the cloister grounds before dinner. A few hiked the rough trails carrying big sticks to ward off mountain lions or rattlesnakes who might be out sunbathing in the dappled evening light.

I soon embraced the walking ritual. I enjoyed the open space after the nearness of the enclosure and luxuriated in dramatic weather that was hot, sunny, and clear one moment, foggy and chilly the next. The quality of light, the color of the water, and the kiss of the air all felt heightened here. Or were my senses heightened? Maybe Catherine's paintings and the Big Sur landscape were teaching me how to see just as the cloister silence had taught me to listen.

Of course I stopped to watch the sunset at the monastery. It became the obvious thing to do when there was no phone buzzing, no assignment to race through before deadline, no adjacent apartment building to block the view. There was just God's majesty sinking slowly over the

Pacific, the colors so brilliant they looked counterfeit; some retouched postcard that, unable to approach the real thing, overdid it with dazzle. No picture could truly capture the vista any more than my photographs could accurately represent the genius of my sister's paintings—paintings that I now realized found direct inspiration in such a sky.

Walking along the cloister road before my departure interview with Mother Benedicta, I was as taken with the view as the day I'd come. I inhaled the ocean breeze and watched rabbits dart out from the underbrush before me. All the rabbits disappeared back into the bushes as a graceful, red fox sauntered across the road a few yards ahead. He paused and looked at me, arresting my own movements with his sheer poise. Then, he swished his tail and moved on.

I sat down on a small promontory rock tucked among reeds and chaparral. A gecko climbed onto the stone beside me. As fog descended below the cliff and erased the water and road below, I felt like I was sitting on the mountain of God looking down over creation. Wanting to leave at least part of myself behind always in this place, I pulled a few strands of hair from my ponytail and let the wind take them, then picked a saffron-colored bloom from a camellia bush and slipped it into my pocket in exchange.

"Two weeks already?" Mother Benedicta asked. We sat in her office where a shocking pink gladiola had replaced the calla lily in the Mason jar. "Are you glad you stayed?"

"Very glad," I said. "Thanks for encouraging me."

"My pleasure. Did you achieve clarity about your vocation?"

"Yes." I snapped the rubber band on my wrist. "As much as I enjoyed my visit, I don't think this is the life for me."

"Very well." Mother touched her cross and leaned back in her chair. "Then I won't elaborate."

"Elaborate on what?" I asked.

"On what we sisters thought about your vocation."

"Oh, I'd like to hear what you thought, anyway." My heart raced. "That is, if you don't mind."

"I don't mind telling you so long as you don't mind hearing it. Typically, we're able to determine if someone is fit for the life after an aspirancy visit. But more than a couple of us are still on the fence about you."

"You are?" I sat up straight. "I'm flattered that you'd consider me at all, given my early scheming."

"Nobody's perfect. You're a complicated young woman, Dorie. One we can't quite figure out. One who can't quite figure herself out."

"I'm feeling pulled in a lot of different directions right now." I rubbed my temples.

"Perhaps you need time to explore some more of them. You're fairly certain you don't want to make a commitment here, and we're not certain we want to ask you for one. But we were going to do something unusual—put you on probation of sorts."

"What does that involve?" I asked.

"It means we aren't rejecting you, but we aren't accepting you either. Whether we eventually invite you to join or not depends a lot on you."

"Me? How so? I mean, were I to consider joining." I spoke out of the corner of my mouth as if worried that someone would hear me. God, perhaps?

"We encourage you to go back to your life and do some soul-searching. Keep up our practice of physical sacrifice and silence as much as possible in the outside world, then return to us when or if you feel ready and we'll consider admitting you. Do you have a spiritual director?"

"No." Sister Barbara, the potter in South Central, leapt to mind as a likely candidate.

"I can recommend a few if you like." The prioress wrote some names on a piece of memo paper and handed it to me. "Vocation or not, a spiritual director can help you with whatever work and life struggles you're having."

"Thank you, Mother." I took the list and stood up. "I appreciate your kindness. I feel like I've wasted your time here."

"Did you do your chores and say your prayers?"

"Yes."

"Then you did as much as the rest of us, and we happen to consider that time well spent." Mother stood and offered her hand. When I accepted it, she pulled me in for a hug. "Goodbye, Dorie. And good luck."

"You too, Mother. I hope you find a solution to your financial difficulties."

"So do I." She touched her stomach and winced. "So do I."

There were no tears when Catherine and I said goodbye. I think we both knew I would be back again before long. Still, it was harder to leave her than I thought. The aching sense that something was missing I'd felt growing up was now replaced by the bittersweet feeling of missing someone in particular.

The world seemed loud during my drive back to Los Angeles. When I reached the busy part of the freeway, the rumble of diesel trucks and the wailing of passing car horns startled me; the merengue music pumping out of a neighboring car blasted through my open windows. Noise I hadn't noticed before now made it difficult to think. I rolled my windows up.

I reflected on my talk with Mother as I drove. After I recovered from the initial shock that the convent might accept me, I was strangely irked by their suggestion of probation. Never mind not wanting the cloistered life, I never considered that I might be capable of it until someone told me I may not be. Now it seemed desirable, if only for the challenge. Or was it desirable for some other reason?

I rolled my windows back down.

CHAPTER TWENTY-TWO

The moment I rattled the key in my front door lock, the apartment door across the hall opened and a bunch of sunflowers popped out. Matt soon followed.

"Welcome back, Dorie." He held out his peace offering. "Listen, I'm sorry I freaked out on you. I had no right to judge you."

"I'm sorry, too." I dropped the duffel inside my apartment and took the cheerful blooms. "Thank you, but I should be buying *you* flowers. You were right. It wouldn't be ethical to publish anything about my sister without her permission, so I won't." I didn't mention that Phil might fire me as a result. "I wanted to do a story on something pure to make up for all the crap I've put out there with my name on it, but exploiting Catherine won't bring me journalistic redemption."

"You hardly need to be redeemed." Matt hugged me. "But you do need to be fed. You feel a little bony around the ribs."

He grabbed his coat and squired me to his Jeep.

Half an hour later, we ate at Hurry Curry. My huge bowl of udon noodles and side of sashimi looked almost obscene. I pushed the food around with chopsticks, unsure what to do with it.

"What's the matter?" Matt asked between bites. "I thought you'd be craving your all-time favorite meal after two weeks of stems and seeds with the vegetarians."

"My stomach must've shrunk." I touched my belly in search of some extra room there. "This would be two days' worth of calories at the convent."

"Want to go somewhere else?" Matt leaned forward on the edge of his seat. "Burgers, Italian, whatever you want."

"No, this is fine. I guess I'm not that hungry after all." I set my chopsticks down. "I'll get a box for it."

When we left the restaurant a few minutes later, I took my to-go container from Matt and went around the corner of the building. I set my leftovers on top of the shopping cart of a homeless man asleep there. When I turned back, Matt stood watching me.

"He probably won't eat sashimi, but maybe he'll like the noodles," I said as we returned to the car.

"How did you know that guy was there?"

"I've seen him around here before." I hopped into the Jeep. "But I never had anything to give him until now."

Back outside our apartment building, Matt took my hand and led me to the ocean. It was our first walk on the beach together since our dating days. Tiny, brown birds with curved beaks ran back and forth with each wave, pecking for dinner in the wet sand. I'd never noticed them or their industry before. On our way back, we stopped at the circle of rock cairns and totems that stood like sentinels and paused to cap them with our own stone additions.

"You're awfully quiet for someone so fond of talking," Matt said, kicking sand at me as he built up a cairn.

"Guess I'm out of practice." I slipped off my flip-flops and kicked sand back, careful not to upset the wobbly balance of rocks on my totem.

"Well, I've got something to say." He stopped working on the cairn and turned to me. "Something to admit, really. I got all high and mighty to scare you out of that trip because I was jealous."

"Jealous?" I laughed. "Of my sister or the story?"

"Both. I'd gotten used to having all your attention. It was hard to see you get excited about someone and something else." He looked out over the horizon. "And then when you went away, I realized that I don't want to live without you."

I lost my balance and took a step back. My totem followed suit—the top rock teetered and fell to the sand with a muffled thud.

"I want to spend the rest of my life with you, Dorie." Matt produced a black, velvet ring box from his shirt pocket and placed it in my hand. "Will you marry me?"

I opened the box to reveal a stunning, emerald-cut diamond ring. I dug my toes into the sand for support and looked around for an answer. The setting sun glimmered on the water, a wave moved in and washed over my bare feet, and the man I'd loved for years stood before me with a shy smile on his face. It was the best and worst moment of my life.

"Oh my God, Matt." My mouth went dry. I licked my lips and tasted sashimi. "I don't know what to say."

"I know it's kinda sudden," he said. "But in a way, it's not. You're my best friend."

"And you're mine. But why now? Why not back when we were dating? If this is what happens when I leave town, maybe I should have done it a long time ago."

"You did more than leave town. You went to a convent. I could compete with another guy, but not with God."

I took a deep breath and snapped the rubber band on my wrist, unready to accept the implication in Matt's words. This wasn't a contest between becoming the bride of a man I loved, but rarely saw, and becoming a Bride of Christ, whom I'd never seen at all. Was it?

"I went looking for my sister who happened to be at a convent and ended up finding out a lot about myself instead. One thing I learned is that I'm not ready to get married. Not to you or God or anybody. Not yet, anyway."

I paused, surprised at myself. The words had jumped out of my mouth before I knew they were in there. "Maybe down the line, but not right now. This last year and especially this trip have made me question my job, my lifestyle, everything. I'm learning about my past and it's having way more effect on my present than I ever imagined. I can't handle thinking about the future on top of that."

I smacked my forehead with my palm. "I can't believe I'm saying this. There was a time when I would've given anything to—"

"I know," Matt said softly.

"You do?"

"I blew it with you a year and a half ago. I've been losing ground ever since, but I didn't realize how much until I saw you get so passionate about researching your roots and writing this article." Matt paused and watched the birds skitter away from the incoming wave. "I guess getting engaged was my last-ditch effort to stop the landslide."

We stood in silence and let the whisper of the surf lull us. I didn't dare try on the ring for fear I'd never want to take it off. Instead I closed the box and offered it back to Matt. He didn't raise his hand to take it. It remained loose in my palm.

"I'm sorry, Matt."

"So am I," he said. "Sorry I ever took you for granted."

"Like I've been doing to you lately?" I asked in an attempt to lighten the moment. "We're both guilty of that."

Matt smiled, gingerly took the box from me, and slid it back into his pocket. He walked back to our building alone.

Not sure what to do or where to go, I sat down among the rocks and tried to make sense of what had just happened. The sun glided across the ocean and dipped behind the mountains, leaving streaks of pink, orange, and purple through smog that managed to make sunsets more glorious than they had a right to be. Eventually, I gave up trying and headed home.

CHAPTER TWENTY-THREE

"*Madre de Dios,* you're so thin!" Graciela gasped when I arrived at the newsroom in baggy khakis, a sweater, and no makeup the next morning.

Two weeks of jeans and T-shirts at the cloister had left me unprepared to face the vast array of my business wardrobe options. Since there was no point in dressing up in order to get fired, I'd decided to save the suits for job interviews.

"Didn't I pack enough Twinkies for you?" Graciela asked.

"You gave me plenty of food." I shifted in my flats and missed the comfort of bare feet. "I felt too guilty to eat that stuff when nobody else there was."

"Wow, that's sacrifice. I can't even be in the same room with a Twinkie and not eat it. At least you had that carton of cancer to keep you going."

"I didn't smoke, either." After setting down my keys, purse, and computer bag, I unpacked Rod's camera, my laptop, cell phone, notebooks, and press pass, struck by the number of possessions it took to get through the day. Even more bizarre was the knowledge that I'd probably take all those items for granted again within a week. "Not after the first day, anyway."

"But you've smoked since you got back, right?" Graciela tapped her own box of menthols.

"I tried one on the way over here." I recalled the open pack of cigarettes I'd picked up off my dresser that morning. "But it was stale and made me kind of sick, so I figure I'll save the money."

"Un momento, por favor. You quit smoking *and* you lost weight? Those two things don't go together."

"They did this time," I said. "I've wanted to kick the habit and lose ten pounds forever. In two weeks, circumstances made it happen without me even trying."

"I hate you." Graciela pulled a cigarette out of the pack with her teeth.

"I'm going to take that as the endearment I'm sure you meant it to be." I smiled. "Anyway, I'm going to lose a lot more than weight and a bad habit when I tell Phil there's no story."

"What do you mean?" she asked. "There's plenty of story. Fulfill your obligation by writing the nice piece like you planned and let him reject it if he wants to."

"I can't. I've decided I'm not going to write anything about Catherine for Phil or any other paper."

"Su hermana said no, eh?"

"My sister managed to talk me out of it without saying a word." I nodded. "And I'm glad. But I'm also about to be unemployed."

"Oh, please. *El Jefe* would never fire you."

"He said he would," I reminded her.

"He lied." Graciela looked at me askance. "Wait a minute. You're glowing. Did you meet a guy or something?"

"Not unless you count Jesus," I joked, eager to avoid the topic of my personal life before Graciela asked about Matt. His proposal seemed so surreal that I wasn't even sure it actually happened. I definitely wasn't ready to talk about it. "Did I miss much while I was gone? Any good libel suits?"

"Nada." The unlit cigarette bounced on Graciela's lips as she spoke. "Just some guy who's mad because we erroneously reported his death. I don't see what the big deal is. His wife got some beautiful flower

arrangements out of it. Anyway, I'm glad you're back. Manipulating Phil isn't any fun without you." Graciela sniffed the air and stashed her cigarette. "Speaking of our editor..."

"Little Virgin Mary's back from the nunnery." Arriving at my desk, Phil sized me up, scratched his chin and turned to Graciela. "She look any holier to you?"

"Nah, just skinnier," my coworker said.

"So what's the dirt?" Phil asked, twirling his cigar like Groucho Marx. "Did you and your sister duke it out, hug it out, or both?"

"We ended up getting along pretty well," I said, focusing on how we left each other rather than our shaky start. "Too well, I guess. I didn't find anything I wanted to write an article about."

"Write it anyway," Phil said. "Didn't pay for your time there so you and your sister could braid each other's hair and sing *Kumbaya*."

"I was, er, kind of hoping you would let me make up the hours," I said.

"Dunno." Phil considered. "Would require me to be charitable, and no one around here appreciates my generosity—"

"That's because you never display any," Graciela pointed out.

"No sense in starting now then." Phil shrugged and turned to me. "Have the story on my desk by the end of the day."

"I'm sorry, Phil," I said, my knees knocking despite my resolve. "I know we had a deal, but I can't write the piece. So, I'm prepared to accept the consequences."

"Really?" Phil looked at me.

I nodded. He chewed on his cigar and whistled.

"Well, then, I guess you're fired, aren't you?" he half asked, half pronounced. He tried to sound cavalier, but his words packed about as much punch as a deflating balloon.

I nodded and managed to remain calm, even slightly relieved. My dismissal forced me to move on—something I'd needed to do for a long time anyway. Graciela almost fell over. Phil ignored her reaction.

"You can finish out the week," he called over his shoulder as he walked off. "Give me a thousand words on the Strip Bar Seniors by five."

"¡Creo que no!" Graciela yelped when he was gone.

"Believe it," I said. The truth was, losing my job paled in comparison to losing Matt. Our friendship had survived a breakup, but I doubted it could survive a proposal. Still, I felt tears well up in my eyes. I didn't want to cry in the middle of the newsroom. "Who the hell are the Strip Bar Seniors?"

"Word is a bunch of little old ladies frequent the Lust Lounge on Melrose every Monday for the lunch special," Graciela said. "How could *el Jefe* fire you?"

"Well, there's that part about me failing to do my job." Trying to stay professional, I pulled up the Lust Lounge on my phone and got directions. "Why would elderly women go to a strip bar?"

"It's a bargain. Where else can an *abuela* on social security get all the mozzarella sticks she can eat for a mere four ninety five? Not to mention live entertainment."

I copied down the strip club's details in a fresh reporter's notebook. Graciela watched my silent tears drop onto the page.

"Can we talk about you now?" She closed my notebook.

"Let me get through the work day first."

I grabbed my keys and raced out of the newsroom, glad I hadn't worn mascara.

I'd regained my composure by the time I returned to *The Comet* that afternoon, thanks in part to the patrons of Lust. The lunch special ladies were charming, and the dancers, meager tips notwithstanding, said they found the polite applause of their female audience a refreshing change from the catcalls and lewd comments of typical customers.

I settled down at my keyboard to write the piece, not quite believing I got paid for such tasks, though not for much longer. I cranked out the story before deadline and then lingered at my desk rereading my cloister journals, marveling at a world so different from the one I now inhabited.

At five o'clock on the dot, Graciela appeared in my cubicle.

"Vamonos, chica," my coworker urged. "Let's go drown your sorrows in sugar."

"I'm actually all right." I tucked the cloister journals into my desk drawer. "Better than I expected."

"I'm not. I can't believe you're going to leave me alone with these sharks and piranhas."

"Graciela, you're *one* of the sharks and piranhas. So am I."

"Details, details." She took my elbow and pulled me up. "Let's get out of here."

I laughed and picked up the photography intern's camera. "Okay. I need to give this back to Rod."

"I'll be out front." Graciela waved her pack of cigarettes and left.

As I walked to the dark room, I remembered that the camera's memory card was full of pictures of Catherine's work. Part of me knew I should erase all the pictures, part of me wanted a personal record of my sister's paintings. I paused. Unwilling to erase them, but unable to hand them over to Rod, I decided I would keep the memory card and buy him a replacement that night. Retreating to my desk, I put the camera in the drawer with my notebooks, then gathered my bag and left.

Suffering from a hot fudge sundae hangover, I yawned and opened my front door the next morning to get the papers. When I saw the latest edition of *The Comet*, my mouth hung open for an entirely different reason.

The tabloid lay face up in the hallway. A full-page, color photograph of Catherine's *Last Supper* masterpiece graced the cover. The headline read, "It's a Miracle! Our Father Paints Through My Sister The Silent Nun, by Dorie McKenna."

My reflexive sense of excitement at seeing my byline in one-inch type was soon eclipsed by confusion and dread. I snatched the paper and pulled it into my apartment before Matt came looking for our shared subscriptions.

Fifteen minutes later, I was in the car and on the cell phone with Graciela. "How did this happen?"

"Apparently Phil saw Rod's print of one of Sister Catherine's paintings, then *el Jefe* found the notebooks and camera in your desk," Graciela explained.

"What the hell was Phil doing in there?" I glanced at the ocean rushing past my window.

"He says he was looking for a pen."

"Looking for a *pen*? In *my* desk?" I snapped my wrist rubber band so hard that it left a red welt on my skin. "Tell him to get his own!"

"I guess his pen drawer isn't as *interesante* as yours."

"But I told him I wouldn't do the article."

"And you didn't," Graciela said. "He figures he saved you the trouble of a story by running segments from your notes, not to mention saving face himself. He didn't want to fire you and now he doesn't have to. He even printed it mostly verbatim, minus his famous editorializing."

"Yeah, I noticed that." I slowed to take a curve and thought back to my cloister journal. I hadn't made my typical, rambling entries at the convent, but instead recorded events in more of a journalistic format. Had I written that way because I still thought of my sister's story as an article even after I decided I wouldn't publish it, or had I subconsciously held out hope that it would somehow make it to print? "Thank God for small favors."

"More like a big favor. We sold out on newsstands by seven-thirty this morning and the online hits are off the charts. Phil's a hero and the owners want to meet you. There's enough in your journals for a whole series of articles."

"Not if I can help it," I said.

"I don't think you can. Anyway, you don't want to stop him. The *Los Angeles Times* has already called asking permission to reprint excerpts."

"They did? What are *LA Times* editors doing reading *The Comet*?"

"Probably gawking at the pictures like everyone else. Those paintings leap off the page. No wonder you've been so obsessed with them."

"They are something, aren't they?"

"Sí, sí, Señorita. And your commentary is *magnífico.* Congratulations."

"Thanks." My guilty conscience was unable to dampen the swell of pride in my chest. "I only wish it didn't have to happen this way."

"Quit your worrying. Who could possibly mind publicity as good as this?"

"My sister, for one." A poky, green Dodge chugged along ahead of me and slowed my progress.

"Oh, she'll love it. When are you coming in to soak up all the glory? I want to bask in the glow of your success."

"Not until later." I put my signal on and changed lanes. "I'm on my way up to the cloister to apologize to the nuns."

"For what?" Graciela asked. "Making them famous?"

"Exactly. I wouldn't be surprised if Catherine sues for breach of privacy. She never signed a release."

"The investors won't care," Graciela said. "Whatever it takes to settle will be worth the ad revenue this thing's generating."

"What have I done?" I wondered aloud.

"You've arrived," Graciela assured me. "Enjoy it."

For a few moments, I did.

CHAPTER TWENTY-FOUR

I pulled up to the cloister entrance just before two that afternoon. The gate seemed more ominous standing wide open in the sunlight than it had when it was locked fast and wrapped in darkness the first time I'd seen it. Sister Teresa greeted me with a smile but considerably less chatter than usual. She quickly ushered me into the parlor.

A moment later, Mother Benedicta entered on the cloister side of the grille. Her tired expression suggested disappointment more than anger.

"Our phones are ringing off the hook." Benedicta sat down heavily. "We've had to unplug them."

"I am so sorry, Mother. I never intended for—"

"I'm sorry, too. Not so much for the article, which was beautifully written, but for the fact of its publication after you promised that you wouldn't. It means you can't be trusted."

"But I can, Mother." I shifted in my seat.

The prioress squinted and touched the cross around her neck. She looked as if she wanted to believe me.

"I didn't break my promise. When I told my editor I wasn't going to write the piece, he found my journals and the photos and ran them without my permission." I sighed and wished I could start over. "Not that my explanation exonerates me in any way. I should have been more careful. What he published was personal. Those were my private thoughts that I had no intention of showing anyone. So on some level I understand the violation Catherine must feel."

"Oh, I doubt that. You saw for yourself during your stay that we have nothing to hide here. I am not against publicity per se, especially during hard times. Lord knows it helps to make people aware of our financial worries. And I happen to agree that the public should be allowed to enjoy Sister Catherine's art."

"You do?" I asked.

Mother nodded. "I've asked her many times for permission to put it up for sale in the gift shop or at a gallery to no avail. I could order her to, but I do my best to honor the wishes of the nuns in my charge. In your sister's case, that means respecting her intensely felt sense of privacy."

"I understand. May I see her? I'd like to apologize."

"I don't know that it will do any good." Mother's lower lip jutted out into a frown. "I'm sure she's asked God to put forgiveness in her heart, but so far I don't believe she's found any."

"I'd like to give it a try anyway."

Mother Benedicta paused. "Very well. I'm not going to force her to come out here, but since you've been inside the cloister before, I will make an exception and let you go to her. I believe she's in her studio."

"Thank you."

I raced to the studio and found the door closed. Before I could catch my breath and knock, it opened. Catherine stood on the other side with her head bowed and waved me inside.

My sister's posture of humility aside, I only needed to look at the latest work propped on the ladder to see how she felt.

The angry, slashing image that glared back at me accusingly depicted Judas turning Jesus over to the authorities. Judas had barely pulled away from his kiss of betrayal and the soldiers were already moving in, yelling and shoving in their blade-colored armor and spiked helmets. Judas' robes had a bruised and bloodied scarlet tint that writhed in tangled chaos, while the soldiers' eyes were white splotches resembling the sightless eyes of the dead. Despite Jesus' expression of weary resignation, the piece warned of a lurking evil. Unseen spirits swirled, moaned, and begged for release. I saw red-hot, super-charged rage, felt waves of a familiar pain. Old wounds ripped open. Our traumatic birth. A glimpse of Hell. The painting seemed to dare me to turn away from its shifting, roiling agony. I could not.

I was speechless at the sight of such pain and anguish, horrified that I had been the cause.

"I... I... I'm so sorry." I finally averted my eyes, which skated around the room in search of something else to rest on. "I never meant for this to—"

Catherine looked up at me. The heat in her normally chilling stare silenced me.

Calm but purposeful, she pulled the huge painting from the ladder and dragged it out of the studio, the red paint on her hands marring the composition. The canvas caught on the edge of the doorframe. Catherine forced it through with a giant heave that gouged the edges.

"Be careful!" I cringed. Disturbing as the image was, it was a powerful painting and I hated to see it damaged. "You're ruining it!"

"It doesn't matter!" an exasperated Catherine snapped in a voice thin and cracked from lack of use. She lugged the lightweight, but awkward, piece down the hall.

I froze. My sister, the silent nun, had spoken. That alone showed how enraged she was. I berated myself and followed her, catching up just as my twin arrived outside the common room. Catherine opened the carved door and slid the painting through this larger threshold without further damage. Then she let the heavy door bang against it and tear the canvas. I swallowed a scream.

Before I understood her intention, Catherine dropped the painting into the massive fireplace and stoked the glowing embers from the previous night's fire. I instinctively moved to retrieve it but was forced back as the oil paint caught quickly. Gaseous flames in sickly, neon-electric hues leapt into the air as the canvas warped. In seconds, the entire painting was consumed. I felt my face twist in horror, but Catherine's expression was one of relief, if not satisfaction.

"What are you doing?" I wrung my hands.

"Giving it back to God." Catherine solemnly watched the ashes rise up into the chimney. "It doesn't matter if anyone else sees it, as long as He has."

"Doesn't *matter?*" I flailed my arms in frustration and paced. "You're insulting God by abusing your talents!"

Catherine shook her head and pointed an accusing finger at me.

"No, *you're* insulting God by giving me the credit for His gift. That article raises me up in the eyes of people, when all I want is to be humble in the face of the Lord. If I have to destroy the results to avoid the praise, then that's what I'll do!"

I looked at her in disbelief, unable to fathom such a sentiment.

"God forgive me." Catherine recoiled and covered her mouth with her hand. "I've broken my silence with angry words. I'm sorry."

A tear rolled down her cheek. Then another. She fell to her knees and wept as the fire subsided.

"You spoke your mind, and I deserved it." I sat down on the worn plaid couch. "I'm sorry for what I've put you through, for making you feel you had to destroy your, I mean, God's, painting to prove your point."

"God didn't paint that one. I did," Catherine said, sitting back on her heels.

I hung my head. Catherine's fury over my article had inspired her first painting not meant to glorify God. The *Jesus and Judas* painting wasn't a prayer, but a protest, and I was at least partially responsible for the shift. It wasn't a good feeling.

"Regardless of your motives, it's a shame to burn it," I said.

Catherine shrugged and wiped away a tear. I marveled at my sister, who didn't mourn the loss of her painting, but instead grieved the loss of her self-control.

"I'm jealous that you inherited our father's talent," I said.

"Why?" Standing up, Catherine pulled the offending newspaper article out of her pocket and waved it at me. "Looks to me like you inherited our mother's."

"Thanks." Her compliment disarmed me, partly because I knew she was right. My article was full of confidence and passion. I did have talent—it had just taken meeting my sister for me to recognize it. "Listen, I didn't mean for this to happen and I'm sorry. I understand why I'd remind you of Judas."

"I'm the Judas here."

I recalled the painting and realized that it was Jesus, not Judas, who had borne the curled right hand before the images of both men burned away a moment before. I shivered despite the blazing fire.

"I betrayed you when I promised Dad I'd look you up and never did," she said, sitting beside me on the couch and staring straight ahead. "I was afraid meeting you would change everything."

"And it has."

Catherine nodded. "For what it's worth, I didn't ask for his talent. I didn't choose painting—it chose me. I don't want it, I don't like it, but I can't avoid it. I'd ignore it, but I can't live without it."

"It's the same with me and writing," I said. "Though I'm guilty of ambition as well."

"Then be careful," she said, turning to look at me. "Dad was ambitious too and enjoyed his fame. When he changed his style and the acclaim went away, he replaced it with alcohol and lost everything, including my respect. I don't want any part of fame or ambition, but I can't avoid painting. So I offered myself up to God as His instrument and the paintings as my prayers. I've given away everything so I could paint in peace, which is why I got upset when you threatened that."

I paused, stunned by all my sister had sacrificed to escape fame. It was still true that Catherine painted for God, but now I saw that as the byproduct of her desire to avoid acclaim, not vice versa.

"I'm so sorry, Catherine."

Behind us, the huge door opened with a shudder. My twin and I rose to our feet the moment we saw Mother Benedicta enter the common room. Several other sisters gathered and watched the commotion from the threshold.

"Sister Catherine! I am appalled by this outburst." Mother peered at Catherine from beneath angry eyebrows and pointed to the smoldering canvas. "You will do double chores this month and ask the forgiveness of your fellow sisters for destroying community property."

Catherine bowed meekly.

"Did you give Ms. McKenna a chance to apologize before this unholy display of temper?"

"We were just..." I stepped in, suddenly protective.

Catherine shook her head.

"I cannot command you to forgive her for compromising your privacy." Mother Benedicta softened her tone. "Whether you do or not is between you and God. But you should know that despite whatever intentions Dorie may have had, the story and photos were published against her wishes. Indeed, if she is to blame, then so am I."

Catherine and I both looked at the prioress, who straightened the folds of her habit and touched the cross around her neck.

"I allowed her to enter the aspirancy program knowing full well that she had a professional interest in your work and a personal interest in you. I believed I saw what might be a true vocation in her, and in my zeal I admitted her without proper forethought as to how her presence might affect your artistic avocation. I'm sorry for whatever pain my decision caused you. I hope you can forgive me."

"And me," I added, choosing to ignore Mother's comment about seeing a true vocation in me because I simply couldn't handle it.

Catherine nodded in acknowledgment of both of us. We watched the embers sputter and die in silence. I rolled back and forth on the balls of my feet before speaking again.

"Unfortunately, there's something else I need to tell you."

Catherine braced her shoulders and waved for me to continue.

"That story was only one excerpt from my notes," I said. "My editor intends to publish the rest in a series of articles."

Mother and Catherine shared a look.

"I spent an hour of the drive up here on the phone with a lawyer trying to figure out how to stop publication, but it doesn't look good. I signed a contract when I got hired granting *The Comet* the right of first refusal on every article I write while on the payroll. Even if I get a court order to stop my boss, it would take weeks, and by that time he'll have published the series anyway. I will do everything I can, but the bottom line is, you're going to get a lot more coverage."

Catherine went pale.

"Courage, Sister." Mother Benedicta put a hand on the artist's shoulder. "If there's nothing she can do, there's nothing *we* can do save accept this as God's will."

My twin closed her eyes and lowered her head.

"After all, we did give up everything when we became Brides of Christ, if not specifically our privacy." Mother turned to me. "As long as she can keep her dignity."

"Absolutely." I bobbed my chin up and down. "I can tell you that it's all very flattering, if that's any consolation."

"Flattery isn't exactly something we seek out, but it beats blasphemy." The prioress sighed.

The first bell rang for the Divine Office of None. Catherine looked to Mother, grateful for the possibility of escape.

"You may go, Sister. I'll see our guest out."

Catherine bowed to Mother and mustered a making-the-best-of-it smile for me before hurrying off to chapel in the wake of the spying doorway nuns who had turned to leave.

"I am so sorry for all of this." I truly was.

"Don't be." Mother inspected the contents of the smoking hearth and reached for a fireplace tong. "I don't regret admitting you to the cloister. For all we know, you're the catalyst God has been looking for."

"I am?" My eyes widened.

"Since you kept your promise not to publish and the story came out anyway, I'm inclined to think God had a hand in this. Perhaps the Lord decided it was high time to share your sister's talent with the public. Just maybe not this picture." The prioress poked at the heap of shriveled canvas before us.

"I guess anything's possible. But she stated her position so convincingly just now that—"

"She *spoke* to you?" Mother asked.

"I forgot to tell you in the confusion, but yes, she did."

"We are talking about Sister Catherine?"

I nodded. "She was pretty furious."

"Whatever it takes." Mother kissed the cross around her neck. "I sometimes suspect that Sister's vow of silence has more to do with avoiding her personal issues than devotion to Our Lord. You moved her to speak her first words outside of prayer in five years. That in itself makes up for your article."

As I watched the last tendrils of smoke rise from the painting my own words had helped destroy, I couldn't help but disagree.

CHAPTER TWENTY-FIVE

"You suck." Arms akimbo, I squared off with my editor in his office that evening.

"Happily, you don't. Those journals are dynamite."

"They're also private."

"Nobody with famous relatives gets to have privacy," he said, reaching into the drawer where he kept his best cigars.

"Regardless, you had no right to—"

"To what? Let you sell it to another paper when you contractually owed it to me?" He unwrapped a Cohiba, lit a match, and took a puff. "Because you're way too driven to let a piece like that go unpublished."

"Typically, yes." I waved the fetid smoke away from my face. "But I gave the nuns my word that I wouldn't print the story."

"All while promising me that you would. You should thank me. Just saved your job and made your career."

"You made me a liar."

"No, *you* did when you promised them something you couldn't deliver."

"I know, I know." I dropped into a chair, deflated. "I need someone to be mad at because I'm tired of yelling at myself." I got up again. "I'm going home."

"Do that. And smile, McKenna. You're a star."

Back in my apartment, I sat on my couch and considered the blank notebook on the wicker coffee table. After the briefest hesitation, I picked it up and wrote. I wrote of the joy of this unbidden, but very real professional success, a shining moment eclipsed by my guilt over hurting my sister in the process. I wrote of my confusion about Matt, about my place in the world, or away from it. I wrote of my wish that I'd never felt compelled to write at all, ever, aware of the irony in finding relief in the very act that brought on the trouble in the first place.

I preferred not to commit words to paper or computer screen, would rather have skipped telling tales of life, choosing instead to live it. But I couldn't help myself. Terrifying as it was, this recording of the world going by and my speculation about it was often the time I felt most alive. Was it possible to live life in an act of creation based on the mere observation of life? Did I exist most fully in the moments when I stopped my own progress to pause and record the past, if only the past of a split-second before, or was it my way of stopping the world and getting off?

Mother Benedicta once spoke of dying to the outside world and its temptations in order to be born into a higher life of contemplation for Christ. Catherine's entrance into the cloister gave her the kind of solitary life that can sometimes make great art possible. It looked to me like the narrow surroundings of my twin's physical orbit opened up a broader canvas for her brush and expanded the prayer life of her fellow sisters. But was that logical, or ironic?

Before I could decide, the doorbell rang.

"Hey, Dorie." Matt chucked me on the shoulder and walked into my living room. His friendly gesture failed to relieve the awkwardness between us, but I appreciated the effort.

"Hey," I managed.

"We wrapped early. I stopped by your office, but they said you'd taken off." He picked up my tennis racket from where it rested near the door and bounced his palm against it as if to check the strings. "I saw your article."

I shut the door and prepared for a lecture. "I never intended for that to—"

"Yeah, I know. Graciela told me what happened. But it looks like old Phil knew better than the rest of us this time. It's a great piece, Dorie. One of your best."

"Thank you." I dropped onto the couch and stared at the floor.

"Are you all right?" Matt reunited the racket with my tennis bag across the room and sat beside me.

I nodded "yes," then shook my head "no" and started to cry.

"Shhhh, it's okay." He put his arms around me and squeezed.

"She burned it," I said, burying my face in Matt's UCLA sweatshirt. "She actually set it on fire."

"Hold on now, slow down." He pushed the hair out of my eyes. "Who set what on fire?"

"The painting. My sister burned a painting in front of me to prove that it doesn't matter if anyone sees it. But it did matter, and now it's gone."

"That's not your fault." He seemed to want to convince himself as much as me. "She's a grown woman who made her own choice."

"It is my fault," I said. "Catherine's painted over things before, but at least they were still there underneath. This one is gone forever as a direct result of my article."

"You don't know that. Most artists would've been thrilled by your coverage. You couldn't have known your sister would react that way."

"Oh, I had a pretty good idea." I wiped my runny nose on my shirt-sleeve. "Don't you want to say I told you so?"

"No reason to." He pulled a clean bandanna out of his pocket and held it to my nose. "Blow."

I complied.

"You had already decided not to write the story," Matt continued. "It's not your fault that your boss got industrious."

"It still feels like it is."

I took the impromptu tissue from him and blew my nose again. I started to hand it back when I'd finished, then decided I'd better wash it first.

"I can't stop you from feeling guilty, but I for one absolve you of any wrongdoing." Matt pulled off his sweatshirt and set it on the wobbly arm of the couch. "Granted I've been skeptical of, not to mention a little threatened by, this whole thing, but now that it's over, I don't think it turned out all that badly."

"I do. And I'm not so sure it is over." I folded and refolded the bandanna. "I've opened a huge can of worms here, and I have a feeling I'm gonna have to go fishing."

"Maybe so. But your writing is getting the attention it deserves, and that's cool."

"Yeah, I'm grateful for that." I wiped my eyes with a clean corner of the bandanna. "Sorry about my blubbering. I'm the last person you need crying on your shoulder these days."

"Oh, I don't mind. But my shoulder won't be available after tonight. Not for a couple of months, anyway." He stood up. "Evan got me a gig on his next film and it shoots in North Carolina."

"That's great, Matt. Let me know how often I need to water your plants and—"

"Actually, um, the kid in that front apartment is gonna do it." He scratched his nose and turned his eyes away.

"Oh, okay." I tried to cover up my disappointment that my customary job had been reassigned.

"Yeah, he's saving up for some Cub Scout trip or something, so I figured I'd give him the chance to earn a few bucks."

"I understand." And I did, all too well.

"So if you'd give him your key next time you see him..."

"Got it." I blinked back fresh tears before Matt saw them. "Hey listen, about last night, I—"

"Don't worry about it. You take care." He retreated out the door and closed it gently behind him.

I watched him go, already missing him. Why was our romantic timing always off? I picked up the notebook again and wrote. The man I'd talked myself out of wanting to marry because I never thought he'd ask had proposed. And I'd said no. Was it him I didn't want anymore, or marriage itself? Matt was the same loving, if absentee, friend he'd always been—not always there when you wanted him, but right there when you needed him. I was the one who had changed. But into whom?

I wrote for hours, until my hand ached and the paper ran out. I flipped through the ink-filled pages and examined the scrawl that grew more illegible when my tired hand couldn't keep up with my thoughts.

All at once the notebook felt like an alien thing with a life of its own. I remembered what happened the last time someone read my private thoughts and vowed that it wouldn't happen again.

I spied Matt's forgotten sweatshirt on the couch, pulled it on, and then grabbed the notebook and walked out into the moonlight. The sand had cooled with the fading sun and tickled my feet. I took care to avoid splinters as I stepped onto the nearest pier and inhaled a lungful of salty air.

I considered the notebook I held for a long time. Then I ripped out the pages and dropped them into the water one by one. As the blue ink bled and the water scrubbed the pages white again, I realized how different my twin and I were. Catherine ruined her work to avoid acclaim, while I did so only to avoid repercussions. I would have embraced the praise if I could have gotten away clean.

Yet I found appeal in my sister's artistic vandalism. I saw it reflected in the paper scraps in the water and the circle of totems on the beach nearby. Detached from the results enough to drown them or let the wind topple them over, finding fulfillment in the process of creation alone, I felt no need for an audience. I didn't know what Catherine's reasoning was, but for me, no audience meant there was no one and nothing to fear.

The next day, I wrote a letter to Matt explaining my feelings as much as I understood them myself. I didn't want the declined proposal to be the end of our friendship but accepted that it probably was and collected his things from around my apartment. I filled a shopping bag with borrowed tools, books, and a spare cell phone charger but found I couldn't part with his sweatshirt. I held it up to my cheek. It still smelled of Matt's woodsy soap. Keeping the fleece, I locked the rest of the items into his apartment along with the letter, and then dropped his house key off with the neighbor kid.

I drove to *The Comet* trying to remember the last time I'd wanted to go to work and couldn't recall a single instance. When had I become so obsessed with being successful that I'd forgotten to stop and ask myself if it was worth it? When I wasn't terrified by it, I still loved to write, but the consequences of publishing now gave me pause. What was the point of professional and material success anyway? Catherine and her fellow nuns seemed to do just fine without it.

Arriving at the newsroom, I muddled through the flood of compliments from my coworkers.

"Way to go, *chica!*" Graciela gushed.

"Great piece," acknowledged the Features Editor, a former *Chicago Tribune* reporter who'd taken the *Comet* job for fun after retiring to California. "We need to talk."

"Dude, you rule," Rod the intern concluded.

It was the kind of praise I'd dreamt about my whole career, but now it produced a knot in my stomach. I sat down to do a follow-up piece on Carmie, the two-headed goat, newsworthy again for delivering seven kids, but found my fingers typing a formal request for a leave of absence instead. I couldn't afford to take unpaid leave, but I needed time to think. If that meant going into more debt, then I would go into more debt.

Letter in hand, I knocked on Phil's open door. He waved me in and continued talking on the phone.

"She's a gem, all right." He winked at me. "Glad you're enjoying the series. Give a call on those ads."

Phil hung up and rubbed his hands together. "How's my star reporter this morning? Seen your latest installment?"

"Not yet."

"Rest of L.A. has. More highbrow than we're used to but damn good. Attracted a whole new readership. People who wouldn't normally be caught dead reading *The Comet* have subscribed. Wouldn't be surprised if some Hollywood type calls about the film rights."

"I'd like to take a leave of absence," I said in my best assertive voice.

"And I'm headlining on Broadway."

"I'm serious."

"You hit your stride and you want to quit?" he asked. For a split second, he looked genuinely concerned about my sanity.

"The employee handbook says I can take up to sixty days of unpaid leave per year."

Phil scrunched up his features in disbelief and then released them with a laugh.

"Not even going to try to understand why you would do such a silly thing but not going to get upset either, considering what you've done for this paper in the past couple of days." He picked up one of my notebooks from his desk and flipped through the pages. "Heck, I'll pay you while you're gone. Got enough material here for two months anyway. Besides, you'll need the time to give interviews."

"Interviews?"

"People want to interview the journalist for a change. Booked you on *Good Day, LA* for Thursday."

"Without asking me?"

"Like you'd turn it down. What kind of journalist doesn't love good press?"

"This thing doesn't need to get any bigger than it is." I snapped the rubber band I still wore on my wrist.

"Sure it does. But if you want to be Miss Prima Donna Garbo about it, go ahead and cancel. Just adds to the mystery, since the word is your sister's not giving interviews either."

"Oh no. Have people been bugging her?"

"Been referring all the interview requests for her to the cloister, so my guess would be yes."

"I've created a monster."

"A very lucrative one." Phil took a cigar from the box in his desk.

I gave him the letter and turned to leave.

"Enjoy your time off." He scanned the letter. "Think about what you want to write for your next series."

I raised my hand in acknowledgment and left.

Graciela sat on the corner of my desk and watched me gather my things.

"I envy you. What I wouldn't give for two months off from this place."

"Compromise your journalistic ethics and you too can feel guilty enough to chuck the whole thing for a while." I stuffed a framed picture of my parents and my Slinky into my computer bag.

"*Madre mia,* I do that every day. It doesn't seem to have the same effect on me."

"You're lucky." I struggled to extricate my laptop's power cord out of the socket under my desk. "This job would be a whole lot easier if I didn't have a conscience."

"No, you're lucky." Graciela reached down and effortlessly removed the cord from the socket for me. "Because you have the nerve to follow yours. I would've quit or changed my m.o. a long time ago if I weren't such a coward."

"It's easy to be brave when you don't have a daughter to support," I said.

As word got around the newsroom about my planned absence, the same coworkers who had congratulated me an hour before now stopped by to say goodbye and wish me well. Few understood why I was going. When they pushed for an explanation, I found I didn't have one.

CHAPTER TWENTY-SIX

"Don't worry, Buckaroo," my Aunt Martha said the moment she saw my agitated expression in the airport waiting area. "Whatever it is, it will work out."

I smiled and relaxed. So much had happened since Martha left for Japan that I didn't know where to begin when she returned.

We spoke very little during her five-hour layover. Martha seemed to sense my inability to articulate what I was going through. We went for a drive and a short walk on the beach and then returned to the airport.

"Love ya, Toots." Martha hugged me as her Phoenix flight was called.

Back at home, I erased five phone messages from Trish lobbying for a gallery show and fixed myself a cup of peppermint tea, only to fall asleep before it finished steeping. Ravenous when I woke up that evening, I ordered a pizza and ate half of it before a glance at the clock reminded me that the sisters had just finished what was no doubt a far more meager meal. I had another slice for them as I pictured the nuns preparing for Compline, the last chapel prayer before they went to bed.

I said a short Compline of my own, examining my conscience and imagining Mother Benedicta blessing me with holy water along with the sisters. I appreciated how the predictability of the monastery routine enabled me to share in the nuns' ritual without physically being among them. There was a sense of closeness and comfort in it that I'd rarely felt before.

Post-pizza, I padded across the hall in my socks to see if Matt wanted to go to a 9:30 movie. Then I remembered he was in North Carolina, and that, even if he were home, he'd probably prefer me to leave him alone. Stopping mid-knock, I placed my forehead and the flat of my hand on his door and let myself miss him.

It was almost midnight when I passed a church on my way home from the movie and thought about the cloistered nuns rising again for Vigils in Big Sur. I pictured them in chapel and sang what scraps of chant I could remember, letting the connection I felt with their midnight prayer envelop me.

Within a week of leaving *The Comet*, I had accomplished ninety percent of all the things I'd been meaning to get around to forever. My apartment was spotless, late birthday gifts were mailed, groceries were bought and eaten before they spoiled. Potted pansies splashed the patio with color while the winged visitors to my new birdfeeder filled it with song. I discovered I now preferred bare feet on the beach and in the house because I wanted to feel rooted to the ground, even if it was the somewhat shaky ground of earthquake-prone California. Daily Mass slipped into my routine almost imperceptibly, as if I'd never stopped going to church in the first place.

I was reacquainting myself with the guitar I hadn't picked up since college when the doorbell rang. I set down the pick I'd managed to pinch between my working right index and middle fingers and rose to answer the bell.

"Hey, Graciela, hi Sophie." I opened the door for Graciela and her shy six-year-old. "What brings you ladies to the neighborhood?"

"You do. *¿Qué pasa?* I've been calling and calling all week, imagining the worst." Graciela fanned herself and dropped onto my couch. "Sophie, would you please get Mommy something to drink? I've been worried sick about you, Dorie."

"I'm fine." I helped Sophie pour sodas in the kitchen. "I got tired of carrying my phone around. But you could've called me here." I pointed to my landline.

"Like I ever bothered to learn that number when you always had your cell glued to your hand. How are you suddenly able to part with it?"

"I discovered that it's kind of nice to be unreachable once in a while."

"Nice for you, maybe. Frustrating as all get out for those of us trying to do the reaching." Graciela took a soda from her daughter. *"Gracias, mi amor."*

"Sorry about that. Would you like a cookie, Sophie?" I held out a plate to the pig-tailed girl behind the long eyelashes. "I just made some."

"You made *cookies?"* Graciela held a hand to her heart. "With flour and sugar and everything?"

"Sort of. I bought that pre-made dough you slice up."

"Even so..."

"Can I, Mom?" Sophie appeared less concerned with the source of the cookies than with their ultimate destination.

"Yes, but just one." Graciela sighed. "You don't want to turn into an addict like your mother."

Sophie grinned and scampered out to the patio with her sugar fix. The birds at the feeder chattered in greeting.

"Amazing." Graciela bit into a cookie. "Next you're going to tell me you've learned how to knit."

"They tried to teach me during the cloister recreation hour, but I was hopeless without enough functioning fingers. I have been playing guitar again." I held up the blistered fingertips on my left hand to prove it.

"That's more like it. The Dorie Homemaker role doesn't suit you. I'm relieved to see you're doing well. You were so unnerved when you left, I thought we'd find you in your bathrobe surrounded by Chinese take-out cartons."

"Only for the first couple of days. Then I switched to Thai."

"Ha, ha." Graciela looked around the uncharacteristically neat apartment. "Did you get a new carpet?"

"No. Why?"

"This one's white. I thought yours was gray."

"That's because it's usually covered with newspapers."

"Oh, right. Have you read your articles? *El Jefe*'s showing some class in his selections and editing."

"I haven't looked at a paper for days." I picked up my guitar again. "But I'm glad Phil's controlling his flashier editorial urges."

"Have you heard from him?"

"He called yesterday to tell me how it was going." I strummed a few bad chords. Out on the patio, I saw Sophie put her hands over her ears. "Ad revenue is way up."

"So is your salary and title if you play this one right, *chica*. This thing's got Feature Editor written all over it." Graciela reached for another cookie. "Do you miss work?"

I shook my head. "It's weird. There was a time when I couldn't imagine life without journalism. It was my whole world. I wondered how people who weren't in the business got along without it—not that I had any time or patience for those people. Now I'm discovering that *those people* probably had it right all along."

"I'm not going to say our jobs aren't warped, but we do some good, too," Graciela said through a mouthful of chocolate. "Look at all the people you're reaching with this series."

"But look who, and *what*, got burned in the process." Graciela, Trish, and Matt were the only people I'd told about the burned painting.

"You apologized, right?" Graciela reached for another cookie. "Though I don't know why, considering the good publicity you're giving her."

"Yes, I did." I struck a dissonant chord. The guitar twanged as if in pain.

"And she accepted?"

"Under duress, but yes." I stopped strumming. Graciela looked relieved and I saw Sophie unplug her ears outside.

"As long as you apologized, you've done your part."

"I suppose." I set the guitar down. "I'm definitely going to miss her. I'll miss all of them."

"Who says you can't go back and visit?" Graciela asked.

"After what happened?"

"*Because* of what happened. You told me yourself how happy the prioress was that you got Catherine to speak."

"Yeah, but—"

"Yeah, but nothing. This is a good thing, Dorie, no matter how much you want to believe it's not. It's bringing your writing to a new level. Hell, it's bringing *The Comet* to a new level. It's bringing out your sister, whether she admits it or not. And I bet you dollars to donuts it's going to generate the money that cloister needs in the long run."

"Maybe you're right." I hugged my knees. "What does dollars to donuts mean, anyway?"

"*Yo no sé*. But don't donuts sound good right now?"

"Graciela, you're eating a cookie," I said.

"And your point is?"

Forty-five minutes later, Graciela, Sophie, and I stood in line at Krispy Kreme.

"Thanks for making the pilgrimage with us." Graciela sniffed the sweetly scented air.

"If you're going to eat donuts, you may as well do it right. Matt loves this place." I reached the counter. "A dozen glazed, please."

"How is that *muchacho*? I haven't seen him in a while."

"We haven't talked much since he proposed," I said without thinking. I nearly swallowed my tongue.

"Since he *WHAT?*" Graciela yelled and flapped her arms like a spooked chicken. Sophie covered her ears again.

"Please don't mention it to him or anyone else." I took the green, polka-dotted box of sugared salvation from the cashier.

"Don't *mention* it?" Graciela flapped some more. A red-faced Sophie placed her mother's arms at her sides and held them there.

I shook my head, paid for the donuts, and steered Graciela outside where fewer eardrums were at stake. "I'm serious, Graciela."

"To *anyone?* I take it that means you said no."

"Yes."

"Yes, you said 'yes' or yes, you said 'no'?"

"Yes I said 'no'."

"No comprendo." Graciela waggled a manicured finger at me. "First, you get all this recognition at work only to take a leave of absence. Then, your best friend in the world proposes and you turn him down. Worse, you keep it a secret from your other best friend in the world."

"I didn't say it made any sense." I took a bite of my donut and let the glaze melt in my mouth. "But you have to admit his proposal came out of left field."

"Left field? It came from outer space." Graciela finished her second donut and reached for a third. "I don't blame you for turning Mr. Married-To-His-Job down. You two make better friends than anything else. But I do blame you for not telling me."

"I'm sorry. The whole thing was so bizarre that I needed some time to let it sink in. And I don't think we are friends anymore. He was pretty upset."

"Maybe, but better to be honest now than marry him and be sorry later." Graciela wiped some icing off of Sophie's chin.

"The thing is, I don't think I would be sorry. Of all the guys I've known, he's the one I'd most want to marry, at least if he were around more. I'm just not sure about the wife part."

"Don't ask me to recommend it. My particular stint as a wife was not fun. The mom part, on the other hand..." Graciela reached out and waggled her fingers like she was going to tickle Sophie, who burst into giggles and darted out of reach.

As Graciela chased her, I laughed and enjoyed mother and daughter at play, no longer sure wife *or* mother were roles I'd choose for myself. I was even less sure of what roles I'd choose instead.

I decided to get Sister Barbara's opinion on whether she thought my revisiting the cloister was appropriate.

"Of course you should return if you want to," Sister Barbara said as we sorted through donated clothing in her South Central convent house. The potter had a smudge of dried clay in her hair. "The nuns won't hold a grudge. The real question is, why did you leave in the first place?"

"My aspirancy visit ended and—"

"No, not the cloister." Barbara folded a pair of jeans and added them to the pile earmarked for distribution at the soup kitchen. "Why did you leave the Catholic Church? Didn't you tell me you lost your faith at eighteen?"

"I wouldn't call it losing my faith, per se." I held up an infant undershirt with a small stain on the front for the sister's inspection. Barbara sized up the garment and shook her head "no." I tossed the tee into the discard heap. "I stopped going to church and calling myself Catholic, but I've always believed in God and still agree with most Catholic theology."

"Why did you stop going to church if you still believed?" Sister Barbara sniffed a donated pair of socks, scowled, and threw them into the laundry basket.

"Long story." I explained that I'd always had a hard time on my birthdays and never wanted to celebrate them because of my biological mother's death in childbirth. My eighteenth had been especially bad because my adoptive mom had cancer.

"After we'd had cake in her hospital room, I left my dad there and went to Saturday evening Mass," I said. "I didn't want to go home afterwards, so I laid down in the pew and eventually fell asleep. I guess nobody noticed me when they locked up for the night. I must have had some good dreams, because when I walked outside in the morning and saw the church fountain shimmering in the sunlight, everything felt right and perfect in the world. I had hope for my mom and felt spiritually alive. I froze, so happy and at peace that I almost couldn't bear it."

Sister Barbara smiled but didn't say anything.

"When I got home, I found out that my mom had died an hour after I'd left her. So now I have two mothers to grieve every birthday."

"You poor thing." Sister Barbara paused in her sorting. "That's a lot to bear."

"I was pretty furious with God after that and stopped going to services," I said. "Before long, I couldn't stand anything about the church, especially priests and nuns—no offense."

"None taken." The potter put a frayed pair of shorts in the discard pile.

"All through school I'd been shy around the sisters, but once I left the church I couldn't even look them in the eye. I had to force myself to overcome my fear to meet my twin. It was as if I knew religious people like her would look right though me."

"And see what?" Sister Barbara tied together the laces of a pair of men's dress shoes and tossed them in a pile with several other pairs. "Something you didn't want to recognize yourself?"

"Maybe," I said. "It was my first taste of good old-fashioned Catholic guilt. It wasn't a sense that I'd done something wrong—more like I'd avoided doing something right. Nothing has gone quite right since. I look for fulfillment in secular things and sometimes I get a flicker of true serenity when I write, but it's never as strong as it was that morning after Mass before I learned about my adoptive mom's death. Until..."

"Until what?"

"Until I saw my birth father's and sister's paintings, especially my sister's. Somehow Catherine has distilled that tranquility into color on canvas, where it could last forever if she'd only let it." I stopped sorting. "That's what I don't understand. How could she capture the peace and completeness I've been chasing for years and then fail to cherish it?"

"Maybe they've got a surplus of those emotions at the cloister."

"If that's the case, then they should share the wealth."

"Looks to me like they already have," Sister Barbara said. "I'm surprised you never thought of returning to the church. It's a shame you turned away from religion right when it might have given you some comfort."

"I thought about it, but it seemed too overwhelming, not to mention disrespectful to my adoptive mother, the agnostic." I picked the lint off of a wool sweater on the table. "Going to church was my mini-rebellion as a kid. After my mom died, the last thing I wanted was to do something she'd disapprove of. If I hadn't been in church feeling sorry for myself, I would have been there for her last moments. Maybe I could have comforted her, which is more than I was able to do as a newborn when my birth mother died."

I yanked the lint off of the sweater, suddenly anxious. I knew my biological mother had passed away giving birth to us, but somehow I hadn't connected that Catherine and I were probably still in the room when it happened until this conversation with Sister Barbara. My hand injury was the result of trauma in an emergency delivery. I doubted there had been time to whisk us away while they were trying to save her.

I paused and put the sweater down. I didn't know why it had never occurred to me before or why I found the realization so upsetting now. Maybe because it made me feel even more responsible than I already did—not only had I killed her, but I had also failed to console her in the process. I knew this was completely irrational, but I couldn't shake it. I realized, too, that I unconsciously felt responsible for my adoptive mom's cancer, which made even less sense. I picked up the sweater and started tearing at it again.

Sister Barbara looked up, saw my manic movements, and placed a hand on the sweater to slow my busy fingers.

"Children are apt to take the blame," she said. "But I hope you know that neither of your mothers' deaths was your fault."

"I know," I managed to mumble. But my lower lip quivered.

"For whatever reason, God put you right where you needed to be," she said, weaving her head to keep eye contact with me when I tried to look away. "I bet your presence in the delivery room and your prayers during Mass eased each woman's passing."

"I hope so," I said, my quiver turning into bone-deep shudders that rolled through my body in waves. Awash in survivor's guilt, I missed both of my mothers with a primal fierceness that exhausted me. Tears fell down my cheeks and dropped onto the sweater.

"It's not your fault," she said again, holding me by the shoulders to calm my trembling.

Her touch made the trembling worse, yet suddenly it was okay to tremble, okay to feel everything that I kept hidden even from myself most of the time. I started sobbing—my nose running, my jaw taut in an anguished grimace, my voice keening. So much time had passed before I was old enough to understand how my birth mother died that no one had ever thought to tell me it wasn't my fault. The guilt was such a part of me that I assumed everyone else blamed me too.

When my sobs turned into quick, shallow breaths, Sister Barbara pulled me in for a hug and began taking in long, deliberate lungfuls of air.

"Slow down," she said. "Deep breaths."

Fighting off panic and dizziness, I made myself match her breathing.

"You're going to be okay," she said. "You can let the guilt go."

I stood there embracing her, somehow lost in grief with this woman I hardly knew—a woman about the age both my mothers would have been had they lived. I imagined I was hugging them, hearing them say through her that they didn't blame me, that they knew I loved them whether I was able to tell them at the end or not. That they were still here with me—always. Had Sister Barbara said that?

I hugged her tighter.

CHAPTER TWENTY-SEVEN

I took Graciela and Sister Barbara's advice and went back to the cloister for a visit, eerily aware that, as *Comet* subscribers read about my first two weeks there, the story continued to unfold. I wondered how it would end.

More cars than usual occupied the parking lot during the 9:00 a.m. Sunday Mass. I hoped their owners were there to pray rather than pry. The crowd of Mass attendees turned out to be well behaved, except for the boy who made crayon drawings on the pew instead of in his coloring book while his parents' heads were turned.

After the service, I found Sister Teresa running herself ragged in the gift shop.

"Our gift shop volunteer moved to Utah." Teresa sold a Mass card to a well-dressed woman. "Wanna job? The pay stinks."

"I'll take it. When do I start?"

"Five minutes ago. I've got to visit the little girl's room something fierce," Sister Teresa whispered. "Back in a jiffy."

The extern was gone before I could ask her how to operate the cash register. I turned to the next customer in line, a fortyish man with a bald spot, too-tight jeans, and a professional camera, and instantly recognized him as Pete Billings, a pushy photographer from *The Comet*'s rival, *The Blaze.*

"I don't suppose you sell cigarettes?" The photographer eyed the shop's meager offerings with obvious contempt.

"Um, no, we don't," I said, avoiding his eyes.

"Dorie?" He squinted at me.

"Hi, Pete." I declined to offer my hand. He didn't seem to notice.

"Well, I'll be damned. Haven't got enough of this place yet, eh?"

"I'm just helping out."

"Helping out? Looks like you're moving in for the kill," he said from behind his knuckles. "Exploit your relationship with your sister to get her to confide in you and then really stick it to her, eh?"

"Not exactly. What are you doing here?"

"Same as you." He picked up a rosary and swung it around his finger. "Following up on your story. Gotta milk this puppy for all it's worth. So you gonna help me get some access here or what?"

"Why would I help someone from a rival paper?" I caught the rosary as it spun, pulled it away, and returned it to the display.

"Because I'm such a nice guy."

My flesh crawled. I was amazed he could say the words with a straight face. But was I any better? It hadn't occurred to Pete to exploit a nun until I set the precedent.

"Sorry. Can't do it," I refused. "These women already have more press than they can stand."

"So that's how it is. You bleed them dry yourself and then get all high and mighty about their privacy."

"What can I say?" I threw up my hands and forced a smile.

"I'll get what I came for with or without you." He slung his camera over his shoulder and turned to leave. "And I'll remember this the next time you need help with a piece."

I dreaded the day I'd again have to write the kind of story that required favors from people like Pete. The photographer nearly knocked over Sister Teresa as they passed each other in the doorway. He left without apologizing to her.

"I can't believe that character is back again," Teresa said as she shook off the encounter and looked at me.

"He's been here before?" I asked.

"Caught him scaling the cloister wall earlier this week trying to get pictures. He won't get far today. I called the police when I saw him arrive." The extern rang the next customer's Bible purchase. "Thank you and God Bless."

"Have you been getting a lot of extra visitors since the articles began?"

"A few looky-loos at Mass and reporters here and there, but nothing we can't handle. The, er, fortress-like nature of a cloister has inaccessibility in its design, don't forget."

I smiled in spite of myself, secure in the knowledge that the sisters could take care of themselves.

"It's good to be back here," I said. The cloister itself now gave me the same good feelings that the paintings did. "I wasn't sure I'd be welcome after the mess I made last time."

"So you shook things up a bit." Sister Teresa rattled her keys and smiled. "I happen to think we needed it. We definitely need your help now. Way things are going, every little sale we make in this shop matters."

"Your finances are still bad, huh?"

"Worse than they've ever been." Teresa frowned and then brightened. "Mind you, the Lord has helped us out of tough spots before. No reason why this one should be any different."

Sister Teresa's tone may have been optimistic, but I could see in her worried expression that the situation wasn't good.

In order to volunteer at the cloister gift shop during my leave of absence, I had to shorten the commute. I hired the same neighbor kid who worked for Matt to pick up my mail and water the plants, and then packed for Big Sur. Since the inn was too expensive and the weather was mild, I bought a tent on sale and moved into a campsite in nearby Big Sur National Park.

Once I'd parked my car at the campsite, I didn't move it. The two-mile hike up the cloister driveway every morning was my favorite part of the day. A tangle of scrub oak, chaparral, and a riot of wildflowers decorated the roadside as the now-familiar red fox, numerous rabbits, geckos, and various birds greeted me along the way. The walk back down the hill in the evening was equally stunning. Mist often shrouded the dusky cliffs, as if the mountains conceded the spotlight to sunset's blazing spectacle over the Pacific.

Between the campsite pay phone's intermittent service and the cloister's emphasis on quiet, I checked my voicemail once a week rather than once an hour and turned off my cell phone since there was no reception, anyway. Most of the messages were from members of the media looking to capitalize on the success of one of their own either through a favor, an interview, or both. Happy to observe the cloister rule about limited phone use, I didn't return those. The other calls were from Graciela, Trish, my Aunt Martha, and worried friends who thought I'd lost my marbles. Mutual friends assured me that Matt was well, but I missed him anyway.

I didn't have any direct contact with Catherine or the other cloistered nuns, but I helped Sister Teresa weed the public side of the garden, sold books and religious knickknacks in the gift shop, set up the altar for Mass, and had long talks with Mother Benedicta in the visitors' parlor.

"Contemplation is beyond our knowledge, beyond explanation, beyond our own self," Mother explained as we sat in the parlor one afternoon. "It's a largely solitary endeavor, yet we're all connected by the power of prayer. You surrender yourself to the working of God in your life and see what happens."

"But how do you surrender?" I tried not to think about how much my questions had changed since my first visit to the monastery. "Where do you begin?"

"All aspirants ask the same things," Mother said with the voice of long experience. "I'd write out the answers, but they're different for everyone. And the moment you work them out for yourself, they change. At least they have for me."

"Great." I folded my arms.

"Just embrace the mystery and stumble through as best you can." Mother chuckled. "That's what I do."

"Kind of like I stumbled through kitchen duty?"

"Exactly like that. Contemplative prayer is about taking risks, being willing to move beyond your comfort zone. It can be both exhilarating and terrifying, and, when nothing seems to be happening, it's downright dull. That's usually because you're trying too hard."

I nodded. "It's the same with writing. You can surrender to the flow, or you can push-pull yourself to death and get nowhere. The moment you let your mind overrule your heart, your work suffers."

"As does your prayer."

"I imagine it's true for painting, too." My thoughts were never far from my sister. "How is Catherine doing? I haven't seen her since the day I—"

"She's fine." Mother clasped her hands in her lap. "Just worried about our financial situation like the rest of us."

"I understand things are getting worse."

Mother touched her stomach and closed her eyes for a long blink. "We didn't get the loan."

"But I thought you were approved last week?"

"For the two smaller ones. The big one didn't come through, and that's the one we can't do without. All the banks are playing it safe and loaning almost two million dollars to a bunch of women who'd need a hundred and ninety-five years to pay it back based on current earning capacity just wasn't a good bet."

I unconsciously glanced at Sister Catherine's latest painting on the wall behind the prioress, a luminous portrait of Mary being assumed into Heaven.

"I know what you're thinking." Mother tipped her head back to indicate the artwork. "I've thought about it, too. But Sister Catherine has always been adamant about not showing her work. It wouldn't be fair to make her life with us conditional upon her ability to support the community with her art when no other sister is required to do anything of that sort."

"I understand." Wary of the idea of a gallery show even when I endorsed it myself, I was definitely against it now that I knew Catherine's artistic temperament. "What are you going to do?"

"Abandon the monastery."

"But..." My heart sank.

"We've found an old parish house outside Carmel. It'll be cramped, but we'll manage. We've signed a lease to move in four months from tomorrow." The prioress pulled a bottle of Mylanta out of her drawer, cracked the seal, and took a tablespoonful. "It'll take that long to put the house in order and close this place up."

"Will you be able to return here?" I asked.

"No." A tear glistened in her eye. "The wilderness reclaims land like this quickly. By the time we raise the money we need for repairs, there will be new damage as a result of our not being here to maintain things. I've lived on this hill for forty-five years. But achieving detachment from places and things is part of our vow, so I suppose I'll go quietly." Mother's tear grew heavy. She wiped it away before it could slide down her cheek. "At any rate, it's something you should know if you're still contemplating joining us. Are you still considering a vocation?"

"I have been thinking about it," I admitted both aloud and to myself for the first time, gaining some small relief from the burden of the internal struggle I'd been having over the subject. Lately I'd let myself entertain the idea of becoming a nun since the financial impossibility of it made it safe to consider. "But it isn't feasible until I pay off my school loans, and since that's not going to be for another five years, I've pretty much given up on the idea."

"Unfortunately, we can't take on anyone with outstanding debts." Mother sighed. "Time was, we could find the money to pay for the education of any sister who pursued one. Those days are long gone. Still, if you're meant to be with us, it will happen. These things have a way of working out."

"I hope so." Then I qualified. "I mean, I'm not sure I want to join, but it would be nice to have the option."

"As far as we're concerned, you have it. We reviewed your candidacy and have decided to extend an invitation to you to join us if and when you are ready."

"Thank you, Mother." I flushed, grinned and panicked all at once. "It's an honor."

"You can thank me by making the decision that's right for you, not the one you think we expect."

"I have to admit I still find the whole idea pretty disturbing." I squirmed and snapped the rubber band on my wrist so hard that it broke and flew through the air. Mother ignored it and I decided not to replace it.

"So did Mary when she was told she'd bear the Son of God. If you didn't feel some resistance, I'd question your calling. Just keep thinking about it. The answer will come."

"Odd that a lack of money is one of the barriers keeping me from entering into a life of poverty," I said.

"The Lord works in mysterious ways." The prioress looked heavenward and frowned. "Some of which frustrate the daylights out of me."

As I descended the cloister driveway en route to my campsite that night, I suddenly realized that I *did* have the financial means to get out of debt and enter the convent, probably with enough money left over to take a chunk out of the nuns' debt as well. I just wasn't sure I had the willingness to part with the one possession that had ever mattered to me.

CHAPTER TWENTY-EIGHT

As my leave wound down, I tried and failed to think of ways to postpone going back to work at *The Comet*. Ultimately, I resigned myself to leaving the place I'd rather stay to return to a place I'd rather not go.

I would especially miss the sisters, many of whom I'd gotten to know as I worked in the gift shop and attended the Daily Offices from the public side of the chapel. Even if it was just a smile or a nod through the cloister grille, I was happy to realize that most of the nuns seemed to have come to accept and respect me as I did them.

I gained no further insight into Catherine, who withdrew into silence after my apology and kept her eyes down whenever I saw her. I was glad to hear from Sister Dominica that my twin was painting more than ever. Whatever injury the article inflicted on Catherine's creative process seemed to have healed.

Just when I'd given up on ever speaking to my sister again, I heard my name called as I set up the altar for morning Mass. I turned from marking pages in the lectionary and saw Catherine beckon to me through the grate that divided the altar from the cloistered section of the chapel. I closed the book and walked over to the grille.

"Do you really think the paintings could make the kind of money we need for the cloister repairs?" Catherine's voice sounded reedier than I remembered as she stood grasping the metal bars that separated us.

"Yes, but—"

"I'm ready to sell them. I want to do that gallery show you mentioned."

I stood there for a moment in silent awe; well aware of the fear and personal conviction Catherine had overcome for this change of heart.

"Are you sure?" I asked. "You hated the attention you got from my articles. If you do a show, it'll be ten times worse."

"I know. But we need the money. I thought I could make my contribution in other ways, but no matter how many extra meals I cook or floors I scrub, chores won't pay for repairs. The paintings can."

"Okay." Despite my stomach twisting at the prospect, I knew she was right. "I'll handle the logistics so you can focus on your painting."

"Thanks." She looked at the floor. "I've always told myself it was God's will for me to keep the paintings unseen, but maybe I was wrong. Maybe selling them is His will. Or maybe I don't know *what* His will is."

I certainly didn't know.

"Do you think I could at least be anonymous?" she asked.

"I'll see what I can do," I said.

Our eyes locked in a mental handshake as we mirrored each other on either side of the grille. Catherine's distressed expression reflected my own fear that the show might have consequences far beyond what either of us wanted to imagine.

After Mass, my emotions alternated between excitement and concern. Thrilled as I was at the prospect of sharing more of my sister's work with the public, I was wary of that same public and wished there was a way to show the paintings without exposing the artist. Just as I was slowing down my own life, everyone and everything around me seemed to be speeding up. I wasn't sure that was a good thing.

Mother wasn't sure either.

"I've never insisted Sister Catherine sell her work because I didn't want to corrupt such a beautiful form of prayer," Mother said as we met in the parlor after services. "But now that she's suggesting it herself—"

"I think the show has real potential to inspire others to pray, not to mention make money for the cloister, but the publicity it generates will be a mixed blessing," I said. "My articles have already attracted visitors with things other than contemplation on their minds."

"There have been a few interesting characters appearing around here of late, but not so many as to disrupt our way of life." Mother made the sign of the cross and looked heavenward.

"You don't have a choice, do you?" I asked.

"I'm afraid not. Even if we move, we still won't be out of the financial woods. Sister Catherine knows how bad things are and I suppose that's why she's changed her mind about selling her artwork."

"Then I guess it's settled." I looked at the Sacred Heart of Jesus picture on the wall and hoped He approved.

Ten minutes later, I dialed Trish from Sister Teresa's office phone as Mother stood by. I'd never seen the prioress on the public side of the convent before. She looked smaller and more vulnerable.

"You go, girl!" Trish prattled on the phone. "I knew you could wear her down!"

"Actually, she approached me. The cloister is really hurting financially, so the sooner the better. Any chance you could pull it off within say..." I looked at Mother, who held up three fingers. "Within three months?"

"Sure, sure. It'll be tight but we can do it. And we can work the struggling nuns angle into the promos."

"I was hoping to avoid that." I wound the phone cord around my hand. "Catherine wants to remain anonymous."

"We use her name and her story or it's no deal," Trish said flatly. "I'm not about to let all that beautiful publicity go away without capitalizing on it."

"The work stands on its own."

"That's true for a lot of artists, but that doesn't mean their stuff sells. We have an angle here, Dorie. We need to use it."

"But—"

"Do you want your sister to make money or not? This is the art world we're talking about. It's fickle. It's trendy. It's downright impractical. When people buy a painting, they need to feel like they're getting a piece of the artist as well or it's not worth it."

The gruesome image of people scavenging Catherine's live body for religious relics came to mind. I shook my head to banish it.

"I'll talk to her," I said.

"Good. There's a space at Bergamot Station that doesn't have anything scheduled after this month because it's going up for sale. Maybe they'll let us rent it for a few weeks. And I'll need to find a photographer right away to shoot in high resolution for the promotion."

"I already have someone in mind for that," I said.

"Who?"

"You haven't heard of him. But he's cheap and he's good."

"He'd better be. And what I save on him I can pay you, since I assume you'll want to write the accompanying text."

"I think I can manage the catalogue descriptions." I looked at Mother, who nodded in silent agreement.

"We won't have time to publish a complete catalogue, but we can throw together some glossy tri-folds. I'll drive up tomorrow to see the paintings. Meanwhile, you should—"

"Whoa, whoa, whoa, slow down." I took a breath on Trish's behalf. "Catherine's just agreed to this. We can run around all we want behind the scenes, but we need to give her some time to get used to the idea before you pounce on her."

"Fine. I'll be up the day *after* tomorrow. But no later. If we're going to put this together fast, we're going to have to get our butts in gear."

The campsite pay phone was ringing off the hook when I returned to my tent for the night. The other campers ignored it.

"It's for you," a backpacker in a hemp jacket and cargo pants informed me without getting up from his bedroll. "Some jackass has called for you six times in the last hour."

"Sorry." I watched an earthworm swim in a puddle of soapy water beside the outdoor shower stall and picked up the phone. "Let me guess. Phil?"

"How'd you know?"

"How did you get this number?"

"Your friend Trish called and spilled the beans about the gallery show. Wanted me to get in touch with you."

I rolled my eyes. "Of course she did."

"Write your next series about the show—the convent's financial troubles, the prep, how your sister feels about it, and all that crap. Make sure you put in the part about her burning that painting. Can't believe you didn't tell me that, you sly dog."

"Don't you think people have had enough by now?" I asked, kicking myself for telling Trish about Catherine's creative bonfire. I should have known she wouldn't be able to keep such a juicy detail to herself.

"Not at all. Series ended yesterday, hundreds of calls and emails wanting more today. Already had inquiries about syndication."

"That's great, Phil. But I'm not sure another series is—"

"Triple your salary. Been meaning to do that anyway. Even throw in a stipend for you to stay up there and write it. Three pieces a week instead of five."

Visions of paying off my debts without having to part with my father's painting swirled in my brain, not to mention the prospect of the extra time I'd get to spend at the cloister. I bumped my forehead with the receiver to bring myself back to reality. My ability to justify ethically dubious career moves had become far too honed for my liking. I watched the earthworm wiggle away from the water and burrow back into the mud.

"I can't, Phil. I don't want to do anything that might lead to more trashed artwork."

"You won't. She's agreed to do the show, which means she's agreed to have her work seen, photographed, and talked about. Media's going to be all over this thing whether that nun likes it or not. We're not going to be left behind. Not when we, er you, started it."

"Can't you get Graciela or somebody else to write it?" I asked.

"Has to be you. You're as much a part of the story as your twin. If the cloister is serious about selling those paintings, they're going to have to submit to the publicity machine. They already know what coverage from you will look like. Bet you could get exclusive rights for a song."

"Let's not get too greedy."

"Why not when it's so much fun?"

"I'll need some time to think about it."

"Nothing to think about. Just get writing." Phil hung up.

I put down the pay phone and wished I could pick it back up and dial Matt for his opinion. I already knew what he'd say, or did I? Maybe it was different now that the first series had benefited the sisters by introducing Catherine's talent to the public. But was it right?

Neither Mother Benedicta nor I sat down during our next meeting in the parlor. Instead, we paced our respective sides of the grille.

"My editor wants me to write a series about the show." I turned and strode the other direction. "I told him I wasn't sure. What do you think?"

"It's going to be written by somebody. I'd prefer it to be you. You know us better than anyone else." Mother clutched her stomach and kept pacing. "In fact, I was going to ask you to do something of that sort."

"Okay, I'll do it, then." I still wasn't excited about writing the series, but I was relieved to have the prioress's approval if not downright encouragement. "I was planning to go back to Los Angeles in a couple of days, but now that I'm writing more articles, I'll be staying around until the show opens."

"Well, we can't have you stuck at that campground the whole time."

"The paper's going to give me a stipend, so I'll be able to move into a hotel."

"Nonsense. You can stay in the visiting priests' quarters. I don't know why I didn't think of it before."

"I don't want to impose," I said.

"You don't need to spend your money on a hotel when you're here most of the day anyway. And it'll give us more time to get to know you."

"But..."

Mother raised a hand to silence me. "Just accept the offer."

"I will. Thank you."

"Since it's convent business, you may also have cloister access to and from the studio and business office to help Sister prepare for the show."

"That will help. I'll make sure to stay out of the other areas."

"Very good. What else do we need to do?" Mother asked.

"Let's see. We'll have to put the paintings somewhere accessible so Trish can look them over."

"There's a garage with a loading dock that we can use for the purpose."

"That'll be fine."

We stopped pacing and looked at each other.

"Are we doing the right thing?" I wondered aloud.

"I wish I knew." Mother sighed and touched her cross.

CHAPTER TWENTY-NINE

Outdoors, the wind that whipped over the autumn landscape left me feeling spiritually dry. Indoors, Catherine's art drenched me in inspiration.

A *Joan of Arc* portrait depicted the saint astride her high-stepping horse, her right hand resembling my own as it curled around the flag she held up to God in triumph. The sun's rays winked off of her studded armor like stabs of light thrown off a sparkler, short-lived but beautifully daring, like drops of rain falling up. The flag snapped in the breeze, the bright blankets on the horse glowed in lustrous hues, and the saint carried herself with the confidence that only comes with believing God is on your side.

The sheer monumentality of the composition challenged the viewer to leap headlong into passion, anticipation, fearlessness. I suddenly felt battle ready. Maybe we could pull off this show without doing too much damage to my twin's artistic process.

As I helped Catherine sift through her work in the studio that night, I was soon saturated by my sister's genius. Still, considering Catherine's output, the actual number of completed canvases was smaller than I had expected, thanks, or, no thanks, to their constant reuse.

Several of the pieces were painted over with completely new work since my last studio visit two months earlier. Others were dramatically altered. In one painting, a formerly gray-toned Sea of Galilee now glistened under a cool blue wash. In another, shepherds now joined

Mary, Joseph, and the cattle at Jesus' Nativity. A few pieces remained unchanged, but I feared not for long. I couldn't find a single blank canvas in the place.

"I assume these are all complete?" I hoped beyond hope.

"I guess." Catherine shrugged. "They're never *really* done."

"I'll take them out to the garage then." I was anxious to remove pieces from the room before she had any more urges to recycle. "Are there any that you want to hold on to? We shouldn't show Trish anything you don't want to sell."

"Take them all." Catherine turned away from the paintings. "They're not mine to keep."

"I'd hate to do that. Why don't we ask Mother Benedicta and the other sisters to choose a few for the cloister first? Then Trish can pick from the rest."

Catherine nodded.

"Oh, hey." I picked up the nearest canvas, saw something missing and set it down again. "You forgot to sign this one."

"I never sign them."

"Ever?" I was surprised I hadn't noticed before.

Catherine shook her head. "It won't matter since I'm going to be anonymous, right?"

"Unfortunately, you won't be able to be anonymous after all," I said. "Trish thinks we should take advantage of the publicity you've already received and—"

"I'm not the one who put those pictures in the paper!" Catherine walked in circles in the small room.

"Neither am I, though it's my fault and I am sorry." *You have no idea how sorry,* I thought. "But the more people know about the artist, the more interested they are in buying her art."

I sat down, tired of being the bad guy despite originating the role.

"I don't have a choice, do I?" Catherine stopped circling.

"I don't think so. What Trish wants is pretty much the way it has to be, and I know she'd want you to sign and date them somewhere."

Catherine considered. "Would a symbol on the back be enough?"

"A symbol and the date should be fine." I started counting canvases and marking them in my notebook. "But we'll have to use your name in the literature."

Catherine took up a thin brush and dipped it in black paint. She carefully painted a small crucifix on the back of each canvas along with the year. At first I thought her decision to use the symbol of Christ offering Himself on the cross reflected the vulnerability she felt about showing her work in public. Then I realized she was signing God's name instead of her own.

Goosebumps rose on my arms. I stopped taking inventory and watched in silence. After signing about a third of the paintings, Catherine straightened up.

"Maybe I would like to keep some," she said.

"Of course." I leapt up to help her. "Which ones?"

"All of them." Her mournful eyes told me that she wasn't joking.

"How do you go from being ready to give them all away to wanting to keep every one in five minutes?" I asked despite guessing the answer.

Catherine used the brush to draw a signature in the air.

"I'm sorry. I know how hard it must be for you to sign them." I picked up as many of the signed paintings as I could carry without damaging them. "I'll return the ones Trish can't use in a day or two. Meantime, I'll buy some fresh canvases in Carmel tomorrow in case you want to start something new."

Catherine resumed her task, and then paused again.

"Maybe I'll just make a few changes first," she said.

She grabbed her palette and a larger brush and reached for the *Joan of Arc* canvas. Unable to accept the loss of any existing pieces, I held her arm and stopped her.

"Let's leave these as they are," I urged. "At least until Trish sees them."

My twin twirled the brush in her hand before tossing it aside with a scowl.

"It's not fair. People design plenty of buildings that never get built, compose operas that never get sung, write books that never get published. Why do these paintings have to be seen just because I had the means to bring them into complete being?"

I hoped her question was rhetorical, because I couldn't answer it. Yet I spoke anyway.

"It's okay to be afraid, you know," I said, kicking myself for how preachy it sounded.

"No, it's not." Catherine shook her head. "Dad wasn't scared."

"What makes you so sure?" I asked. "I didn't know him, but I'm guessing he didn't drink himself to death because he was thirsty."

"Good point," Catherine said.

I picked up her discarded brush, handed it to her, and then looked around at the paintings.

"On second thought, I don't see any harm in you keeping a canvas or two to work on."

My sister smiled at the small gesture. I wished I could have done more, and then remembered again that I might in fact do much, much more. I could sell *Shift* and use the proceeds to help the nuns, not to mention free myself up financially to join their community if I decided to. I dismissed the thought, as fearful as the rest of my family.

The next day, Catherine was temporarily excused from her regular duties to focus on painting.

"The rest of us will pick up the slack on her chores until after the gallery show," Sister Teresa explained as we arranged the paintings around the garage in anticipation of Trish's visit. "Whatever God asks us to do, we'll do."

"I'm sure Catherine will make good use of the extra time, especially since I brought her a ton of new supplies this morning." I hung a small painting on a nail. "Would you mind if I went to see if she needs anything else? We're pretty much done here."

"Go ahead. I'll hold down the fort."

"Thanks." I hurried out.

When I arrived at the studio, I found my sister placing the last blank canvas on the easel as her customary candle burned in the corner of the room. The other canvasses sat around the room in various stages of completion.

"I knew you'd be busy, but this is ridiculous," I joked. I couldn't see my twin's face. "At this rate you're going to run out of supplies again by tomorrow."

"I'm going to redo all of them," Catherine said with a quiet vibration in her voice. She pointed to the new canvases. "After a mistake, I have to let the paint dry before I can go over it."

She dropped her plastic palette. It smeared wet color on the unprotected hem of her habit before it hit the ground. I rushed to help her.

"It's all right, it's my spare." Catherine wiped at the stains. She looked up and I saw that she was crying.

"Never mind the habit, are *you* all right?"

"I've never cared how the work turned out before." She shook her head. "Now I'm trying to anticipate what people might want, and nothing seems right."

"You're giving the public too much power. Forget about the people and forget about the show. No one can compromise your painting unless you let them," I said.

"I've always felt guilty that I don't show the artwork to outsiders, but I don't know how to do that and still paint honestly. Now that I'm showing the paintings, I feel guilty because it infringes on the prayers I intended for God alone. I don't feel God in these." She waved toward the new paintings. "He's not here."

I took a closer look at the canvases and realized that they all had the same subject: Jesus' agony in the Garden of Gethsemane.

In one painting, Jesus' expression conveyed the dread of His pending crucifixion. Though He looked up toward the sky in hopeful entreaty, His whole face was pulled down in emotional pain—eyes half closed, lips pursed, chin strong but ready to tremble.

Another piece communicated His insecurities through the canvas itself. Catherine had scarred and distressed it to resemble an artifact painted on a dissolving sheet of rusty metal, its subject likely to fade away at any moment. It didn't look like a comfortable space to occupy.

In a third, the landscape seemed to mock Jesus' prayers for release from His destiny. His stark, staring eyes and weather-beaten face looked at a candy-colored garden, complete with a theme-park blue lake where I half expected to see pleasure boats bobbing, their captains beckoning me with the promise of a margarita in a plastic novelty tumbler.

The confidence I'd seen in the *Joan of Arc* portrait the day before was gone. Catherine was right. Interesting as they were, I couldn't see God's hand in these new paintings despite having Jesus as their subject. God was crowded out by the staggering fears of the artist.

"You worry too much," I said, rattled but trying not to show it. "Even if you don't paint another thing, you've got more than enough to show Trish."

"But what if no one likes those?"

"Everyone who's seen your work likes it," I reminded her.

"Everybody liked Dad's paintings too—until he changed his technique. Then the critics panned his new stuff even though it was amazing."

"I read about that," I said.

"So he changed back to his old style to please the public. He also started drinking." Catherine shuddered. "After he drank himself to death trying to stay inside that little box the critics put him in, those same critics declared the panned paintings brilliant. Now they sell for three times what his others sell for."

"I know," I said. "He left me *Shift*."

A smile of recognition broke up the moody purple clouds on Catherine's face like a glorious sunrise. "I remember when he painted that. It was a real breakthrough and we both loved it." The clouds rolled back over Catherine's expression. "Everyone else hated it."

"Not anymore," I said. "Sometimes it takes the public a while to catch up."

"Yeah, well, they did plenty of damage in the meantime. And now here I am trying to please that same public. I'd be disgusted with myself if I wasn't so busy being terrified." Catherine looked over her work. "Maybe if I could just do a few more..."

"If you like. But paint for yourself and for your God," I said. "God is the only audience that matters."

Catherine took a deep breath and turned to face the canvas. I could see the pressure weighing on her shoulders and regretted the part I had played in placing it there. It was time to do what I had to do.

CHAPTER THIRTY

I waited for Trish in the cloister parking lot that afternoon and accosted her the moment she stepped out of the car.

"I want you to look for a buyer for my Wagner."

"What?" Trish's head reared back. "Why? The taxes aren't due until April, and the way your career is going, you'll have the money to pay them without selling the painting."

"I know, but I have school debts too and—"

"So? You're paying those off on schedule, right?"

"Yeah, but—"

Trish looked at the cloister behind me and smacked her forehead. "Oh, Jesus. This isn't about your loans or the taxes, is it?"

I didn't say anything.

"Listen to me, Dorie." Trish looked me right in the eye. "It's not your job to save this place. You didn't put these nuns into debt. Don't throw away your security on a bunch of women you hardly know."

"Those women include my sister."

"You mean the sister who broke a promise to your dying father and ignored you for nine years?" Trish asked.

My face fell. Catherine had apologized for not contacting me, but the jellyfish sting of rejection still left my whole body prickling every time I thought about it. I wondered if it would ever not hurt.

"I hate to be a bitch, D, but there it is. You don't owe her anything."

"It's not about owing," I said.

"I don't get it. You gave these nuns an opportunity to get out of debt when your articles introduced Catherine's art to the buying public."

"Yes, and the thought of that same public is killing her creativity," I said. "If she's sacrificing, so can I."

"That painting is your only link to your father."

"Sister Catherine connects me to my birth father far more than a piece of canvas."

"Fine, whatever." Trish rolled her eyes. "If you're going to reduce it to a piece of canvas, then let's consider the money. *Shift* represents financial freedom for you. It could pay for time off to write that novel you always talk about, or establish a healthy retirement portfolio, or—"

"I know, I know. I've thought about all that. But this is what I want, and there'll be enough for the convent *and* me. If you don't want to help me, I can always find another dealer who will." I hoped she wouldn't call my bluff.

"Of course I'll help you. I just want you to think about what you're doing. At the very least, let's hold off a few weeks. Your Wagner will command a much higher price if we wait until Catherine's show generates some renewed buzz on your dad."

"I don't want to wait."

"Clearly." Trish shook her head. "Fine. I'll start looking."

"Thanks."

"Now let's go see if your sister's stuff is everything you say it is."

"They're even better than I imagined." Trish took in the garage full of Catherine's art. "I'll take them all. Has she got any more?"

"Not at the moment," I said while Mother Benedicta stood by. The prioress and the community had decided not to hold any paintings back. Instead, they would keep whatever remained unsold after the show.

"Well, I hope she's getting busy." Trish examined another canvas. "Is she fast?"

"I don't have any basis for comparison. Mother Benedicta?"

"Nor do I." The prioress shrugged.

"Can she produce a painting a week?" Trish asked.

"Sure," I said as Mother nodded in agreement. "Sometimes she does one in an hour. But others take several days or even—"

"Good, because I could use about fifteen more."

"That many?" Mother's eyes crinkled. She looked worried.

"But there are at least forty paintings right here." I gestured around at the art. "How big is this gallery space you leased?"

"Fairly small, but I like to have additional pieces available in the back to show prospective buyers."

"I don't know if three months are enough for her to finish that many paintings," I said.

"It's really more like ten weeks." Trish whipped out a tape measure and checked the dimensions of a canvas. "I need to have everything completed two weeks before we open."

"I'm not going to pressure her," the prioress said. "She's anxious enough about this show as it is."

"Maybe I should talk to her," Trish whispered to me. "I've dealt with my share of temperamental artists."

"Well, you're not going to deal with this one until it's absolutely necessary." Mother Benedicta furrowed her brow. "Sister Catherine is more than temperamental, she's downright fragile."

"Then I'll trust you to tell her what she needs to do." Trish turned to me. "Can you get that photographer of yours up here to shoot what we've got so far?"

"He's coming tomorrow."

"Good. If I don't like his work, I'll still have time to hire someone else before we print the tri-folds."

"Is there anything else we need to do?" I asked.

"Think about a name for the show. I'll get the title wall painted in mid-November. Based on Catherine's palette, I'm thinking a cool gray for the gallery walls." Trish flipped through several canvases. "Or should we do something warmer? Maybe I'll paint each room a different color. Does she require any special conditions for display?"

"Like what?" I asked.

"Like how they should be framed, if at all, lighting, a specific amount of space between the paintings...that sort of thing."

Mother Benedicta and I looked at each other before I replied for both of us. "I'll ask her, but I doubt it."

"Well, if she does have any preferences, make sure you find out what they are. Any chance she'll come down to oversee the installation?"

"I'd allow it since it's cloister business," Mother said. "But I have a feeling she'll decline."

"That's fine," Trish said. "As long as she comes to the opening."

"She'll be there," Mother answered.

"I still can't believe that an artist of this caliber is completely unknown." Trish shook her head. "Not that I'm complaining. It's a coup for me and it's going to be a boon for this convent."

"We hope so." Mother balled her hands into tight fists. "We could use a break."

"How much can they expect to make on this show?" I asked the question so the prioress didn't have to.

"Depends. It's hard to price a new artist. Then again, my clients are used to paying top dollar." Trish closed her eyes and did the math in her head. "I'd say if two thirds of these sell, less expenses and my percentage, you're looking at roughly a half a million."

"That much?" Mother asked.

"More like that little. Believe me, buyers are getting a bargain. I've seen stuff half as good sell for twice as much. But since it's her first show, I have to go in a little low and price them to sell."

"Five hundred thousand dollars is enough to make the basic repairs that will enable us to stay here." Mother touched her cross. "And showing the bank we have a viable income should convince them to loan us the rest of what we need."

"Glad to do my part to keep you sisters happy. And I know it'll put a smile on my face. I love it when everybody wins."

I hoped that would be the case.

"I've got to sign the lease for the gallery and start planning the layout." Trish air kissed me. "See you later, Dorie." She shook Mother's hand. "It's been a pleasure meeting you, Mother Benedicta. I look forward to working with you."

"You too, Trish. God bless you."

"Uh, thanks." Trish headed back to her Range Rover outside the loading dock door. "I'll need those images by Friday, Dorie."

"No problem." I waved as my friend climbed into her car and drove off.

"Well then," was all Mother could say.

"She was on her best behavior in your honor," I said.

"The habit has that effect on people."

CHAPTER THIRTY-ONE

That night, I returned to the priest's quarters I'd moved into the day before and reveled in a long, hot shower after almost two months of the campground's al fresco cold water stalls. Then I sat down in front of my laptop to write the first of the new series on Catherine's show. The pressure I'd seen Catherine put on herself as she tried to paint for the show began to weigh on me, too. Raising my hands to the keyboard seemed almost impossible.

A jagged fingernail sent me jumping up to rummage through my toiletries for a file, desperate for any distraction. As I repaired that nail and reshaped the rest, I wondered if I could match the open style of my personal journals.

I doubted it. Even though I'd written my cloister journal more or less in article format, the content was personal. Writing for myself was much different than writing for a readership of three hundred thousand. Interesting that I did my best work in a journal no one else would have read if Phil hadn't printed it, just as Catherine did her best painting in isolation until I exposed her. Exposed myself and well aware of the vulnerability of my subject, I wasn't ready, much less willing, to write that way again.

I struggled to draft something about Catherine, the gallery opening, and the cloister that readers would want to know but didn't compromise my sister or her community.

Several minutes of flurried fingers clicking across the keys resulted in one long keystroke on the delete button. Again, I experienced the relief Catherine must have felt whenever blotting out an image. There was a certain appeal to spilling your guts, then retrieving them and neatly sewing them back into your body before anyone noticed. Tempting as such surgery was, I couldn't do that now if I was going to give the nuns the publicity they had expressly asked for.

I switched from typing on the laptop to writing longhand in my notebook to fool myself into thinking that I was writing for only myself and maybe God. I wasn't fooled, nor was God. The words didn't express the ardent wonder I felt writing the first series, much less capture the lighter-than-air depth of Catherine's art.

Eventually, I managed to string together several dozen phrases capably enough to have something worth sending to Phil. My editor might notice a difference in the tone, but it should be sufficient for an audience already hooked on the subject matter.

Visiting an exhausted Catherine in the studio the next morning, I scanned the results of a full night of painting and recognized the same fear in her completed works that I'd felt in my writing. Not wanting to overwhelm her, neither Mother Benedicta nor I had told Catherine that Trish expected a dozen more paintings, or even that the art dealer wanted all of the pieces she'd seen so far, leaving Catherine unable to rework any of them. Yet my sister seemed to know it. This latest completed painting depicting the miracle of the loaves and the fishes was beautiful and very capable, but the airy lightness had been replaced, if not by darkness, then a pointed sadness.

Rod, the photography intern, arrived that afternoon with five different cameras and a carload of rented lighting equipment.

"I'm sorry Phil saw that photo of the painting after I promised you I wouldn't show anyone," Rod said right away, as if he'd been waiting to get it out. "It was on my computer screen when he walked into the darkroom and he zeroed right in on it. Then he found that memory card in your desk and I—"

"Don't worry about it." I carried a backdrop screen into the garage. "Looks like it all worked out."

"Yeah, I guess so." Rod mounted a light on a C-stand. "Thank you so much for giving me this gig."

"My pleasure. I figure you've been working for free long enough, and anyone who appreciates Sister Catherine's stuff the way you do should get to photograph it."

"Right on." The intern checked the aperture on his first camera. "I just hope I can do her justice."

"So do I," I said more to myself than to Rod.

As the weeks passed, I found it much easier to write the second series of articles in the studio while Catherine painted. Fortunately, my sister now welcomed my presence there. Somehow our fears weren't as overpowering when we faced them together. Whatever unspoken competition we'd felt before now dissolved in the giddy fizz of our common purpose.

Yet those fears were still there. Catherine was not only aware of my presence where she had been oblivious to it in the past, but she also talked about the future patrons of her work crowding the room with expectation. As I watched this human audience emerge in her mind, the only presence worth hosting, the spiritual one I'd found so powerful when I first witnessed Catherine's artistic process, continued to fade.

I no longer peppered Catherine with questions, choosing to quietly cherish her hard-won trust instead. Ironically, the more subdued I was, the more she opened up.

"It's funny," Catherine observed as we spent recreation hour in her studio one night. "Everyone says I'm humble because I keep my eyes on the floor, but it's not about humility. I'm studying the patterns and colors of the tiles for painting ideas."

"I see." I smiled in my corner chair and put down the pen I'd been using to scribble nothing worth keeping. It was still rare for her to speak. "And you never bothered to correct them?"

"It's easy to let assumptions go when you don't talk." Catherine picked up a new brush. "Now I look down to avoid the eyes of all those people I imagine will be critiquing the paintings at the show."

"Is that why you paint over your pieces? To make sure nobody sees them?" I asked.

"It didn't start out that way, but yeah, sort of," Catherine said. "I didn't get interested in painting until high school, and by then Dad was drinking and money for supplies was tight. So I painted his blank canvases when he wasn't around, then re-primed them for him to use. Usually he was so drunk he didn't notice."

"So a lot of his paintings have your paintings underneath?"

Catherine nodded.

"That's so sad that you never kept anything."

"It was hard at first, but I trained myself not to care. I didn't know if I was any good, but I was sure that if I was talented, I didn't want anyone to know. I didn't want my life to turn out like Dad's."

"You made sure of that when you became a nun," I pointed out.

"Yeah," Catherine nodded. "I wanted to be as unlike him as possible. He craved the spotlight, so I wanted to hide in the convent. When I got here, I kept recycling canvases even though I didn't have to anymore. I was afraid to let the images matter to me. The sisters thought my reuse of finished canvases was a little odd at first but accepted it when I said I did it to save money. They also liked that I dedicated the process to our Lord. I figured He'd remember the images He created through me whether I painted over them or not."

"I'm sure He does," I said, further confirming my hunches about Catherine's artistic choices.

"I hope so." A light shone in Catherine's eyes. She blinked it away. "But it's different now that I know we need to sell the artwork. As soon as I try to paint things meant to last, God drops the brush. Maybe He's punishing me for trying to create art for self-glorification rather than His own."

"You said yourself that this show isn't about you," I said. "If it were, you would have sold your paintings a long time ago."

"Maybe it wasn't always, but I'm starting to make it about me. And now I'm wondering if I can replace them." Catherine scanned the walls crowded with artwork. "I've never worried about that before."

"Don't psyche yourself out. Selling paintings you'd only intended for prayer is assuming some control, but you're also giving away control by inspiring other people to glorify God in their own way."

"Maybe." Catherine set the brush down. "I used to love coming in here."

"I used to love writing in this." I tossed my notebook on the table. It fell with a clunk. A long silence followed before I spoke again.

"You don't have to do this, you know. It's not too late to cancel," I said, meaning it. Trish hadn't sold my Wagner yet, but she'd assured me there was interest and it would sell soon. "I have some other ideas on how to come up with the money."

"Yes, I do, and so do you." Catherine handed my notebook back to me and picked up her brush again, swirling it in a blob of pigment. "I just pray that God will meet us on the other side."

CHAPTER THIRTY-TWO

As December arrived and the sisters lit the first Advent candles in preparation for the birth of Christ, Catherine turned in fourteen capable, though less spirited, paintings, and I turned in a series of informative, yet guarded, articles. Invitations were mailed, caterers hired, and advertisements appeared in newspapers and on public radio. Trish and I rushed around making preparations. Once the paintings were shipped, Catherine had very little to do except pray.

Pray she did, along with the rest of the convent. On the day of the opening, the sisters offered special intentions for the success of the show during morning Mass. When it was time to leave, everyone lined up at the cloister entrance to send Catherine and Mother Benedicta off with a blessing.

"We always travel in pairs." Mother slipped into a pair of clogs for the journey. "Like shoes." She winked.

"Glad to have you," I said as we exited the building.

When Mother and I crossed into the public garden, Catherine hung back in the doorway.

"I, um, hate to skip any more of my cloister duties," she stalled.

"At the moment, attending the opening *is* your cloister duty." Mother turned to her. "You started this, and you need to see it through."

Catherine hesitated to leave the safety of the enclosure. Mother went over and took her hand.

"Don't worry, Sister," the prioress reassured her. "Just pretend we're taking our annual trip to the dentist."

Catherine frowned and touched her mouth.

"Right. Bad example, given your bridge work last year." Mother considered. "I know. Let's ask God to widen the cloister walls today to encompass the whole state of California."

Catherine put on a brave face and slid awkwardly into her borrowed clogs. She stepped outside and the three of us walked to the parking lot together.

I chose the scenic route along the Pacific in hopes that the soothing blue vastness would help calm my sister's last-minute nerves. Except for the sound of chewing our dinner bread, cheese, and apricots, and our recitation of the Divine Office, we were silent on the drive down. Catherine and Mother Benedicta stared out at a world they rarely saw. It was only when I turned onto Olympic Boulevard and neared the Bergamot Station gallery complex that I offered some coaching.

"There may be a couple of reporters at the opening," I warned as we waited at a stoplight. "Just try to relax, don't let the press rattle you. They'll take your picture and ask a few questions, but you don't have to respond to anything that makes you uncomfortable."

I turned down the access road leading to the converted trolley station's entrance and found a line of two dozen cars ahead of us.

"Wow," I said, surprised and pleased by an even better turnout than I'd expected. "This looks promising."

We inched toward the cluster of galleries housed in corrugated metal buildings.

"That's quite a crowd." Mother scanned the people milling around in the full parking lot. "Are there any other events going on?"

"No, just Catherine's."

I heard my sister's breath quicken behind me.

"I'll have to park across the street." I signaled and pulled over to the curb. "I can let you off here if you want."

"That sounds fine." Mother opened her door.

Catherine froze in the back seat.

"Or maybe we'll just stay with you until you park." Mother stayed in the car and slammed her door harder than was necessary.

I found a spot at the palm-lined Ralph's Supermarket parking lot nearby. The prioress and I got out of the car. Catherine made no move to join us.

"Ready, Sister?" Mother opened the back door so my twin could exit.

Catherine shook her head and kept her eyes on the floor mat. Mother pursed her lips, threw up her hands, and looked skyward. "Help me out here?"

I was about to respond when I realized the prioress was talking to God rather than me. Mother Benedicta clutched her stomach and took a few deep breaths, and then leaned down beside the car to face Catherine again.

"I'm afraid I must insist, Sister." There was an edge to Benedicta's voice I'd never heard before. "We all do our penance sometime, even if it's just insurance for sins we haven't committed yet."

I looked at the throng across the street and then back at my twin. I took Mother's arm and pulled her aside.

"She doesn't have to come in if she doesn't want to. I'd rather have her in her own time and on her own terms than force her into this mob before she's ready," I said.

"Sister Catherine is never ready for small crowds, much less large mobs."

"Well, then it's better if she stays in the car." I pointed to the winding line of patrons and press waiting to enter the gallery. "If she's in the wrong frame of mind, she could do more harm than good."

"Very well." Mother took a bottle of Mylanta from her pocket and chugged it directly from the container. "You know more about these things than I do."

"Not by much, but thanks for trusting me."

The prioress shook off her frustration as we walked back toward the car.

"Join us later if you feel like it, Catherine," I said. "Just don't go hot-rodding in my car in the meantime."

Catherine's shoulders relaxed as she settled in to wait. We left the car and the artist behind and headed for the gallery complex.

"Are you sure about this?" Mother peered back over her shoulder. "We didn't come all this way to..."

"She'll be there." I pressed the button for the crosswalk. "She's got to be curious about how her work looks in a professional space."

"That's true." The prioress took another swig of Mylanta before pocketing it, and then closed her eyes and touched her cross. It seemed to calm her down. "Everything will be fine."

Drivers waiting at the light stared at Mother Benedicta's habit as we crossed the street before them. Their gazes shocked me into recognition of a nagging fear of my own. I'd been so preoccupied with putting the sisters at ease that I hadn't dwelt on the fact that my humble, holy friends from Big Sur were about to bump up against my brazen, stylish friends in Los Angeles. Would they get along? I wasn't sure the simple black dress I'd chosen to wear could successfully bridge the gap between the two worlds, much less the rest of me.

I didn't have time to dwell on it. The moment Mother Benedicta and I arrived on the other side of the street, photographers and news reporters made a beeline for the prioress.

"How many years have you been in the cloister?"

"Where did you get your artistic training?"

"Is this your first time out in public since you joined the convent?"

"I'm not the nun you want." Mother held up her hand, but this crowd didn't quiet down.

"Where's Sister Catherine?" a ball-capped cameraman called out above the din.

"She may arrive later." I kept walking.

"How much later?" a coifed reporter asked. "We want this for the soft feature on the seven o'clock news."

"I'm sorry, but I can't be any more specific than that." I tried to push through the multitude toward the gray gallery stairs.

Mother Benedicta stepped in front of me and the sea of humanity miraculously parted for the nun.

"I should get out more often." Mother went inside with me right behind her.

Entering the gallery, I scanned the space for Graciela or Trish to no avail. Wall-to-wall people dressed in the art industry's requisite black crammed the room. Noisy conversation, classical music, and the wet, woolen smell of too many bodies in too little space filled the air. The wait staff had given up trying to move champagne and hors d'oeuvres through the crush and waited on the sidelines for hungry and thirsty people to come to them. The members of the string quartet played with their elbows pinned to their sides to avoid poking passersby with their bows.

It was impossible to see one's own feet, much less get a clear view of the paintings on display. The dizzying swirl of black-clad humanity mingled with white walls and glimpses of colored canvas made the paintings come alive with a vibrant, pulsating presence. The room seemed to pitch and roll, yet buoy me up, leaving me feeling seasick and exhilarated all at once.

Mother and I were able to move through the crush and search for Trish, but only after the prioress had the wherewithal to hold up a scribbled cocktail napkin that read "I am not the artist," thus ensuring the respect her habit commanded without the pesky interest that accompanied genius. Late afternoon rays of sun shone through the center skylight, spotlighting those people caught in the beams in a dazzling square of what looked like heaven amid the chaos. Was God in attendance? I hoped so.

We found Trish introducing Rod to the petite photography editor of *Art World* magazine.

"Megan Brown, meet Ray Mallory." Trish gave Rod a motherly nudge to shake Megan's hand.

"It's Rod," Rod corrected.

"Right, right." Trish put an arm around the intern. "I discovered Rob slaving away in the bowels of *The Comet*'s darkroom and rescued him."

"Nice job, Rod." Megan examined the promotional tri-fold. "Your shots really capture the essence of the paintings."

"Uh, thanks. But it's easy when the subject matter is so—"

"There you are." Trish drowned out Rod when she noticed Mother Benedicta and me. She left the editor and the intern in her wake and hugged us. "Where's our Sister Catherine?"

"Not ready to meet this mess." I shook my head.

"No matter. We're doing great without her." Trish waved to passing patrons. "I've sold three paintings and there's interest in several others. People are offering above the list price to outbid other buyers."

"Is that ethical?" I asked.

"Well, it's not typical, but anything for the nuns, I say." Trish giggled and looked around. "Which reminds me, the reps from the Getty Trust wanted to discuss a couple of pieces. I hope they're still here."

She flitted off, insofar as it was possible to flit in a packed crowd.

"I'm going outside to get some air and some quiet if there's any to be had." Benedicta fanned herself with her cocktail signage.

"I'll join you in a minute." I spied the rest of the *Comet* crowd: Graciela, Phil, and Phil's peroxided wife, Melissa, in a knot by the bar. I was about to make my way over to them when someone tapped me on the shoulder and I turned to find Matt standing there. I tried and failed to hide my surprise.

"Hi, Dorie." Matt looked far more composed than I felt.

"Hey, Matt." A nervous shiver ran through me.

"You remember Evan Cole." Matt indicated the man radiating movie star presence beside him.

"Of course." I offered my left hand to the actor who I'd met while visiting Matt on the *Obsessed* film set a few months before, glad I didn't get star struck. Keeping my composure around Matt was hard enough. "Hello."

"Nice to see you again, Dorie." Evan grasped my hand in both of his between flashing grins for passing photographers. The actor was clearly practiced at granting picture requests before he was asked so photographers wouldn't interrupt his conversation. He nodded toward the paintings. "Looks like you've been busy."

"Yeah, well, I can't exactly take credit for them," I said.

"But you wrote about them." Evan signed an autograph for a weak-kneed teenager. "And your words made this show possible."

"That's what I told her," Matt chimed in. "Though neither of us were sure it was a good idea at the time."

"I'm still not sure." I looked at the packed crowd. "It's been tough on my sister. But with all the repairs their monastery needs, it was this or move out of their home."

"They won't have to worry about money anymore." Evan spoke with the authority of someone who could make such statements. "I plan to buy up as many of these paintings as I can."

I gulped. "You don't have to do any favors for—"

"Believe me, they're doing me a favor. I've got a new house in Mexico to decorate, and this stuff is *tight*."

I stifled a laugh at the thought of what Catherine would think of a twenty-something movie star calling her paintings "tight."

"Her use of light and spatial relations is inspired." The star ignored a fawning photographer in his enthusiasm. "I majored in art history and I've studied a lot of paintings. It's rare to be able to say so much with so little paint. And the brushwork..." Evan shook his head. "I've never seen such texture."

"She's an original." I was sobered and pleased to realize that Evan knew what he was talking about. "I'm sure Catherine will be glad to hear that some of her work will be going to someone who enjoys it so much."

"Some of it? I'm buying the whole collection." The actor held out his arms expansively. "Whatever I don't hang in the house I'll give as Christmas gifts."

Matt and I shared a look in quiet observation of the vast chasm that separated the very rich from the getting-by in Los Angeles.

"Well, then you'd better hurry, because the dealer's already sold at least three." I indicated a painting with a small red sticker on the wall beside it.

"Point the way," Evan said, suddenly agitated.

"That's her over there with the red hair and the black-rimmed glasses." I indicated my friend with a nod of my head. "Her name's Trish Reed."

"I know." Evan's eyes squinted in recognition. "I'm a big fan of your father's work, too. When I heard Trish repped Rene Wagner's daughter, I called her hoping she might have some leads on your dad's stuff, but she didn't."

"Really." My blood burned. Trish had more than a lead on a Wagner—she had mine to sell. That same blood rimed over with frost when it hit me that selling the painting meant giving it up. I shook off the chill.

"Yeah. It's a drag," Evan said. "I've been trying to add a Wagner to my collection for years, but they're rarely up for sale. Hey, if *you* hear of anything..."

"Will do," I said, afraid to mention my painting to him before finding out why Trish hadn't. Maybe there was a good reason she didn't want to tell him about it, though I couldn't think of one. "Matt's got your number, right?"

"Yeah. Thanks," Evan said. "Guess I'd better talk to Trish before I miss out on another Wagner's stuff. You take care, Dorie."

"Bye," I managed as the actor hurried off in Trish's direction.

"I wasn't sure if I should tell him about yours or not," Matt said after Evan was out of earshot. "Since I don't know what you've decided to do with it."

"I'm going to sell it," I said.

"You are? Then why didn't you—"

"I probably will, but today is about Catherine," I said, stifling my fury at Trish lest I take it out on Matt. I changed the subject. "Evan's a nice guy."

"He is." Matt nodded. "He offered me a job as his personal assistant after we wrapped in North Carolina."

"Well, if a movie star has to monopolize your life, I'm glad it's him."

"I turned it down. I've been working on my short for the last month."

"No way!"

"Way." Matt grinned. "I finished shooting last week and I start editing tomorrow."

"That's great!" I hugged him as much as the crush of bodies would allow. "It's so good to see you. Thanks for coming tonight, not to mention bringing Mr. Moneybags with you."

"*You* brought Mr. Moneybags," Matt replied. "Evan read your articles and suggested coming, then I reminded him you and I were friends."

"Really?" I was glad Matt still considered me a friend.

"Your words inspire people just like these paintings do, Dorie." Matt chucked me on the shoulder. "Watching you chase this story is what finally got me off my ass and doing my movie. And, if I may be so bold, you need to go after what you want, not to mention turn down what you don't want, after all this is over."

"I'm so sorry if I hurt you, Matt." I felt tears well up in my eyes.

"No sweat." Matt automatically wiped my falling tears away with his thumb and then pulled back, awkward, and shoved his hands in his pockets. "It was my fault for choosing the absolute most inappropriate time to propose. Just when you were getting some clarity on where your life is headed, I tried to get to you to change direction." He sighed. "Just promise me that once you're sure what your vocation is, if you'll excuse the word choice, you won't waste years putting it off like I did."

I gulped. Deep down, I was already sure. "I promise."

As I spoke the words, the room's noise level rose and flashbulbs illuminated the gallery entrance.

Unable to see above the crowd, I ventured a guess. "Must be another celebrity coming in."

"One in the making, anyway." Matt's six-foot-three frame gave him a superior view. "I think your sister just arrived."

CHAPTER THIRTY-THREE

Craning my neck, I climbed a nearby set of stairs for a better look and saw what a modern-day picture of martyrdom might look like.

A clearly terrified Catherine, hands covering her ears, wore the same shocked expression she had when she first caught me taking pictures in the little studio. Instead of arrows, microphones were aimed at her chest while the glare of camera lights poured down on her shoulders like so much boiling oil. I leapt off the steps and rushed over as fast as the surging crowd would allow. Trish excused herself from a conversation with Evan and fell in step alongside me.

"Why didn't you tell Evan Cole about my Wagner?" I hissed.

"Because last week he would've offered half of what he'll offer after this show," Trish muttered without a trace of conscience.

"But that's not—"

"That's business, D. Get used to it," Trish said as we neared Catherine. "Besides, he won't miss any meals. Now let's get to the Wagner at hand."

I stood there, deflated, as Trish waylaid Catherine.

"Here's the woman of the hour." Trish put her hands on Catherine's shoulders for a photo op. "Let me introduce you to one of your biggest fans. Now where did he go?"

As Trish glided off with Catherine, I mouthed the words, "Are you okay?" to my twin. She tried to reply but got swept up in the crowd.

"The noise level in here is bad for the average person." Mother

Benedicta arrived beside me and put her hands over her own ears. "Take that and magnify it ten times and you might have an idea how jarring it sounds to someone accustomed to silence."

I watched, angry and numb, as a few yards away Trish presented Catherine to Evan like a trick pony.

"Catherine, I'd like you to meet *Evan Cole*," Trish said with such treacle that it dripped off her sycophant's tongue.

"Nice to meet you, Evan," Catherine said, polite but distant.

Catherine obviously had no idea who Evan was. Trish's head reared back in panic. How would a movie star react to someone not recognizing him? Would he be insulted?

He was delighted. In fact, he blushed.

"The honor is mine, Sister Catherine," Evan said with a small bow that wasn't so much theatrical as respectful. "I love the paintings."

Catherine grinned. I could tell she appreciated Evan not referring to the paintings as hers. He'd done his homework. Trish just looked bored and nudged the photographers toward the pair. The paparazzi snapped shots of the famous actor with the soon-to-be famous artist. Not far behind, more fans descended on my twin with a flood of superlatives.

"Fantastic."

"Inspired."

"Pure genius."

"A miracle."

Catherine nodded her thanks, but the tilt of her eyebrows suggested that she was having a hard time determining whether these people were serious. Her body stiffened as people shook her hand, hugged her, or kissed her on both cheeks. For someone who rarely encountered strangers, it must have been incredibly stressful. Sweat poured from Catherine's temples.

"Are you all right?" a concerned Evan asked her. "You look like you need some air."

"She's fine," Trish said and then yammered on. "I'm asking buyers to let me keep the show up for a few months so the public can see this important work." Trish pointed to the paintings like a flight attendant indicating exits. "All I can say is, thank God the cloister is in financial crisis. If it weren't for this year's mudslides wreaking havoc on the convent's facilities, this show never would have happened."

A man with pince-nez and an attitude to match agreed.

"Talk about good things coming out of bad situations," he said. "If this is what happens when it rains in Big Sur, I hope it floods."

Catherine stared at the man with an appalled expression. As the jostling crowd, unbearable noise, and thoughtless comments hit critical mass, she walked away from a mid-sentence Trish. Evan held two prying photographers back as my twin, bumping elbows and upsetting drinks, pushed through the throng in an attempt to escape. Catherine lost her footing in the clogs and tripped halfway to the back exit. Picking herself up, she yanked the fabric of her habit free from under someone's shoe with a rip and continued on. Finally she disappeared through a rear door. I did my best to follow.

Spilling a few drinks myself as I made my way through the mob to the back door, I couldn't help but pause when I noticed an auburn-haired young woman who looked captivated by the *Joan of Arc* painting. As she stood there gazing at the painting, I saw in her fascinated expression the same awe I'd felt when I first encountered the *Madonna and Child*. I wanted to stay and watch her, to reexperience Catherine's work for the first time through her eyes, but there wasn't time.

I found my sister in the tiny gallery bathroom, leaning over the toilet, throwing up.

"Dad used to puke at shows, too," she said between gags. "Even before he drank."

"Oh, Catherine." I locked the door behind me. "I'm so sorry."

She finished vomiting and turned to me with sweat pouring down her face and a wild look in her eyes. I grabbed some paper towels and mopped her brow. I held her veil back and away from her face, but the white wimple that covered her head, neck, and ears made it impossible for her skin to breathe.

"Screw it." I dropped the veil. "Let's get this off you."

Catherine didn't protest as I pulled out the three straight pins securing her veil. Next I unfastened the white wimple and slipped it off of her head to reveal her thick, brown hair cut mercifully short. Catherine closed her eyes in apparent relief as the air reached her, but she looked far from peaceful.

"Did you hear what they—"

"Forget them." I folded the veil and wimple in my hands the way I'd seen it done in the cloister laundry. "Sometimes people don't think about what they're saying."

"Is anything selling? Did this save the cloister?" She stood and cupped her hands to gulp water from the tap, swishing it around in her mouth and spitting it into the sink before sliding down the wall to sit on the floor again.

"I believe it did." I recalled the mesmerized young woman studying the *Joan of Arc* and hoped the show had saved a few souls as well. I checked outside the door. "Wait here while I see if Graciela can drive around back and sneak you out through the alley."

Catherine looked too tired to argue. Kicking off her shoes and resting her head on the wall, she smiled for the first time that night.

"My job is done," she murmured.

As I nodded reassuringly at my sister, weak and exposed as she huddled bareheaded and barefooted on the floor, I knew the task was far from over.

"Thanks for the ride," I said when Graciela dropped us off at my car a few minutes later. I was grateful the press hadn't noticed us. "Tell Trish I'll call her tomorrow from Big Sur."

"You're going back *esta noche*?" Graciela flicked cigarette ash onto the pavement outside her window. "Why tonight when you could stay in town and drive back in the morning?"

"Catherine is anxious to get home and share the good news." I looked to my pale but giddy sister, who nodded as she and the prioress climbed into my car.

"As am I," Mother Benedicta agreed with a grin that crinkled her eyes. "But only if you're not too tired to drive, Dorie."

"I'm fine," I reassured Mother. "I'm amped on adrenaline."

"How are you going to get your article done by deadline if you're driving?" Graciela asked.

"Oh, no." I smacked my forehead with my hand. "I completely forgot." I peered at Catherine curled up in the rear seat, already nodding off. "I'll call it in on the way up."

"Like that would be safe." Graciela didn't miss a beat. "Don't worry about it. I'll do it."

Even though I had initially suggested to Phil that Graciela write the second series, I paused before accepting her offer to pinch hit. The piece about Catherine's successful opening was arguably the most important one of them all and I wanted to be the one to write it. But Graciela was right. There was no way I could dictate a decent article and drive Mother and Catherine safely back to Big Sur at the same time. Could I hire them a driver?

I looked in on Catherine again, now asleep in the back seat and knew the answer. Being ferried home by a stranger would freak my twin out, and she'd been spooked enough for one day.

"That would be great," I said to Graciela. "Do you think Phil will be okay with—"

"*El jefe* will just have to deal." Graciela tossed her cigarette onto the pavement.

Crushing the cigarette under my shoe, I permitted myself a sigh of relief and then got into my car. "Thank you."

"You're welcome. Be careful driving." Graciela honked and drove off.

"May I borrow your cell phone?" Mother checked the time on the car clock. "I'd like to call Sister Teresa before Grand Silence begins in three minutes."

"Sure." I grabbed my phone, went to hit the speed dial button to the monastery and then paused and chuckled in disbelief.

"Is something wrong, Dorie?" the prioress asked.

"No. I just never thought I'd have a monastery on speed dial." I remembered my promise to Matt, took a deep breath and turned to Mother Benedicta. "And I never thought I'd ask this, but now is as good a time as any. May I have an application to become a sister at the cloister?"

"Of course."

"I can't guarantee I'll actually fill it out, so please don't expect—"

"I don't. Your vocation is between you and God. I'm just the secretary handling the paperwork."

"Thanks."

I sat there smiling and cradling the phone for several seconds before Mother spoke again.

"Can I make that call now?" she asked.

"Oh right. Sorry." I hit the monastery button and handed her the phone. "It's ringing."

"Sister Teresa?" Mother said into the mouthpiece. "We should be back around three-thirty...Very well...See you then."

After the prioress hung up, we practiced our own Grand Silence in the car. Anxious to forget the implications of what I'd just asked for, I spent the time reviewing the events of the gallery opening. The show was every bit the success, yet every bit the mistake I had thought it would be. The paintings had saved the cloister, but at what price? Was God happy with the outcome? It seemed to me that the cloister should be saved simply as a house of worship, not as a nice home for an artist making important contributions. If only it worked that way.

Then again, if others had been moved half as much as the young woman I'd seen responding to *Joan of Arc*, then perhaps the show served God's purpose on a level beyond my understanding.

At midnight, Catherine's internal clock roused her and she recited the first Divine Office of Vigils with the prioress. I followed along with their prayers as best I could while I drove. When they finished, Catherine went straight back to sleep and our Grand Silence resumed.

I pulled up to the monastery gate at 3:45 in the morning. As Sister Teresa opened the creaking gate, Mother Benedicta reached back and nudged Catherine awake. My sister rubbed her eyes and stirred.

Emerging from the car to the soothing hum of cicadas, I looked up to find the entire community assembled in the garden awaiting news. Respecting that Grand Silence was still in effect, the sisters didn't speak but looked to Mother for some sign of how the opening had gone. The prioress frowned and then smiled and gestured that they should ask the artist. Everyone turned to Catherine, who responded to their questioning expressions with thumbs up and happy tears in her eyes.

Tears welled up in my own eyes as I watched the community erupt in silent celebration. Sister Teresa hugged Catherine, Sister Scholastica broke into a tuneless jig, and Mother Benedicta and several others fell to their knees in gratitude. Even Penguin the cat leapt into the air to swat at the flower petals that Sister Dominica threw like confetti.

A few minutes later, the sisters went inside for another hour of sleep before they rose for Lauds. As I turned to walk to my guest quarters off the public courtyard, I saw the first news van labor up the bumpy cloister drive.

CHAPTER THIRTY-FOUR

By the time I helped Sister Teresa open the monastery gate to the public at 5:30 a.m., ten television vans lined the driveway. Dazed reporters, photographers, and cameramen who must have traveled straight from the gallery tumbled out and roamed the parking lot. More vultures than usual hovered overhead.

Enough rumpled journalists crowded into the pews of the public chapel to leave the regulars without seats for Lauds, Mass, and Terce. I stood in the back with the locals, who looked unsure of what to make of this sudden intrusion upon their home church. Despite Father Charles' pithy one-word sermon, "Behave," a murmur of discontent arose when Catherine failed to appear for the morning services. Several photographers stuck their lenses through the enclosure and took pictures of the sisters who *were* in attendance. None of the journalists left. They simply settled in to wait.

As the nuns filed out after Terce, Mother gestured to me from behind the chapel grille.

"It seems we've become quite popular," the prioress said once I'd made my way through the stuffy public sanctuary and met her at the grille. "Can you stay a few more days to help us handle the press?"

"I'm due back in the newsroom tomorrow, but I'm sure my editor will want continued coverage given these developments." I heard stomachs rumble amid the unshaven and unfed journalists camped out in the pews behind me. "I can arrange to stay another week or so."

"Excellent. I'll extend your access to the cloister. Meet me in the business office after breakfast." Mother closed the wooden shutters and disappeared behind them.

I downed a granola bar in my room and went to the office. There I found the prioress and Sister Dominica struggling to keep up with the faxes and emails pouring in while Sister Scholastica manned the telephone.

"*Time, Newsweek, The Atlantic Monthly* and *60 Minutes* all called requesting interviews," Sister Scholastica said as the phone trilled again. "Is Sister Catherine willing to talk to them?"

"I don't want to snub the media, but I don't want to overtax Catherine either." Mother Benedicta turned to me. "What do you advise, Dorie?"

"Tell them you'll organize a press conference for three o'clock tomorrow afternoon. That way, she can respond to all of them in one fell swoop. I'll write up a statement for her to read. Where is she?"

"Still napping." Mother yawned, her own lack of sleep catching up with her. "I excused her from morning offices so she could rest. And I suggested that she participate in afternoon prayers from the infirmary window until things die down a little."

The infirmary window was a small opening set high along the back wall of the altar, originally designed to hold spotlights in the chapel's prior incarnation as a theater. A sister too ill to leave her bed, or, in Catherine's case, too popular to appear in church without disrupting services, could hear the chanted prayers through this window connecting the second-level sickroom with the vaulted chapel.

"That makes sense," I agreed. "Give her a break from the media until the press conference anyway."

"Here's a fact sheet on the cloister that might help you write the press statement," Mother said as she pulled a document from a drawer and handed it to me without letting the other sisters see it.

"I'm not sure I really need..." I looked down at the document and realized that what the prioress had handed me wasn't a fact sheet, but a cloister application. "Oh."

"You don't have to use it." Mother winked. "Just take it in case you need it."

"Thanks." I reddened and shoved it into my pocket.

Clanging out of key with the ringing telephone, the second bell pealed for the Divine Office of Sext. Sister Scholastica stopped mid-reach for the receiver, rose, and exited the room. Dominica and Benedicta also dropped their tasks and left with no regard for the jangling phone. It was nice to see some things hadn't changed.

That afternoon, tourists began arriving in droves, their cars crunching up the already tenuous road. Those visitors who couldn't fit into the packed chapel wandered the grounds, startling the wildlife. When the parking lot was full, they left their vehicles in the middle of the driveway, resulting in an angry blaring of horns every time someone trying to leave discovered the blocked exit. So much for silence.

I walked out to the public courtyard and found Sister Teresa handing out water in paper cups to the people trampling her flowers. A line formed in the garden for the single accessible public bathroom. One teenager, unwilling to wait, relieved himself behind a tree.

"Please stay off Sister Teresa's flowers," I called out to no one in particular. A few people chose their next steps more carefully, but most ignored me.

"Not my flowers, never were." The extern's dismayed expression belied her cheerful tone. I saw her mouth droop when a middle-aged woman in neon pink shorts stepped on a hydrangea bush to peer through a first-floor window nearby. Teresa appeared to resign herself to the desecration and mustered a smile. "I'm just grateful I'll be here in a few weeks to replant them. Meantime, I can't keep up with the demand for water."

"Let me help you." I set out more cups on the extern's gardening bench.

"People are asking where the vending machines are, as if we had those. What should I tell them?"

"Tell them to go to hell," I muttered under my breath, forgetting that nuns accustomed to silence had very keen hearing.

"That's not a destination we particularly endorse," Teresa said.

I broke out into a loud guffaw in spite of myself.

Just before 7:30 Compline, Sister Teresa, the local sheriff, and I managed to wrangle the last of the reporters and tourists out of the parking lot and lock the gate. I was glad it was too dark to see the damage the crowd had done to the grounds.

I spent most of the night drafting a statement for Sister Catherine to read at the press conference the following day and then went to the studio at two a.m. to have my sister check it over. For the first time since I'd discovered her tiny workshop months before, Catherine wasn't there.

The next day, I again looked around anxiously for my twin. Aside from fleeting glimpses of a black veil through the infirmary window during the Divine Offices, I hadn't seen her since our return from the gallery opening and had no idea how she was handling the attention.

I finally found Catherine in her studio around two thirty in the afternoon. She looked more calm and refreshed than I'd ever seen her. Unlike the dark under-eye circles and sallow skin I now wore, her blue eyes were clear and her cheeks a healthy pink. She didn't stand at her easel painting as usual but sat in the broken office chair in apparent contemplation.

"I wanted to show you the press release in advance in case you'd like to make any changes." I handed her a sheet of paper. "It's up to you whether you want to take questions or not."

Catherine read through the page and nodded.

Within minutes, my sister, Mother Benedicta and I stood before a knot of microphones in the public courtyard. Catherine set my lengthy typed statement aside and spoke in her own words.

"I am pleased that the gallery show has been such a success," she said with the composure of a seasoned politico. "And thrilled that we sisters now have the financial means to stay in our home. I wish to take this opportunity to rededicate my paintings to God. I remain His humble servant. Thank you."

I stared at my sister, unable to fathom that this poised creature was the same woman who'd fled from the press like a spooked rabbit two days before.

"What are you working on now?" a reporter shouted out.

A flash of pain crossed Catherine's face before she said, "I have nothing further to add."

As my twin turned and reentered the cloister, the journalists latched onto me.

"What about you, Ms. McKenna?" someone asked. "Do you have anything to say?"

"I um, er..." I tried to form words and failed. "No."

As Mother Benedicta stepped up to the microphones to answer questions, I ran inside and caught up to Catherine just outside her studio.

"That was great!" I was breathless from effort. "You sounded like a—"

"Fraud." She stepped into her workshop and shut the door.

CHAPTER THIRTY-FIVE

The Monastery of the Blessed Mother had always hosted large crowds for midnight Mass on Christmas Eve, but with the holiday arriving shortly after the gallery opening, attendance shattered all records. Nevertheless, the sisters managed to keep the focus on the birth of Christ with a beautifully unaffected service.

The day after the holiday, the nuns returned to the recreation room for another business meeting and Mother gave me permission to attend.

"It's been almost two weeks since the gallery opening and the crowds are getting larger rather than smaller," Mother said to the assembled community. Catherine stood near the ping pong table with her chin tucked into her chest.

"Grateful as we are for the success of the show and for the increased interest in our monastery, we need to address the crowds," the prioress said. "What's the visitor situation, Sister Teresa?"

"There aren't many reporters coming anymore, but more and more tourists show up every day," the extern answered. "We don't have enough receptacles for all the trash piling up, and people are picking through the dumpsters we *do* have in search of paintings they think Sister Catherine might have thrown away. As for our lack of bathrooms, visitors with RVs are charging a fee for use of their on-board latrines. Those who don't want to wait in line for our single public toilet or pay a fee are relieving themselves in our gardens."

"Sister Scholastica, have we received sufficient gallery revenue to provide more facilities?" Mother inquired.

"More than enough. In addition to the paintings' proceeds, donations are pouring in from everywhere. The problem is, while we have the means, we no longer have the access." Scholastica pushed her round glasses up the bridge of her nose. "Our driveway was in poor condition before, but with all the recent traffic it's become barely passable. Until we clear the road and fix it, the construction trucks can't get up here to make urgent building repairs, much less construct extra bathrooms."

"What about the fire road?" Sister Carmella asked, her hands busy mending an altar cloth. "Didn't the delivery trucks use that when Highway One was closed?"

"Yes, but using the fire road adds four hours to the drive and the grades are too steep for the construction vehicles anyway," Sister Scholastica said. "But if we don't begin the building retrofits soon—"

"We won't be able to stay here during rainy season," Mother concluded. "Money or no."

"That's right." Sister Scholastica nodded. "The only way we can accomplish the repairs in time is by drastically limiting the number of visitors per day."

"But how?" Sister Teresa asked. "These folks are determined."

"We'll have to set up a reservation policy and hire a guard to enforce it," Scholastica replied.

I saw Catherine roll her eyes.

"We'll need two guards," Mother said. "One to monitor the gate and one to make sure visitors stick to the parking lot, the public courtyard, and the chapel. All the foot traffic on the grounds has done irreversible damage to the wildlife. We don't really have a choice, but I'll conduct a vote anyway. All in favor of establishing a visitor reservation policy and hiring guards for crowd control please raise your hands," Mother ordered.

After a pause, most of the sisters raised their hands.

"Good." Mother touched her cross. "In other news, I'm happy to report that we've had a major increase in vocation inquiries since all this began."

"How many of them are for real?" Carmella asked, completing a stitch.

"Probably about as many as usual—twenty percent or so. Which is fine, since we have room for only one or two more novices anyway. As you may have guessed, Dorie McKenna is among the interested candidates." The prioress smiled at me. "She's displayed both an aptitude and a desire for the life in these last months."

I blushed crimson as the sisters murmured their approval.

"That's all the business we have to discuss," the prioress concluded. "Enjoy the rest of recreation hour."

"So you're going to be a nun?" Catherine approached me after Mother had finished.

"I'm thinking about it. If I can pay off my debts, that is." I didn't tell her I planned to sell my Wagner. "I'm dreading going back to work at *The Comet* tomorrow, but I can't put it off any longer."

"You'll find your way back to the monastery. I'm just sorry I won't be here."

"What are you talking about?" I looked at her, alarmed.

"I have to go. The special treatment I get isn't fair to the other sisters, and the cloister is designed to focus on prayer, not tourists."

"No one is losing their focus," I argued.

"I am." Catherine looked at the floor. "Painting has always been my prayer. Ever since I agreed to do the show, I've lost my connection with God. Even the paintings reflect it."

"That's not true," I lied.

"Did you hear me at the press conference? I took credit for the canvases, called them *my* paintings. And in that moment, I believed it. I don't deserve to wear this habit or paint ever again."

"That's ridiculous," I said.

"Not to me. I'd leave tonight if I could, but I have to get dispensation from my perpetual vows."

"How long will that take?"

"A few weeks. Mother has to write to the Cardinal."

"I don't believe this." My voice rose and a few sisters turned to look. I lowered it to a whisper. "This is your home."

"I never really belonged here." Catherine watched the other sisters knitting, chatting, and playing cards. "It was just a break from not belonging anywhere. The only place I've ever been at home is on the canvas."

"And you don't even let that be permanent."

"I'm not sure I'm capable of permanence." Catherine shrugged. "I made my perpetual vows, but deep down I always knew I couldn't stay."

"Why not? Who's making you leave?"

"You, actually."

"Me?"

"Not you exactly, but the me I see reflected in your eyes."

I shook my head. "I'm not following."

"I can lie to myself, but not to my twin. I never looked for you because I knew you'd see who I really am and I wasn't ready to be that person."

"How could I possibly know who you really are?" I asked. "I don't even know who I am."

"You know enough. You know I'm a coward who broke a promise to our father by not looking you up and a fool who defies God by shunning the responsibilities of talent."

"I never said that!"

"Not in so many words. But you recognized that the paintings should be seen and I knew you were right. I also know fame can destroy me like it ruined Dad." Catherine sighed. "Even so, I have to go learn to face it."

"Why do you have to leave the cloister?" I asked. "You can be famous from here."

"I might if the old ways were still working, but they aren't. In order to become comfortable with people knowing who I am, I need to get to know myself first in ways that I can't from inside the cloister. Maybe being out among people will help diffuse the power the public has over me and help me reestablish my connection with God."

"But you're such a good nun."

"Am I? My relationship with God is grounded in painting, not piety. I strive for holiness, but obedience is an easy price to pay to paint undisturbed."

"It doesn't matter what the relationship is based on so long as it's a strong one," I argued. "I feel God's presence in your studio."

"I'm pretty sure it's you bringing God into that studio these days."

As the bell rang for Compline and Catherine exited with the other nuns, I realized I'd avoided contacting my twin for the same reasons she'd avoided meeting me.

CHAPTER THIRTY-SIX

When I entered the newsroom the following afternoon for the first time in over five months, I was met with applause from my coworkers and a bear hug from my boss.

"Surprise!" Phil yelled. "Congratulations on a great series, McKenna. And you didn't think there was a story there." He puffed up with pride.

I smiled, bewildered by this show of affection, as Phil popped a bottle of bargain basement champagne. The pink suds ran down the bottle and soaked his arm to the elbow before splattering on the floor. The industrial gray carpet was too threadbare to soak up the moisture. I watched the sticky liquid pool atop older stains already ground into permanence in the fibers.

"Here's to the most popular series in *Comet* history," he said.

Phil raised the foamy bottle and poured it into Graciela's waiting coffee cup. Nearby, Rod held out his mug with the kind of enthusiasm only a minor can summon for cheap alcohol.

"As a little token of appreciation for the attention your articles have brought to the paper, here's a bonus for your trouble." Phil reached into his pocket and pulled out a check.

I took it and raised my eyebrows at an amount that exceeded my annual salary. In the past I would have taken the money without a second's hesitation, but now I paused.

"What? Not enough?" Phil joked.

"Too much." I tried to hand it back. "Everybody else here works as hard or harder than I do and—"

"And everybody else here can thank you for healthy raises this year due to the skyrocketing subscription rate your articles generated." Phil pushed my hand back toward me.

I kept the check. Then Phil opened his mouth again.

"As the *coup de grace* to an outstanding, not to mention lucrative, series, let's all look forward to Dorie's article about her sister being banished in scandal." Phil took a long pull directly from the champagne bottle and immediately spit it out. "This is crap."

"Scandal?" I asked. "Please tell me you're joking."

"Heard about what a zoo it's become up there." He wiped his mouth with the back of his hand. "Rumor is it won't be long before they'll have to kick her out just to keep the peace. Right?"

I glared at him. "If she leaves, that won't be the reason."

"No? Then let's make up a better one. Your twin can take a little good-natured ribbing at this point." Phil scratched his chin and thought. "Maybe we could make her pregnant by that movie star who bought most of her stuff. What do you think?"

"I think I quit." I handed back the check. Phil took it this time.

"That's loyalty for you." The editor tossed the half-full champagne bottle into a nearby wastebasket while Rod eyed it with underage longing. "Just because the *Times* and *Chronicle* are knocking your door down doesn't mean you drop the paper that gave you your start to trade up."

"It's not like that at all." Among others, the *Los Angeles Times had* called a few days before, but at that point I would have left *The Comet* with no prospects.

"It's not?" Phil looked surprised. "Hell, that's what I'd do."

I'd already removed most of my personal things from the newsroom when I took my leave of absence. Now I collected the remainder from my desk—a favorite pen that leaked, my thesaurus with the ripped cover, and a chipped tea mug. I saw Graciela's chin tremble. I hugged her.

"I'll call you later," I said.

Graciela nodded. I hugged Rod next.

"Thanks to you I start a job at *Art World* next week," Rod said with a heartfelt squeeze.

"Thank my sister." I turned to go.

The entire newsroom broke into applause again as I left. I picked up my pace. The combination of admiration and jealousy I read in my coworkers' expressions made me uncomfortable, giving me some idea of how Catherine must have felt at the gallery opening and how Evan Cole must feel every day. I stifled the family urge to vomit.

Once outside, I wondered if I'd made a mistake in turning down the bonus money. If nothing else, I could've donated it to the convent. Just as I turned to go back inside and ask Phil for the check, my cell phone rang. It was Trish.

"Hello?"

"I just sold your Wagner to Evan Cole for two and a half million."

I didn't bother going back into the newsroom. I was too busy throwing up.

CHAPTER THIRTY-SEVEN

"So what now?" Sister Barbara kneaded air bubbles out of a lump of clay at the wedging table in her South Central pottery studio a couple of weeks later. A forgotten plastic holly wreath adorned the wall.

"That's the problem," I said. "I'm not sure. Here I am right where I always thought I wanted to be. I've got financial security, the respect of my professional community and a job interview with the *Los Angeles Times*, not to mention a marriage proposal."

"But it's not what you want any more, is it?"

"You know, I don't think it is. The more I get, the less I seem to need."

"Was it hard to part with your father's painting?" she asked.

"Yes and no. *Shift* introduced me to my birth family. But owning such a valuable thing always made me nervous. And now I've got all this money to deal with," I said. "Don't get me wrong, the money's wonderful. I paid off my debts, made a big donation to the convent, and still have a ton left. But wealth is stressful in its own way. When I see those nuns so content with living simply, it makes me wonder if I've been going after the wrong things. God, I must sound so ungrateful."

"Sounds to me like you've got your head on straight," Barbara said.

"Oh, I'm all talk. Entering the convent was easy, even fun, to think about when it wasn't a financial possibility, but now that I'm actually in a position to do it, it's—"

"Terrifying?"

"Yes. This is my whole life we're talking about."

"Not really." Sister Barbara popped a bubble in the clay. "It's a year. That's when you take first temporary vows, and it goes in stages from there. You don't make perpetual vows until you've been there three-and-a-half years, and even those you can get out of under certain circumstances."

"Like Catherine's." I picked up the blue pot I'd admired on my previous visit. "In a way that's a relief, but I don't want to go in with the plan of getting out. I just wish I could be sure I'm doing the right thing before I even try. What if I turn out to be a terrible nun?"

"Mother Teresa once said that God does not call us to be successful, only to be faithful." Sister Barbara pressed her palms into the clay, turned the lump over, and rotated it clockwise on itself.

"Speaking of being 'called,' I don't know that I ever have been," I said. "The nuns I've met said they experienced a direct invitation from God to serve the church. Did you?"

"Not exactly. I was unhappy with my life and needed to make a spiritual change. 'Call' or no 'call,' you'll never be sure about the decision. That's where trust comes in. Do you meet all the requirements?"

"Mother Benedicta said the sisters were seriously considering my vocation, so I must. I'm debt free thanks to the sale of the painting. I'm the right age and I've been celibate longer than I care to remember. How do you deal with the celibacy thing anyway?" I asked without thinking. "I'm sorry, I don't mean to be nosy."

"Everybody's curious about that." Sister Barbara laughed. "I don't really miss sex so much as I miss closeness with another person. Now I strive to achieve closeness with God through prayer. And staying single gives me a lot of freedom, but I have to be careful not to become self-absorbed. Parenthood teaches a kind of selflessness that I'll never achieve."

I felt a twinge in my gut at the thought of never having children.

Then I recalled how my birth mother fared in childbirth. I put the blue pot back on the shelf.

"Sister Cindy was a vocation director before she took over the soup kitchen. I think she has some materials in here somewhere." Barbara wiped her hands off on her jeans and rummaged through a dusty cardboard box in the corner.

"Here we are." The sister pulled out a dog-eared directory of religious communities. "Let's see—Monastery of the Blessed Mother. Okay." She found the page. "Requirements include a high school diploma and some work experience preferred, which you've got. You should be healthy, which you are. You should love God, the church, and all people, and attend Mass regularly."

"I try, and I am."

"Finally, you'll need the stamina for hard work and a strict schedule, not to mention a sense of humor in close quarters with all those people."

"It's pretty cozy. But so far I've managed on my visits."

"Then it sounds like you're a good candidate." The potter put the book back into the box. A cloud of dust puffed into the air as she closed the lid.

"I was afraid you would say that. I wish someone would tell me what to do so I don't have to decide for myself."

"When I was discerning, my spiritual advisor had me write a letter to God listing all my concerns and then write God's reply to me with my weak hand," Sister Barbara said. "The reply business seemed silly until I did it. I received insights on my vocation that I hadn't had before."

"Like what?"

"Like it was okay if God's will differed from my parents' expectations." The sister took the chunk of clay from her wedging table and sat down at the pottery wheel. "Before writing the letter I wasn't even aware that was an issue for me, especially since I was almost forty when I became a sister."

"It's definitely an issue for me, and my parents aren't even alive anymore."

"Maybe writing a letter to God will give you some clarity on that." Barbara spun the wheel and molded a chalice out of the clay.

"I'll try it."

I smiled, but Sister Barbara seemed to sense my skepticism. She stepped away from her work, pulled the small blue pot I liked back down from the shelf, and gave it to me.

"For you. Put all your concerns into this pot and ask God to handle them."

"Thank you." I touched the glaze's satiny finish. "It's lovely."

"God Bless you, Dorie. I'll keep you in my prayers."

"Thanks, Sister." I exited the studio clutching my pot and went home to change for the *Los Angeles Times* interview I didn't want to attend.

"Your work speaks for itself, Ms. McKenna." The *Times* Associate Features Editor fanned through a pile of my clips and chewed on the end of his Cross pen with the ferocity of a former smoker.

I reached to snap my rubber band in subconscious solidarity and then remembered I no longer wore one.

"If you can raise the bar like this at a tabloid, imagine what you could accomplish here," he said.

I liked this editor. In his tiny office cluttered with books and a wrinkled blazer hanging on the door handle, he seemed like the kind of boss I would enjoy working for.

"I had to pull some strings," the editor said. "But I'm pleased to be able to extend to you the best package I've ever negotiated for a young journalist."

He handed me an offer letter and then leaned back in his creaky, antique desk chair and waited for my reaction.

Just as I hesitated to try on Matt's engagement ring for fear that I'd never take it off, I dreaded reading the details of a job offer I might not be able to refuse. I took a cursory look at more zeroes than had ever graced one of my tax forms and closed my eyes for a long blink before answering.

"I'm flattered, but I can't accept it."

I handed the paper back to him. The pen fell out of his mouth.

"But you hardly read it." He perused the letter himself as if reading it for the first time. "This offer is beyond generous–"

"Yes, and I appreciate that, but I'm considering a career change." I stood up on wobbly legs and offered my hand. It wasn't every day that I turned down the job of a lifetime. "Thanks again, sir." It took all my effort to exit as he watched, dumbfounded.

I couldn't believe it either.

That night, I sat in bed considering the pros and cons of entering the cloister. The cons: loneliness, loss of freedom, no journalism, no sex, no husband, no children, no junk food, risk of burnout, all seemed to outweigh the pros: a life spent serving God, time for contemplation in a beautiful landscape, a close-knit community. Yet I found myself unable to decide. To my frustration, the cloister managed to be both the most practical and impractical life I could imagine. It attracted me but had I been "called" to become a nun?

I had no trouble writing a letter to God that included the list of pros and cons but couldn't bring myself to write God's reply. It felt too ridiculous. I tucked my letter into the pot Sister Barbara gave me, turned out the light, and tried to sleep.

Three hours later, I was still tossing and turning.

"All right, all right!" I flicked on the light sat up. "Pushy, aren't You?"

Pen poised, I stared at the blank page a moment before remembering to switch to my disabled hand. I secured the pen between my index and middle fingers, and with some leverage from my pinched right thumb, I managed to write "Dear Dorie" in a childlike scrawl. As I examined the jagged script, my mind wandered back through images of my biological family's paintings and came to rest on the one I had inherited and subsequently sold—my father's *Shift*.

I pictured the black, white, and gray circles of paint that floated up from a murky swath of ebony on that work of art. Lamenting that I would never see the image in person again, I suddenly realized I had seen it years *before* I encountered it on canvas. Those circles of paint suggested drops of water caught in the sunlight—not just bubbles at a first swim lesson or splashes from a lawn sprinkler, but drops of water emanating from a church fountain the day I experienced real joy for the first time.

I understood then that the rapture I'd experienced the morning after my eighteenth birthday came from a moment of true communion with God. I shivered. I may not have *seen* Him until I looked at Catherine's paintings that night in her studio, but I had *heard* God's call to spend my life in prayer then and there at the church fountain. At eighteen, the invitation had seemed too overwhelming. Rather than heed the call, I blocked it out and used the excuse of my mother's death to walk away from the church. At twenty-six, I didn't want to lose that mental image or the serenity it engendered ever again.

Stirring from my reverie, I looked down and saw that my disabled hand had written the perfectly legible words, "Say Yes."

I stopped, surprised and alarmed, but all the fear and anxiety I'd been carrying suddenly left me. Tired of fighting it, my whole body trembled with relief and I was filled with a sense of peace. Even my twisted hand relaxed a little. Tears ran down my face as I smiled and whispered, "Yes," and then laughed when I realized I'd yelled at God a moment before.

Sister Teresa would be so proud.

"Since when do people eat cactus?" My Aunt Martha eyed the menu at the Border Grill suspiciously.

"Since forever, I imagine." I placed my napkin on my lap and tried not to squirm. I'd had a few days to sit with my decision but was still nervous about telling my aunt.

"It's very good." The server tapped her pencil on her pad.

"Well, far be it from me to be left out. I'll have to try it." Martha handed the waitress the menu. "Course, I'll probably take one bite and leave the rest," she added the moment the waitress hustled off with our order.

"Fine with me." I grabbed a chip and dunked it into the tomatillo salsa. "I'm glad you came for a real visit so we don't have to rush through another airport layover."

"Amen to that." Martha eyed the arriving margaritas with anticipation.

I was also happy to be in the socially trendy, visually funky, and acoustically challenged nouveau-Mexican restaurant. I'd chosen the place in hopes that the overall din would drown out the sound of Martha's wailing and gnashing of teeth when she learned about my plans to become a nun. Even liberals had their limits.

"Of course I'm here." She squeezed the lime wedge into her drink. "I had to take my wildly successful niece out to celebrate her recent accomplishments! I'm very proud of you, Dorie."

"Don't be so sure." I clinked glassware with her.

"I hear a confession coming on." Martha set down her drink. "Spill it."

"For starters, I quit my job."

"Good for you." She patted me on the back. "You said yourself that *The Comet* was a rag. Do you need some help until you find something else?"

Martha rummaged through her rucksack and pulled out her checkbook.

"Not exactly," I said. "I sold *Shift*."

"What? Why?" she asked, returning her checkbook to her pack. "You loved that painting!"

"I still do," I said. "But owning something that valuable doesn't fit into my current plans."

"What plans are those? Will you look for another job right away or take it easy for a while?"

"I've checked out some jobs. I got an offer from the *Los Angeles Times*." I crunched a tortilla chip between my teeth. "And a couple of other nibbles."

"Have you accepted a position?"

"Sort of." I watched her stare at me with rapt anticipation. I took a long sip of my margarita for courage. "I've decided to enter the convent."

For once, Martha had nothing to say. She finished her drink in one gulp and hailed for another.

"Would you please say something?" I pleaded.

"I thought this might happen," she said.

Now I was speechless but only for a moment. "You did?"

"I've watched you moving in this direction for years. In fact, your father and I were surprised you left the church in the first place."

"But Mom—"

"Died on your birthday, yes. And it wasn't fair. But she wouldn't have wanted you to leave the church you love right when you needed it the most." Martha took my weak hand from across the table and held it between hers. "Look here, Dorie. I don't pretend to know if your parents are slaving away in hell, whistling Dixie in heaven, or simply fertilizing the cemetery grass. I do know they'd never want you to compromise your dreams in order to honor the dead. Do what you need to do. It's your life, not theirs, not your biological parents', not even your sister's. And religion is part of your story. Always has been and always will be, whether you choose to recognize it or not."

"You're right," I said.

"'Course I am. Connor and Hope may not have shared your beliefs, but they respected and admired your commitment to them and that they would support you now. And so do I." Martha sighed. "I wish I had that kind of faith in something."

Relieved, I reached over and hugged her, taking care not to stick myself on the arriving cactus salad. "Thank you."

Two hours later, I stood before my adoptive parents' graves. I didn't say anything, just dropped glassy tears onto their headstones and silently thanked them, too.

CHAPTER THIRTY-EIGHT

As promised, Mother Benedicta and the rest of the nuns approved my application to join their community. I spent the next month in a flurry of phone calls, cloister visits, and paperwork for both my new life and the life I was about to leave behind.

Catherine's circumstances changed as well. The Cardinal approved her dispensation request and released her from her vows. After eight-and-a-half years in the cloister, she was free to go.

Consequently, my visit to the monastery that rainy February afternoon had a dual purpose—to go over the final details of my approaching admission to the convent and to help Catherine move out.

I arrived at the sawhorses blocking the base of the monastery driveway and rolled down my window. I was a recognizable regular to the new security staff.

"Afternoon, Ms. McKenna." The clean-shaven young guard stepped out of the makeshift plywood kiosk and leaned down to face me.

"Hi, Michael. Looks like you're busy despite the weather."

The advance booking policy for visitors had been in place for weeks, but people without appointments still waited in their cars on the side of the highway behind me, hoping for a cancellation. A few hardy souls with umbrellas hiked up the sharp incline on foot. Reservations weren't required for pedestrians.

"Always busy," Michael said. Juicy raindrops spattered on the gatekeeper's clipboard as he checked my name off the reservation list and moved the sawhorses aside. "Enjoy your visit."

I chugged up the driveway, careful to avoid the black, red, and blue umbrellas of the hikers bobbing up the side of the road. Yellow police tape marked the edge, reminding pedestrians to stay off the wild grass and chaparral. Clods of dirt dropped by a construction truck melted on the patched asphalt.

I remembered the first time I'd arrived at the cloister in the rain a million years before, curious and terrified all at once. I wasn't curious anymore, but I was still terrified—this time for a whole new set of reasons.

I found Sister Teresa in the public courtyard taking advantage of a break between cloudbursts to repair a trampled flowerbed.

"There she is," the extern said when she saw me. "How's my favorite future nun?"

"Nervous. How's our favorite artist?" I asked.

"Sister Catherine's all right, considering." Sister Teresa wiped her hands on her garden smock and frowned. "We've got the tourist thing managed here, but I don't know what she'll do once she leaves. We can't protect her privacy anymore."

"With luck, the tourists won't know she's gone until long after I've snuck her past them." I'd brought a blanket in my car for just that purpose. "I made Trish promise to keep mum for at least a month so Catherine has time to adjust."

Another cloud crossed the sun and threatened more moisture. Teresa and I stepped under the covered walkway for shelter.

"We hate to see her go. She says she's leaving because of the tourists, but that's merely an excuse." Keys jingled as the extern removed her smock and set it on the gardening bench. "Catherine's hit a rough patch in her prayer life is all. Happens to everybody. I don't think one bout of spiritual dryness is reason enough to rush back out into the world."

"I'm not sure she's *ready* for the world," I said.

"Neither am I, but we can't force her to stay. I suppose it's in God's hands now." Teresa made the sign of the cross. "What about you? Ready for your interview?"

"Ready as I'll ever be," I said.

"Alrighty then."

A clap of thunder rumbled in the distance. The nun led me inside as the rain resumed.

Soon I sat before Mother Benedicta and Sister Scholastica in the parlor, far more apprehensive than I'd been in my *Los Angeles Times* interview.

"We know you so well that the personal interview is largely a formality," Mother Benedicta said. "So just relax and be yourself."

I nodded, though relaxing was the last thing I was capable of at the moment.

"Still, it's a necessary evil before you begin your religious formation as a nun, so we might as well get it out of the way before you spend time and money taking all the tests," the prioress added.

"Tests?" I sat up straight.

"Don't worry. You won't have to study." Mother's gray eyes crinkled. "We require candidates to undergo medical and dental exams as well as personality and intelligence tests. A psychologist will conduct a behavioral assessment and review your personal and educational background."

"Wow. I had no idea."

"Given that we live, pray, *and* work together, we have to be a little more thorough than your average potential employer," Scholastica explained. "The tests also give you a chance to examine your vocation decision from a different perspective."

"That makes sense."

"We had some real adventures with candidates before we implemented this screening process." Benedicta shook her head.

"We'll also need documentation of your citizenship, credit record, proof that you've been confirmed in the Catholic Church, et cetera." Sister Scholastica handed me a manila folder full of forms through the slats of the grille. "You have been confirmed, haven't you?"

"Yes." I took the folder. "In seventh grade."

"Good. That's one less hoop you'll have to jump through," Mother said. "I believe that does it for the technicalities. The real question on our minds is your reason for joining us."

I looked at the women, confused.

"We want to make sure you're not entering the convent out of some sense of guilt over Sister Catherine's pending departure." Sister Scholastica pushed her glasses up the bridge of her nose. "She's made her own decision to leave despite our best efforts to convince her to stay."

I nodded. "I understand that, but I still feel guilty since I was the one who made the public aware of her talent."

"If you hadn't introduced her art to the world, someone else would have." Mother Benedicta touched the cross around her neck.

"Very likely," Scholastica said.

"Despite what's happened, I can honestly say I'm here of my own volition and on my own terms," I said. "I'll admit that it was Catherine who drew me here at first, but as Mother pointed out, that could have just been God's way of calling me. I still love my sister and her paintings, but now I love this place, your way of life, and what you stand for, too. I do wish Catherine would stay. I can't imagine leaving such a beautiful place."

"It is beautiful here, but monastic life isn't easy," Mother said. "There are always new challenges—some big, like finances, others small, like construction. In order to keep our vow of seclusion, we've had to alter our schedule to avoid the workers making repairs inside the cloister. As for our finances, the proceeds from Catherine's paintings and the recent donations, yours among them, will enable us to stay in Big Sur indefinitely, thank God." Mother looked skyward and clasped her hands together.

"I'm glad. But I'd follow you wherever you go," I said.

"What about a husband and children?" Scholastica asked. "How do you feel about never getting married or becoming a mother?"

"Okay at this point," I said. "I'm not very good at romantic relationships. From the sisters I've spoken to, I understand that the real grief about never giving birth or having a family comes later, so I guess I'll have to deal with the issue then."

"That's true," Scholastica said. "And there's no way out of the pain but through it. Most sisters survive and remain here, strengthened by the struggle."

"Right now I'm more worried about missing the family and friends I already have," I said.

"Will the monthly Visiting Day be enough for you?" Mother looked worried.

"I think so." I hoped so.

"We understand that you sold your father's painting for quite a sum," Sister Scholastica said. "How will you handle material temptation? What's to stop you from walking out of here and enjoying your money?"

"Absolutely nothing," I said. "I don't know how I'll resist temptation until I'm faced with it, but I'm hoping God will help me out there. Besides, Mother got a glimpse of life in the fast lane at the gallery opening, and I'm sure she'll agree that it isn't all that."

"Indeed," Mother nodded. "The rich and famous are a noisy bunch." The prioress stood up. "Well, since we've covered most of the relevant issues in previous discussions with you over the past months, I think we can conclude this interview. Welcome to our community, Dorie."

"Thank you, Mother." I dried my sweaty palms on my skirt before I stood and shook their hands through the grille. "I'm honored."

"Oh, and regarding temptation, we recommend that you hold onto your home, car, and bank account for six months to a year after you've entered so you'll have something to go back to if you decide the cloister life isn't for you," the prioress said.

"So I've heard," I said as we exited. "I know someone who can make good use of them in the meantime."

An hour later, I went back to the parlor in search of Sister Teresa but found Mother Benedicta, Catherine, and Father Charles there instead. The priest handed some official-looking documents through the bars to the women on the cloistered side of the grille.

"Oh, I'm sorry." I backed out of the room. "I was looking for—"

"Can she stay?" Catherine asked. She wrung her hands and fidgeted.

"I don't see why not." The prioress pulled a small table from the corner, placed it near the grille and set the paperwork on it. "It's unusual to have a secular person witness these proceedings, but if it makes you more comfortable—"

Catherine nodded.

"Is that all right with you, Father Flash, I mean, Charles?" I turned beet red when I realized I'd used the nickname the nuns had given him.

"Fine by me, though I can't promise it'll be as speedy as my sermons," the priest reassured me with a relaxed smile. "Come on in, shut the door, and we'll get to it."

I closed the door and joined Father Charles on the public side of the grille.

"Those are your dispensation papers, Sister Catherine." The priest pointed to the documents as Mother organized them on the table. "Look them over carefully. Once you sign them, you are released from your religious vows. That means you will no longer be a nun or a member of this religious community. If you ever change your mind and want to return to religious life, you're free to reapply here or at any order you hope to join, but there's no guarantee you'll be accepted. Do you understand?"

Catherine nodded and looked at the ground.

"Canon law requires me to ask if you thoroughly examined your conscience and sought God's guidance with this decision," Father Charles said.

"I have," Catherine replied with a slight quiver in her voice.

"Okay. After you sign on the dotted line there, Mother and I will both sign as witnesses."

The priest passed a silver fountain pen through the grille. Catherine took the pen and signed with a shaky hand.

Frowning as she took the pen from my twin, Mother paused and gave Catherine a searching look.

Catherine looked Mother in the eye and nodded.

Mother sighed, added her own signature and then handed the pen and papers through the grille to Father Charles. The priest took them and signed.

"That'll do it." Father Charles folded the documents and put them in his jacket pocket. "I'll send this off to the archdiocese right away."

"Thank you," Catherine managed to say.

"Yes, thank you, Father," the prioress said.

We all stood avoiding each other's gaze until I couldn't stand it anymore.

"I brought you some clothes." I handed a Gap bag to Catherine through the grille bars. "I hope they fit."

Catherine took the bag and left the parlor. Mother Benedicta, Father Charles, and I waited in silence until my sister reappeared a few minutes later looking very young and boyish in a T-shirt and jeans. Without the habit, she was thinner than I'd realized and the clothes hung on her frame. A red kerchief covered her short hair. She carried the pair of sandals I'd bought her in one hand and her carefully folded habit in the other. As she handed the habit, her wedding band, and her rosary over to Mother, Catherine hesitated for the briefest moment. Benedicta smiled and put a hand on her shoulder.

"It's all right, Catherine." The prioress gently took the wedding ring and habit from the now-former nun but closed the rosary back into my sister's hand. "Keep the rosary to remind you of your time here. And I have something else for you."

Mother turned and removed Catherine's cleaned, pressed, yet paint-splattered habit from the chair behind her and held it out to the artist. "The laundry never did get the paint out of your spare, so you may have it as a keepsake if you like."

Catherine took the habit with a nod of thanks.

"I'll pack the car while you say goodbye." I was eager to escape the sad scene. "Where are your things?"

Catherine picked up a small gym bag from the floor and handed it to me through the grille.

"That's it?"

She shrugged.

"Well, I guess that's good considering how small my car is."

Catherine shook hands with Father Charles through the grille and then turned to leave.

"God bless you, Catherine," the priest called out.

Catherine mustered a small smile before exiting the parlor with the prioress.

After saying goodbye to the priest myself, I took the gym bag and waited for Catherine at the cloister door. When it opened, I saw all the sisters in the community assembled at the threshold to send my twin off. Catherine didn't look at them as she made her way toward me, but then she returned to the nuns and hugged every one of them.

"Keep an eye on the bread, the ovens run a little hot," she told Sister Dominica.

"Good luck with the ping pong," she said to Sister Carmella.

When Catherine hugged Teresa and Scholastica in turn, the extern shook with heavy sobs and Sister Scholastica had to clean her tiny glasses because her tears had fogged them up.

Catherine remained dry-eyed until she got to Mother Benedicta at the end of the line. Then the formerly silent nun again lost her words and wept.

"Oh, you dear child." The prioress hugged Catherine. Tears welled up in Mother Benedicta's eyes and this time she let them fall without wiping them away. "We will miss you and pray for you. Come back to see us any time."

A lump lodged in my throat as I watched Mother and my sister say goodbye.

Catherine slid into the sandals I'd bought her and stepped through the cloister door to the world outside. Aside from holding my arm for support, she carried herself with aplomb as we walked from the hallway into the public courtyard. We passed by the wandering visitors unnoticed, as no one expected to see the famous nun in secular clothes. Once we were in the car, she hid under a blanket in the back seat for good measure. I navigated past the tourists along the driveway and highway shoulders.

"My place is pretty small, but we'll only be sharing it for a couple of weeks, so we shouldn't drive each other *too* crazy," I said when Catherine emerged from beneath the blanket once we were well down the road. "I just wish you were going to be in the cloister with me."

"I wish you would stay out here with me." Catherine climbed into the front passenger seat and stared at the Pacific outside her window.

I smiled. Our relationship had come a long way since the days when Catherine had hesitated to *meet* me, much less trust me.

"You'll be fine, and so will I." I hoped I was right for both our sakes. "I'll do everything I can to help you get set up before I go. What will you do for money? I'd be happy to share the wealth."

"No, thanks," she said. "I should be okay. The community gave me a little and Trish said she's got someone who wants to commission a painting. But I've never handled my own finances."

"We'll work out a budget for you. Can you drive?"

Catherine shook her head.

"You should learn. Public transportation is lousy, but you'll have the use of my car. As far as my rent-controlled apartment goes, we'll have to..." I stopped when I noticed Catherine's eyes glaze over. "Are you sure about this?"

"I'm sure." She seemed resolute. "If part of me hadn't wanted to do the show to begin with, I never would've agreed to it, and if part of me wasn't ready to leave the convent, I'd still be there. Given that I lost my connection to God while inside the cloister walls, I have to believe that He's calling me to search for Him elsewhere, at least for now."

"If you don't belong in the convent, then neither do I," I said. "I didn't seek out a vocation. I came looking for you and found God along the way. At least I hope I did, or I'm making a huge mistake."

"It's not a mistake." Catherine shook her head. "At least my devotion to painting helped bring you to your vocation."

"And my lust for professional recognition drove you away from yours." I didn't want to believe that my vocation came at a cost to Catherine, but it was hard not to.

"Maybe we were meant to have each other's lives and were holding places for each other in the world," she said.

CHAPTER THIRTY-NINE

There were no paparazzi awaiting us when Catherine and I arrived in Venice that evening.

"Looks like your departure hasn't leaked to the press," I said, parking the car outside my apartment. "Let's hope it stays that way."

Catherine nodded and exited the car. She bypassed my front door and headed straight for the rock totems and cairns on the beach, apparently as fascinated by them as I'd always been.

"I love these," she said, admiring them. The sun was setting behind the mountains, framing my sister and the totems in golden light.

"Aren't they cool?" I asked, catching up. "The wind blows them down most nights, and every morning, people come by and build them back up."

"The ultimate in temporary art," Catherine said. She had already begun building one of her own. Unlike me—whose impatience and grand plans often made building totems a frustrating, toppling business—my sister's artistic, steady hand soon built an elegant tower of stone. Sisyphus would have approved.

"For you," she said, gesturing toward her creation. "Happy Birthday."

"Oh, my God." I sat down next to a cairn. "It is, isn't it?"

Catherine nodded and seated herself beside me, burrowing her feet into the sand. "I don't usually celebrate."

"Me neither. In fact, I try to block it out." It was comforting to talk with someone who shared at least part of my birthday losses. "I wonder what our mother was like. Have you seen any pictures of her?"

"No. Dad found it too painful to keep any around, but he said she looked like me, I mean, us, freckles and all. And that she snorted when she laughed in a really endearing way that totally horrified her. Oh, and he said she was brilliant. More talented at writing than he was at painting."

"Have you ever read her poetry?"

"No." Catherine shook her head. "But I lost two teeth trying."

I looked at her askance.

"Dad told me he'd boxed it all up along with the pictures and gotten rid of it after she died," she said. "I didn't want to believe him, so I spent years looking for it around the house. When I was about eleven, I saw a couple of boxes up in the rafters of his studio and was convinced I'd hit the jackpot. I got up on a ladder and fell trying to carry them down, knocking out my teeth. Stupid boxes had old eight track tapes in them."

"That's horrible," I said.

"I survived. Flaws are interesting, so I liked the gap, but Mother Benedicta decided the cloister should spring for a bridge last year." She pointed to her left canine and the adjoining bicuspid. "It does make it easier to chew, but it doesn't bring me any closer to finding Mom's poetry."

"I would've loved to have read it," I said.

"Me, too. I'm still convinced it's out there somewhere. I wish I could have known her." Catherine turned to me. "I'm jealous that you got to grow up with a mom. Dad sometimes had girlfriends, but I didn't let myself get close to them because they were never around for long. What was it like?"

I paused, taken aback. It hadn't occurred to me that the twin our father kept might be jealous of my adoption. I was suddenly very grateful for both of my parents.

"It was...safe," I said. "We were very different and fought all the time, especially when I was a teenager. But that's to be expected. Puberty sucks."

Catherine nodded.

"Try having your famous father buy your first feminine products for you," she said. "Two different women recognized him while we stood there, clueless, in the tampon aisle. He ended up asking one of them for advice. I wanted to crawl under the display shelf."

"No thanks." I laughed. "But as much as we sometimes struggled to get along, my mom was always there for me. Whenever we hugged, all this love came gushing out of her and went straight into me."

"Sounds amazing."

"It was." I nodded. "I wish I had told her I loved her more often. She died on my, I mean our, birthday too. Our eighteenth."

"No way. That's awful."

"Yep." I stood up, jiggling my car keys and willing myself not to cry. "C'mon. It's time we had ourselves a party."

It was dark by the time Catherine and I sat eating a King Sooper's birthday cake directly from the box on the well-worn grass beside Lucy and Rene Wagner's graves. Paint brushes and flowers left by admirers leaned against Rene's simple headstone. Our father's fame made the spot a bit of a tourist attraction, but we were the only ones there at that late hour.

Catherine glanced around the cemetery. "This is my first time back since Dad's funeral. I looked for you at the memorial service. I knew he hadn't told you about us, but I thought maybe you'd figured it out on your own."

"No, but it's possible all three of us were here for her funeral," I said, pointing to our mother's headstone. "He didn't place me for adoption until we were six weeks old."

"Sounds likely, then." Catherine laid her palm on the grass over our mother's grave. "I feel like I have to make something of my life, since she lost hers."

"Me, too." I caught myself shrugging off a shiver and consciously sat up straight instead. "But you know what? I bet all she'd really want is for us to do something that makes us happy."

"Well, if that's the case, I'd say we're doing all right," Catherine concluded. "Even if we're screwing up, nobody can say we didn't try."

I took some of the flowers decorating our father's memorial, placed them before our mother's unadorned one, and hoped Catherine was right.

"What was he like?" I asked, picking up a paintbrush and brushing the grass with it. "I always wished for a birthday card from him even though I knew I would never get one."

"He was the classic, tortured artist, but he did his best," Catherine said as she licked frosting off of her plastic fork. "For the first few years we lived in his studio and ate a lot of beans."

"Wow," I said. "The estate lawyer mentioned that he was struggling back then, but I always tend to think of him as rich and famous."

"Not at first, but we managed. He was doing what he loved and we were happy. There wasn't money for extras so, on special occasions, Dad would draw chalk art advertisements for shops in exchange for a birthday cake or a Christmas dress for me. Then when I was about six, his career started taking off. We were still happy and he was still doing his thing, only now we had more than enough. Somewhere in there he started relying on the money and acclaim to make him happy. That worked fine until some of his new paintings were poorly received, and then he... Well, you know the rest."

She set down her fork, wrapped her arms around her knees, and looked away. Unsure of what to say or do, I put a tentative hand on her shoulder and looked at the ground.

"I'm sorry," I managed.

"It's okay. I got through it. He talked about you constantly at the end."

My head snapped up. "He did?"

Catherine nodded. "He didn't tell me about you until a week before he died, but he told me everything he knew, and he knew a lot."

I was shocked.

"Like what?" I asked as every neuron in my body shorted out. Tendrils of nervous energy emanated from my fingertips. What did he know? How did he learn it?

"He knew you were an honor student at Calabasas High and wrote for the school newspaper. He told me all about your hand. He said that despite the doctor's prognosis when you were a baby, it had never gotten better."

"So he must've seen me at some point." I flushed, feeling exhilarated and exposed at the same time.

"We both did."

"Really?"

"Uh huh," Catherine said. "But I didn't know who you were. Every spring, we had lunch on Saturdays at the park across the street from your house. Once in a while, you and your parents would be outside doing yard work."

"Man, I hated gardening." I laughed, marveling as the memories of those dreaded Saturdays rewrote themselves with the knowledge that my birth family sat just a few yards away. "That was my least favorite chore."

"It looked pretty good to me. The part about you having two parents, not the yard work," Catherine said. "Anyway, Dad would just sit and stare. Sometimes he'd mutter, 'She's better off without me.' I figured your mom was a long-lost girlfriend or something. I didn't know he was referring to you until he told me when he was dying that I had a twin with a disfigured hand. Then all those Saturdays when we drove miles to picnic at your park made sense."

"I had no idea. And he never introduced himself, which I gotta say is kinda creepy." Anger pursed my lips. "He could have saved me a lot of wondering if he had."

"I think he was afraid." Catherine plucked three blades of grass and braided them together. "Afraid of how all of us would react, including your parents."

"I would have been scared, too, considering," I admitted. "Technically, he wasn't supposed to contact me. My parents said I could look for him if I wanted to, but I thought it would hurt their feelings if I actually did."

"He was worried about that also, especially since he didn't know if they'd told you that you were adopted. Not all parents told their kids back then and he said he didn't want to flip anybody out."

"Oh my God." I dropped the paintbrush as my hand went to my mouth. "That never occurred to me. My parents told me I was adopted as soon as I was old enough to understand, but how could he have known that? No wonder he stayed away."

In that instant, all my anger and confusion about my adoption disappeared. I inhaled an expanse of air and let it out slowly through my mouth, breathing deeply for what felt like the first time. As my lungs relaxed, I felt a clean, open space under my rib cage that had never been there before. The mythic figure I had made my birth father out to be was replaced by a fallible human being worthy of compassion. He had loved me when I was born and continued to love me after he'd let me go—that was clear now. Because he loved me, he did what he thought was best for me regardless of his own feelings. Because he loved me, I could, in that moment, finally love myself.

The open space under my ribs extended to the rest of my body and into the air beyond. I chuckled, reveling in my new freedom to think, do, and feel without this central question informing my every thought and action without me even being aware of it. Until that moment, I had achieved an approximation of living, but now I could quit faking it and simply exist. My chuckle morphed into a full-blown laugh that left me shaking with relief.

Catherine tipped her head and looked at me. "What's so funny?"

"Nothing," I said. "I'm just glad to be here."

CHAPTER FORTY

For the next few days, my sister and I prepared to switch places. I took personality tests and got measured for my postulant uniform; Catherine studied for her driver's license exam and tried on new clothes at the mall. I closed my checking account as she opened one.

"What do you eat?" Catherine asked one night as she rooted around in my nearly empty refrigerator and bare freezer. "I'd like to cook something for us, but there's nothing in here."

"I live on take-out. I'd buy frozen entrees, but my freezer doesn't work." I waved a pile of delivery menus from the table where I sat at my laptop transferring my utility and phone bills into Catherine's name. "It's so weird writing your name as Candace instead of Sister Catherine."

"You can still call me Catherine if it's easier."

"Definitely easier," I said as I deleted another spot on the transfer form where I'd typed "Catherine" and then replaced it with her given name. "Are you okay taking over these bills? I don't mind helping you out with them while you're first starting out."

"No, thanks." Turning her attention to the cabinets, Catherine located a dusty box of cereal and pitched it into the trashcan. "I need to learn how to take care of myself."

"Are you sure?"

"Are you? You're walking away from a lot of menus here."

"No, I'm not sure. But I'm going to do it anyway." I signed my name on another form. "Because knowing what I know now, I can't go on living the way I used to, even if I don't have a true calling."

"Trust me, you do," Catherine said. "If it weren't real, you wouldn't have been fighting it for so long."

"Who says I've been fighting it?" I asked.

"Your apartment, for starters." Catherine gestured toward my food-free kitchen and my simple living space. "You're already living like a nun. It's not lack of decorating savvy that keeps this place so plain, or that guy Matt's workaholism that's kept you from a romantic relationship, or even a tough economy that's kept your career stalled until now."

"Oh, no?" I was both annoyed and intrigued by her pat assessment.

"No. It's you and your epic struggle with the Man Upstairs." Catherine looked around. "You must be exhausted. Good thing you finally answered the call so you can get some rest."

"Amen, Sister," I said.

Two weeks later, Matt heaved my duffel bag into his Jeep.

"The nuns claim I won't need most of this stuff, but I don't buy it." I pointed to my bag.

"You won't be buying much of anything on your new salary," Matt joked.

"Am I an idiot?" I wondered aloud.

"Some would say yes." Matt wedged my duffel among the basketball, hockey sticks, and other sports equipment crowding his car. "Given that you've chosen poverty at a cloister over six figures from the *Los Angeles Times.*"

"What do you think?" I asked.

"I think you're crazy." He slammed the back door shut. "In an inspiring sort of way."

"Thanks, I guess." I rolled my eyes and grinned.

"You're welcome." Matt looked away. "Not sure how I'm going to live without you, Dorie."

"Same here." I hugged him. "You'd better come to visit."

"Absolutely." He seemed to have trouble letting go of me. "And don't worry about my new neighbor. I'll watch out for her."

"Would you?" I was relieved. The easy rapport Matt and Catherine had enjoyed since they'd met two weeks before made them fast friends, and Catherine needed friends. "She left on a walk about an hour ago without saying goodbye. I wish she'd come back to the cloister with me, but I can't tell her what to do."

"She'll be fine as soon as she learns how to parallel park. Is anybody coming to see you off?"

I shook my head. "I told them to come visit me in a couple of months instead. Seeing everyone would be too hard right now."

"Then do you want to get going?"

"I guess so." I climbed into the car and took a good long look at my crumbling building.

As Matt turned to back out of the driveway, Trish drove up and blocked him in with her Range Rover. Trish, Rod, Graciela, and her daughter, Sophie, piled out of the vehicle while Catherine emerged from Matt's apartment with a lopsided cake.

"You didn't think you were going to get away clean, did you?" Matt asked.

"Drink up." Rod, who had recently turned twenty-one, proudly wielded tequila and limes. "After this it's just communion wine for you, Missy."

"I can't believe you're doing this." Trish downed a shot. "I really thought you'd change your mind at the last minute."

"It's still not too late!" Matt looked wistful, but resigned, as he winked at me.

"We put together a little collection at the paper and came up with this donation for the cloister." Graciela handed me a check. "Make sure we get some quality prayers for our money."

"Phil needs all the help he can get," Rod said.

"So do my dessert skills." Catherine presented me with the tilting cake. "We didn't bake many sweets at the cloister."

"Stick to painting, honey," Trish said. "We'll both be happier."

"Speak for yourself." Graciela sampled the icing and gave a taste to her daughter.

I didn't say anything. I stood crying and smiling at the same time.

Temples aching from the tears, I closed my eyes and rested my head against the seat for the drive up to Big Sur. After what seemed like only a blink, Matt gently shook me awake.

"Is that it?" Matt glanced between his directions and a spot up the hill from the highway.

I roused myself, looked, and nodded.

"Oh, man." Matt stared as much as the winding road would allow. "It's gorgeous."

Wearing its garland of flowers, the cloister rested on the rugged cliff overlooking a sparkling blue-green Pacific bejeweled by the midday sun. In that one glance, all of my doubts disappeared and I knew I was home.

The sawhorses and the guard were gone from the monastery driveway. The news of Catherine's departure wasn't public knowledge yet, but the crowds had thinned to a manageable level on their own. A few tourists wandered around as Matt parked at the top of the hill. I was barely out of the Jeep before Sister Teresa was there to hug and greet me.

"Welcome, Dorie! Welcome Home!" The extern watched Matt get

my bag out of the back. "And who's this strapping, young candidate for the priesthood?"

"Hardly." Matt grinned. "I'm just the chauffeur."

"Sister Teresa, this is my friend, Matt."

"Pleased to meet you, Ma'am." Matt offered his hand to Teresa. "Take good care of my girl, here."

"Don't you worry about that," Teresa said. "The Lord takes care of all of us, including you."

Matt blushed. I jumped when something warm and furry wound around my legs. I looked down to find Penguin the cat oozing affection for me.

"And here's our president of the Welcome Wagon." The nun tipped her head toward the feline.

"I didn't think she liked me." I picked up Penguin and scratched her behind the ears. "She usually glares and switches her tail at me."

"Oh, she was just hazing you," Teresa said. "She does that to all the new recruits."

Given the way the cat purred in my arms, I believed it.

CHAPTER FORTY-ONE

My first six months in the cloister passed in a blur. Other than visits from friends and my Aunt Martha, I don't remember words or events, just feelings. Good, strong, happy ones. God lived here, that I knew, whether I was watching the sunset over the ocean or appreciating the beautiful spareness of my postulant's cell.

I found the theological coursework challenging, the disciplined work routine invigorating, the call to constant prayer inspiring. There were periods of intense doubt and extreme loneliness, but then I remembered that I had experienced those same feelings in the outside world as well. There were times when it seemed too easy and times when it was impossibly hard. I wondered if I was running away from life or simply taking a new approach as I learned to live for myself and my God rather than constantly striving for affection or achievements.

I fell in love. Not with a man but with God and prayer. My prayers felt trivial some days, leading to fear that they would always seem that way, only to have the same words be rapturous and fulfilling the next day.

As I swabbed the hallway tiles one morning, my shoulders aching from the weight of the industrial-sized mop and my hands chapped from the harsh detergents, I realized that I was happier than I'd ever been.

September's Visiting Sunday fell a week before I was scheduled to receive my new name and the habit of a novice. Trish and Graciela met me in the parlor with decadent care packages I had to refuse.

"Can't blame a girl for trying." Trish tucked the bottle of Grey Goose vodka back into her bag.

"I guess I won't bother to offer you these then." Graciela displayed a stack of gossip magazines, cigarettes, and Twinkies.

"I'm sorry." I laughed from the cloistered side of the parlor grille. "I appreciate the thought, but vodka and cigarettes don't have a place in here, and they're not exactly appropriate resale items for the gift shop."

"No problema," Graciela assured me. "We made a point to bring stuff we liked in case we were *forced* to keep it ourselves."

"Funny, Matt and my aunt did the same thing with the gifts they brought last month. Oh hey, did you know that Matt's short got into Sundance?"

"I heard it's pretty good." Trish nodded.

"You heard right," Graciela confirmed. "It's *fabuloso*."

"I'm glad. He deserves it." I turned to Trish. "What about you? Are you still looking for a gallery to buy?"

"I closed on a space at Bergamot Station last month," she said.

"That's great!" I said. "Congratulations."

"Thanks," Trish replied. "It sat empty for so long that they finally came down to a price I could afford. You've seen it—it's the one I rented for Catherine's show. I'll have to renovate it, but the location is perfect."

"How is Catherine?" I asked. "I've been writing to her but haven't heard back and she hasn't come to visit."

"She's okay," Trish said.

Trish, who now served as Catherine's manager, had told me on prior visits that when the press found out Catherine had left the cloister, she was big news again. At first it had been so disruptive to the neighbors that Trish thought Catherine might have to move somewhere less accessible. But the hoopla had died down fairly quickly when Catherine figured out how to elude the news vans and continued to decline interview requests.

"I got PBS interested in giving her an art show of her own a few weeks ago," Trish continued.

"Really? That's amazing!" I said, continually impressed by Trish's powers of persuasion.

"Yeah, it would have been. But she bombed the screen test, so we can forget about tie-ins," Trish concluded.

"But how is *she* doing?" I wanted to know.

Graciela and Trish looked at each other.

"Not very well, I think," Graciela admitted. "Matt and I check on her as often as we can, but we're both so busy that—"

"She's your typical, reclusive artist," Trish interrupted. "Which would be fine if she were a productive one. Then the work could speak for her. But right now she's not producing much, and the fact that she's no longer a nun means that she's no different from the dozens of other non-productive, reclusive artists in town. I've been letting her use the gallery as a studio until I get the money together to renovate the space, but she's rarely there."

"So she's not painting?" I asked.

"Nothing she's willing to finish or let me sell. The gallery is full of half-done canvasses." Trish took off her glasses and ran a hand through her red curls. "She says she tries and it's no good. Not that it has to be. I could sell her stuff on name alone, but she won't have it. I've had to turn down clients who want to commission work because I can't guarantee Catherine will produce any."

"I tried to convince her to come here with us today, but she declined." Graciela ignored Trish. "I'm worried about her, Dorie."

I was worried too.

That evening, I took a long walk on the property. The fog rolled in, largely obscuring the ocean views, but leaving what water was still visible a bright aquamarine close to shore and dark navy farther out. I could no longer see the waves crash against the rocks, but I could hear them from my spot 1300 feet above the shoreline. A bluebird danced across my path and I spied one of my favorite hummingbirds busy among the tea roses. I wished Catherine were there to enjoy it with me, wished I could see her and judge for myself how she was coping.

I didn't have to wait long. As I walked back to the convent, my Jetta struggled up the driveway with my sister behind the wheel.

Since meeting visitors on the grounds was against cloister rules, I rushed into the parlor and waited. Catherine soon entered on the public side wearing a backwards baseball cap.

"Nice hat." I hugged her through the grille.

"It's yours." Catherine turned it around to reveal the *LA Dodgers* logo on the front. "I'm not about to start doing my hair now."

"I definitely don't miss that." My own hair was tucked under my postulant's veil. I felt the fabric of my blue jumper. "Though I'm finding that polyester doesn't breathe very well."

"The novice habits are cotton," she said.

"Good." I fanned myself with my strong hand. "I'll look forward to that."

"I'm sorry I didn't visit sooner," Catherine said. "This has all been a lot to get used to."

"No problem. I'm just glad to see you now."

"I've never been on the visitor side of this room before." She took a seat and looked around. "Weird."

"For me, also. If anyone had told me two years ago that I'd be joining a convent, I would have laughed."

"How's it going?" Catherine asked.

"Great," I said, sitting down myself. "Everything about it feels right.

I went to confession for the first time since college, and even *that* went okay. Father Flash went easy on me."

"He's a softy." My sister smiled.

"I'm writing more than ever. Nothing for publication, just personal stuff. When I shut up and listen, God tells me what to put down on the page."

"I'm not surprised."

"And with all this manual labor my arthritis is getting better rather than worse." I wiggled the functioning fingers on my weak hand. "Go figure."

"Oh, I figured," Catherine said. "You look radiant."

"Isn't it wacky?" I touched my flushed cheek. "How is it that a former tabloid writer like me can feel so comfortable in a convent?"

"That's easy. You belong here."

I nodded as Catherine's words settled into the core of my being and made themselves at home.

"How's it going for you?" I was almost afraid to ask.

"All right. I'd forgotten how many people there are in the world." Catherine kicked off her sandals and touched the hardwood with her bare feet. "It's all so noisy and strange. No offense, but I wish the media didn't exist."

"None taken. After seeing how the press treated you, I don't like them much anymore either. A couple of journalists showed up here when they found out I'd entered the convent, but Mother turned them away."

"I can't believe how nosy they get in interviews. They act like they know me. Someone actually asked me if I was a virgin."

"I'm sure they did." I folded my arms, annoyed with my former profession.

"Or they'll want my opinion on political issues I know nothing about. Shouldn't they go to experts for that?"

"Unfortunately, a lot of people would rather know what celebrities think than what the experts say."

"Even when they ask questions about the paintings, which I should know the answers to, I'm tongue-tied." Catherine pulled off her cap and fiddled with the brim. "I hold the brush, God paints, what else is there to say?"

I bristled on my sister's behalf. "You can turn them down."

"I tried that," she said. "They just made up stuff about me."

"I guess not talking only works as a survival tactic in here, where a vow of silence makes you sympathetic. Out there, it makes you a target."

"I wouldn't mind interviews if I were better at them. I have the time to give them now that I'm not painting."

"So you're not painting at all?" My eyes widened. "Trish said you weren't doing much, but I hoped maybe you were painting without telling her."

"There's nothing to tell since I started speaking again. The more I say out loud, the less I have to say on the canvas." Catherine paused and looked out the window. "Not that I haven't tried. I've got a pile of lousy, unfinished paintings to prove it. I did my best to make the process a silent conversation between God and me the way I used to, but there are too many other voices now. I end up not being able to paint—which means I'm not able to pray."

"Your whole life is a prayer. You're an inspiration to the other sisters."

"Maybe the paintings were." Catherine chewed on her lip. "I've lost my connection with God."

I didn't know what to say. My twin's art had saved the cloister, but if that was God's will, why did He turn His back on the artist once she'd done her duty?

We sat in silence for several minutes.

"Are you doing okay with your finances?" I finally asked.

"Sort of." She looked down at the cap in her hands. "Not really. I got a job as a prep cook at a diner, but I couldn't handle all the swearing on the line."

"I wish you would let me help you," I said. "I need to give away my money before I take the vow of poverty. I'd love to set up an account for you."

"No, thanks," Catherine said. "I want to make it on my own."

"I know a sister who might be able to find you a suitable job." I thought of Sister Barbara in South Central. "I'll give you her number. Better yet, have you considered coming back here now that the excitement has died down? We've kept your studio intact and all the sisters miss you."

"I miss them too, but I can't come back." Catherine put the ball cap back on. "I was never much of a nun. I was just a painter who found a good setup."

"Oh, please." My voice rose. "You have the strongest spiritual connection I've ever witnessed. Sitting in your studio while you worked was a transforming experience for me. I wish I could express myself in images."

"And I wish I could express myself in words. It would give me a new way to pray now that I can't paint." Catherine paused before she spoke again. "I feel as if painting has taken me as far as it can for now, but you sound like your best writing is just beginning."

I shifted uncomfortably. Was what I'd gained worth what Catherine had lost?

"It's not a trade-off," I insisted. "God doesn't work that way."

"It's as it should be." The artist put the ball cap back on. "I'm full of desires now. That's why I had to go."

"You're being too critical of yourself."

"I don't know how to be any other way." Catherine nudged her sandal around on the floor with her bare foot. "It's time to lose my ego and open myself up to God again."

"How will you do that?" I asked.

"I'm going to quit trying so hard. I left the cloister intending to get to know the audience for the artwork, but instead I hid out and attempted to create my own little cloisters inside your apartment and Trish's gallery. The more I sought inspiration in solitude, the more elusive it became."

"There's grace in the struggle too, you know," I said.

"Oh, I'm not ashamed of my efforts. I did my best, but it's time for a different approach. Every minute of my life was preplanned inside the cloister, but now that I'm out, I have to embrace the unknown, scary as that may be. I need to offer up those uninspired paintings to God as a symbol of my struggles and my willingness to put Him first again. Then I can move on without any expectations of myself or my Creator and see what happens. If moving on means giving up painting for a while as I learn to interact with people and see how I can be of service in the world, then I'll give up painting for a while."

As I heard the unmistakable ring of hope, not to mention the relief of surrender, in my sister's voice, I realized that God had never left Catherine. He'd just changed course, opening up new paths for her to choose from. I wondered what road a mystic would take.

"My clothing ceremony is next week," I said. "Will you come?" I wanted reassurance that I'd see Catherine again soon.

"Yeah, sure." Catherine blinked and looked away. Her twitchy body language belied her casual response. I knew she wouldn't attend the ceremony but decided not to push it.

"I'm supposed to make a private retreat of silent prayer and meditation this week in preparation for it," I said.

"Do me a favor?" Catherine slipped her sandals back on. "Pray for me?"

"I always do."

"Thanks. With you here, part of me still feels a connection with this place whether I'm inside the walls or not. Goodbye, Dorie."

There was a ring of finality to her voice that scared me. I grabbed the bars of the enclosure.

"Why don't you stay overnight in the priest's quarters?" My voice was high and shrill. "You don't want to turn around and drive all the way back to Venice. I'm sure everyone would love to see you in chapel for prayers."

"Prayer isn't my strong suit these days." She hugged me through the grille. "I'll be fine."

I was afraid to let go of her. "Mother and the sisters will be upset when they find out they've missed you."

"They'll forgive me. That's what nuns do." My twin pulled away and walked out.

"I'll see you soon." I called after her.

I sincerely hoped that I would.

CHAPTER FORTY-TWO

The sunset sent colorful stained-glass shadows splashing across the walls as I entered the chapel for my clothing ceremony. I stood beside the altar in my postulant's navy blue jumper while the sisters nodded to me from behind the grille. Aunt Martha, Matt, Trish, Graciela, Sophie, Rod, Phil, and Sister Barbara waved from the public area. A couple of reporters were also in attendance. A careful scan of the public pews confirmed what my gut already knew: Catherine wasn't there.

A bell rang. Everyone stood as Father Charles entered. The priest spoke a few words, but I didn't hear them above the clamor of the blood pumping between my ears. Halfway through the ceremony I was too distracted to absorb, Mother handed me the gray habit and white veil of a novice and I mechanically left the chapel to change.

Sister Teresa helped me dress in the vestry just off the chapel.

"Was Catherine out there?" I whispered as I pulled the coarse, cotton habit over my head. "I didn't see her."

"I'm sure she's on her way," the extern murmured through gritted teeth to keep the straight pins in her mouth from falling out. She secured my new wimple around my head, neck, and ears and then fastened the white novice veil to it.

I hoped Catherine was all right. Excited as I was to take the next step in my religious training, uneasiness washed over me whenever

I thought about my sister. I cinched the knotted linen cord around my waist, hooked a set of rosary beads to it, and tried to ignore the nausea roiling my belly.

I told myself that my twin was simply running late, yet I couldn't shake the sense that something was wrong.

My temples ached as I reentered the chapel. I wished Catherine were there, though in my heart I felt her spiritual presence despite her physical absence. It was as if she were trying to tell me something. But what?

I roused from my reverie when the nuns and members of the congregation each lifted a hand toward me in blessing. I kneeled while Father Charles read from a leather-bound book that lay open on the lectern before him.

"Dorie Elizabeth McKenna, do you seek admittance to the cloister as a novice?"

"I do, Father."

"And do you invite the Lord Our God into your heart?"

"Yes, Father."

"Do you promise to honor the principles of monastic life and obey the holy rule for the next six months as you continue to discern your religious vocation?"

"To the very best of my ability."

"And do you accept the name of Sister Clare?"

"With gratitude."

"May the Lord who has thus called you bless you and keep you as you grow in faithfulness." Father Charles made the sign of the cross over me. "We pray this in the name of the Father, the Son, and The Holy Spirit."

"Amen," the congregation replied.

"You may rise and join your sisters in community."

"Thank you, Father."

As I stood up, I felt a sharp pain and tasted the stinging, metallic tang of blood in my mouth. I touched my lips with my hand. There was no gore, no injury, just a phantom ache. I tried to ignore it as I walked over to the sisters behind the grille.

The short walk was difficult. I paused, suddenly feeling dizzy and hot. I wondered if I had inhaled too much incense smoke and continued walking.

As I approached, Mother Benedicta unfastened an interior latch and a door-sized portion of the grille swung open to allow me to enter. I took a deep breath and stepped through on shaky legs. I'd been inside the cloister before, but this time was different. This time it was for good.

The prioress closed the grille and offered me an unlit candle. As I held out my right hand to receive it, I noticed that all the sisters were staring at the candle. I wondered why, then realized that they weren't staring at the candle at all—but at my right hand—a hand whose fingers were fully extended. I wiggled my fingers in astonishment. The muscles were withered and the joints knobby, but I could bend and stretch all my digits for the first time in my life.

I stood there, so happy and stunned that Mother had to nudge me to continue the ceremony. I struck a match to light my candle, marveling at my newfound dexterity. The sulfur oxidized in a dazzling, blue flame that startled me before it dulled to a steady orange glow. It reminded me of the flames that leapt from Catherine's *Jesus and Judas* painting the day she set it on fire to make her point. In that moment, another realization dawned.

CHAPTER FORTY-THREE

I went straight to the cloistered side of the parlor after the ceremony and found Matt among the visitors on the public side.

"Well, if it isn't Sister Clare." He smiled and offered me a bouquet of sunflowers through the bars that now divided us. "Congratulations."

"Thank you."

When I held out my open palms to receive the blooms, Matt dropped the flowers and took my right hand into his, where he turned it over and back again, looking at it from all angles.

"Oh, my God." He pulled me in for a hug through the bars.

"That's the only explanation I can think of." I looked over his shoulder for Catherine.

"This proves it," Matt said. "You're exactly where you belong, Dorie."

"It feels right." Grateful as I was, I scanned the room anxiously. "But something else feels wrong. Is Catherine here?"

"She should be by now. She wasn't going to come, but then she changed her mind at the last minute." Matt's expression darkened when he saw my concern. "When I offered to drive her, she said she had some work to finish first and would catch up later. Why?"

"Call the Santa Monica Fire Department."

According to the report, fire trucks screamed toward the orange glow on Olympic Boulevard in time to save the gallery structure, but not the art or Sister Catherine. No bodily remains survived except her dental bridge and a scrap of paint-splattered habit among the charred canvasses, malfunctioning fire extinguisher, and shards of broken glass from the shattered skylight.

I remembered the skylight from the gallery opening and its resemblance to a sunlit portal to heaven. Now the vision of the gray ashes from Catherine's unfinished paintings rising up through the opening against a square of night consumed my mind. I imagined these attempted paintings returning to their Creator as Catherine's artistic sacrifice—one that I hoped wasn't intentional.

At first I worried that Catherine might have burned another painting only to have the flames get out of control. When investigators found the fire's point of origin at a scorched electrical outlet, I heaved a sigh of relief. Trish got enough insurance money to replace the faulty wiring, repair the gallery damage, and do the renovations she'd been saving up for anyway.

Mother Benedicta requested special permission from the diocese to bury Catherine's scant remains among the departed nuns in the cloister cemetery. Remembering the connection my sister said she still felt with the place when I last saw her, I knew that being buried where she'd found so much divine grace in life would make her happy in death.

Something in me didn't think she *was* dead. With the kind of biological conviction felt only by those who have shared a womb, I believed a burnt scrap of habit and a well-placed piece of dental work enabled my twin to walk away and fade back into the obscurity she craved.

After the fire, Sister Catherine's cloister studio was returned to its original use as a broom closet. Mops and sweepers resumed their places against the walls; bleaches and solvents reestablished residency on the shelves. As time went on, many sisters forgot the space had ever been otherwise. But for me, it would always be the place where I first saw God.

EPILOGUE

Seven months have passed since the fire, and Catherine hasn't resurfaced. I still believe she's alive, but I now accept that the world may never hear from her again.

I stopped talking the day we buried those negligible remains, but my penance brings me no peace. Now I am trying another—the one my sister would choose.

I've written this manuscript by hand, pen on paper, feeling closer to brush on canvas than typing ever could. The book I once dreamed of writing has now written itself, the story not one I could have imagined. It may be my best prayer, this Act of Contrition, now that I've learned to hear the words that God whispers in the silence.

When I put my pen down, I will pick up this manuscript, feeling its satisfying heft as I carry it over to the stone fireplace, where just enough embers remain to set the pages alight. Then I will watch them burn, white ashes against a black hearth, as the words float up to the heavens.

ABOUT THE AUTHOR

Maura Weiler grew up in Connecticut and earned her BA and MA in English Literature from the University of Notre Dame and the University of Chicago, respectively. She is a former columnist for *The Connecticut Post* and a trash artist whose work has been featured on NBC Television and in galleries and shows across the country. As Director of Development at Blue Tulip Productions, she helped develop the screenplays for such films as *Speed, Twister, The Paperboy* and *The Minority Report. Contrition* is her first novel. For more information or book club queries, visit www.mauraweiler.com.

If you liked "Contrition," we invite you to try books by these other Infinite Words authors.

THE TROUBLE *With* THE TRUTH

by Edna Robinson

Available from Infinite Words

Set in the 1930s, this poignant, funny, and utterly original novel tells the American story of one lost girl's struggle for truth, identity, and understanding amidst her family's nomadic, unconventional lifestyle.

What's the right way to behave, to think, to feel—if you're always the new girl? How do you navigate life when you're continually on the move? Do you lie? How do you even know if you're lying? What's the truth anyway?

It's 1928 and nine-year-old Lucresse Briard is trying to make sense of life and the jumbled, often challenging family it's handed her: a single art-dealer father who thinks nothing of moving from place to place; her brother, Ben, who succeeds in any situation and seems destined for stardom; and their houseman, Fred, who acts like an old woman. As Lucresse advances through childhood to adolescence, she goes from telling wild lies for attention to desperately seeking the truth of who she is as a sophistication-craving teenager in the 1930s.

Told from Lucresse's perspective as a grown woman, *The Trouble with the Truth* transcends its time in the late 1920s and '30s, and weaves the story we all live of struggling to learn who we are and the truth behind this human journey.

PATIENCE, MY DEAR

by Bower Lewis

Available from Infinite Words

In this quirky, romantic novel, in the irreverent spirit of Christopher Moore's national bestseller *Lamb*, a young woman is getting texts from an iPhone-obsessed God, and she's not okay with that. Her handsome new neighbor tries to intervene in the dispute, but is he on her side, or the Almighty's?

Patience Kelleher doesn't want to be a soldier of the Lord. She doesn't want His voice in her head, and she certainly doesn't want Him texting her emoticon-laden messages about boy band singers and sinister solar power corporations. What would a cranky, twenty-three-year-old waitress know about preventing the Apocalypse? He's got believers for that sort of thing, or the Army. All Patience wants is to keep a job she actually likes, and to avoid falling for her confounding new neighbor, if at all possible. When the Lord enlists said neighbor to convince her to step up, it doesn't brighten her mood. That was dirty pool.

Zane Grey Ellison doesn't particularly want to be a soldier of the Lord either, but he's keeping an open mind. His world's been pretty skewed since he abandoned his father's estate, and his preoccupation with the waitress across the street hasn't helped him regain his equilibrium. The messages she's receiving from a text-happy God don't seem all that much more wondrous to him than his discovery of diner food, or the realization that not every girl in the world can be impressed by a Bugatti Veyron. In fact, if Patience would just stop bickering with the Lord for a minute, he believes they might even get the job done.

Patience fights to keep her sanity as Zane fights to keep the peace, determined not to let the world die...not when it's just getting good.

Shifting Time

by Kelly Bennett Seiler

Coming Soon from Infinite Words

In this entertaining and thought-provoking novel, a thirty-something woman wakes up one day to discover her long-lost love has come back to life. But is this new reality truly the answer to her heart's desires?

Despite her great life in New York City as a prestigious book editor, Meade Peterson can't shake the heartache of losing her high school sweetheart. Fifteen years after his death, she still thinks about all the things—love, family, happiness—she'll never have, now that Daniel's gone. That is, until a new man, Tanner, enters Meade's life and brings her the kind of joy she hasn't experienced in years. She's torn, though, over whether she can bear giving her heart away again. Taking time to reflect, Meade returns to her hometown of Austin for what should be a relaxing visit—but instead, she becomes the victim of a violent crime.

Upon waking from her real-life Texas nightmare, Meade finds herself in another world where she doesn't recognize anything, until she realizes the man in bed beside her isn't a stranger—it's Daniel. Meade has awakened into an alternate existence where Daniel is very much alive, and has been part of her life for the past fifteen years.

Meade can't believe her good fortune—she's finally experiencing the life she's always wanted! Or is she? As Meade quickly learns, if one thing in your life changes, nothing else may stay the same. And now she's forced to face the question: Is what she's gained worth what she's destined to lose?